MADELINE BAKER

**Winner of the *Romantic Times* Reviewers'
Choice Award for Best Indian Series!**

**"Madeline Baker is synonymous with tender
Western romances!"**
—*Romantic Times*

DREAM LOVER

His lips were firm, sensual, and when he smiled, as he was smiling now, it made her wish that he was a man of flesh and blood and not just an image conjured from the fathomless depths of sleep.

He came toward her, one hand out in a gesture of welcome, but still, in his eyes, she saw the same silent plea for help. And yet, how could she help when she couldn't help herself?

"Lady...." His voice was deep and rich, like chocolate velvet.

"I'm coming," she called. "Wait for me."

Yet even as she hurried toward him, his image faded, like an old painting left too long in the sun, and then he was gone from her sight.

"Your name," she murmured sadly. "I don't even know your name."

A sob rose in her throat, waking her, returning her to the ugliness of her prison cell, and a pillow soaked with tears.

MADELINE BAKER

Beneath A Midnight Moon

LEISURE BOOKS NEW YORK CITY

A LEISURE BOOK®

September 1994

Published by

Dorchester Publishing Co., Inc.
276 Fifth Avenue
New York, NY 10001

The name ''Leisure Books'' and the stylized ''L'' with design are trademarks of Dorchester Publishing Co., Inc.

Printed in the United States of America.

To Hilda Laselette, Bev Lippincott, Lucy Byard
Helen Brown, and Marian Kelly
for all their encouragement, support,
reassurance, and gentle criticism.

And to Mary, because she likes it even though
it isn't a Western.

Prologue

He came to her in dreams, always different, yet always the same, his fathomless gray eyes filled with quiet desperation and a silent plea for help.

Was he real, this dark-skinned man with the long inky black hair, or only a dark image sketched from the paint box of her imagination, a phantom warrior woven into the shadowed tapestry of her nighttime fantasies . . .

Chapter One

She was walking through a deep green forest dappled by shimmering fingers of sunlight. The air was warm, fragrant with the aroma of a thousand exotic ferns and flowers. She heard the joyful songs of birds praising the birth of a new day, the distant whisper of a waterfall tumbling over stones.

Deeper and deeper she penetrated into the heart of the emerald forest, her footsteps muffled by a thick carpet of pine needles as she explored this strange new world that was so different from her own.

She saw a black-faced doe picking its graceful way along a narrow path, saw a pair of red-tailed squirrels chasing each other across the forest floor, saw a bird with bright yellow plumage flitting lightly from tree to tree.

And then she saw him, the man who lived only in her dreams. Her gaze moved over him with undisguised admiration. He was large of stature, his massive shoulders and well-muscled arms and legs accentuated by the gauzy white shirt and tight buff-colored breeches that he wore.

His eyes were gray, the color of clouds on a winter day; his hair fell to his waist, as deep and black as the Caves of Mouldour. His skin was the color of dark honey, smooth and unblemished. His nose was long and straight; his cheekbones prominent and well defined; his jaw strong and square.

His lips were firm, sensual, and when he smiled, as he was smiling now, it made her wish that he was a man of flesh and blood and not just an image conjured from the fathomless depths of sleep.

He came toward her, one hand out in a gesture of welcome, but still, in his eyes, she saw the same silent plea for help. And yet, how could she help him when she couldn't help herself?

"Lady . . ." His voice was deep and rich, like chocolate velvet.

"I'm coming," she called. "Wait for me."

Yet even as she hurried toward him, his image faded, like an old painting left too long in the sun, and then he was gone from her sight.

"Your name," she murmured sadly. "I don't even know your name."

A sob rose in her throat, waking her, returning her to the ugliness of her prison cell, and a pillow soaked with her tears.

Chapter Two

She stood in the middle of the inquisition chamber, her wrists tightly lashed to a thick iron bar suspended above her head.

"You will tell us what we wish to know," the Lord High Sovereign's interrogator demanded brusquely. "You will tell us today, or you will die tomorrow."

Kylene shook her head. She'd been imprisoned for almost a fortnight, and she still had no idea why they thought she could help them find the elusive Hardane.

"The lash is a crude weapon," the Interrogator mused. "Crude, but effective."

He nodded in the Executioner's direction and Kylene's body tensed as she waited for the lash to fall. The thick leather strap cracked through the air with the sound of thunder, biting deep into her skin, sizzling like summer lightning.

"Dying under the lash is a most unpleasant way to perish," the Interrogator remarked. "A way that, if done with care, can take a very long time."

It was an effort to hold her head up, to stay the words of pleading that rose in her throat. It was fortunate she didn't know where Hardane was, she thought, for she feared she would tell the Interrogator everything he wished to know if it would spare her the pain of the lash. But she could tell him nothing.

"Where is he?"

The whip fell again, and then again. Tears stung her eyes and clogged her throat. The blood trickling down her back felt like sunfire. A red haze hovered before her face, making everything else seem distant and out of focus.

Trembling convulsively, Kylene closed her eyes, and he was there, standing before her, his slate gray eyes warm with compassion. His hand reached out to her, the touch of his fingertips as soft as fairy mist as he gently wiped away her tears.

"Lady, come to me . . ."

Startled by the sound of his voice, so near, so real, she opened her eyes.

And he was gone.

Mad, she thought. I must be going mad.

And yet his voice seemed to linger in the room, surrounding her with its strength, cocooning her in its warmth, lessening her fears, easing her pain.

"Where is he?"

The Interrogator's voice cut through the silence, sharp as a blade.

Slowly, sadly, Kylene shook her head. "I don't know. I don't know who Hardane is. I don't know where he is."

The Interrogator nodded and the whip fell again.

She heard the sibilant hiss, felt it strike across her shoulders. From deep within her mind, she heard a low-pitched wail, like that of a man sobbing with fury.

As if from far away, she heard the Interrogator order the Executioner to put away the lash.

Sick with relief, she closed her eyes and surrendered to the darkness that dragged her down into blessed oblivion.

Chapter Three

It was dark and she was alone beside an iridescent waterfall. Moonlight danced upon the face of the ink-black water. Countless shooting stars chased each other across the indigo sky. A night bird lifted its voice to the heavens, its three-note mating call begging for attention.

Sitting alone on a flat gray rock, she searched the darkness, a nameless fear making her shiver with apprehension.

There was a soft rustling in the underbrush as a huge black wolf materialized out of the shadows, its dark gray eyes fixed upon her face.

She should have been afraid. In her own world, she would have been afraid. But here, suspended in a dreamworld of illusion, she held out her hand.

The wolf drew closer, close enough to touch. A

low whine erupted from its throat, and then it lowered its head and licked the palm of her hand. The velvet stroke of its tongue coursed through her, hot as molten lava, sweet as sunbaked honey.

A soft sigh of pleasure escaped her lips. And then, to her disbelief, the wolf changed shape, its image blurring, until a man stood before her. A man with hair the color of pitch and eyes the color of storm-tossed clouds.

"You." The word whispered past her lips.

"My lady . . ."

"Your name," she begged. "Tell me your name."

"Search your heart, lady. You know who I am."

"I don't. Tell me, please."

She wanted to plead with him, to tell him that it had to be now, this very night, because it was to be her last night. But the words seemed trapped in her throat.

And then he was touching her, his big, callused palm cupping her cheek, his dark gaze lingering on her face, as warm and sweet as a caress.

"I won't leave you alone, lady."

She heard the promise in his words, the underlying anguish in his voice.

He gazed deeply into her eyes, her soul. "Only swear you won't betray me."

"I swear," she murmured.

His smile pierced the dark clouds of her despair, and then he was gone, leaving her alone once more, left to wonder how she could possibly betray him when she didn't even know his name . . . when she was condemned to die on the morrow.

Chapter Four

They came for her at dawn. A priest of the Holy Brotherhood of Mouldour blessed her soul, and then her wrists were bound and she was led away to the inquisition chamber once again.

The Interrogator stood in the middle of the room, appropriately clad in funereal black from head to foot. He was a tall man, thin but with no hint of weakness. His eyes were cold and blue, like the Inland Sea. His hair, cropped short, was thick and blond. He would have been handsome but for the hideous scar that angled across his left cheek.

"This is your last chance," he warned as Kylene stepped into the room. "Where is Hardane?"

"I've told you and told you, I don't know who he is, or where he is."

"Shall I refresh your memory for you? It is said that Hardane of Argone possesses mystical powers. His great grandmother's mother was a Wolffan . . ."

Kylene frowned. "A Wolffan, my lord?"

The Interrogator shook his head impatiently. "Yes, a Wolffan, believed to have evolved from the union of a wolf and an Argonian woman. He's a shapeshifter, as you well know."

"I know nothing of the kind."

"Perhaps she speaks the truth," the Executioner remarked, idly tapping the butt of his whip against a well-muscled thigh.

The Interrogator stroked his jaw thoughtfully. Was it possible the Princess Selene didn't know of Hardane's whereabouts? But that was impossible. She was Carrick's seventh daughter, betrothed since birth to marry Hardane. It was a match that had been prophesied by the White Witch of Mouldour on the eve of Selene's birth. According to the prophesy, a marriage between the seventh son of Argone and the seventh daughter of the rightful heir of Mouldour would produce twin sons who would one day rule the warring lands of Argone and Mouldour, thereby bringing eternal peace to the two countries.

Such a marriage would signal the beginning of the end of Bourke's reign as Lord High Sovereign.

The Interrogator drew in a deep breath and let it out in a long, shuddering sigh. If Bourke were destroyed, the Interrogator's life would also be forfeit, for he had sworn a blood oath to follow Bourke not only in life, but in death, as well. Bourke, the reigning Lord High Sovereign of Mouldour, had stolen the title from his elder brother, Carrick, through trickery and deceit. Carrick's whereabouts were presently unknown, though it was feared he might be trying to muster an army in an attempt to regain his throne.

At the moment, Carrick was no threat. Bourke was confident that he could defeat his brother in battle, but an alliance between Carrick's daughter and Hardane of Argone would be the first step in fulfilling the ancient prophecy. It was possible that the people, superstitious fools that they were, would read more into the marriage than there was. Weary of war, the common folk desired peace. But there was no profit to be made in peace, and neither Bourke or the Interrogator would rest secure until any possible alliance between Mouldour and Argone had been thwarted.

Permanently.

"She must know Hardane's whereabouts," the Interrogator insisted, his voice cracking with tension. "How could she not know? She is betrothed to the man."

"You speak foolishness," Kylene said. "I am betrothed to no one save the Sisterhood."

"So you keep saying, but it is well known that you are Carrick's daughter."

Kylene frowned. "His daughter, my lord?"

The Interrogator took a step closer. His frigid blue eyes narrowed, his breath mingling with hers.

"I grow weary of these games. If you value your life, you will speak the truth. Are you not Carrick's seventh daughter?"

"No."

"No?"

"Has your hearing gone amiss, my lord?"

The Interrogator whirled around, his ice-blue eyes boring into the pale brown eyes of the Executioner. "Have you brought me the wrong woman?"

"I brought the woman you described," the Executioner said quickly. "A woman with hair the color of dark fire and eyes the color of newly turned earth." His voice softened with obvious admiration. "A woman with skin like alabaster come to life. . . ."

"I did not ask you to praise the girl's beauty," the Interrogator replied brusquely.

The Executioner shrugged, the movement causing the coarse material of his shirt to pull taut over his massive shoulders. Who could help but be spellbound by such a rare creature?

"Where was she found?"

"Cos and his men found her gathering herbs near the Motherhouse at the farthest reaches of Carrick's holdings."

Near the Motherhouse? The Interrogator muttered a mild oath. Was it possible that Carrick had returned to Mouldour? Was he even now plotting to depose his brother and regain the crown?

The Interrogator shook his head. Even if Carrick had returned, it was unthinkable that he would allow his daughter to prowl around the countryside alone, gathering herbs, of all things!

His gaze moved from the Executioner's pockmarked face to Selene's. For the first time, he began to think the girl might be telling the truth, that they did, indeed, have the wrong woman.

"She fits the description," the Executioner remarked.

"Aye," the Interrogator agreed absently. "Tell me, girl, if you are not Carrick's daughter, who might you be?"

"I am a foundling, my lord, allowed to live on the outskirts of my chieftain's lands. I would have taken my final vows so that I might join the good sisters who raised me if your men had not abducted me."

Kylene's heart began to pound erratically as confused looks spread over the faces of both men. Did they believe her? Would they now let her go?

The Interrogator stroked his bearded jaw thoughtfully. It was possible they had taken the wrong woman. It was just as possible that she was lying.

"Kill her," he said curtly. "If she is the wrong woman, it matters not. If she is the right woman, so much the better."

"And if Lord Carrick learns her fate?"

The Interrogator shrugged. "He need never know. Indeed, if she is not his daughter, he will not care."

The Interrogator walked swiftly toward the door, only to pause with his hand on the latch. Glancing over his shoulder, he fixed his accomplice with a hard stare. "Attend me in my chambers when it is done."

"Aye, my lord."

With great deliberation, the Executioner secured Kylene's hands to the iron bar, took a step back, and raised the whip.

"Do not make her passing too easy," the Interrogator warned. He turned his narrow-eyed gaze on Kylene. "You should have told me that which I desired to know, princess."

With a courtly bow, he left the room, closing the door behind him. He had hoped to locate Hardane's whereabouts that he might procure for himself the secret of shape-shifting, but he dared not wait longer to dispose of the Princess Selene, if indeed that was who she was. It seemed unlikely now. Perhaps her resemblance to Selene was mere happenstance. Perhaps not.

Still, he could take no chances. Better the woman die now and forever put an end to the possibility of her bearing the twin sons that had been prophesied. Each day she lived put Bourke that much closer to being deposed.

The Interrogator smiled faintly. There was still a chance that they would discover Hardane's whereabouts. He fingered the ugly scar that puckered the skin on his left cheek. It would give him great pleasure to slay Argone's heir to the throne. But before he took Hardane's life, he would discover the shapeshifter's secrets.

Chapter Five

Kylene closed her eyes, her fingers curling around the iron bar over her head as she waited for the lash to fall. How many strokes before the pain would drive her to unconsciousness? she wondered morbidly. How many strokes would it take to steal the breath, the very life, from her body?

Why didn't he begin?

She opened her eyes and looked over her shoulder. The Executioner was standing motionless, his head cocked to one side, as if he were listening to voices only he could hear.

He was perhaps the ugliest man she had ever seen. His hair was lank and brown, his face scarred by the pox. His lips were thick, his nose decidedly crooked. He had massive shoulders, a bull-like neck, and huge, hairy hands that could break her in half as easily as she might snap a twig.

She stared at him, wondering why he didn't begin and get it over with. He nodded once, briefly, and then released her hands from the bar, though her wrists were still bound together by a narrow cord.

"Follow me," he said.

She hesitated only a moment. Perhaps he still meant to take her life, but, be that as it may, she was grateful for the reprieve, however short it might be.

He opened the heavy, iron-barred door, turned left, and started down the narrow corridor, his footsteps as wary as a wolf on the prowl. Not once did he turn to see if she followed, yet she knew he was aware of her every move, her every breath.

Swift and sure, he made his way along the corridor and up a winding staircase until they reached the rear entrance of the dungeon. Without hesitation, he opened the heavy iron door and stepped outside.

Kylene drew a deep breath as she crossed the threshold, feeling as if she had just crossed the boundary from death to life as she breathed in the sweet, clean scent of fresh air, of trees and earth.

"Hurry," the Executioner said.

Kylene hastened after him, wishing he would stop long enough to free her hands. But then, perhaps he didn't mean to free her at all. Perhaps he only meant to use her for his own amusement before carrying out the Interrogator's orders.

The thought brought her to an abrupt halt.

Immediately, he whirled around to face her. "What is it?" he demanded curtly. "Why do you tarry? Is it your wish to die at the hands of the Executioner?"

Odd, Kylene thought, that he should speak of himself in such a way.

"No," she replied. "I have no wish to die at your hands, nor anyone else's."

"You will not die by my hand, lady." He glanced at her bound wrists as if noticing them for the first time. Muttering an oath, he drew his knife and cut her hands free. "Hurry now, before our escape is discovered."

"*Our* escape?"

"Trust me a few more minutes," he urged, "and all will be explained." He cocked his head to one side. "They're coming," he said, and he held out his hand.

In that instant, Kylene knew that she *did* trust him, though she couldn't help shuddering with revulsion as his thick, hairy hand closed over hers; then they were running up the hill, over the crest, and down the other side.

Two horses, saddled and bridled, awaited them.

"You can ride, can't you?" the Executioner asked.

"Of course I can ride," she said quickly, fearing that if she told the truth, he would leave her behind.

The Executioner looked skeptical; then, with a shrug, he lifted her onto the back of a long-legged gray mare.

Swinging aboard a big black stallion, he pounded his heels into the animal's flanks.

The gray mare needed no urging. She raced after the other horse, almost unseating Kylene, who grabbed the saddle horn with one hand and the horse's mane with the other, and held on for dear life. In truth, she had never ridden before; there had been no horses at the Motherhouse.

The Executioner glanced over his shoulder from time to time, no doubt to make sure she still followed him. She toyed with the idea of trying to get away from him, but it would be night soon, and she had no desire to ride through the forest alone. She would be easy prey for the many outlaws that roamed the countryside after dark.

After what seemed like hours, the Executioner drew his horse to a halt. Dismounting, he lifted Kylene from the back of her mount, tethered the horses to a sturdy tree, then led the way up a short steep cliff toward a small cave.

"We'll stay the night here," he said.

"And then what?"

"At dawn, we'll ride for the Sea of Mouldour. My men have a ship waiting to take us to Argone."

"Argone." She spoke the word in the same tone she might have used if he'd told her they were going to Perdition's flames.

"You object?"

"Would it do me any good?"

A wry smile tugged at the corners of his mouth. "No, lady, it would not."

He gathered a handful of leaves and twigs and carried them into the cave. Moments later, a small, cheerful fire chased away the darkness.

Kylene stood at the entrance to the cavern. The fire's warmth beckoned her even as the Executioner's ugliness repelled her.

He glanced at her, a hulking shape in the dancing shadows cast by the flames.

"Come, warm yourself." He looked at her askance when she hesitated, one grizzled brow quirked in amusement. "You still do not trust me?"

"Yes . . . no . . . I don't know."

Rising to his feet, he walked slowly toward her. "Trust me, lady, I will do you no harm."

Removing his fur-lined cloak, he placed it over her shoulders.

"Who are you?" Kylene asked. "Why are we going to Argone? Why have you brought me here?"

"I will answer your questions in good time, lady. For now, I would know who *you* are."

"It is as I told the Interrogator. My name is Kylene, and I am a foundling. The Sisterhood has cared for me since I was a child. I want only to take my final vows and join their holy order."

He shook his head in disbelief. He had saved her life and she still didn't trust him with the truth. And yet, he could understand her reluctance. He was, after all, in the guise of a stranger.

"Why would a woman as lovely as you seek such an existence?" he asked, willing to play along for a moment.

"I wish to embrace their way of life, to know the kind of peace that they enjoy."

"What kind of life is that? To hide yourself behind high walls for the rest of your days?"

Kylene lifted her chin defiantly. "It is my life. What is it to you how I wish to spend it?"

"You are a woman of rare beauty. They will clothe you in shapeless black robes, cut off your hair, and cover your face with a veil." Slowly, he shook his head. "It is a waste, to hide such perfection in ugliness."

Kylene felt her cheeks grow warm under his praise. She had little experience with men, still less with worldly compliments.

"So," he mused, "you are not the rightful Mouldour's daughter, but a foundling."

Kylene went suddenly cold. Would he kill her, now that he was convinced she was not Carrick's seventh daughter?

She stared at him, mute, wondering if she could buy a little more time by lying. A sudden weariness overcame her. Lifting her chin defiantly, she stared at the Executioner.

"I am not his daughter," Kylene said. "I have seen Lord Carrick but once, and from a distance. If it is your intention to kill me, then do it, but, pray, do it quickly and be done with it."

He grinned, amused by her unexpected show of temper. "Why did Lord Carrick offer you sanctuary?"

Kylene shrugged. "I am told he is a kind man."

"Kind, perhaps, but you cannot rule a country and maintain a throne with kindness."

He thought of the waste brought about through war with Mouldour, the lives sacrificed on the field of battle, the homes and crops that had been destroyed. Of course, Carrick couldn't be held entirely responsible. He had wanted peace. He had willingly agreed to see his daughter betrothed to the house of Argone in hopes of achieving peace.

But he had not been strong enough to keep the throne of Mouldour. Unfortunately, Bourke and his advisors seemed determined to keep the ancient feud alive, to seek the revenge that the ruling house of Mouldour had long felt was its due, and all because Hardane's great-grandfather's father had chosen to marry a Wolffan princess instead of the Mouldourian princess who had been selected for him. The Lord High Sovereign of Mouldour had been insulted when his daughter was passed over in favor of a woman he considered to be less than human. The Wolffan were an alien race. They were rumored to prowl the woods at night, slaughtering cattle and sheep and wild animals, stealing young children from their beds to be sacrificed to their heathen gods. The cry of war had been raised, and there had been war ever since.

"My people have never known kindness from any of Mouldour's monarchs," the Executioner remarked. "Surely Bourke does my liege no kindness by holding him prisoner in the dungeons on the Isle of Klannaad."

Kylene leaned forward, fear for her own life momentarily forgotten. No place in all the known world was viewed with such horror as the dungeons located in the bowels of Castle Conn on the barren Isle of Klannaad. It was said that to be imprisoned there was to look into the face of certain death.

"Your liege is Lord Bourke's prisoner?" she queried, frowning. "How can that be? Do you not serve Lord Bourke?"

"No, lady," he said, tiring of the game. "I serve only my father, the Lord High Ruler of Argone."

Kylene drew back as, quite unexpectedly, the Executioner's gruesome face and form began to change.

Her breath caught in her throat as the man who lived in the shadow world of her dreams stood before her, his eyes as dark and stormy as winter clouds. His hair was long and sinfully black, his skin the color of wild honey.

"You." The single word whispered past her lips.

He inclined his head, the ghost of a smile hovering on his lips. "My lady."

"Who are you?" She felt her mouth go dry as her gaze moved over him. Surely there could be no harm in looking, for he was beautiful enough to tempt Saint Lorinda herself.

"I am your betrothed, lady," he said with a soft smile. "Hardane of Argone."

Kylene shook her head. "I am not the woman you seek, my lord." But now, looking at his broad shoulders, at the wide expanse of his chest, she felt suddenly envious of the woman who was destined to be his bride.

"Impossible," he retorted sharply. "We have met often in your dreams."

Kylene nodded. "That's true, but I am not your betrothed. The Princess Selene is Carrick's seventh daughter."

Hardane grunted softly. Selene. Kylene. "What is the color of her hair, her eyes?"

"I know not. I have never seen her . . ." Kylene's voice trailed off. "It was Selene you meant to communicate with, wasn't it?" she asked, unable to stifle her disappointment.

The man of her dreams had become flesh—only he belonged to another. It was just as well, she thought, hoping to console herself. She had vowed to unite with the Sisterhood, to devote her life to easing the pain and suffering of others. There was no place in her future for a man, especially one who was heir to a throne.

"You can tell me the truth, lady. Surely you know I mean you no harm."

"I am telling the truth," Kylene replied quietly. "The Princess Selene is the woman you want."

Hardane shook his head in confusion. It wasn't possible. Only his betrothed, the woman destined to be his life-mate, had the power to receive his essence.

If Kylene was not the woman meant for him, how then to explain the fact that she had seen his *tashada*, his spirit, in her dreams?

Chapter Six

"Gone?" The Interrogator glared at the Executioner in disbelief. "What do you mean, she's gone?"

The Executioner shrugged helplessly. He could not explain what he did not understand. The last thing he remembered was being sent after the woman. He had gone to the dungeon, the key to her cell in his hand. After that, he remembered nothing until he woke, lying on the bed in her cell. Heart pounding with dread, he had hurried to find the Interrogator, curious to learn what had happened to the woman while he had been unconscious.

The Interrogator paced the floor, his brow furrowed in an angry frown. "When I left you, she was securely bound. How did she get away?"

"When you left me, my lord?" the Executioner queried.

"Yes, you idiot! This morning, in the interrogation chamber, I told you to dispose of her, but not too quickly. Don't you remember?"

"Nay, my lord."

A wordless cry of frustration rose in the Interrogator's throat. "Start from the beginning," he said, taking a deep, calming breath. "What do you remember?"

"I remember being told to bring the woman to the interrogation chamber."

"Yes, yes, go on."

The Executioner shook his head. "I went to the dungeon and then . . ." He shrugged again, his hand massaging the large lump on the back of his head. "The next thing I knew, I was lying on the cot in her cell and she was gone."

"That's impossible! You were here, in this room. I saw you. . . ." The Interrogator swore a vile oath. "Hardane! It had to be Hardane."

The Executioner looked bewildered. "My lord?"

"He took on your shape, you fool." The Interrogator dragged a hand across his jaw, his expression thoughtful as he stared out the window. "So, we had the right woman, after all. I hold you responsible for this," he said, whirling around to face the Executioner.

"But my lord—"

"You will never fail me again," the Interrogator said curtly. "You are hereby banished to the Isle of Klannaad."

"No! My lord, please, I beg of you. I've served you well, done all you ever asked of me."

"It is done. You leave on the morrow. Pray I never see your face again."

Madeline Baker

Heavy shoulders slumped in despair, the Executioner left the Interrogator's chambers.

Banished to the Isle of Klannaad. It was a sentence of living death.

Chapter Seven

Hardane sat with his back against the cave wall, his gaze straying once again to the woman sleeping beside the fire. He had never seen anything so lovely, he thought, as Kylene's face in the firelight. Her hair was as red as the flames, her skin as smooth as Argonian silk. Her brows were delicate crescents, her lashes dark fans against her pale cheeks. And her lips . . .

He cursed softly as he felt a sudden tightening in his loins.

She is not for you. He repeated the phrase in his mind, over and over again, hoping to cool his rising passion, but to no avail. He had dreamed of this woman, yearned for her, imagined what it would be like to possess her. No matter that she insisted she was not the woman he thought her to be, he knew he couldn't be wrong. He couldn't be. . . .

And yet, when he probed her mind, he knew she was telling the truth, that she was not Carrick's seventh-born daughter.

He stood abruptly, his hands curled into tight fists as he walked to the entrance of the cave and drew in a deep breath.

He had never had a woman. His life had been spent in studying, in training for battle, in the subtle nuances of ruling Argone so that he might be prepared to take his father's place when the time came. But a knowledge of women had been denied him.

He glanced over his shoulder, overwhelmed with a sudden urge to disregard all he had been taught and trained for, to run his hands over her skin, to taste the certain sweetness of her lips, to bury himself in her warmth and learn the hidden mystery of her femininity.

Body rigid with desire, he stared at her, at the steady rise and fall of her breasts, at the long, shapely outline of her legs beneath his cloak. The need to mate burned strong within him, and only the knowledge of what would be lost kept him from crossing the short distance between them.

With regret, he drew his gaze from Kylene. He was Hardane, heir to his father's throne, his country's only hope for a lasting peace between Argone and Mouldour.

He had been betrothed since birth to marry Lord Carrick's daughter. On the seventh day of the seventh month, he would take her to wife and plant his seed within her. According to prophesy, twin sons would be born of their union, sons who would

38

one day rule the lands of Argone and Mouldour, thereby putting an end to the ancient feud.

He gazed at Kylene once more. Was Selene as fair of face and form? Was her hair as soft, her skin as translucent? Would his body burn for his betrothed as it burned for this woman who had pledged her life to the Sisterhood?

A soft oath escaped his lips as he left the cave, hoping the cold breath of the night wind would cool his heated flesh.

Kylene stared at the earthen ceiling overhead. Where was she?

A sound drew her attention and she saw Hardane outlined in the entrance to the cave. It all came back to her then, their wild ride through the night, his transformation, the knowledge that he had mistaken her for someone else. Strange, the pain that lanced her heart when she thought of him with another woman.

She stared at him, mesmerized by the sheer masculine beauty of the man. She'd had little contact with men. Those she had seen now seemed ordinary when compared with Hardane. Almost without exception, the men of Mouldour were fair of hair and skin. Few were as tall as Hardane; none wore their hair long.

She fought an almost uncontrollable urge to go to him, to run her fingers through his long black hair, to caress the broad expanse of bronzed flesh visible beneath the black leather vest that he wore. Black breeches hugged his long, muscular legs; soft black leather boots covered his feet.

Hardane endured her scrutiny in amused silence. Though he had little experience with women, he had no trouble reading the blatant admiration in Kylene's eyes. For one brief, unguarded moment, he let himself imagine what it would be like to take her in his arms. Would she fight him? Would he let her go if she did?

He shook the thought from his mind. There were women who would assuage his hunger if he couldn't wait until his wedding night. Thus far, he had managed to keep his baser needs under control. But Kylene's mere presence was a temptation he was hard-pressed to resist. The shapeless brown wool dress, with its high neck and loose-fitting sleeves, did little to disguise her soft, sweet curves.

"It's time to go, lady," he said, his voice strangely thick.

She ignored the hand he offered her. Scrambling to her feet, she groaned softly. A night spent on cold ground had left her stiff and aching. When she tried to give him his cloak, he shook his head.

"Put it on," he said tersely. And turning on his heel, he left the cave.

Kylene frowned, puzzled by his curt tone, and then she sighed. No doubt he was angry because he had put his life in danger to rescue her, only to discover that he had rescued the wrong woman.

Wrapping the cloak around her shoulders, she hurried after him. It wouldn't do to make him more angry than he was. She had no wish to be left behind, no wish to fall into the hands of the Interrogator once more. She wondered briefly what Hardane had done to the real Executioner.

Had he killed the man? There were times when she looked into his eyes that she thought him capable of such a thing, and yet, at other times, he seemed the most gentle of men.

At the foot of the hill, he lifted her onto the back of the gray mare, then mounted his own horse, swinging effortlessly onto the stallion's back.

It took only a moment for Kylene to realize that sleeping on the cold ground hadn't eased the awful ache in her thighs, back, and buttocks. Every step the mare took added to her discomfort, making her wonder if she would still be able to walk when the journey was over.

It was an hour's ride to the Sea of Mouldour. Clinging to the horse's mane, Kylene closed her eyes, grateful that her torment would soon be over even though she dreaded the thought of a sea voyage, dreaded the thought of days spent upon the water, helpless, prey to wind and weather. She'd been terrified of the sea since childhood, though she didn't know why.

The Sea of Mouldour loomed ahead, a vast expanse of bright water sparkling in the sunlight. A small ship rocked gently in a quiet inlet.

Kylene felt a shiver of apprehension at the thought of spending days, perhaps weeks, aboard ship.

Numb in mind and body, she followed Hardane down the narrow winding path that led to the bay.

A half-dozen men hurried toward them when they reached the dock. Smiles wreathed the men's faces as they welcomed Hardane, slapping him on the back, shaking his hand, grabbing him in fierce

41

hugs. Only when their exuberance began to wane did they take any notice of Kylene.

As one, the men turned to stare at her.

"She's a beauty, my lord." The tall, bearded seaman spoke for them all. "You're a lucky man."

"This is not the Princess Selene," Hardane said gruffly.

"Then who might she be?"

"Her name is Kylene, and you will treat her with the same respect you would have given to my betrothed." His cool gray eyes rested on each man. "Is that understood?"

"Aye, my lord."

"Let us be under way, then." He glanced at Kylene, then started up the gangplank.

Kylene hesitated only a moment, her fear of water overcome by her fear of being left behind. Lifting her skirt, she hurried after Hardane.

She stood at the rail as the ship left the bay, her gaze sweeping over the shore. She was leaving Mouldour, leaving the only home she had ever known, perhaps never to return.

An hour later, her melancholy was forgotten, swallowed up in the sure knowledge that she was going to die. Her stomach churned, her throat burned with bile, and her head ached. She clutched the rail, afraid to move, afraid she'd be thrown overboard into the white-capped waves that sucked at the ship's sides.

With a groan, she closed her eyes and prayed for death.

That was how Hardane found her a few moments later.

"Lady, are you ill?"

Kylene nodded, thinking that ill didn't begin to describe how she was feeling. And then she brightened. Perhaps he'd brought good news. Perhaps the ship was going down. Drowning seemed a vast improvement over what she was feeling now.

Frowning, Hardane put his arm around her shoulders and eased her away from the rail. "Have you ever been on a ship before?"

"No."

He grunted softly as he swung her into his arms and carried her down the sturdy ladder to his cabin. Gently, he placed her on the narrow bunk. She tried to bat his hands away as he began to unfasten the stiff collar of her high-necked brown dress.

"Lady, be still," he admonished. "I'm not going to hurt you."

The sound of his voice soothed her and she ceased her struggles.

Closing her eyes, she gave herself up to his ministrations, sighing as he removed her sturdy black shoes and thick wool stockings, then sponged her face and neck with a cool cloth.

She heard him leave the cabin, but she was too miserable to wonder where he'd gone. The thought crossed her mind that if, by some miracle, she reached Argone alive, she would have to spend the rest of her life there, because she was never going on board a ship again.

Hardane returned a few moments later. Urging her to sit up, he thrust a cup into her hands. His face was near, his beautiful gray eyes filled with concern. Perhaps he didn't hate her, after all.

"I'm sorry to be so much trouble," she murmured groggily.

He nodded. "Drink the broth. There's ginger in it. 'Twill make you feel better soon."

She did as she was told, her gaze fixed on his. His eyes were as changeable as the sea, she thought, sometimes dark and stormy, sometimes soft and gentle.

"Rest now," he said. Setting the cup aside, he drew a heavy blanket over her, tucking it under her chin. "You'll get your sea legs in a day or two."

"And if I don't?"

His smile was kind. "Then you'll probably wish you'd died at the hands of the Executioner."

"What's to become of me?"

"Lady?"

"When we reach Argone?"

He nodded with understanding. "No harm will befall you, lady. You may stay with us, if you wish. If not . . ." He shrugged. "You will be free to leave."

Free, she thought. Would she ever be free again? She was a fugitive now. If she returned to Mouldour, she would be forever looking over her shoulder, waiting for the Interrogator to find her. And if she stayed in Argone, she would still be a prisoner of sorts, trapped in an alien land among alien people.

"Rest now," Hardane said again.

And she obediently closed her eyes, seeking oblivion in sleep.

She was drowning. Salt water clogged her nose, burned her eyes. She opened her mouth to scream, and sea water filled her mouth and throat. She flailed her arms and legs in a wild effort to gain the surface, but her frenzied motions were of no avail and she felt herself sinking deeper, deeper . . .

"Kylene. Kylene!"

His voice penetrated her terror. Opening her eyes, she saw him leaning over the bunk, his face hovering over hers, his eyes hooded with concern.

"Kylene?"

"I . . . I had a bad dream. I was drowning . . ." She shuddered with the memory. "I'm all right now," she said tremulously.

Hardane nodded. He was about to leave the cabin when he noticed the fear that still lurked in the depths of her eyes. Her face was pale, sheened with perspiration. He could see that she was trembling beneath the blanket.

Taking a deep breath, he gathered her into his arms, blanket and all, and carried her to the big leather chair in the corner of the room. Sitting down, he settled her in his arms as if she were a child.

"My lord . . ." Kylene tried to free herself from his hold, but his arms tightened around her.

"Go to sleep, lady," he said, his voice gruff. "Nothing will harm you while I'm here."

She stared up at him. She was still trembling, but it had nothing to do with bad dreams, and everything to do with the feel of his arms around her.

"Go to sleep, lady," he said again, and this time his voice was as soft as a caress.

His arms were comforting, the rocking of the ship soothing, now that she was no longer afraid. Her eyelids fluttered down and she snuggled against him, feeling as safe as a child in its father's arms. Nothing could hurt her now.

Chapter Eight

He had never feared anything in his life, but now, as the shores of the Isle of Klannaad came into view, the Lord High Executioner felt a shiver of apprehension. Klannaad, the Isle of Living Death. Traitors were sent here to die. Outcasts. Those who were in disfavor with the Lord of Mouldour, or with the Interrogator.

It was a bleak land, gray and barren. There was no water on the island save for that brought by ship each month. The men lived on the victuals that were brought with the water ration, and what they could catch in the sea. Those who were lucky were allowed to roam free; others were confined in the bowels of the prison, never again to see the sun.

The Executioner wondered how long he would survive in such a desolate place. He was accustomed to rich foods and fine ale, to comfortable quarters and garments custom-made to fit his oddly shaped form. Though his occupation was viewed with loathing, he had still been respected, for he was good at what he did, and his loyalty to Mouldour was above question or reproach. It was unfair that he had been banished from service to the royal house for one mistake.

Looking back, he tried to remember what had happened that fateful day, how he had been taken unawares. He hadn't seen anyone else in the dungeons . . . ah, but he had. And yet, the man had been dressed as a guard and so he had paid him no mind. Only now did he realize that it must have been the shape-shifter, Hardane.

"Damn you," the Executioner murmured as he watched the ship catch the tide. "Damn you, Hardane. You'll rue the day you crossed my path."

He stood there for a time, watching the ship grow smaller and smaller, and then he smiled. It was Hardane who had caused his banishment; it would be his hatred for Hardane, his need for revenge against the Lord of Argone, that would give him a reason to survive on this accursed island.

Chapter Nine

She stood on the shore beside a quiet pool, her eyes drinking in the beauty of the crystal clear water. Hardane stood beside her, his hand reaching for hers. She smiled as she followed him into the depths of the pool, shivering a little as the cool water closed over her.

But she wasn't afraid, not even when the water rose over her knees, her hips, her waist. She was never afraid when he was beside her.

"Trust me, lady," he said, and lifting her into his arms, he carried her into the depths of the water and taught her to swim.

It was wonderful, being in his arms, floating beside him, seeing the approval in his dove-colored eyes.

They swam for hours, going deeper and deeper into the pool. And she was never afraid, because he was there beside her. . . .

A ray of sunlight tickled Kylene's eyelids. Reluctant to awake from such a beautiful dream, she snuggled deeper into the blanket. Her eyelids flew open when the bed beneath her moved.

Only then did she realize she wasn't in bed at all, but in Hardane's arms.

Only then did she realize she had spent the night in his lap, wrapped in his arms.

How handsome he was! His lashes rested like black fans on his tanned cheeks. His nose was wide and straight, his lips full and well formed, tempting her touch.

Unable to help herself, she lifted her hand, one fingertip extended, reaching to trace the curve of his mouth. . . .

She quickly withdrew her hand when she realized he was no longer asleep.

He stared up at her through heavy-lidded eyes. "Good morrow, lady," he said, his voice raspy.

"Good morrow," she replied, embarrassed to have been caught staring at him while he slept. She felt her cheeks grow warm under his knowing gaze.

"Did you sleep well?"

She nodded. With each passing moment, she grew more and more aware of the intimacy of their position. But when she started to rise, his arms tightened around her, holding her in place.

"Let me up, please."

"Are you not comfortable here?" he asked, his eyes dancing with amusement.

Too comfortable, she thought irritably. "I . . . please, my lord."

He knew he should let her go, but he continued to hold her, liking the weight of her in his lap. Her scent, warm and womanly, filled his nostrils. Mesmerized by her nearness, her beauty, he traced the soft curve of her cheek, ran the back of his hand down the slender column of her neck.

His body reacted immediately, filling with warmth, pulsing with need.

Abruptly, he stood her on her feet and headed for the door. "I'll have one of the men bring you something to eat," he said, not looking at her. "And water for a bath," he added, and then he was gone.

On deck, Hardane endured the speculative looks of his crew, but only Jared had the nerve to approach him.

"I trust you slept well, my lord," he inquired cordially.

Hardane glared at the man who had been his friend for more than twenty years. "Well enough."

Jared grinned at Hardane. They had grown up together, always conscious of the fact that Hardane would one day be the ruler of Argone, yet it had never hindered their friendship. Jared readily accepted the fact that one day Hardane would be his liege, but it never stopped him from speaking his mind, nor did he ever forget to give Hardane the respect that was his due. Respect that had been earned on the field of battle where they had fought side by side.

"She's a pretty wench," Jared remarked.

Hardane scowled at his friend. Jared was a handsome young man, tall and lanky, with dark brown hair and eyes that always carried a hint of laughter. Women had always flocked to Jared, fawning over him, eager to share his bed. And, gentleman that he was, Jared always obliged them, effortlessly seducing them, the married and the unmarried alike.

Jared's easy conquest of anything in skirts was one topic that wasn't often discussed, the one subject where Jared tread softly, always careful in his choice of words. The fact that Hardane had never had a woman was something they rarely discussed, except obliquely. And yet, on occasion, Jared could not help but give in to a little lighthearted teasing.

"Was the bunk a tight fit?" Jared asked, his voice deceptively innocent.

"What?"

"Surely you did not make the wench sleep on the floor."

"Of course not."

A smile tugged at the edges of Jared's mouth. "We will be long at sea," he mused. "You are indeed fortunate to have such a delectable creature to cuddle with."

Hardane made a sound of disgust low in his throat. "Don't you have something better to do than worry about how I spent the night?"

"Aye, my lord," Jared replied with a grin. Turning on his heel, he sauntered across the deck, whistling softly.

For Hardane, the hours seemed to pass with unusual slowness. Usually, he enjoyed being aboard ship, exulting in the power of the waves beneath him. The sea air was invigorating and he loved nothing more than running into the wind, or facing the challenge of a gale, pitting his wits against the elements.

But now he could think of little but the woman who occupied his cabin. Time and again he made excuses to go below decks—he needed a drink, a compass, his charts. Each time, he lingered longer than necessary in his quarters. Each time, he was struck anew by Kylene's beauty.

She was still seasick, though not as bad as the day before. He sent her broth laced with ginger, and warm watered wine. And each time he saw her lying in his bunk, his body reacted in the same way. It was ridiculous, he thought. She was fully clothed, indifferent to his presence as she tried to conquer her aversion to the sea, yet his loins swelled with longing and a traitorous voice in the back of his mind whispered that she was his prize, that he could take her at any time.

It was on his fourth trip to his cabin that he found her on her knees, her head bent over a bucket as she vomited her supper.

She glanced up, her pale cheeks stained with embarrassment, when she saw him watching her.

He swore softly as he knelt beside her, one arm going around her shoulders, supporting her as she began to retch again.

When the spasm passed, he helped her to the bed, wiped her mouth, offered her a drink of water.

"I'm sorry to be so much trouble," she mumbled.

"You're no trouble, lady."

Her gaze slid away from his, only to return, her eyes drawn to his face like a fox to its hole. A faint flush warmed her cheeks. There was an odd feeling in her chest, like butterflies dancing.

She was acutely conscious of his hand supporting her back. His scent filled her nostrils, the combined odor of man and sea making her senses reel. He was near, so near.

She pushed the cup away, knowing she could never swallow past the lump in her throat.

Gently, he took her into his arms and carried her to the window seat in the stern.

"Here," he said, opening the jade green curtains, "keep your eyes fixed on the horizon."

"Why?"

Hardane shrugged. "Sometimes it helps when nothing else will."

She didn't think anything would help, but then common sense won out. He was a sea captain, after all. Surely he knew about such things.

Sitting in his lap, with his arm around her waist, Kylene gazed out the window. The water was calm, restful. Hardane's fingertips were gentle as they massaged her brow, his touch both soothing and arousing, making her long for a way of life that was forbidden to a member of the Sisterhood. Making her yearn for a man's love, for a home of her own, children.

"Rest, lady," he urged.

His voice was as deep as the sea, as soothing as warmed wine. She felt a sense of peace as she gazed out the window, at the blue-green of the sea and the deeper blue of the sky.

Her eyelids fluttered down as she gave herself up to his touch. The rocking of the ship and the gentle murmur of his voice lulled her to sleep, to dream of a vine-covered cottage, and a tall, dark-skinned man with hair like liquid ebony and eyes as gray as the stones that flanked the chapel at Mouldour.

Hardane paced the windward side of the quarter-deck, confident no one would dare invade what was traditionally the captain's private domain. His eyes were gritty with the need for sleep, his body tense from wanting what he could not have. He knew every man on board was wondering if he had finally broken his lifelong vow of celibacy and bedded the wench . . . bedded Kylene.

How easily her name fell from his lips, how readily his mind conjured her image.

The mere thought of her, of bedding her, was enough to bring a fine moisture of sweat to his brow and make his body throb with desire. He paused at the rail, staring blankly at the sea, his hands clenched so tightly they ached. He had promised his mother he would abide by the ancient law of the clan, that he would remain celibate until he took a life mate. It was for the good of the people, she had assured him when he looked doubtful, and for his own good as well. He would expect his bride to be nothing less than a virgin; should his future wife have any reason to expect less?

Hardane groaned softly. What if Carrick's seventh daughter did not stir his blood? What if Selene's eyes were not as warm and brown as the sun-kissed earth of Argone? What if her

hair didn't shimmer like a flame in the moonlight?

What if he'd waited so long to possess a woman
that his body wouldn't function at all?

Chapter Ten

Kylene knelt beside the hard wooden bunk, her head bowed, her hands clasped, her eyes closed in prayer. But try as she might, she couldn't concentrate on the words of the Morning Prayer that she had recited at every dawn since she had taken her first vows in the Motherhouse. Instead, Hardane's dark visage danced before her, his deep gray eyes mocking her attempt to pray.

How could she devote her life to service to others if she could not banish one man's image from her mind? How could she take her final vows of obedience and chastity when some wayward part of her, some wicked little corner of her mind, wanted only to feel Hardane's hands in her hair, to know the taste of his lips?

Had such sinful thoughts always been there, lurking deep in the dark corridors of her mind?

57

And how did one banish them once and for all?

She pounded her fist on the floor, willing his image to depart and leave her in peace, but to no avail. She had no sooner managed to utter the first few words of the prayer when there was a knock at the door and she heard his familiar voice calling her name, telling her the morning meal was ready.

With a sigh, Kylene rose to her feet and opened the door. As always, she was astonished anew at how handsome he was, how tall, how broad. Shirtless, his legs encased in tight breeches, his feet shod in soft leather boots that hugged his calves, he exuded strength and power and sheer, overwhelming masculinity. For one whose only contact with the male of the species had been a gray-haired Confessor of the Sisterhood, Hardane of Argone was indeed a sight to take a woman's breath away, to make her sinfully, painfully, happily aware of the vast difference between men and women.

"My lord," she said, hardly able to speak the words, so intent was her gaze upon the vast expanse of his dark-furred chest and muscular shoulders.

"Are you ready to break your fast, lady?"

Kylene nodded, little tremors of pleasure skittering up her arm as he took her hand in his and led the way to the galley.

During their first few days at sea, she had eaten in Hardane's cabin. But now that she'd gotten her sea legs, they took first meal in the galley each morning, just the two of them, though sometimes Hardane's friend Jared joined them. Being seated between two such virile men, listening to their easy camaraderie, was almost more than she could endure. Strict silence had been observed at all meals she had shared with the Sisterhood. Idle conversation was to be avoided, just as one abstained from laughter and gluttony, greed and strong drink.

Today, they dined alone, just the two of them.

Kylene kept her gaze upon her plate, acutely aware of the man who sat across from her. She could feel him watching her, waiting for . . . for what, she didn't know. His scrutiny, indeed, his very nearness, made her feel clumsy and ill-at-ease.

She uttered a small cry of despair as she reached for the teapot, only to have it fall from her hand. A flood of hot spiced tea spilled into her lap.

Hardane was beside her in an instant, lifting her to her feet, dabbing at the dark stain on her skirt. "Are you hurt, lady?"

"No."

Like a child drawn to a promised reward, her gaze lifted to meet his. She felt a sudden warmth, a sweetness, as she saw the concern reflected in the depths of his clear gray eyes.

For a timeless moment, she let herself bask in the warmth of his gaze. Pleasure unfolded within her, uncurling like the bud of a flower opening to the light of the sun. Never had anyone looked upon her with such caring, such concern.

She had no memory of a mother's love, no recollection of a father's devotion. Always, she had been alone. Even in the abbey that housed the Sisterhood, she had been aware of a gulf between herself and the others. They had seen to her needs, provided her with nourishment and shelter, protected her from the outside world, but no one, man or woman, had ever looked at her as Hardane was looking at her now.

Lifting her onto a dry corner of the table, Hardane pushed Kylene's skirt and petticoat out of the way, exposing long, slender legs. She wore no stockings, only calf-high leggings made of heavy black cotton.

Alarmed that he would dare to take such a liberty, Kylene batted his hands away. "What are you doing?"

"Checking to make sure you're not burned."

"I can do it."

He nodded in agreement, but instead of moving out of the way, he bent to his task once again.

Hot color flooded Kylene's cheeks as he gently examined her right thigh. She gasped as the touch of his callused fingertips ignited their own brand of fire.

Hardane drew back, his brows rushing together in a frown. Her heavy skirt and thick petticoat seemed to have protected her delicate flesh from harm. No redness marred the ivory perfection of her skin, yet she shuddered at his touch.

"Are you in pain?" he asked.

"No," Kylene answered, and quickly drew her petticoat and skirt down over her exposed thigh.

Hardane swore under his breath, suddenly aware of the tension that hummed between them. He had never seen a woman's bare legs before, never realized what an impact it would have on his senses.

Kylene flushed under his probing gaze. It was hard to breathe, impossible to think, when he looked at her like that. The touch of his hand made her thigh throb with a fire that had nothing to do with scalding tea. Her heart was beating wildly.

Hardane took an abrupt step backward, then turned away from Kylene lest she see the effect her nearness had on him. By Romar's Beard, but he was tempted to throw away all restraint, bend her back on the table, and bury himself in her sweetness. Only the oath he'd made to his mother, and the knowledge that Kylene would never forgive him, kept him from surrendering to the lust that was roaring through him with all the ferocity of a maddened beast. For the first time in his life, he realized what a powerful force desire could be. Little wonder that men left thrones and countries for the love of a woman, that they turned their backs on wealth and power. At the moment, he would gladly give all he had, all he would ever have, to take Kylene in his arms and unlock the eternally sweet mysteries of womanhood.

"Finish your meal," Hardane said curtly, and stormed out of the room before the tiger rampaging in his blood made him do something he would forever regret.

Jared glanced up, his expression mirroring his surprise, when he saw Hardane striding toward him. It had been Hardane's habit to spend the morning hours with the wench. In the two weeks they'd been at sea, the heir of Argone had rarely made an appearance on deck before midmorning.

"What is it?" Hardane snapped, annoyed by Jared's probing gaze.

"Nothing, my lord," Jared replied. "How soon will we reach home?"

"In another week, if the weather holds." Hardane grunted softly, irritably. Another week of sleepless nights and tormented days.

He stared at the sea, thinking how pleasant it would be to dive overboard and cool his heated flesh in the chill water, to let himself sink into the sea's all-encompassing embrace and drown his problems once and for all.

"What's wrong?" Jared asked. "Did you have an argument with the lady?"

"No."

Jared cocked his head to one side, a knowing grin tugging at his lips. "You want her, don't you?"

"Of course not."

Jared snorted. "Don't lie to me, my friend. I've known you too long. She's a comely wench, and you're long overdue to sample a maiden's wares."

Hardane swore a vile oath. Was his need for the woman so obvious that everyone saw it?

Jared laid a sympathetic hand on his friend's shoulder. "Perhaps it's time to . . . to . . ." He cleared his throat. "There are many beautiful women in the House of Karos. All would be willing to, uh, initiate you."

"No."

"It's her you want? Kylene?"

Hardane nodded, his gaze still on the sea. "Even if I could bring myself to break my oath, she's a maiden. I couldn't . . ."

"I'd be glad to break her in for you."

Jared had spoken the words in jest, hoping to brighten Hardane's bleak mood. Too late, he realized he had made a serious error. With a roar, Hardane's hand closed around his throat, choking off his breath.

"You will not touch her," Hardane warned in a voice as hard and implacable as iron. "I will geld any man who dares lay a hand on her. Do you understand?"

Jared nodded, knowing, in that moment, that he was as close to death as he'd ever been.

He gasped with relief when Hardane released him. For a moment, he rubbed his neck, his expression thoughtful.

"I meant no disrespect," he said, his tone filled with the formality and deference due Hardane's position.

"I know," Hardane muttered, refusing to meet his friend's eyes. "Forgive me."

"I think it's more than mere lust that troubles you," Jared mused.

Hardane ran a hand through his hair. "Don't you understand? I can't allow myself to feel anything for her!" he exclaimed bitterly. "I am betrothed to another. I have given my pledge to marry Carrick's seventh daughter. I have made a sacred oath to my mother that I will live like a eunuch until the day I wed."

Jared dragged a hand across his jaw. Unlike Hardane, he had been born to poverty. His early years had been spent begging in the streets. As he grew older, his pride rebelled at begging and he turned to stealing, finding it more satisfying, less humiliating. He'd been almost sixteen when he had tried to lift Hardane's purse. To his eternal gratitude, the heir of Argone had not had him arrested but had instead taken Jared into the castle, accepting his word that he would steal no more. From that day onward, Jared had sworn allegiance to Hardane. Jared had never really understood why Hardane had spared his life. When asked, Hardane had only shrugged. Later, Hardane had confessed that, though he had six older brothers and a younger sister, he felt the need for a confidant closer to his own age.

Jared crossed his arms over the rail. "So," he asked after a while, "what's your next move?"

Hardane shrugged. "The Isle of Klannaad."

"To rescue your father?"

"Aye."

"No easy task, that," Jared mused. "The dungeon is well fortified, the prisoners as dangerous as the guards."

Hardane nodded. "Aye, and then I must return to Mouldour to find my betrothed." He spoke without enthusiasm.

"And what of Kylene?"

"I have promised to give her sanctuary on Argone, or to return her to Mouldour. The choice is hers."

Standing there, staring into the sea's blue depths, Hardane wondered which would be worse, having her leave, never to see her again, or having her stay, her nearness tormenting him like the fiery darts of Gehenna.

Chapter Eleven

The storm rose without warning, the waves battering the ship's sides with watery hands of fury.

At first, Kylene had cowered in the bunk, her knuckles white as she clung to the side rail, her stomach heaving in rhythm with the churning waves. She'd retched until her stomach was empty, grateful that Hardane had the foresight to send a cabin boy to empty the malodorous bucket.

At the time, she'd been certain she was going to die, but the thought hadn't frightened her as it should have. Indeed, she would have welcomed death if it meant an end to the horrible nausea that assailed her.

But then Hardane had come, offering her a cup of broth heavily laced with ginger. She had drunk it eagerly, remembering how quickly it had settled her stomach a few days earlier.

Hardane had stayed with her while she drank the broth, then remained a few moments longer, wiping the perspiration from her face and neck with a cool cloth, assuring her that everything would be all right.

She'd felt bereft when he left her with a sympathetic smile and a promise that she'd feel better soon. That had been over an hour ago, and she did feel better.

With a sigh, she closed her eyes, wondering what he was doing on the storm-tossed deck, wondering if it was just wishful thinking on her part or if the storm was lessening.

She heard the cabin door swing open, heard Hardane mutter a foul oath as he stepped into the room.

"By Romar's Beard," he muttered, "it smells like the bottom of a privy in here."

"Sorry."

"I'm not blaming you," he said with a wry grin. "I'm only glad you're feeling better."

"Will we reach Argone soon?"

He shrugged. "Depends on how long the storm lasts." Crossing the room, he studied her for a moment, noting that the color had returned to her cheeks. "Get some rest. I'll look in on you again in an hour or two."

A sudden gust of wind rocked the ship and Kylene grabbed the side rail, her knuckles white. "Don't leave me," she begged plaintively.

He hesitated only a moment; then, taking her hand in his again, he sat on the edge of the bunk.

"Tell me of Argone," Kylene said, hoping the

sound of his voice would keep her fear of a watery grave at bay.

"It's a beautiful country, all green and gold, with rolling hills and lofty mountains. There are lakes and rivers everywhere, and trees like you've never seen before."

Kylene closed her eyes as she tried to imagine such a place. Mouldour was a dark country, flat, arid. Houses were made of brick and stone because of the scarcity of timber.

Another wave crashed over the bow and Kylene clutched the bunk's rail as the ship rocked violently. Timbers creaked as the ship bucked the wind.

"You've never been at sea before," Hardane mused aloud. "I don't suppose you know how to swim, either."

Kylene shook her head, her heart pounding at the implication. Did he expect the ship to go down?

"Don't worry," Hardane said, smoothing her hair back from her brow. "Kruck's at the helm, and he's the best quartermaster in the fleet."

Kylene nodded, though his words did little to reassure her. "I guess it doesn't matter to you if the ship goes down," she muttered. "You'll just turn into a whale and swim away."

Hardane chuckled softly, surprised she could find humor in the situation when she was so obviously frightened.

She grinned faintly. "Or maybe you'll change into a bird."

"I think not," he allowed with a grin. "I fear I can't change into anything so small as a bird."

67

"Really?" She stared at him curiously, her fear of imminent death temporarily forgotten. "I thought shape-shifters could turn into anything they fancied."

"Perhaps some can," Hardane said, serious once more. "But, other than the wolf's form, the Wolffan can only assume human shapes."

A wolf, she thought, remembering her dream. A black wolf with dark gray eyes.

Hardane smiled at her. "Fear not, lady. If the ship sinks, I'll make sure no harm comes to you."

She nodded, fascinated by his ability to change shape. "Do it," she urged. "Change now."

Hardane frowned. "Shape shifting is a gift, lady, one that takes a great deal of concentration. It's not a game."

"I'm sorry," she said contritely. "I didn't mean to offend you."

She gasped as the ship seemed to fall out from under her. They were going to die. She knew it. Weary of waiting, of being afraid, she wished the ship would just sink and be done with it.

She closed her eyes, praying for strength, for courage, only to open them with a start when a low whine sounded near her ear, followed by a sudden breath of heat.

Alarmed, she opened her eyes to find a wolf standing beside the bunk. A black wolf with dark gray eyes.

For a moment, she stared at the animal; then, tentatively, she reached out to stroke its neck, but a sudden overpowering fear made her snatch her hand back.

The wolf whined again, poking its nose over the side of the bunk, butting its head against her hand in a silent plea.

"Hardane?" She whispered the word as she laid her hand on the wolf's head and scratched its ears.

The wolf whined again, the sound distinctly one of pleasure. For a moment, the wolf gazed into her eyes, its pink tongue lolling out of the side of its mouth in a canine grin, and then it pulled away from the bunk to stand in the middle of the floor.

And while she watched, the wolf began to change, taking on the shape of a man, and Hardane stood before her, fully clothed as before.

"Does it hurt?" she asked.

"Not in the way you mean."

"How long can you stay in another form?"

"It depends. If I'm under stress, or in pain, it's very difficult to hold another shape for more than a few hours."

"How do you do it?"

"I'm not sure I could explain it to you. I think it, and it just . . ." He shrugged. "It just happens."

Kylene sat up, everything else forgotten in her fascination with the man before her. "Can you change into things that don't exist, like a three-headed dragon?"

"I think not. I was often tempted to find out when I was young, but my mother advised against it, warning me that I might change into a shape and not be able to change back." Hardane grinned. "I know now that she was teasing me."

"You? Afraid? I don't believe it."

Hardane shrugged. It was true whether she

believed it or not. There were old legends of shape-shifters who had tried to use their gifts for nefarious means, who had sought to pervert their gifts for riches or power. All had come to a bad end, dying horrible deaths, or finding themselves forever trapped in the body of some hideous beast.

"Have you ever assumed the shape of a woman?"

"No."

"Can you?"

"I don't know. As I said before, it's not a game. It's a gift, one I've not used over-much."

"The wolf is the easiest, isn't it?"

"You're very perceptive. The wolf is my *tashada*, the spirit of my maternal ancestors. It's the only shape I can hold indefinitely, without conscious thought." He dragged the back of his hand across his jaw. "I'd appreciate it if you didn't tell anybody what I've told you."

"Why? Isn't it common knowledge?"

"No. There are rumors that I have the power, but except for my family and a few others, no one has ever seen me do it."

She wondered about those "few others"; wondered if they were still alive to tell the tale.

"Do I have your word, lady?"

Kylene nodded, more intrigued by the man than ever before. She studied him for a long moment, the turbulent sea and the intricacies of shape shifting forgotten as her gaze moved over him, lingering on his broad chest, the width of his shoulders, his flat, muscular stomach and long legs.

Hardane frowned, wondering what she was thinking, until he looked into her eyes. And then he smiled. She might be an innocent, she might be promised to the Sisterhood, but she was still a woman, with a woman's desires, a woman's hungers.

For a moment, he contemplated climbing into the bunk beside her, taking her into his arms. She probably didn't even realize that her eyes were burning with a sweet, hungry flame, a flame he would be only too glad to extinguish. He imagined her lying beneath him, her hair like a splash of red against the pillow, her eyes smoky with desire, her skin warm and tingling beneath his hand . . .

With an oath, he forced his thoughts away from such a dangerous path, reminding himself that he was promised to a woman he'd never met, that the woman he wanted was betrothed to the Sisterhood.

But he had no desire to wed the woman who had been chosen for him.

And Kylene might never be able to return to Mouldour.

But they were here now.

Alone.

Together.

"Listen!" She cocked her head to one side, a wide smile playing over her lips as the roar of the wind and the waves diminished.

She swung her legs over the edge of the bunk and hurried to the porthole. Standing on tiptoe, she peered outside. The sea was calming, the waves less fierce, less threatening.

71

"Do you think it's over?" she asked.

"Aye, lady," he replied, thinking that the storm that had raged outside was as nothing compared to the tumult raging in his loins.

Hands coiled into tight fists, he let out a sigh. The gale was over. It was time to go on deck and assess the damage.

It was just as well, he thought as he left the cabin and closed the door firmly behind him. Had he stayed a moment longer, he had no doubt he would have done something he would have regretted later.

They arrived in Argone two days later. Kylene stood at the rail, mesmerized by the beauty of the land. There were trees everywhere—graceful willows that swayed gently in the breeze, tall oaks and pines. In the distance, wildflowers covered the hillside like a multicolored blanket. There were lacy ferns and climbing vines, bloodred night-blooming roses and bright yellow dandelions.

She took a deep breath, her nostrils filling with the scent of sea and earth, flora and fauna. She slid a glance at Hardane, who stood at the windward side of the quarterdeck, one hand shading his eyes, the other clinging to the mast. His hair, as black as the sea birds that hovered over the ship, billowed behind him like a battle flag. Days at sea had darkened his skin. He looked wild and untamed and outrageously handsome.

She forced the thought from her mind. He was not for her. Even if she wanted him, which she most decidedly did not, he belonged to another.

But she could not draw her gaze from his broad back, from the way the sun danced in his hair. He shifted his stance, and the sight of corded muscles rippling beneath sun-bronzed skin made her stomach curl in a most peculiar fashion. She felt her mouth go dry, felt her palms itch with the need to run her fingers through his hair, to measure the width of his shoulders, to map the unknown terrain of his broad chest and ridged belly.

"Stop it!" She muttered the words under her breath, chastising herself for letting her mind wander down a path that she had no business navigating.

With an effort, she drew her gaze from Hardane and stared over the rail again as the ship glided effortlessly into port.

A half hour later, Hardane was leading her down the gangplank. It seemed odd to be standing on solid ground again. She'd just gotten her sea legs, she thought wryly, and now it felt awkward to be on land again, to be able to take a step without worrying about being thrown off balance by a sudden swell.

Men called to Hardane as he passed by, their voices filled with respect as they welcomed him home. Women smiled at him, sometimes coyly, sometimes brazenly, but all with an unspoken invitation in their eyes.

Hardane accepted their adulation as his due, she noted waspishly, smiling and waving, occasionally pausing to speak to this one or that one.

Kylene stood mute, feeling like a crow in a flock of parrots. She'd never seen such beautiful clothing. Silks and satins in bright reds and blues and greens—stripes and plaids and gaudy prints. She wondered that such bright hues didn't completely overpower the women who wore them. The women. She had never seen such lovely women, with their dark skin and hair and sparkling dark eyes. The women of Mouldour could not begin to compare with the women of Argone.

She didn't argue as Hardane took her arm and handed her into an open carriage drawn by a matched pair of blood bays.

In a short time, they had left the seaport behind and now they were traveling through a land of gently rolling hills.

"It's beautiful," she murmured, hardly aware that she'd spoken aloud. "It looks like . . . like Paradise."

"Aye," Hardane agreed. *And you look like a seraph who hasn't yet tried her wings.*

"Where are we going?"

"Home."

Home, she thought, and the word twisted through her like a hot knife. She'd never had a real home. The only place that had come close had been the gray stone abbey of the Sisterhood, and now that was forever lost to her. She had no place to call home, no one to call friend, except . . . She glanced furtively at Hardane. He had treated her kindly on board ship, looking after her needs, calming her fears. Surely that qualified him to be her friend.

"What will happen when we get to your home?" she asked tremulously.

"What do you mean?"

"Will you send me away?"

Hardane let out a sigh. Send her away? That was the last thing he wanted. "Is there somewhere you'd rather go?"

She shook her head quickly. "No."

"My people will make you welcome, Kylene. My mother has always longed for another daughter. She will receive you with open arms."

"I hope she'll like me."

"She will. And you'll like her."

"Does she look . . . different?"

"Different?"

"Someone once told me she was a descendant of the Wolffan."

"As I am." Hardane smiled wryly. "You needn't expect to find her with fangs and claws and blood dripping from her mouth."

Kylene stared up at him, mute, a flush of embarrassment staining her cheeks. "I didn't mean to offend you."

"You didn't. She has no fangs, Kylene, no claws, only a rather sharp tongue when she is angry. But she is rarely angry."

"Will we be there soon?"

"By nightfall."

"Oh."

"Don't be afraid, lady. My people are not savages. They do not eat helpless women or small children."

Kylene's cheeks burned hotter. Even in the relative solitude of the Motherhouse, she had overheard tales of Argonian treachery, of Mouldourian babies snatched from their cradles and fed to Wolffan young. Often, the Sisterhood had united in prayer for the poor lost souls of Argone who were doomed to burn in the fires of Gehenna for their brutality.

They traveled for some distance in silence. Kylene stared at the passing countryside, wishing she could run barefoot through the tall green grass, stop to touch the petals of a flowering shrub, splash her feet in one of the numerous blue-green pools that glistened in the bright sunlight.

They passed through several small villages. The houses were all neat, the yards well tended. The people they saw smiled and waved. Some flagged the carriage to a halt and plied them with warm wine and bread and cheese, baskets of sweet rolls, bowls of fruit. If they stared at Kylene, it was only with friendly curiosity, but the main focus of their attention was Hardane. That he was loved by his people was evident in every look, every gesture, every offering of goodwill.

How different from the attitude of the people of Mouldour toward Bourke, she mused. She had heard it said that he dared not travel unescorted, that he feared to eat the food that came from his own kitchens until it had been first tasted by another to make certain it hadn't been poisoned.

It was near dusk when they started up a steep, winding hillside. No trees grew along the narrow pathway, and when Kylene remarked on the lack, Hardane said it had ever been so, that no shrubs or trees were allowed to grow close to the road because of the danger of ambush in times of war.

It seemed they'd been climbing for hours when the road straightened and Kylene saw Hardane's ancestral home for the first time.

A soft sigh of wonder escaped her lips as she stared at the beautiful edifice. Constructed of white stone, it seemed to shimmer with a pale golden light in the last rays of the setting sun. Blue and white flags fluttered from the towers.

As they drew near, she saw that there was a wide moat, an enormous drawbridge, a well-fortified gatehouse. Mounted men wearing the blue and white of Argone rode out to meet them, escorting them across the bridge.

Two men hurried up to the carriage. One took the reins; the other helped Kylene out of the coach. They bowed respectfully to Hardane before leading the horses toward the stable.

As Hardane and Kylene neared the entrance to the castle, a tall, gray-haired man opened the door. He bowed low, then informed Hardane that his mother could be found in the Blue Tower.

Hardane smiled reassuringly at Kylene, then held out his hand. "Ready, lady?" he asked.

Kylene took a deep breath. "Ready," she said, and placed her hand in his, praying all the while that she wouldn't do or say anything to embarrass him, that his mother would like her, that she might stay here, in the heart of Paradise, forever.

Chapter Twelve

Kylene stared at Hardane's mother. Perhaps, deep down, she *had* expected to find someone who resembled a wolf, but the woman who fairly flew across the room to greet her son didn't resemble a wolf in the least. She was small-boned, petite, with waist-length black hair and eyes as dark as midnight. Her skin was golden brown, smooth and clear.

"Hardane!" she cried, and threw her arms around her son, tears of joy welling in her eyes. She held him for a long time, her face buried in his chest.

Kylene felt a tug at her heart as she watched the two embrace. Hardane bent his head, his cheek pressed to his mother's, his eyes suddenly bright with unshed tears.

Feeling as if she were intruding, Kylene backed toward the door, only to be brought up short by the sound of Hardane's voice.

"Mother, I've brought a guest." He raised his head and smiled at Kylene over his mother's shoulder. "Kylene, this is my mother, Sharilyn. Mother, this is Kylene of Mouldour."

Sharilyn dabbed at her eyes with a delicate kerchief. "Forgive me, Kylene, but I've not seen my son for several months."

"Of course," Kylene said. She curtsied as she had been taught. "I am pleased to meet you, my lady."

Sharilyn smiled. Gliding across the floor, she took Kylene's hand in hers and gave it a squeeze. "We're not very formal here, child. Please, call me Sharilyn. Everyone does. She's lovely, Hardane. Have you made plans for the wedding?"

"Wedding?" Hardane stared at his mother blankly for a moment, and then muttered an oath. "She's not Carrick's daughter."

"She's not?"

"No."

Sharilyn's gaze darted from her son's face to Kylene's. "Then who is she?"

"A foundling, my lady," Kylene replied. "Lord Hardane rescued me from the hands of the Executioner."

Sharilyn shook her head. "I don't understand."

"It's a long story, mother mine, and we've been on the road since dawn."

"Of course." Sharilyn smiled at Kylene. "No doubt you'd like to bathe and change your clothes." She clapped her hands twice. Immediately, a young girl dressed in a long brown tunic hurried into the room. "Hadj, take our guest upstairs and make her comfortable. She'll want hot water for a bath, and a change of clothes. Brushes, soap, toweling."

"Yes, my lady," Hadj replied. Turning to Kylene, she offered a tentative smile. "This way, miss."

Kylene looked at Hardane, reluctant to leave his presence, afraid she'd never see him again.

"Go with Hadj, lady," he said. "I'll send for you as soon as Cook has prepared us something to eat."

Stifling the urge to seek shelter in his arms, she followed the maid up a long, winding staircase, down a wide, well-lit corridor, and into a room that was almost as large as the Motherhouse at Mouldour.

"Make yourself comfortable, miss," Hadj said. "I'll be back soon with water for your bath."

"Thank you."

"You'll like it here, miss," Hadj said with a reassuring smile. "Lady Sharilyn is very kind."

"I'm sure she is. And Lord Hardane, is he also kind?"

A dreamy expression softened the girl's features. "Lord Hardane is most kind," Hadj murmured. "All the people love him."

And so did Hadj, Kylene thought.

Kylene was wondering if the serving girl was going to spend the rest of the evening contemplating the heir to the throne of Argone when Hadj apparently remembered where she was. With a smile of apology, she hurried out of the room to do her mistress's bidding.

* * *

Sharilyn frowned as Hardane's story drew to a close. "So, she is not Carrick's seventh daughter, but a foundling raised by the Sisterhood." Sharilyn shook her head. "How can that be? How is it she received your shade if she is not your betrothed?"

Hardane spread his hands in a gesture of bewilderment. "I know not. Have you had any word from my father?"

"No. But he still lives, Hardane. I would know if it were otherwise."

Hardane nodded. The bond between his parents was unusually strong. In days gone by, they had often communicated without speaking, a gift which Hardane and his sister had viewed with mixed feelings of admiration and jealousy.

"How soon will you return to Mouldour?" Sharilyn asked quietly.

"Within the month. We'll set sail as soon as the necessary repairs have been made on the *Sea Dragon*."

"Did you hear any mention of your father while you were in Mouldour?"

"No." Hardane took his mother's hand in his. "But, like you, I'm sure he still lives. If not . . ." He took a deep breath, his jaw clenching with determination. "If not, Bourke will rue the day of his birth, and Carrick will pray for death a thousand times before it finds him."

Sharilyn's smile was rueful. "He's too valuable a hostage for them to eliminate, Hardane."

"Perhaps. But if my father dies, I will not let his death go unavenged. If the Wolf of Argone must be unleashed, so be it, but my father's blood will be avenged."

"As you will, my son, only remember, there is no pain greater than the pain of taking a life."

"I hear you, mother mine." He drew a deep breath, exhaled it slowly. "Let us speak of happier things. How are my brothers?"

"Very well. Scattered to the four winds, as usual. Dirk and Garth are at Fescue trying to settle one of the endless boundary disputes between Clannon and his uncle. Dubrey and the others have gone to Chadray."

Hardane grunted softly. The people of Chadray sometimes forgot to whom they owed their allegiance. Twice each year, the men of Castle Argone went to Chadray to remind them who ruled the land. "And my sister?"

"I had a message from her only yesterday. She said the babe thrives, and she prays she will see you soon."

Hardane grunted softly. He had not seen his sister, Morissa, since her wedding to Eben, Lord of Kyle, almost six months ago.

It had taken more than a month to learn that his father was no longer imprisoned in the dungeon at Mouldour, and another month to discover that he had been moved to the Isle of Klannaad, and then, when he had been about to launch a rescue, he had sensed that his betrothed was in mortal danger. Saving her life had taken precedence over freeing his father.

Due to foul weather, it had taken longer than usual to cross the sea to Mouldour to rescue his betrothed, only to learn that the woman he had snatched from beneath the very nose of the Interrogator was not his bride after all.

He shook his head in confusion. Why had he sensed that Kylene was in danger? If she was not his betrothed, why, when he sent his shade to seek his future bride, had he been directed to Kylene instead of Selene?

Hardane frowned. Was there an evil wizard at work, casting some sort of spell to cloud his powers so that he was drawn to the wrong woman, thereby making it impossible for Hardane and Selene to wed on the seventh day of the seventh month? Was the Interrogator behind all this? Had he used witchcraft to summon Hardane to Mouldour to rescue the wrong woman?

He swore softly. He would have to go back to Mouldour and find Selene before the auspicious date set for their marriage passed, but first he must rescue his father.

His crew was already at work, refitting the ship. They would lay in supplies, make the necessary repairs, patch or replace the sails. When all was in readiness, he would sail to the Isle of Klannaad and free Lord Kray from the dungeon.

Kylene stood at the window, gazing down into the courtyard below. Hardane was there. Shirtless, his long legs clad in black leather breeches, his hair flowing down his broad back like ebony-hued silk, he faced a good-looking young man with dark brown hair and dark eyes. She thought it might be Jared, but she couldn't be sure. It was odd, she thought, that she had no trouble recognizing Hardane, and it occurred to her that she would know him even in the dark. The sunlight danced and shimmered on their swords as they lunged and parried.

Both men moved with innate grace and remarkable speed, yet there was something about Hardane's movements that set him apart. He moved with catlike ease, supple, lithe. Power radiated from him as he launched a bold attack, driving his opponent back. The corded muscles in his broad back and shoulders rippled with each lunge, and he wielded the blade as though it were a part of him, an extension of his hand.

She heard the sound of his laughter, deep and rich, filled with exultation as his opponent lowered his sword in defeat.

And then he looked up, his gaze meeting hers as he lifted his sword in a salute. Light and fire seemed to fill her whole being when he looked at her. And then he smiled, and it was as if she'd been struck by a thunderbolt. Oh, she thought, the power in that smile. It could melt stone.

His smile broadened, as though he knew exactly what kind of effect he was having on her. Then he turned away and draped his arm over his companion's shoulder, and they walked toward the well in the center of the courtyard.

She couldn't stop watching him. She watched the muscles ripple in his back and shoulders as he raised the bucket, then took a long drink. Filling the dipper again, he poured the water over his head. To her chagrin, she envied the drops that sluiced down his face and neck, trickling down over his shoulders, his chest. That broad chest, lightly furred with curly black hair that tempted her touch even from a distance.

The mere thought caused her heart to pound in her chest, and she turned away from the window, chiding herself for such improper thoughts. She was bound to the Sisterhood. She had vowed to obey their laws, to be chaste. Somehow, she would find her way back to Mouldour and take her final vows. She would don the heavy black habit of the order, embrace their rules, and forget this man who filled her mind with thoughts she ought not have, who followed her into her dreams, dark sensual dreams that made her wake in the night, her body sheened with perspiration, yearning for things she did not understand.

The next few days passed quietly. She developed a deep admiration for Hardane's mother, sometimes pretending that Sharilyn was the mother she had never known. Hardane was devoted to his mother. He spoke to her always with love and respect. Kylene envied the bond between them, envied the hugs they exchanged morning and night, the easy affection and gentle repartee they shared. She had never been a part of a real family, never known what it was like to receive a mother's love, a father's esteem. The Sisterhood had nurtured her. They had treated her with kindness, with respect, but they had never indulged her, never showered her with affection. Only now did she realize how much she had missed. She felt a yearning to be hugged, to be held.

She took her meals with Hardane and his mother, spent her days working in the flower garden on the east side of the castle, or doing needlework, or simply standing at her window watching Hardane and his friend Jared practice with the sword.

For Kylene, who was accustomed to being busy, to long hours spent washing and mending, cooking and scrubbing, it seemed a life of idleness. In the Motherhouse, one never had time to merely sit and contemplate life, to watch the clouds drift across the sky, to walk through a meadow and gather an armful of flowers. But here, in Hardane's home, there were servants to do the cooking and the cleaning, to make the beds and change the rushes, to make candles, to beat the dust from the carpets and draperies. Servants to draw water for her bath, to lay out her clothes, to help her dress and arrange her hair.

Sharilyn had given her a dozen gowns, beautiful gowns in rainbow colors, but Kylene could not bring herself to wear them. Colors were forbidden to the members of the Sisterhood. The novices wore brown, the professed wore black. Kylene had looked at the bright reds and blues and greens with covetous eyes, and then, regretfully, had begged Sharilyn's understanding and asked for a simple dress of plain brown wool.

Sharilyn had not argued. She had provided Kylene with several dresses of different design in varying shades of brown, but she had insisted that Kylene keep the other dresses as well.

And now it was evening and they were gathered in the dining hall. Sharilyn sat at the head of the table. Hardane sat at her left, Kylene at her right. She tried to concentrate on the meal, but, as always when he was near, she was aware of Hardane's proximity. The sound of his voice, deep and mellow, tugged at her heart. The knowledge that she could reach across the table and touch him made her pulse race. And when he looked at her, as he was doing now, all coherent thought fled and she was conscious only of the magnetism of his gaze, the timbre of his voice, the blatant maleness that seemed to fill the room, dwarfing her, making her feel vulnerable and somehow empty inside.

"You look pale, child," Sharilyn remarked. "Hardane, why don't you take Kylene riding tomorrow? No doubt she's weary of my company. Perhaps a ride to the cove. It will be cool there."

"There's no need," Kylene said quickly. "I'm sure he'd rather spend the day with Jared. And I . . . I should . . ."

Sharilyn made a gesture of dismissal with her hand. "Nonsense. You're our guest. A ride will do you good, put some color in your cheeks." She looked at Hardane. "What say you?"

A shadow passed over his face, and then he smiled. "It would be my pleasure, mother mine. Perhaps Nan will pack us a lunch."

"I'll see to it," Sharilyn said, smiling benignly.

The rest of the meal passed in a blur. Kylene could think of nothing but the coming day, of spending it alone with Hardane.

She excused herself immediately after dinner and hurried to her room, only to pace the floor, her stomach a knot of anxiety.

A day, alone with Hardane.

It was a dream come true.

It was a nightmare.

It would be too soon upon her.

Chapter Thirteen

Hardane paced the floor as he waited for Kylene. How could he spend the day with her, be near her, and not touch her? Thoughts of women often filled his meditations. He had admired them, lusted for them, but never before had he been plagued with such soul-wrenching desire as he was now. He had only to look at Kylene to want her. Her image filled his dreams so that he tossed and turned night after night. When the wanting got unbearable, he left the castle, running through the darkness until he was exhausted, but no matter how far he ran, he couldn't outrun his desire.

The sound of footsteps drew his attention, and he glanced up to see Kylene standing at the head of the stairs. She was wearing a dark brown riding habit that would have been drab on any other woman, but the earthy color enhanced the red of

Kylene's hair and deepened the color of her eyes.

Kylene smiled tentatively as she started down the stairs, unable to shake the feeling that Sharilyn had maneuvered Hardane into this outing against his will.

"We don't have to go if you'd rather not," she said when she reached the bottom of the staircase. "I know how busy you are."

Hardane shook his head, then held out his hand. "The horses are waiting, lady."

Kylene placed her hand in his, noting how large his was, how dark the skin compared to her own, and then his fingers closed over hers and all thought fled her mind as a soft golden warmth crept up her arm and spread through her, filling her with sunshine.

Her gaze darted to his face. Did he feel it, too, that slow heat that sent shivers along her spine whenever he was near, whenever he touched her? She stared at him in confusion, her nerve endings tingling, her whole body yearning toward that which she did not fully understand.

Hardane sucked in a ragged breath. He looked down at her hand, so small, so delicate, compared to his own. Heat radiated from her touch, pulsing through him to settle in his groin, hot and heavy.

Wordlessly, he led Kylene outside and lifted her onto the back of her horse. She was like a feather in his arms, soft and light.

Swinging aboard his own mount, Hardane headed toward a verdant valley a short distance behind the castle.

Kylene held her horse back a little. She needed some distance between them, a space of time to collect her thoughts, to remind herself of her obligations, her vows to the Sisterhood—especially the vow of chastity.

She tried to concentrate on the beauty of the passing countryside, the lush grass, the flowers that grew in bright profusion on every peak and hill, the trees clothed in every shade of green imaginable—but time and again her gaze was drawn to Hardane—to the incomparable width of his shoulders, the way the morning sun made blue highlights dance in his hair, the way he rode his horse, tall and straight and proud, like the warrior prince he was. His sleeveless jerkin exposed his arms—strong, well-tanned, well-muscled arms. His legs, clad in supple black leather, guided his horse with the ease of long practice.

He was like a hawk, wild and free, master of his own life, his own fate, and she was like a wren, dull brown and ordinary, easy prey for cats and wolves . . . and hawks.

She drew her gaze from his broad back and began to mentally recite the rules of the Sisterhood, but, somehow, she couldn't seem to concentrate on promises of obedience, poverty, chastity, and service to others. They were promises she'd made when she was hardly more than a child, when she didn't fully realize that there was a whole world waiting outside the walls of the Motherhouse, when she didn't fully understand the implications of chastity. She knew now that it meant more than staying chaste. It meant giving up all hope of a husband, a home of her own, children. . . . It meant denying herself the pleasure of a man's arms around her, a pleasure she had never contemplated until she met Hardane of Argone.

Lost in thought, she was hardly aware that he had come to a stop until he reached out and grabbed her horse's bridle, bringing the animal to a halt.

She blinked up at him, felt the full impact of his gaze as his eyes met hers. Those eyes, deep and dark, which were sometimes as gray as thunderclouds and sometimes the soft hue of a dove's wing.

"We're here," he said, and swinging from the saddle, he lifted her from her horse's back and placed her feet on the ground.

For an endless moment, they gazed at each other, a mere breath of space between them.

She saw the sudden heat that flared in his eyes, the fine lines around his eyes, the steady beat of the pulse in his throat. She hadn't seen many men in her life. Those on board the *Sea Dragon* had been plain, of no consequence. Hardane's friend Jared had been comely enough, but surely no man in all the world was as handsome as the one standing before her.

Hardane felt his body respond to Kylene's perusal. The touch of her golden brown eyes was like the touch of fire, snaking along his nerve endings, igniting the coals of desire until he thought he might burst into flame. It had been sheer folly to agree to bring her here. He was a man grown, a man destined to rule Argone, and yet he had no more knowledge of women than a lad.

The fire in his body raged hotter and hotter, fueled by the faint hint of longing that sparked in Kylene's eyes.

Take her now.

He clenched his fists to keep from doing just that, but he didn't turn away. Fool that he was, he continued to stand close to the flame, tormenting himself like a moth that knows sure destruction awaits but is drawn closer and closer to the fire.

And then he heard his mother's voice whisper in the back of his mind, warning him, reminding him of the promise he had made to her years ago.

Like a splash of cold water, it cooled the flames, though the spark still burned. With an effort, he took a step back, putting distance between them.

"Are you hungry?" he asked.

Kylene released a deep breath, feeling as though she had just been rescued from the edge of a precipice. "Not yet."

"Thirsty, perhaps?"

She nodded, her gaze following him as he removed a flask and two goblets from his saddlebags. He filled one and handed it to her, then filled the second for himself.

Kylene took the goblet, grateful to have something to do with her hands. She sipped the wine slowly, feeling it spread through her, warming her, relaxing her.

"It's pretty here," she remarked, looking around. "Do you come here often?" *Do you bring women here often?* was what she really wanted to know, but didn't dare ask.

He shrugged. "This was my favorite place when I was a boy. I used to spend hours here, walking through the woods, watching the waterfall yonder, fishing, dreaming."

"Of what did you dream?"

A faint smile tugged at the corners of his mouth. "Of being a great warrior. Of saving a princess from an evil wizard."

Selene. The name slithered into the back of Kylene's mind. Selene was the princess he was destined to rescue.

"And now your dreams are coming true," she murmured. "Jared told me you are a great warrior. And soon you'll have your princess."

A shadow darkened Hardane's eyes. He had forgotten about Selene.

"No doubt she's very beautiful," Kylene said.

"Perhaps," Hardane remarked, and knew that it wouldn't matter. Beautiful or ugly, he didn't want her. He wanted the girl standing before him, wanted her with such soul-searing desire that he was tempted to turn his back on all that he was, to break the promise he'd made to his mother, just to possess her, if only for a day, an hour.

Kylene stared at him over the rim of her goblet. She could feel his desire reaching out to her, tangible, alive. It should have frightened her; instead, for one brief moment, she welcomed it. He desired her. Perhaps he thought her pretty. It was a heady thought, one that filled her heart and soul with joy, and then guilt overshadowed her joy, reminding her that she had vowed to take her place in the

Sisterhood, that pride was a sin, that the yearnings of the flesh were of the most wicked kind, for which she would have to do hours and hours of penance when she returned to the Motherhouse.

A little seed of rebellion, nurtured by distance and watered by desire, suddenly sprouted in the back of her mind, reminding her that she might never return to the Motherhouse, that she might never have the opportunity to take her final vows.

And for the first time, she let herself think of what it might be like to live as other women lived, to love, to marry, to share her life with a man. She tested it, tasted it, and found it sweet. And then, like a bit of meat chewed too long, it lost its flavor and she knew she was only deceiving herself. Hardane was the only man she wanted, the only man she would ever want, and he was betrothed to another, just as she was betrothed to the church.

Saddened, she turned away from him and walked toward the sound of rushing water.

Frowning, Hardane stared after her, wondering at the play of emotions that had flitted across her face. Her hips swayed seductively as she walked. In any other woman, he would have said it was a deliberate ploy to entice him, a feminine art well practiced, but not in Kylene. She was artlessly seductive, completely unaware of her beauty.

Muttering an oath, he followed her down the path that led to the waterfall.

He found her a short time later, sitting on a large boulder that overlooked the river. The sound of the falls was like thunder as the water rushed over the edge of a high rock-faced mountain to crash into the river below.

"It's lovely," Kylene murmured. "So powerful."

Hardane nodded. "It's said that a Wolffan warrior once fell over the edge in the dark of night. He was riding to save his beloved from marrying another man and in his haste, he misjudged his distance from the edge. Unable to stop, he plunged to his death. When his beloved learned of his fate, she donned her wedding gown and rode her horse over the edge and joined him there at the bottom of the falls. You can see them sometimes, sitting together on that rock down there."

Kylene stared at the rock he indicated and then gazed up at Hardane. Her mind told her such a thing was impossible, but her heart wanted desperately to believe that the lovers had been reunited.

Hardane smiled down at her, mesmerized by the faint gleam of tears in her eyes, by the way the sunlight shimmered in her hair.

He had a sudden, strong urge to sweep her into his arms. Instead, he used his forefinger to brush a tear from the corner of her eye.

"You needn't weep for them," he said, his voice low and husky. "They're quite happy."

"You've seen them?"

Hardane nodded. "Often, on cold winter evenings when the moon is full and the night is quiet."

"Is it another of your gifts, to be able to see ghosts?"

He shrugged. "Perhaps. Perhaps it's only because I believe."

He bent toward her, his face filling her gaze, his scent surrounding her. "What do you believe, lady?"

"I . . . what do you mean?"

"Do you believe in the Sisterhood? Do you truly wish to take your final vows, to lock yourself behind cold stone walls, to grow old there, alone and unloved?"

"You have no right to ask me such questions."

"I saved your life," he reminded her quietly. "I have every right."

"I gave my word to abide by their rules. I'll take my final vows when I return."

"If you return."

"When I return," she said firmly, and knew a sudden need to return to the safety of the Motherhouse, to be away from dark, probing eyes and a voice that ensnared her like a silken web, urging her to turn her back on all that she was, all that she had promised to be.

Hardane looked deep into her eyes for a full minute and then, with a muttered oath, he stood up and walked away, away from tantalizing rose pink lips and golden brown eyes that silently begged for his touch even though her words pushed him away.

Kylene watched him go, aware of a sudden emptiness that seemed to creep into every part of her heart and soul. She had to find her way back to Mouldour, she thought desperately; she had to get away from this man who played havoc with her heart. Once she returned to the Motherhouse, she would find the security she had once known, the inner peace she craved. She didn't want to be tormented by dreams of strong brown arms and stormy gray eyes. She wanted only to be left alone to pray and serve others. Didn't she?

For a long while, she sat on the boulder, gazing at the waterfall as it rushed down the mountainside, wondering at the woman who had loved a man so much that she had joined him in a watery grave rather than live without him. Such devotion was foreign to her. The only love she knew was the love of the Sisterhood, her love for Him who was the Father of All. She had no knowledge of the kind of love shared between a man and a woman. Indeed, she had never given much thought to carnal love until Hardane walked into her dreams.

Hardane. He was so handsome, so brave and strong. Surely he had known many beautiful women. She saw the way the maids at the castle looked at him, their eyes wide with admiration and adoration, the way they hurried to do his bidding, vying for his attention. No doubt women were constantly throwing themselves at his feet, yearning for his touch . . .

She heard the sound of his footsteps behind her, felt her cheeks flame with embarrassment because she had been thinking of him.

She glanced over her shoulder to see him standing behind her, a large basket over his arm.

"Perhaps we should eat now," he suggested.

His voice, rich and deep, made her skin prickle.

"I . . . yes," she stammered, "perhaps we should."

"Do you want to eat here, or over there in the shade?"

"In the shade, please."

With a curt nod, he spread a blanket under the leafy canopy and began to empty the basket.

Feeling somewhat ill at ease, Kylene sat down beside him, accepting the plate he offered her. Nan had sent along a veritable feast: sliced venison, biscuits, a loaf of brown bread, a variety of fruit, tea cakes, and ale.

Kylene ate slowly, ever aware of Hardane's nearness. It was an uncomfortable meal. Try as she might, she could think of nothing to say to break the awkward silence between them. She wondered if he was having the same trouble, or if his lack of conversation meant he was angry with her.

Once, glancing up, she caught him watching her, a bemused expression in his eyes. She looked away quickly, but not before she felt the heat of his gaze, the spark of desire that seemed always to vibrate between them.

Later, sated and drowsy, she curled up on the blanket and closed her eyes. The sound of winged insects and the distant song of a bird lulled her to sleep.

And he was there, walking through the corridors of her mind, his gray eyes warm with desire. Murmuring her name, he took her into his arms and kissed her, gently at first, and then with a spiraling intensity that left her breathless.

Be mine, lady, he coaxed. *Admit that you're Carrick's daughter, and let us be wed in the seventh month, as planned.*

She gazed into his eyes, wishing she could say the words he longed to hear, wishing that she

Madeline Baker

were, indeed, his betrothed. Here, in his arms, with her heart pounding and her blood racing, she put all her lies behind her and knew that it wasn't the peace and security of the Motherhouse she wanted, but the love of the man who held her in his arms. For an instant of time, she considered lying to him, considered telling him that she was indeed Carrick's seventh daughter.

I can't wait until the time of ripe fruits, she wanted to cry. *Marry me today. Now. This minute.* But the words would not come. She could not lie to him. Much as she wished it, she could not pretend to be someone she was not.

He drew her close, crushing her breasts against the solid wall of his chest, letting her feel the heat of his desire. With a wordless cry of pain, she pressed her lips to his, the ache of needing him bringing tears to her eyes.

Do not cry, lady, all will be well.

"Do not cry, lady."

His voice penetrated her dream, and she opened her eyes to see Hardane stretched out beside her, so close that his breath fanned her face.

For a timeless moment, they gazed into each other's eyes, and then his hand slid around the back of her neck and his mouth closed over hers.

It was a gentle kiss, as light as thistledown, and yet the wonder of it, the beauty of it, suffused her from head to foot, making her heart pound and her blood sing a new song.

She felt bereft when he took his lips from hers. In her mind she heard the echo of his words: *Be mine, lady. Be mine, be mine . . .*

100

It was tempting, so tempting. But she wasn't a princess and she couldn't say she was. As much as she yearned to belong to Hardane, she could not live a lie, could not spend the rest of her life pretending to be Selene, no matter how tempting the thought might be. And, sooner or later, he would discover the lie and she would be exposed as a fraud. It was a humiliation she could not begin to imagine.

Aware of his gaze, his disappointment, she stood up, her fingers worrying the folds of her skirt. "I wish to go back now."

He rose lithely to his feet, his gaze never leaving her face. "As you please, lady."

Moments later, he lifted her onto the back of her horse. For a long moment, he remained at her side, his eyes searching hers, and then he turned away.

As they rode back to the castle, Kylene had the feeling that she had lost something precious though it was never meant to be hers.

Chapter Fourteen

Hardane stared at Jared, a frown creasing his brow. "What are we doing here?"

A hint of mischief danced in Jared's brown eyes. "It's what you need, my friend."

Hardane sent a dubious glance at the pleasure palace. It was a large square building made of dark stone. There were no windows, only narrow slits that admitted a minimum of light during the day. A narrow iron door was the only entrance.

He let out a quick breath. He had never been inside such a place, though he had heard tales of what went on inside. Anything a man desired could be his for the right price. Women of all sizes and shapes, all colors and ages. The finest ale, the softest beds, the most willing courtesans in all of Argone.

"It's what you need," Jared said again. "I know,

I know, you promised your mother to live like a monk until you wed, but you're not a monk, my friend. You're a man, with a man's needs, a man's desires, and it's time you had a woman."

Hardane stood there for a long moment, torn between the need to relieve his sexual frustration and his determination to keep the promise he'd made to his mother. But his mother was not a man. She couldn't know how painful it was for him, wanting a woman, needing a woman. Until Kylene entered his life, he'd been able to keep his sexual tension under control by constantly keeping busy, by training for battle, by working such long hours during the day that he went to bed utterly exhausted.

But now, no matter how hard he worked, how tired he was when he sought his bedchamber, there was no respite from the hunger that plagued him. Surely it wouldn't hurt to give his body the release it needed just this once.

"Well?" Jared looked up at Hardane, his fists resting on his hips. "Are you ready to be a man?"

"Yes."

A broad smile played over Jared's lips as he opened the iron door and ushered Hardane inside. He felt no guilt at urging Hardane to break the promise made to Sharilyn. He understood Sharilyn's reasoning, but he also felt a strong loyalty to Hardane and it grieved him to see his friend hurting when there was no need for it. Sometimes a man needed a woman, any woman.

Hardane noticed the smell first. The heavy mixture of perfume and powder and the faintly pungent scent of incense. A tall, yellow-haired woman came forward to meet them, her lithe body enveloped in a gossamer gown of purple silk.

"Jared," she purred, extending a slender hand. "How good to see you again." She saw Hardane then, recognition and surprise flickering in her eyes.

Before she could speak Hardane's name and thus draw attention to the future ruler of Argone, Jared said, "Susna, this is my friend, Brayce. He's visiting from Chadray."

"I see," Susna murmured, a knowing smile playing over her lips as she realized she would be well paid to keep Lord Hardane's visit a secret. "Welcome, Brayce. I hope you'll come back often."

Hardane nodded, his senses reeling.

"What type of woman do you prefer?" Susna asked.

"He wants a redhead," Jared replied. "About this tall, with brown eyes and pale skin. Young. Not too experienced."

"I see." Susna smiled at Hardane. "You'll find what you're looking for upstairs in room seven." She glanced at Jared. "Mina is waiting for you."

Jared slapped Hardane on the back. "Shall we?"

Heart pounding, Hardane followed Jared up the long staircase, then down a dark hall.

"This is it," Jared said, stopping in front of a blue door. "Room seven. I'll meet you downstairs in . . . an hour?"

Hardane nodded, then watched as Jared continued down the hall, stopping in front of a yellow door.

Glancing over his shoulder, Jared grinned at Hardane, then opened the door and stepped into the room.

Hardane took a deep breath. What was he doing here? He was about to turn away when the door opened and he found himself staring at the most beautiful woman he had ever seen. Her skin was like porcelain, her eyes a deep brown, her body ripe and firm. A curtain of red hair fell over her breasts and down her back, almost to the floor.

"Come in," she murmured, her voice low and husky. "I've been waiting for you."

When he hesitated, she took him by the hand and led him into the room, softly closing the door behind her.

His gaze darted around the room. It was blue—floor and walls and ceiling. There was a large mirror on one wall, a small chair and a table in the far corner. And a bed, the biggest bed he had ever seen, covered with a blue counterpane.

"Have you been here before?" the woman asked in the same sultry voice.

"No."

She closed the distance between them, her hips swaying provocatively. "Tell me what you want, and it's yours." Her arms slid around his neck, her breasts pressing against his chest as her mouth covered his.

With a cry of desperation, Hardane put his arms around her and kissed her back. His nostrils filled with the scent of perfumed hair and the musky scent of a willing woman. Her skin was warm under his hands, her lips pliant, her body humming with readiness and desire.

And he felt nothing but disgust.

For the woman.

For himself.

With a low growl, he twisted out of her arms and backed away, his mind filling with Kylene's image. He didn't want to bed an experienced courtesan; he wanted to share Kylene's sweet innocence, to savor her virginity as he lost his own.

The woman looked up at him, confused. "What is it?"

He shook his head. "I . . . I can't."

"Can't?" Her gaze moved over him, coolly assessing his masculinity. "Is there something wrong with you?" she asked candidly.

The back of his neck felt suddenly hot and he flushed under her probing gaze.

"There's nothing to be ashamed of," she said. "Lots of men have . . . trouble. That's why they come here."

"There's nothing wrong with me," he said curtly.

"Perhaps the fault lies with me. Perhaps I don't please you?"

"You're very beautiful, but . . ."

She smiled sagely. "But I'm not her?"

"No, you're not."

"She's a lucky woman," the courtesan murmured. "Perhaps, if things don't work out between the two of you, you'll come see me again."

"Perhaps," Hardane replied, but he knew it was a lie, and so did she.

Without another word, he left the woman's room.

In the hall, he drew a deep breath and exhaled it slowly. Other men might find relief here, but he felt degraded, unclean.

Downstairs, he ordered a flagon of ale, then sat in a dark corner to wait for Jared, wondering how his friend could find pleasure in the arms of a woman who sold herself to any man who could pay the price.

He was half asleep when Jared entered the room, a grin stretching across his face.

"Well, aren't you the quick one," Jared remarked, slapping Hardane on the back. "Been waiting long?"

"No. Shall we go?"

"In a minute. How was she? Did she give you your money's worth?"

"I learned what I needed to know," Hardane replied ruefully, and wondered if he'd perform any better with Selene than he had with the woman in the blue room.

And if he didn't, what then? What of the prophesy that foretold the birth of twin sons? How could he hope to produce an heir when his body refused to respond? Perhaps there was some flaw in his masculinity, perhaps he could only be aroused by a woman he couldn't have . . . Kylene.

He cursed softly as he felt his manhood stir to life. He had only to think her name, he mused, and desire ran through him, as hot and swift as lava spewing from a volcano.

Kylene.

He hurried to his horse, Jared and the woman in the blue room forgotten in his haste to return home, to see her face, hear her voice.

He railed at the cruel hand of fate that had played him such a cruel trick, and then he forgot everything but the need to be with her, the woman who held his heart.

Kylene. The one woman who could never be his.

Chapter Fifteen

Hardane left Jared to look after the horses and hurried into the keep, driven by an uncontrollable urge to see Kylene, to hear her voice. He needed the company of her sweet presence to banish the last vestiges of the pleasure palace that lingered like a dark memory in the back of his mind.

The castle had never seemed so huge as it did now as he walked through it room by room.

He found her in the small sala in the far reaches of the keep, a delicate piece of lace embroidery in her lap, a faraway look in her eyes as she gazed out the open door into the gardens beyond.

He stood inside the doorway, just watching her, for a long moment before he spoke her name.

Kylene's heart fluttered with excitement at the sound of his voice. All day, she had been thinking of him, wondering where he had gone, when he would return. It baffled her, how eagerly she had awaited his return, how empty the hours seemed when he was not there. And mingled with that bewilderment was a strong sense of guilt because she spent so much time thinking of him, only him, when she should be examining her soul, seeking penance and forgiveness for her wayward thoughts.

She laid the needlework aside as he crossed the floor to stand beside her. She tilted her head back so she could see his face, mesmerized, as always, by his rugged good looks.

Hardane stared down at her, suddenly at a loss for words now that he'd found her. The sunlight streaming through the open door made her skin glow and cast golden highlights in her hair. But it was the look of welcome in her eyes that brought a smile to his lips.

He nodded toward the gardens. "Do you . . . would you care to take a walk?"

"Aye, my lord."

He offered her his hand and helped her to her feet, pleased that she was a woman who knew her own mind, that she didn't feel the need to be coy, or to play silly games.

Outside, they walked along the wide paths that wound in and out of the gardens. The flowers were in bloom and a rich sweet fragrance filled the air.

Kylene surveyed the gardens in wonder, captivated by the shrubs that had been cut and shaped to resemble animals—wild cats, horned leopards, snarling wolves . . .

She slid a glance at Hardane, remembering how he had appeared in one of her dreams in the shape of a wolf. He was remembering, too; she could see it in his eyes. But, more than that, she felt it in her thoughts. And then, to her surprise, the image of the black wolf appeared briefly in her mind.

Kylene came to a halt and stared up at him. "How do you do that?"

"Do what?"

"You know very well what. You were reading my mind. You planted the wolf's image there."

"Did I?"

"You know you did!" she exclaimed. "Didn't you?"

"Aye, lady," he admitted with a roguish grin. "I did. I sensed you had a fondness for the beast."

Kylene dropped her gaze, embarrassed to recall how pleasurable the touch of the wolf's tongue upon her palm had been.

"You can deny it all you wish," Hardane mused, "but I know that you're Carrick's daughter, else you could not receive my thoughts, nor could I read yours."

"If you can read my thoughts so easily, why can't I read yours?"

"Have you tried?"

"Of course not," she retorted. Her first reaction was horror at the mere idea, but then . . .

"Try," Hardane urged.

She gazed into his eyes, those fathomless gray eyes, and tried to see what he was thinking. But all she could think of was how handsome he was, how much she wished that she was indeed the woman he thought her.

"You must concentrate on my thoughts," Hardane remarked with a knowing grin, "not the color of my eyes."

She flushed from the soles of her feet to the crown of her head. "Stop that!"

"I'm sorry, but some thoughts are easier to read than others, especially those that concern me."

"It's . . . it's indecent."

"Indecent, lady?" he asked wryly.

"It makes me feel naked." She clapped her hand over her mouth. Mortified at what she'd said, she stared up at him, waiting for him to make some ribald suggestion.

Instead, he took her hand in his and held it over his heart. "You need never hide your thoughts from me, Kylene. I will never betray you, or shame you."

His gaze met hers, held it, and in that moment she knew that he desired her, heart and soul, and that he would never do anything to hurt her.

Overwhelmed with the depths of his desire, not knowing how to respond, she started walking again. He quickly fell into step beside her, shortening his long stride to match her shorter one.

They walked in silence for a long while, weaving through the garden paths until they came to a maze. Kylene hesitated a moment, and then continued on. In moments, she could see nothing but green on all sides.

"Why, lady?" Hardane asked at length. "Why do you continue to deny me?"

"Why, sir, do you continue to plague me? I've told you and told you, I'm not Lord Carrick's daughter."

She came to an abrupt halt and turned to face him. "Don't you think I'd admit it if it were true? Even if I didn't find you . . ."

"Attractive?" he supplied, stifling a smile.

"Attractive," she admitted. "I'd be a fool to refuse all of this." She made a broad gesture that encompassed the whole of the castle. "I've lived in poverty all my life. If it were up to me, I would gladly stay here. But it isn't up to me. I have sworn fealty to the Sisterhood, and you're betrothed to the Princess Selene. It's your duty to wed her, just as it's my duty to honor the vows I've made."

Hardane felt a rush of admiration for the woman standing before him. She was honest. She was loyal. She would, he thought, have made a valiant knight.

He dismissed her protestations that she wasn't Carrick's daughter. Whether she denied it from fear or pretended ignorance, he knew it to be a lie. And yet, when he probed her mind, he found nothing to indicate she was other than she claimed to be, a foundling raised by the Mouldourian Sisterhood. Still, deep inside his own soul, he knew she was the woman destined to be his. And he would prove it. One way or another, he would prove it.

Kylene held Hardane's gaze a moment more, and then she began walking again, conscious that he was there beside her.

A short time later, they reached the heart of the maze. "Oh," Kylene exclaimed. "It's beautiful."

And yet beautiful didn't begin to describe it. A crystal geyser bubbled from an underground spring. Huge lacy ferns and wondrous flowers grew in profuse abundance. A small stone bench was shaded by the leafy umbrella of an ancient willow tree. A golden shrub grew beside the spring. Cut in the shape of a unicorn, it seemed vibrant and alive.

It was like being in a different world, a magical world where dreams could come true, where the innermost desires of one's heart might be granted.

Slowly, she turned around, not wanting to miss the smallest detail, until she came face-to-face with Hardane.

For a timeless moment, they gazed at each other.

And then, wordlessly, helplessly, he held out his arms.

And she, willingly, eagerly, stepped into his embrace, lifting her face for his kiss.

He lowered his head, blocking the sun, the sky, until there was nothing in all the world but the man bending over her. With infinite tenderness, his lips claimed hers. Feather-light, no more than the merest whisper of his mouth on hers, yet the heat of his touch engulfed her like a living flame, consuming every thought, every emotion.

Unaccountably, the image of a black-haired, gray-eyed wolf padded quietly down the corridors of her mind, and she felt the palm of her hand tingle, felt a rush of pleasure that was as warm and sweet as the finest Mouldourian wine.

Too soon, he took his mouth from hers, and yet, in that one brief instant, Kylene knew her whole world had been changed forever.

With a sigh, Hardane let her go.

With a sigh, Kylene took a step backward.

And yet his arms still felt the warmth of her body, the softness of her skin.

Her lips still tingled with his touch, his taste.

For the first time, he wondered if it might be possible to break his betrothal if Kylene proved to be a commoner, as she claimed.

For the first time, she wondered if she had truly been called to the Sisterhood.

Because he had to touch her again, Hardane reached for her hand, his fingers curling lightly around hers.

"We should go back," he said reluctantly.

"Yes."

His gaze moved over her face, resting briefly on her lips. "Kylene . . ."

She smiled up at him, knowing that everything she was feeling was reflected in her eyes. "My lord?"

Slowly, he shook his head. "Nothing, lady. I wanted only to say your name."

His words pleased her beyond measure, making her heart swell with an emotion she had never before known.

A pleasant warmth filled her as they left the maze, walking in companionable silence back to the castle. She very carefully stored the memory of his kiss, the sound of his voice, the look in his eyes, into a corner of her mind. No matter what the future held, no matter if she spent the rest of her life in a tiny cell within the confines of the Motherhouse, she would always have the memory of this day to keep her warm.

Chapter Sixteen

Sharilyn stared at her son in alarm. "You cannot love her, Hardane. It's impossible."

"I'm afraid it's very possible, mother mine."

"But the prophesy . . . it must be fulfilled. Only your sons can bring an end to the constant warring between Argone and Mouldour. Would you let hundreds, perhaps thousands, of others suffer simply to satisfy your lust?"

She held up her hand to silence the protest that sprang to his lips. "Yes, lust, that's all it is."

"No!"

"Hardane, you're a man, a warrior. Perhaps it was wrong of me to invoke your promise to remain celibate until you wed Carrick's daughter. But I wanted only the best for you, and for Selene. No matter what others say, a man who can control his appetites is a man to be reckoned with."

"Jared—"

"Jared is not the heir to the throne of Argone. It matters not if he spills his seed like water upon the ground."

"I hear you, mother mine," Hardane said, his voice heavy. "I hear you."

Rising, he began to pace the floor, his long strides carrying him effortlessly across the room as he sought to sort through his thoughts, looking for a way to make his mother understand what he felt. Always, they had shared a close bond. In days past, they had assumed the shape of the wolf, cavorting in the moonlight as they listened to the ancient songs that only they could hear.

He had to make her understand. He drew up before her and took one of her hands in his. "What if Kylene is the woman spoken of in the prophesy?"

"Where did you get such an idea?"

He shrugged. "I can't explain it, but deep inside, I know she was meant to be mine, that we're destined to be life-mated."

Sharilyn placed her hand over her son's. "I think you feel it because you want it so badly."

"Then why can I read her thoughts? Why can I walk in her dreams? When I send my shade to mingle with my betrothed, it's Kylene who receives me, no other."

"I can't explain it," Sharilyn replied. "I only know that you must wed Carrick's daughter on the seventh day of the seventh month, or all hope for a lasting peace will be forever lost."

Knowing there was no point in arguing further, Hardane left the room.

Somehow, he would prove Kylene was meant to be his.

Until then, if he could not possess her in the flesh, there were other ways.

He was walking in her dreams again.

She was sitting beside the waterfall, watching the torrent cascade over the mountainside, and suddenly he was there beside her. The sunlight glinted off his raven-black hair and kissed his skin like a lover who had long been denied his touch.

He stood before her, his deep gray eyes alight with a fierce glow, a hunger that filled her with fear, and excitement.

He held out his arms, a question lurking in the depths of his shadow gray eyes. "Lady?"

Without a second thought, she slid off the boulder and walked into his arms. "My lord?"

"Will you be mine?" he asked, his voice low and husky.

She hesitated a moment, only a moment, even though she knew it was wrong. But she wanted him, needed him, so desperately. "Aye, my lord," she murmured softly.

For these few moments, she would be a woman like any other, free to love a man, to hold him in her arms, to savor the sweetness of his kisses.

His hand moved lightly over her shoulders and down her arms. "I've never had a woman," he said, his gaze burning into hers.

The thought that he was as innocent as she filled

her with exquisite pleasure. "I have never had a man."

"I know." The words were barely audible, made harsh by a sudden soul-wrenching uncertainty.

Her hand reached up to cup his cheek. "You will be my first," she said tremulously. "My last. My only."

"Kylene . . ." He whispered her name, and then his mouth slanted over hers and he kissed her, ever so lightly at first, his lips as light as dandelion fluff.

But it was not enough. She leaned against him, her breasts pressing to his chest, her hips arching toward his. A low moan rose in her throat as his mouth crushed hers, the tip of his tongue sliding over her lower lip, until her mouth opened under the constant pressure.

Sparks. Lights. Comets. The tail of a hurricane. Her whole body throbbed with fire and silent thunder as he kissed her again and again. Carefully, he lowered her to the ground, his weight a welcome burden.

His hands were trembling as he caressed the clothing from her body. She should have been embarrassed, mortified. No one, man or woman, had seen her naked since she was old enough to dress herself. But she felt no shame as his gaze moved over her, his gray eyes alight with something akin to reverence.

His hand traced circles on her belly as she undressed him, and then he was pressing her close once more. She let her fingertips explore his hard-muscled body boldly, shamelessly, delighting in his solid strength, in the way he trembled at her touch, at the low moan of pleasure that rumbled deep in his throat.

And he was touching her, discovering the silken hills and soft valleys, learning what made her purr with pleasure, what made her shiver with delight.

And then, when he was shaking with need, when she was trembling with desire, he parted her thighs and found his way home.

Warmth engulfed him. Heat surrounded him. And he began to move inside her, reaching for the sun.

And she gave it to him. Bright, shattering light that exploded through him and spilled into her like a million shards of silken sunbeams.

He cried her name as tremors racked his body, his voice a low growl of pleasure as his arms crushed her close.

And she arched up to meet him, drawing him deeper, deeper, knowing that never again would she feel as loved, or be as complete, as she was at that moment.

And it was only a dream . . .

She couldn't face him in the morning. No dream, no reality, had ever been as soul-satisfying as the image that had made love to her in the night. She couldn't stay here any longer, couldn't see him every day, couldn't hear his voice, see his smile, and not throw herself into his arms. Not after what had passed in her dream the night before.

If she stayed, that dream was certain to become reality and, as tempting as the thought was, she couldn't let it happen. She could not break the vows she had made to the Sisterhood. To do so would leave her soul forever damned, doomed to wander in darkness throughout all eternity.

She woke early and went to Sharilyn's room, lightly knocking on the door.

"Who's there?" inquired a sleepy voice.

"Kylene, my lady."

"Kylene? Is something wrong?"

"I need to speak to you."

"Come in, child."

Hesitantly, Kylene opened the door and stepped into Sharilyn's bedchamber. It was a large room, filled with large dark furniture. Wine red draperies covered the windows; thick fur rugs covered the floor. She was relieved to find Hardane's mother alone in the room.

"What is it, child?" Sharilyn asked.

"I came to ask a favor."

Sharilyn sat up, her back propped against the high curved headboard. "Ask."

"Hadj mentioned that there's a sisterhouse not far from here. I wish to go there."

Sharilyn's brow furrowed at the girl's odd request. "Is something wrong?"

"No, my lady. It's just that I'm uncomfortable here, surrounded by servants and . . . and wealth. I've taken vows of poverty and chastity and . . ."

"I see," Sharilyn said. And, indeed, she did see. Hardane was not the only one smitten. "I think, perhaps, it would be best for everyone if you took refuge at the Bourne Sisterhouse."

Kylene nodded. Sisterhouse or Motherhouse,

though called by different names, both were places of refuge and retreat, and she dearly needed a place to hide. "I should like to go as soon as possible."

"Within the hour, if you like."

"Thank you, my lady. And . . . I . . . that is . . ."

"I understand, my dear. Hardane needn't know where you've gone."

"Thank you, my lady."

"I shall miss you, Kylene," Sharilyn said sincerely. "I wish you every happiness in the life you've chosen."

Kylene nodded, unable to speak past the sudden lump that rose in her throat.

"Hadj will attend you," Sharilyn said kindly. "And Teliford will escort you to the abbey when you're ready."

Kylene nodded again and quickly left the room before Hardane's mother could see the tears brimming in her eyes.

"Gone!" Hardane exclaimed angrily. "Gone where?"

Sharilyn shook her head, unruffled by her son's outburst. "It was her wish to leave, a wish I respected. And you will, too."

"No!"

"If she had wanted you to know her destination, she would have told you."

Hardane swore under his breath as he began to pace the Hall's polished wooden floor. She had run away from him, run just as fast as she could. Why? Had his shadowed lovemaking been so repellent that she'd feared he might invade her dreams again?

He shook his head, knowing even as the thought crossed his mind that it wasn't true. She had returned his love, every touch, every thrust. He could not be mistaken about that.

Then why had she left the castle like a thief in the night?

He paused to stare out the window, and the answer came to him, quietly and without doubt. She had not run away from him at all, but from herself. She was an honorable woman and she had chosen to leave him rather than risk breaking her vow of chastity to the Sisterhood.

As if he would take her by force, he thought angrily.

And yet, wasn't that just what he'd done?

Selfishly, his need more urgent than his concern for her welfare, he had slipped into her mind and ravished her soul as surely as if he had raped her body.

But he couldn't forget how she had welcomed him, how she had unfolded to his touch, willingly, eagerly, drawing him to her without doubt, without hesitation . . .

A harsh cry erupted from his throat as he turned on his heel and left the Hall. Outside, he walked into the woods, seeking solace in the solitude of the forest.

Closing his eyes, he willed his body to take the shape of the wolf and then he began to run, loping with long-legged ease through the dappled shadows of the forest.

He loved being the wolf, loved the sense of freedom, the ability to run tirelessly. The wolf's nose picked up a myriad of scents: earth, trees, the smell of other animals, man . . .

And Kylene. He slowed as her scent was carried to him on the wind. She had passed this way not long ago.

At a trot now, he followed her trail, a low whine coming from his throat.

She had been here. He sniffed the ground and the air, howling with frustration. She had been here.

He followed her scent for miles, followed it to the edge of the woods. In the distance, set atop a shallow rise, he saw the stark outline of the Bourne Sisterhouse.

Sitting on his haunches, he stared at the high stone walls, a low howl rising from his throat as he heard the bells chime, calling the sisters to afternoon prayers.

Kylene's head jerked up as she heard the wolf's howl again.

It was him, she thought. Hardane. Somehow, he had followed her.

She shivered as another howl rent the stillness of the chapel. Never, never in all her life, had she heard a cry filled with such sadness, such anger, such despair.

She had arrived at the sisterhouse only a few hours ago, but it seemed as if she had been there forever. The ways of the Bourne Sisterhouse were different from the Motherhouse in Mouldour, and yet not different at all.

The same stillness permeated the rooms. The sisters wore the same look of serenity, their eyes filled with a deep inner peace. Their voices were soft, never raised in anger. They moved through the corridors on silent feet, accomplishing the tasks that needed to be done, feeding the hungry, the homeless, tending the sick, praying for those who were dying.

They had welcomed her with open arms, without question, apparently recognizing her immediately as one of their own.

The howl of the wolf came again, louder, closer. Kylene glanced around the candlelit chapel, but none of the other sisters seemed affected by the savage howling. Indeed, if they heard it at all, they paid it no mind, so caught up were they in their prayers, in their own private meditations.

Resolutely, Kylene clasped her hands and bowed her head in prayer, seeking the deep inner peace that had once been hers. But it remained out of reach, a shadow without substance, a chimera, like swamp gas on a cool summer night.

Desperate, her eyes damp with tears, she tried to find her own inner stillness, but it was gone, perhaps forever, shattered by the remembered touch of a man's hands on her too willing flesh, and the heartrending lament of the wolf.

That cry, that haunting, lonely cry, followed her the rest of the afternoon and into the quiet hours of the evening, penetrating every thought.

That night, when she crawled into bed, she was determined to stay awake, afraid he would steal into her dreams and take her unawares, afraid that, if he but spoke the word, she would turn her back on all she had promised to be, to do, simply because she wanted so badly to indulge her fantasies, to feel his hands in her hair, his lips caressing her flesh.

Wicked, she thought helplessly; such thoughts were so very, very wicked.

She closed her eyes and tried to pray, but her ears were filled with the anguished sound of the wolf's howl.

She remained awake as long as she could, but gradually her body's need for sleep overcame her and she tumbled over the brink into oblivion.

In her sleep, she wept, because he was not there.

Chapter Seventeen

"It was what she wanted, Hardane," Sharilyn said gently. "The vows of poverty, chastity, and obedience are not given lightly, and, once given, must not be broken."

"I know."

He sat with his head cradled in his hands, his shoulders slumped. She had never seen him look so defeated, so thoroughly discouraged.

"Hardane . . ."

"I'm all right, mother mine. Don't worry about me."

Indeed, she thought. When had she ever done anything else? He had been an adventuresome child, walking when he was only eight months old, climbing, exploring. No matter how many times he fell, how many bumps and bruises he sustained, he never gave up. Nothing frightened him—not fire, not water, not threats of dire punishment. What he set his mind on, he achieved. And yet, for all his willfulness, he had never been mean or disrespectful. When he did something wrong, he admitted it and took his punishment without complaint.

Now, for the first time in his life, he wanted something and he couldn't have it. Most people learned early in life that they couldn't have everything they wanted. Sharilyn admitted it was partly her fault that it was a lesson Hardane was learning only now. But he had been her last-born son, the seventh son of a seventh son, and because she had known of the hardships that awaited him, she had cherished him and spoiled him beyond measure. She knew now that it had been a disservice to let him believe he could have everything he wanted simply because he wanted it.

Hardane rose to his feet heavily, crossed the floor, and gazed out the window, staring at the forest. Beyond the trees lay the tall gray buildings of the Bourne Sisterhouse. And Kylene.

He had spent a sleepless night, tormented by his longing to walk in her dreams and the knowledge that he had no right to violate her. She had fled the castle to escape him, and he would respect her wishes. But the knowledge that he could go to her, that he could touch her again, hold her in his arms, even if it was only in her dreams, was tearing him apart.

He sensed his mother's presence behind him, felt her arms circle his waist. "It will pass, Hardane. Only give it time."

He nodded bleakly, not believing her.

"Won't you trust me, son?" she asked quietly.

"I love her. I . . . I did something I shouldn't have."

Sharilyn's arms tightened around Hardane's waist. "Tell me."

"I seduced her."

"No!"

"Only in her dreams, mother mine, but it could not have been more real if she'd been in my arms."

Sharilyn uttered a wordless cry of despair. For the Wolffan, the line between reality and dreams was very fine indeed. Sometimes, what happened in the netherworld of sleep was more meaningful, more significant, than anything that happened in the clear light of day.

"I'm going after my father," Hardane said. "I've already alerted my men. We leave on the evening tide."

"Can you not wait for Dirk and Garth to return? They should be home within a fortnight."

Hardane shook his head. Much as he would have liked to have had his brothers at his side, he couldn't wait.

Sharilyn nodded, knowing there was nothing she could say to change his mind. And perhaps, she thought, it was better not to try.

With a sigh, she pressed her cheek to his back. "Be careful, Hardane," she murmured. "Your people are depending on you."

He nodded, but she knew him too well. He wanted the danger, the adventure, seeking it as an alternative to the pain he was feeling, as men had always run toward danger when they were running away from a deep inner hurt.

"Be careful," she repeated, and then he was gone.

He stood on the quarterdeck of the *Sea Dragon*, gazing out across the water, his face into the wind. Kylene had run away from him, run to the safety of the Bourne Sisterhouse, knowing he could not follow her there. He could not blame her, not after what he'd done, and yet the thought that she'd run from him hurt as few things in his life had hurt.

He was the seventh son of a seventh son and as such, he was heir to the throne. And because he was to be the next Lord of Argone, little in life had been denied him. He'd never thought of himself as being pampered but, in retrospect, he supposed he had been. People had always deferred to him. At first it had been because he was the heir, but later, as he grew to manhood, he had earned their respect, earned it with his sword on the battlefield; on shipboard, with his crew; and, more recently, in running the affairs of the land while his father was imprisoned. He had always done what was expected of him, always done what was right even when it wasn't what he, himself, wanted.

He wanted Kylene.

With an oath, he began to pace the quarterdeck, relishing the sting of the wind in his face, the smell of the salt air. Perhaps two weeks at sea would clear her image forever from his mind.

And perhaps the sea would freeze over and the sky would melt, he thought ruefully.

The bells. Her life was ruled by the bells. Five bells roused her from her hard, narrow cot in the morning, four sent her to prayers, three directed her to the refectory for the morning meal. Another four bells sent her back to the chapel for mid-morning prayers; two told her it was time to take her place in the laundry room where she helped one of the Holy Sisters of Bourne wash the heavy black habits of their order. There was a brief pause for the midday meal, more prayers, and then it was back to the laundry until the ringing of the bells sent her off to the refectory again.

Idle speech and laughter were to be avoided in the sisterhouse. Their rule was one of work and prayer. They followed a schedule that never varied, summer or winter, rain or shine. Sunday was a day of rest, a day to be spent in constant prayer and meditation.

Kylene slipped into the life of the Bourne Sisterhouse without causing a ripple. She purged her mind of all worldly thoughts, all memories of a tall, well-muscled warrior with copper-hued skin and hair the color of pitch and eyes as gray as the stone walls of her tiny cell.

She prayed constantly for strength, for forgiveness for the lustful thoughts that had plagued her while she had been in Hardane's company.

And if she sometimes wondered at the wisdom of her chosen vocation, if she questioned what good could come of spending one's life closed behind high stone walls, of denying oneself the companionship of a husband, the joy of children, she kept such thoughts to herself, certain that, if she tried hard enough, she would learn to control her thoughts. Surely, in time, Hardane's image would become less clear, the remembered touch of his hand would lose its power to make her tremble with longing. Surely, in time, she would forget the sound of his voice, forget how masterful he looked standing on the quarterdeck with the wind whipping through his hair. She would forget how he had comforted her and held her and . . .

She was lying to herself, and she knew it. She would never forget him, not if she lived a thousand years. The color of his eyes, the breadth of his shoulders, the soft husky timbre of his voice were forever imprinted in her mind and her heart.

With a sigh of resignation, she bent to her task, trying to concentrate on scrubbing the dirt from the heavy black habit in the tub. But the color of the cloth reminded her of the ebony hue of Hardane's hair, and the water sloshing against the wooden sides of the washtub reminded her of the sound of the sea. . . .

It took almost a week to reach the distant Isle of Klannaad. Hardane dropped anchor several leagues off shore. At dusk, he slipped over the side and swam to the island.

Upon reaching land, he overpowered a convict he found relieving himself near the water's edge, bound the man's hands and feet, and then grinned wryly as he took on the familiar shape, wondering, as he did so, what the Executioner had done to merit being sent to this wretched place.

No one bothered him as he made his way toward the small stone castle that was situated on a low rise. The citadel had once been a monastery, but a plague had wiped out all human life and the castle had fallen into ruin. The island had been deserted until Bourke became Lord High Sovereign of Mouldour.

Hardane paused to scan the area. Fire and neglect had ruined the upper two floors of the castle, though the ground floor was still habitable. The dungeon, located below ground and made of stone, was a honeycomb of small cells where those accused of treason or treachery were imprisoned.

Where his father was imprisoned.

Hardane passed several small groups of men as he climbed the rock-strewn ridge. He guessed there were less than twenty prisoners roaming the island. He could tell, by the way they deferred to him as he walked by, that the Executioner had already established himself as a man to be reckoned with.

On reaching the top, he melted into the shadows. And waited. An hour later, one of the guards left the castle and made his way into the darkness. On silent feet, Hardane slid up behind him and rendered him unconscious. And once again, he changed shape.

Approaching the castle, he stepped inside and looked around. In the next room, he could see six cots placed at intervals along the far wall. Men slept in four of them.

Only one man occupied the anteroom. He sat behind a badly scarred table, halfheartedly sharpening a long-bladed knife.

The guard looked up as Hardane stepped into the room. "Everything quiet out there?"

Hardane nodded. He stood in the doorway for a moment, wondering if it would cause suspicion if he went down to the dungeon. The guard made it easy for him.

"It's time to check on the prisoners," the man muttered, checking the sharpness of the blade with his thumb. "Take care of it, will you?"

Hardane grunted. Then, his heart hammering, he took a torch from the nearest wall sconce and made his way down the narrow stone stairway.

The stink of urine and vomit and unwashed bodies hit him even before he reached the bottom of the stairs. Voices called out to him, begging him for food, for water, for mercy.

He walked slowly down the corridor, peering into each cell, appalled by the gaunt faces, the sunken eyes devoid of hope.

He found his father in the last cell on the left. For a moment, he could only stare in horror at the human skeleton that sat huddled on a filthy pallet. A heavy chain secured Kray's right foot to an iron ring in the wall.

Anger churned through Hardane as he took in his father's ragged clothes, his bare feet. His long black hair and beard were matted with filth. His father had always been a proud man, careful of his appearance, conscious of his station in life. He was the Lord High Ruler of Argone. As such, he should have been treated with respect.

"You'll pay for this, Bourke," Hardane muttered under his breath. "By damn, you'll pay!"

At the sound of Hardane's muffled words, the prisoner looked up. Hardane watched in amazement as a change came over his father. Kray lifted his head, his black eyes blazing with contempt. Gone was the forlorn prisoner of a moment before and in his place sat the Lord High Ruler of Argone, haughty, defiant, as though he were sitting on his throne instead of a rank pile of straw.

Hardane couldn't stay the grin that tugged at his lips. He had thought his father cowed, beaten, humbled. He should have known better.

"Father."

Kray leaned forward, his eyes narrowed. "Why do you call me father?"

"Because it is better to die as a wolf than live as a dog," Hardane whispered, quoting an old Wolffan proverb.

"Hardane!" Rising to his feet, Kray closed the distance between them.

"Are you well, my lord?"

"Well enough. How's your mother?"

"Anxious to see you again."

Kray smiled, the expression softening the harsh lines of tension around his mouth and eyes.

"I'll have you out of here soon," Hardane promised.

Kray nodded. He didn't ask questions. There was no need.

"How many guards on the island?"

"Six, I think. They're well armed, but lazy."

Hardane grunted softly. "Look for me tomorrow night at this same time."

"Take care," Lord Kray urged. He reached through the narrow barred opening and placed his hand on Hardane's shoulder. "Your mother will never forgive me if anything happens to you."

"Nothing will happen." Hardane placed his hand over his father's and gave it a squeeze. "Until tomorrow."

"Until tomorrow," Kray repeated softly, hopefully.

Kray stared at the bleak walls of his prison, the heavy chain that hampered his movements. Locked in the dreary cell, his leg shackled to the wall, he had wished, endlessly and uselessly, that he could somehow escape.

But now Hardane was here and he knew that freedom was at hand. True, all his sons were brave, fierce, loyal. He knew each of them would willingly risk their life to save his, but, of them all, Hardane had the best chance of success. It was only his youngest son, his seventh son, who possessed the special Wolffan gift.

"Until tomorrow . . ." Lord Kray smiled as he repeated Hardane's parting words.

For the first time in months, he had hope again.

"Tomorrow." He breathed the word aloud as he sank down on his straw pallet once more.

Like a magic talisman, the word hovered in the

air, keeping all his nightmares at bay, repeating itself in his mind until he fell into a deep, dreamless sleep.

Tomorrow . . .

Chapter Eighteen

Under cover of darkness, Hardane and his men
went over the side of the *Sea Dragon*, swam to
the Isle of Klannaad, and made their way ashore.

Leaving his men well hidden behind a jumbled
mass of boulders, Hardane did as he had done
the night before. He overpowered a prisoner who
had wandered away from the others and rendered
him unconscious. After assuming the man's shape,
Hardane moved up the ridge toward the abandoned
castle that housed the dungeon.

Lurking in the shadows, he waited for one of the
guards to step outside; then he quickly disarmed
the man, bound his hands and feet, and changed
shape once again.

There were two guards playing dice in the dungeon's antechamber. They looked up only briefly
as Hardane entered the room.

He acknowledged them with a nod, then took one of the torches and started for the stairs.

"Crill, where are you going?"

Hardane glanced over his shoulder, his fist tightening around the torch. "To check on the prisoners."

The guard shook his head. "It isn't necessary. Hanse went down a few minutes ago."

Hardane grunted. "I've got nothing else to do," he remarked. "I'll just see if he needs help."

The guard looked at him suspiciously for a moment, wondering at Crill's sudden ambition, and then he shrugged.

Hardane waited, but when there were no objections, he descended the stairs. His men would be storming the island in a quarter of an hour. He had to get his father out of the dungeon before then.

He saw the light from the guard's torch at the far end of the corridor. Frowning, he watched the man for several moments, and then he grinned as he saw the man tip a bottle to his mouth. Apparently the guard kept a flask hidden in the dungeon.

The guard looked up, a guilty flush staining his cheeks, as Hardane walked up to him.

"Oh, Crill," the man muttered in relief. "I thought—"

Hardane never discovered what the man thought. Drawing back his fist, he flattened the guard with a single blow to his jaw. He caught the torch before it hit the ground.

There was a stirring from within the nearby cells as the prisoners saw one guard strike another.

Hardane paid them no mind as he hurried toward his father's cell. "My lord?"

Lord Kray approached the door cautiously. "What is it?"

"Better to die as a wolf than live as a dog."

"Hardane!"

There was a world of relief, of hope, in the older man's voice as Hardane slipped the key into the lock and opened the door.

For a brief moment, the two men embraced; then Hardane thrust the torch into his father's left hand and the fallen guard's sword into his right.

"We've got to go," he said tersely.

"I'm right behind you," Kray said, and quickly followed Hardane down the corridor toward the narrow winding staircase.

Hardane heard shouts of alarm, the hoarse cries of men in pain, and the harsh clash of metal striking metal as he reached the top of the staircase.

"We're under attack!" One of the guards shouted the warning as he slammed the door that led outside. "Crill, arm yourself. . . ."

The guard's voice trailed off, his expression changing from concern to confusion when he saw Kray standing behind Hardane, a sword in his hand.

The second guard stood up, his hand resting on the hilt of his sword. "What's going on?"

"You're under attack in here, too," Hardane replied calmly. "Drop your weapons, both of you."

The two guards exchanged glances and then they both lunged forward.

140

Hardane engaged the man on the left, and soon the air rang with the harsh clang of metal striking metal. For a moment, his attention was divided between the guard and concern for his father, but soon he had no time to think of anything but his opponent, who wielded his sword with great skill. The guard managed to draw first blood, but it was Hardane who landed the fatal blow, his sword driving into the man's chest, piercing his heart.

Withdrawing his blade, Hardane whirled around in time to see his father deliver the fatal blow to the second guard.

"Let's get of here," Hardane said, assuming his own form so his men would not mistake him for the enemy.

"Wait!" Lord Kray took hold of his son's arm. "You're hurt."

Hardane glanced at the blood dripping from his left shoulder. "It's nothing."

Lord Kray started to protest that the wound needed to be bound up, at least, but it was too late. Hardane was already out the door.

Whatever fighting had taken place outside the dungeon was over. Jared and the others stood in a ragged half circle, their swords drawn. The surviving prisoners were huddled together, their expressions malevolent as they waited to see what would happen next.

Jared smiled as he saw Hardane and Lord Kray emerge from the dungeon. Lord Kray paused to speak to some of the crewmen, while Hardane continued on toward the shore. Jared started forward, intending to pay homage to his liege, when a ferocious cry rent the stillness of the night.

All eyes swung toward the sound.

Too late, Hardane saw the Executioner bearing down on him.

Too late, Jared saw the huge, scar-faced man hurl himself at Hardane. The impact knocked Hardane off his feet and sent the sword flying from his grasp.

Muttering an oath, Jared sprinted across the uneven ground, knowing, even as he did so, that he wouldn't get there in time.

Lord Kray watched in horror as the scar-faced man plunged a crudely fashioned knife into Hardane's chest.

And then Jared was there, his finely honed saber cutting through the air like a scythe, cleanly severing the Executioner's head from his body.

Heedless of the shocked gasp that hissed from the prisoners, he hurried to Hardane's side. Lord Kray was already there, his face pale as he cradled his son's head in his lap.

"Is he . . . ?" Jared looked into Lord Kray's eyes, unable to say the word.

"No, only unconscious. We must set sail for home at once."

Jared nodded. Rising to his feet, he ordered the prisoners into the antechamber and locked them inside so that they could not swarm the ship in a bid for freedom. It wouldn't take them long to break down the door, but the *Sea Dragon* would have set sail for home by then.

Lord Kray packed the wounds in Hardane's chest and shoulder with damp sea moss, then ripped his shirt into strips and bound the wounds. When that was done, several of the crewmen carried Hardane toward the shore.

A short time later the *Sea Dragon* was running before the wind, her course set for Argone.

Lord Kray paced the captain's quarters, his gaze never leaving his son's face. He was free at last, he thought, but at what a price!

Kylene sat up in bed, her face and body drenched in perspiration, the sound of her own anguished cry still ringing in her ears.

She had been dreaming of Hardane, dreaming that they were walking hand in hand through a shady glen, when suddenly she had heard a wolf's agonized cry.

Instantly, the images of her dream had vanished and she had seen Hardane lying on the ground, his shirt covered with blood, his eyes closed, his lashes like dark fans upon his pale cheeks.

She glanced around the small, barren cell that was hers, her heart pounding. She'd had the same dream for the past four nights.

Rising from her narrow cot, she went to the window and gazed out into the darkness. Low clouds shrouded the moon and the stars. The only light visible came from the garden below where a single candle burned before a life-size statue of Saint Hadreas, the patron saint of the Bourne Sisterhouse.

"Please let it be a dream," Kylene murmured, yet even as the words left her lips, images of Hardane lying helplessly in bed surrounded by candles flooded her mind. A bloody cloth was bound around his chest; his face was as white as the coarse linen nightgown that covered her from neck to heels. He tossed restlessly on the big four-poster bed, his hands clenching and unclenching. He was in terrible pain, feverish. She saw his lips move, heard the harsh rasp of his voice as he whispered her name over and over again.

It wasn't a nightmare at all. She knew it with a sudden heart-wrenching fear. Hardane was hurt, perhaps dying, and he needed her.

"Hardane, hear me."

She didn't realize she had spoken aloud until she heard the sound of her own voice. She frowned, confused by the inexplicable inner prompting that had forced the words past her lips.

"Hardane, I'm coming. Wait for me."

Kylene spoke the words with fervor, willing them across the miles to Castle Argone, repeating them again and again without knowing why.

And then, in her mind, she saw her words encircle Hardane like a soft blue flame. A deep sigh escaped his lips; his body stopped its restless churning.

She was surprised to find herself dressed and standing before the Holy Mother a few minutes later.

"What is it, sister?" the good Mother asked. "Are you ill?"

"I have to leave."

"Leave? Leave the Sisterhouse?"

"Yes. Right away."

"I'm afraid that's impossible."

"I have no time to explain, Mother, but I have to go. Immediately."

The Holy Mother frowned in consternation. "You realize that, once you leave the order, you cannot return?"

Kylene nodded. There was no time to ponder the wisdom of her decision, no time to fret over the future. Hardane needed her, and an inner force she didn't understand was urging her to go to him as quickly as possible.

"Let us pray about your decision, child," the Holy Mother suggested, rising to her feet. "Surely a few days of meditation will help you see things more clearly."

"I don't have a few days," Kylene replied sharply. "I have to leave now, tonight, with or without your blessing."

"I see."

"Is there someone who can take me to Castle Argone?"

"I'm afraid not."

"Can I at least borrow a horse? I'll see that it's returned as soon as possible."

"I'm sorry, child, Lutres took the horse to go into town for supplies. He won't be back for several days."

With a nod, Kylene turned toward the door. She couldn't wait several days. She couldn't wait another moment. She had to go, now, even if it meant walking every step of the way.

"My child, won't you at least wait until morning?"

"I'm sorry, I can't wait."

"Very well. Godspeed, and may the Father of Us All protect you in your travels."

Sharilyn stood beside her son's bed, her head bowed, her hands clasped in prayer. Her husband's homecoming, which should have been a joyous occasion, had been overshadowed by Hardane's infirmity. The gash in his arm, dealt by one of the guards, was already healing, but the knife wound inflicted by the Executioner had festered on the voyage home, and nothing seemed to help. Physicians had been called, prayers had been said, to no avail.

Because she didn't know what else to do, she had turned to the old ways. She burned a dozen blue candles to invite healing and peace into the sickroom, red candles for vitality, black ones to banish illness.

She filled a jar with angelica and mistletoe, flax and trefoil, mugwort and mullein, and placed it beside Hardane's bed in hopes their protective qualities would ward off any evil that lingered in the room.

In desperation, Sharilyn had sent for Druidia, the dark witch of Argone, hoping that the old crone's powerful magic might be able to heal Hardane's wounds. Many of the people viewed witches as evil, but the Wolffan shared an affinity with witches and warlocks, sorcerers and wizards, perhaps because they, themselves, were thought to be evil.

The witch had arrived in a swirl of heavy black wool skirts and the lingering scents of vervain and yarrow. She had nodded in approval at the numerous candles burning around the bed, and then produced one of her own—a long, slender, purple candle specially made to boost her magical powers. She had examined Hardane, withdrawn several packets of herbs from her bag, ground them with mortar and pestle.

The scents of rosemary, sage, rue, and wood sorrel had soon filled the air, mingling with Druidia's voice as she stood at the foot of the bed, chanting softly.

Hardane's breathing had eased almost immediately, the swelling and the redness had faded from his wounds, but he had remained unconscious, tossing restlessly as though he were suffering from some deep inner pain that even Druidia's magic could not reach.

"An illness of the heart, it is," Druidia had decreed. "An emptiness in his soul. Heal the heart, and the flesh will mend."

That had been two days ago. Since then, Sharilyn had been trying to prepare herself for her son's death. Despite all she could do, she feared he would not survive much longer. Druidia was right, she thought, his ailment was of the heart and the soul, not the flesh.

She looked across the bed into her husband's eyes and saw the same awful knowledge reflected in his gaze.

"Kylene." Hardane whispered her name, his voice weak, halting.

"She's coming," Sharilyn said, hoping it would soothe him to think so.

"No . . ." He shook his head. "Betrothed . . . to the Sister . . . hood . . ."

Sharilyn blinked back her tears. He sounded so weak, so forlorn. Perhaps if she sent word to the Sisterhouse at Bourne . . . but even as the thought crossed her mind, she knew it was too late. A low keening wail rose in her throat as she took Hardane's hand in hers, willing him to fight, to live just one more day.

"Kylene . . ." He breathed her name, railing at the Fates that had brought them together only to tear them apart. It was so unfair, he thought. If she was never to have been his, why had he been allowed to see her, hold her, touch her? If she was never to be his, why had their paths crossed at all?

He summoned her image to mind, wishing that he could have made love to her just once. . . . Kylene. Her name whispered through his mind like a prayer.

"I'm here."

Sharilyn whirled around, her hand going to her throat as she stared at the hooded woman standing in the doorway.

A soft cry escaped Kylene's lips as she approached the bed. Was she too late?

Sobbing his name, she knelt by the side of the bed and took Hardane's hand in both of hers. It was cold, so cold. She grasped it tightly, willing her strength, her life-force, into him.

"Hardane! Hardane, come back to me." She pressed her lips to his cheek. "Come back to me, my Lord Wolf," she murmured brokenly. "Please come back to me."

"Kylene . . . is that you?"

"Yes, oh yes." She squeezed his hand as his eyelids fluttered open and she found herself gazing into the gray depths of his eyes, eyes filled with pain and wonder.

"You . . . came back?"

"Yes."

"Why?"

"Because you needed me. Because . . ." She squeezed his hand again, afraid to say too much, afraid her heart would make promises she couldn't keep.

"You'll stay?"

"Yes, for as long as you need me."

He smiled weakly, his eyelids fluttering down once more. "Stay . . . stay . . ."

"I will."

"Always?"

She bit down on her lip, knowing she couldn't promise him always.

"As long as you need me," she said again, but he was already asleep.

"Bless you, my dear," Sharilyn said, placing her hand on Kylene's shoulder. "He's resting peacefully for the first time in days."

Lord Kray came to stand beside his wife, his brow furrowed thoughtfully as he stared down at Kylene, who was still kneeling beside the bed. "Might I have the pleasure of an introduction?"

"This is Kylene," Sharilyn answered. "She arrived here with Hardane some weeks ago."

"Why wasn't she here when we returned from Klannaad?"

"She was at the Bourne Sisterhouse, Kray."

"At Bourne? Why?"

"It's her vocation."

"Her vocation?" Lord Kray exclaimed. "What are you talking about?"

"She's taken the vows of the Sisterhood."

Lord Kray shook his head, completely bewildered.

"Hardane rescued her from the bowels of the Citadel," Sharilyn explained. "He thought she was Carrick's seventh daughter."

Lord Kray frowned. "Isn't she?"

"No."

"Are you blind? She looks just like Carrick."

"Does she?" Sharilyn stared at Kylene. "I've never seen him."

"Oh, yes, I'd forgotten," Lord Kray murmured absently. "Well, I've seen him. This girl has his eyes, his coloring."

"I'm sorry, my lord," Kylene interjected shyly, "but I'm not related to Lord Carrick. I'm a foundling."

"Go on."

"I was given into the care of the Sisterhood when I was very young. I have no memory of any other life."

"How did my son happen to rescue you?"

"I'm not sure. I . . . I saw him in my dreams and then, shortly after I was captured by the Interrogator, Lord Hardane rescued me and brought me here. He thought I was his betrothed, but as I've told you, that's quite impossible."

"You saw my son in your dreams?"

"Yes, my lord."

"You know, of course, that such a thing is impossible unless you're destined to be life mated?"

"So I've been told."

Lord Kray shook his head. Deny it though she might, Kylene was related to Carrick. The resemblance was far too strong to be happenstance.

He glanced down at his son, who was sleeping peacefully. "We will discuss this further in the morning," he decided, taking his wife by the hand. "I suggest we all get some sleep until then."

Kylene looked at Hardane's hand resting in hers. "I'd like to stay here, if it's all right."

"Of course," Sharilyn said. "Bless you, my dear."

Alone, Kylene stared out the window, her mind replaying Lord Kray's words. *She looks just like Carrick . . . she has his eyes, his coloring . . . you saw my son in your dreams . . . such a thing is impossible unless you are destined to be life mated . . .*

Weary and confused, she rested her head on her arm and closed her eyes. Was it possible? Was she Carrick's seventh daughter? But what of Selene? It was no secret that Selene was Carrick's seventh daughter. She had gone into exile with her father, her whereabouts were unknown, but it was common knowledge that she had been betrothed to Lord Kray's son since birth. They were to be married this year, in the seventh month.

"Kylene."

His voice, though faint, made her pulse race with new life. She could feel him watching her and she opened her eyes slowly, wanting to savor the moment when her gaze met his again.

His eyes were clear, as fathomless, and beautiful, as always.

"I thought I had dreamed you," Hardane murmured.

He slipped his hand from hers, then caught her hand in his and pressed his lips to her palm. His touch, though light, spread through her like heat lightning, making her heart sing, bringing a warm flush to her cheeks.

"Are you really here?" he asked, his lips brushing against the sensitive skin of her palm.

Kylene nodded, her gaze locked with his, her mind unable to accept the fact that he was growing stronger before her very eyes. His skin had lost the pale waxy look that had frightened her so. His hand was no longer cold, but cool, his breathing steadier, less erratic. It was impossible, she thought, and yet the proof was before her eyes, a living, breathing miracle.

He stretched, and then he sat up. She was too stunned by his sudden recovery to protest when he lifted her onto the bed, then gathered her into his arms. "How did you know I needed you?"

"I saw you in a dream. I heard you calling my name."

"And I heard you." His hand delved under her hair to stroke the nape of her neck. "I knew if I held the darkness at bay long enough that you would come to me."

"You heard me? What did I say?"

"You said, 'Hardane, I'm coming. Wait for me.' I heard what my father said, too," he murmured, his breath tickling her ear. "Do you still deny that you are my betrothed?"

Kylene nodded. "Aye, my lord. And yet I cannot deny that we are truly bound in some way that I do not understand."

"I understand," he replied quietly. "You are a part of my heart, my soul, my very life. How else can you explain our bond?"

"I can't." She looked at him, her expression troubled.

What if it was true? What if she really was a part of him? What if he couldn't live without her? And what if the reverse was true? Would she somehow die without him? She thought of how lost she had felt while residing at the Sisterhouse at Bourne, how long the days had been, how empty the nights had seemed. Without Hardane, she'd had little appetite for food or drink or for life itself.

The thought of being so closely bound to another frightened her in ways she feared to examine too closely.

"What are we to do?" she asked tremulously.

"I don't know. I only know that you've come back to me, and I won't let you go again."

"Why has this bond made itself known only now?"

"Because the time for mating is approaching. The bond lies dormant until the time of the mating moon."

Kylene swallowed hard. The seventh day of the seventh month would soon be upon them.

Her heart fluttered with excitement at the thought of being his woman, his wife. "And will

153

the bond go away once you've joined with your betrothed?"

"No." His right hand roamed up and down her spine. "Do not be afraid, lady. You cannot change what was meant to be."

With a sigh, Kylene buried her face in the hollow of his shoulder. In spite of what he thought about fate and destiny, in spite of all he'd said about not letting her go, nothing had been settled. He was still betrothed to another, and she was still promised to the Sisterhood. But for now, for this one night, she didn't care. Hardane was here, beside her, and that was all that mattered.

Tomorrow, they would worry about the future.

Tomorrow, she would ponder what Lord Kray had said about her uncanny resemblance to Lord Carrick.

But none of that seemed important now. Hardane was alive and well, and she was in his arms, content to be there for as long as the Fates allowed.

Chapter Nineteen

Selene sat beside her father, listening to his labored breathing. She offered him a cup of cool water, holding his head while he drank. Months of hiding out, of finding shelter in dank caves, of trying to eke a living out of the barren land of the Mouldourian desert had left him weak and disheartened.

Gently, she lowered him down to the blanket once more. Gently, she covered him. He reached for her hand, his long, thin fingers wrapping around her own, and then he closed his eyes.

Selene glanced at the dismal cave that had been her home for the past six months. Once, she'd lived in luxury. She'd had numerous servants to wait upon her, dresses of the latest fashion, the best victuals and the finest wines the land had to offer.

She stared at the tattered hem of her gown, quietly cursing her uncle Bourke's treachery. When she was again in a position of power, she'd see him drawn and quartered for the misery he had caused her. The swine. He'd had a castle that was as big as Castle Mouldour, servants to do his every bidding, enough wealth to last two lifetimes. He'd been Carrick's chief advisor, heir to the throne, Master of the Treasury. He'd had everything a man could want, except the throne and the power that went with it.

Power. She knew how her uncle felt; she could understand why he had done what he'd done. Almost, she could forgive him for what he'd done. Almost.

Day passed into night and she stayed at her father's side, watching the shallow rise and fall of his chest. He was dying, of that she had no doubt. A ghost of a smile tugged at her lips. Soon she would be free, free to pursue the destiny intended for Carrick's seventh daughter.

She wondered absently what Hardane of Argone looked like, if he was kind or cruel, if the blood of the Wolffan truly flowed in his veins. But none of that mattered. She wanted to share his throne. To bear his children. To know, at last, the security that came from belonging to a man who possessed power and strength and knew how to use both wisely.

She stared down at her father, her expression cold. He had always been a kind man, a fair-minded man, but he had been weak and foolish and it had cost him the throne of Mouldour.

Rising, she cast a last glance at the man who had sired her. There was nothing she could do for him now. It was time to look forward, time to go to Castle Argone and claim the prize that she had coveted for as long as she could remember.

Chapter Twenty

Sometime during the night, Kylene awoke, shivering violently, her mind filled with vague images, indistinct images of a man and a woman that seemed oddly familiar though she was certain she'd never seen either of them.

She stared wildly around the room, the covers clutched to her breasts, her heart pounding with an impending sense of doom.

With a hand that trembled, she lit the taper beside her narrow bed, but even the flickering light of the candle failed to dispel the thick darkness that hovered around her.

She whimpered Hardane's name, wishing he was there beside her. The thought had barely crossed her mind when the chamber door burst open and she saw him silhouetted in the dimly lit corridor, his sword clutched in his hand. He was naked save for a bit of cloth that covered his loins.

"What is it?" he asked harshly.

Kylene shook her head. "I . . . I don't know." She lifted one shoulder and let it fall. "Nothing, I guess."

Frowning, Hardane stepped into the room. And then he felt it, an aura of darkness, of evil.

Crossing the floor, he put his arms around Kylene and held her close.

"You feel it, too, don't you?" Kylene asked, her voice filled with wonder and fear.

"Aye, lady, I feel it." His arms tightened around her as the evil in the room swirled around them, growing stronger, more oppressive.

Kylene buried her face in the hollow of Hardane's shoulder, certain that only he could protect her from the unseen menace that seemed to lurk in the shadows, ready to envelop her. His skin was cool against her cheek, his arms solid and reassuring as he held her close.

Abruptly, he swept her into his arms and carried her out of the room into the hallway.

"Where are you taking me?"

"To my chambers."

She stared at him in horror. "No. Please, I . . . what will your mother think? Oh, please, Hardane, don't do this."

But it was like trying to reason with a mountain. He carried her as if she weighed no more than a thistle, his long legs carrying them down the long corridor to his room.

Inside, he closed and bolted the door. Tossing his sword aside, he lowered her to his bed.

Kylene stared up at him, her cheeks flushed with embarrassment. The evil that had engulfed her only moments ago was completely forgotten as she found herself alone in Hardane's room, sitting on the edge of his bed.

Her gaze skittered across the width of his broad shoulders, the vast expanse of bare male chest, a bronzed belly ridged with muscle. Her gaze darted quickly back to his face as a new fear took hold of her, one more frightening, one infinitely more dangerous, than the darkness that had hovered in her room.

"Please, don't." She forced the words from a throat gone suddenly dry.

"Don't what, lady?"

"Don't defile me."

He cocked his head to one side, his gray eyes glittering. "Do you think I would take you against your will?"

"No," she said, her voice barely audible. "But I fear you could make me want you with very little effort."

Hardane stared at her, his heart accelerating at her words. "You do want me," he replied, his tone confident. "You want me as I want you."

Kylene nodded. There was no point in arguing, nothing to be gained by lying, not when he could read her thoughts.

"Lady, there's something I should tell you."

"Tell me, then."

"Kylene, I . . ." Slowly, he shook his head. He couldn't tell her, not now. Instead, he leaned toward her, his gray eyes blazing.

Knowing it was wrong, Kylene lifted her face for his kiss.

He didn't close his eyes as his lips covered hers, nor did she.

She felt the heat of his kiss, saw the bright flames of passion that burned in the depths of his eyes, felt his hands clasp her shoulders. She knew then that she would never return to the Sisterhood, that she was truly bound to this man who could divine her innermost thoughts, who had the power to make her heart soar and her soul rejoice.

Hardane felt the change in her, felt the walls she had built between them fall away, and knew she would be his. A low moan of pained pleasure rumbled in his throat as he drew his lips from hers.

"You have accepted me at last," he murmured, ignoring the voice of his conscience that chided him for being a coward, for not telling her who and what he was.

His fingertips traced the curve of her cheek, and then he kissed her again, savoring the taste of her lips. "Tell me," he whispered, "tell me that you'll be mine."

"I will be yours," she replied breathlessly. "I think I have always been yours."

His smile warmed her as nothing else could. Exultantly, he swept her into his arms and crushed her to his chest, his arms tight around her, his desire for her evident in every taut line of his hard, muscular body.

"Kylene, ah Kylene."

He said her name again and again, the sound filling the room like a prayer and a promise.

Dizzy with happiness, she stared deep into his eyes, wondering if he would make love to her now.

Slowly, Hardane shook his head. "I want to," he said, answering her unspoken thought. "I have wanted you since the day I first saw you, but I cannot. Not now."

Reluctantly, he let her go, his hands curling into tight fists as he fought to keep from laying her back on the bed and burying himself in her sweetness. A low groan that was almost a growl rumbled in his throat as he fought down the urge to possess her, to learn the secrets of a woman's love.

"Go to sleep, Kylene." He forced the words through clenched teeth.

"Perhaps I should go back to my own room," she suggested.

"No. I don't want you to be alone." He drew a ragged breath. "I'll sit there," he said, pointing to the window seat on the far side of the room. "Try to get some rest."

For a moment, she sat there staring up at him. It didn't seem right that she should take his bed and she was about to say so when something in his gaze warned her to keep still and do as she was told.

"Good sleep, my lord," she murmured, and crawled under the covers, pulling the blankets up to her chin.

"Good sleep, lady," he replied, knowing that he would not find any rest this night, not with her lying there in his bed.

Already her scent seemed to fill the room. And

her thoughts, uncertain, filled with a yearning for that which she didn't understand, played havoc with his imagination.

With a great effort of will, he drew his thoughts from Kylene and focused instead on the darkness that had hovered in her room, a blackness fraught with evil. It might have been a sorcerer's spell, he mused, or the ghost of some ancient inhabitant of Castle Argone, and yet he knew instinctively that it had been neither one. It had been the essence of a dark vengeful soul, a festering, palpable hatred that had been directed at Kylene.

But why?

In the morning, Kylene woke to find herself alone in Hardane's bedroom. A dress had been placed on the foot of the bed, along with the necessary undergarments, thick white stockings, a pair of soft-soled white boots, and a length of fine white ribbon.

Kylene stared at the dress. It was made of finely spun yellow wool, pale and soft. The underskirt was a darker shade of yellow, almost gold. The sleeves were long and full, slashed at intervals to reveal a layer of the same dark gold cloth as the underskirt. A froth of cream-colored lace decorated the square-cut neckline.

Sitting up, she let her hand slide over one sleeve. What would it be like to wear such a dress?

Before she could change her mind, she slipped out of bed, threw off her sleeping gown, and donned the exquisite yellow dress. After braiding her hair and tying it with the ribbon, she stood in front of the mirror and studied her reflection. The yellow of the dress made her hair seem redder, her eyes more brown.

With a sigh of resignation, she started to remove the gown, intending to put on the dreary black habit she had been wearing when she arrived from the Bourne Sisterhouse.

"No."

Startled, Kylene sent an anxious glance toward the door to find Hardane standing there, his arms crossed over his chest, his slate gray eyes warm with admiration.

"How long have you been there?" Kylene demanded.

"Long enough to know you'll never wear black again."

"Members of the Bourne Sisterhouse aren't allowed to wear colors," she retorted inanely.

"You're no longer a member of the Bourne Sisterhouse," he reminded her.

"The Motherhouse at Mouldour doesn't—"

"You'll never go back to the Motherhouse at Mouldour, either."

"But I . . ."

Hardane crossed the floor in three long strides and took her in his arms.

"You're mine, Kylene. Have you forgotten what you said last night?"

She hadn't forgotten, but now, in the cold light of day, it didn't seem possible. Even if she wanted him, even if he wanted her, he was betrothed to another.

"You're mine," Hardane murmured again.

164

"Always and forever mine. I'll not let you go again."

His hands slid down her arms, the heat of his touch penetrating her cloth-covered arms, sending shivers up and down her spine. Slowly, deliberately, he took the ribbon from her hair and ran his fingers through the thick braid until her hair fell in a glorious mass around her face and over her shoulders.

Kylene swallowed hard, unable to take her gaze from his face. There was something terribly intimate about the touch of his hands in her hair, something that spoke of possession in the way his hands rested on her shoulders.

Hardane gazed into her eyes, his expression telling her more clearly than words that he found her beautiful, desirable.

"I like it down," he said, his voice husky.

Kylene blinked up at him, her heart fluttering like the wings of a hummingbird. "Then I'll wear it down."

A slow smile curved the corners of Hardane's mouth and then he lowered his head and brushed a kiss over her lips. It was no more than a whisper, a promise, but it sent waves of delight crashing through her. She could feel the pressure of his hands on her shoulders, sense his barely controlled passion.

Without conscious thought, she leaned toward him, her arms wrapping around his waist, and he obligingly kissed her again, his lips lingering on hers as he held her close against him.

With a groan, Hardane let her go and took a

step back. He took several deep breaths to still the pounding of his heart, and then he took her hand.

"My parents are waiting for us in the dining hall," he said, giving her hand a squeeze.

It took a moment for his words to penetrate the fuzzy web of desire that he'd spun around her with only a kiss. "What? Oh . . ."

Hardane chuckled, pleased by Kylene's heated response to his kisses, to the way her cheeks pinked with pleasure.

"Your parents! Oh, Hardane, your mother doesn't want me here."

He wanted to argue, to put her mind at rest, but he could not lie to her. He knew that, as grateful as his mother was for Kylene's help in restoring his health, she would never forgive him if he refused to marry Carrick's daughter. But it couldn't be helped. Knowing Kylene, loving her, he could not wed another.

Kylene stared up at him, her eyes wide. "You love me?"

Hardane grinned at her. "Are you reading my mind, lady?"

"Did you not speak?"

He shook his head, his eyes glinting with delight. "No, lady."

Kylene clapped her hand over her mouth, astonished that she had so easily read his mind.

"It seems our bond is growing stronger," Hardane remarked.

She could think of nothing to say. Hand in hand, they went down the wide stone stairway that led to the dining hall.

Kylene's stomach fluttered nervously when she saw Sharilyn and Lord Kray sitting at the table.

Hardane's parents greeted her warmly. Sharilyn smiled at Kylene, her appreciation for Kylene's help in restoring Hardane's health shining in her eyes.

Lord Kray nodded in her direction, his expression speculative, and Kylene knew he was wondering if she was indeed Carrick's daughter, even though she had told him that such a thing was impossible.

Kylene was decidedly uncomfortable during the course of the meal. Troubled by chaotic thoughts, she was hardly aware of what she ate, if she ate at all. She kept hearing Hardane promise that he would never let her go, that she was his, always and forever. A warmth flooded her as she remembered hearing his words of love in her mind.

They had just finished the last course when a messenger hurried into the dining hall.

"What is it, Parah?" Lord Kray asked.

"We have a visitor, milord," Parah said, his words tumbling forth in a rush. "A most auspicious visitor."

Lord Kray sat forward expectantly. "Who is it?"

Parah took a deep breath, held it, and then let it out in a long, slow sigh, as if he relished the moment of drama and hated to see it end.

"Parah . . ." Lord Kray's voice spoke of his growing impatience.

"Lord Carrick's seventh daughter."

Sharilyn and Lord Kray exchanged astonished glances, and then Sharilyn looked at Hardane, who was frowning.

Madeline Baker

Kylene sat motionless, her face drained of color.

"Show her in," Lord Kray commanded.

The air in the dining hall seemed to crackle with expectation as they awaited the arrival of Lord Carrick's daughter.

Kylene felt as if someone had drained the very life from her limbs. She looked at Hardane, and even as her eyes moved lovingly over him, it seemed to her that he was moving farther and farther away even though he remained seated beside her.

In moments, a lady swept into the room, her bearing regal in spite of her tattered gown.

Kylene gasped as she stared into the woman's face. It was like looking into a mirror.

"May I introduce the Lady Selene," Parah said in his most formal voice.

There was a long moment while everyone in the room looked from Selene to Kylene and back again.

Lord Kray recovered first. "Welcome, Lady Selene," he said, rising to his feet. Crossing the room, he extended his hand.

"Thank you, my lord," Selene replied, dropping a proper curtsey.

"This is my wife, Lady Sharilyn, and my son, Hardane. And this," he said, gesturing at Kylene, "can only be your sister."

"Yes, Kylene," Selene murmured. She stared at her twin for a long moment and then, as if suddenly remembering where she was, she bowed to Sharilyn, then turned the full warmth of her smile on Hardane.

"Twins," Hardane said, glancing from one to the other.

"Yes," Selene said. "Won't you embrace me, sister?" she asked, and held out her arms.

Still stunned at the realization that she had a sister, Kylene crossed the room. For a moment, she stared into Selene's eyes, eyes so like her own, and then she put her arms around her sister. She felt no warmth in the gesture, no sense of unity, of kinship.

And then Selene was hugging her back, and for a moment Kylene felt as if she were trapped in a dark cave.

With a start, Kylene dropped her arms to her sides and stepped away. She saw Sharilyn and Lord Kray smiling at the two of them, obviously touched by what looked like a warm reunion. Kylene frowned. Had she imagined the sense of darkness that had swept over her? She glanced at Hardane, wondering if he'd been aware of it, but his expression was closed to her.

Selene felt a sense of relief as the contact was broken. Turning away from her sister, she smiled at the man she intended to marry. He was more handsome than she had dared hope. Tall and broad-shouldered, he exuded the kind of raw masculinity that was impossible to ignore.

"Selene, won't you please sit down," Sharilyn invited, gesturing at the chair beside her.

"Thank you." Selene sat down and folded her hands in her lap. It was said that the Lady Sharilyn was descended from the Wolffan, but now, looking at the petite woman, Selene dismissed what she'd heard as scullery gossip.

But it was Hardane who held her gaze. "My lord," she murmured. "I hope you will forgive me for arriving without an invitation."

Hardane nodded. For the moment, he seemed incapable of speech as he glanced from Kylene to Selene and back again, wondering if he had imagined the dark pall that had seemed to engulf Kylene when she embraced her sister. Her twin sister. For some inexplicable reason, his shade had been received by the wrong woman.

"You're welcome here, of course," Lord Kray said, frowning at his son's rudeness. "Tell me, where is your father?"

Selene squeezed a tear from her eye. "He has passed on, milord. I came here unbidden as I had nowhere else to go."

"I'm sorry," Lord Kray replied. "Carrick of Mouldour was an honorable man. In another time and place, we might have been friends."

Hardane leaned forward, his eyes narrowing as he studied the woman who was destined to be his bride. "How is it that you and your sister were separated?"

"I hesitate to say, since it makes my father sound quite cruel, but he decided that since I was the eldest, and betrothed to wed into the House of Argone, he would send Kylene to live with the Sisterhood. By so doing, he could enlarge my dowry."

Selene glanced at Kylene, hoping to see the effect of her words, but Kylene's face remained expressionless.

Hardane nodded. It was a common practice for the second sons of the Mouldourian nobility to be given to the church, since they had little hope of inheriting their father's lands. He had not been aware that the custom pertained to women, as well.

Selene smiled benignly. "I am glad to see you again at last, sister. Our father spoke of you often." Too often, she thought bitterly. But all that was over now. She would soon have everything she deserved.

"I am surprised to meet you," Kylene said, her voice curiously flat. "How did our father die?"

"Of a fever. We have been in hiding for quite some time, trying to elude Bourke's men. It was Father's hope to regain his throne, but it was not to be. The Lord High Interrogator executed all those who tried to come to our aid, until our people feared to help us."

Kylene shivered at the mention of the Interrogator. She could well imagine his evil influence striking terror into the hearts of any who opposed him. It occurred to her suddenly that Bourke was her uncle, that her father was dead, that her sister, a sister she had no memory of, was the woman who was rightfully betrothed to Hardane. She felt a curious emptiness inside, a disappointment that she could summon no sense of love or affection for the woman who was her kin, only soul-shattering envy.

Kylene stood abruptly, her legs trembling. "If you'll excuse me, Lord Kray, I think I'd like to go to my room. I'm sure Lord Hardane and my sister have much to discuss, and I . . . I . . ." She sent a pleading glance at Lord Kray. "Milord?"

His eyes were kind as he said, "You have my leave to retire, Lady Kylene."

"Thank you," she murmured, and hurried from the dining hall. Only when she reached the safety of her own room did she let the tears fall.

Chapter Twenty-One

For Hardane, the rest of the day passed in a blur, as if he were seeing it all through a layer of gauze. Selene was given a chance to refresh herself and then, clad in a clean gown of rose-colored silk, she joined the family in the informal sitting room.

Now, two hours after Selene's arrival, Hardane sat beside the fireplace, listening impassively as his mother and Selene talked of the coming wedding. Lord Kray managed to sneak in a few questions about Carrick, about Bourke, about current conditions in Mouldour. Of her own accord, Selene spoke little of her father, his death, or the hardships they had endured since Bourke assumed the throne. She answered Kray's questions, but that was all.

Hardane felt an emptiness inside, a sense that Fate had taken control of his life. His betrothed was seated across from him, the very image of the woman he loved, but he felt nothing for her. Her hair was the same color as Kylene's, yet the red seemed to lack the fire that blazed in Kylene's tresses. Her eyes were the same shade of brown, yet Kylene's were as warm as sun-kissed earth, and Selene's seemed as cold as frozen ground. When she smiled at him, he felt nothing. How was he to bed her, to breed her, when he felt no warmth, no desire?

At length, Selene commented that she was weary and begged to be excused. Apologizing for her endless chatter, Sharilyn escorted Selene to the living quarters upstairs, summoning one of Hadj's cousins to look after Selene's needs, telling Selene to be at ease, assuring her that Castle Argone was her home now.

Hardane stared into the fire. Was it only this morning that he'd promised Kylene that she'd never return to the Sisterhood, that she would be his, that he would never let her go?

He heaved a sigh. The responsibility of his birthright weighed heavily on his shoulders. He was betrothed to Selene, had been pledged to take her to wife since the day of her birth. In spite of what he felt for Kylene, in spite of the promises he had made her—promises he'd had no right to make her—he knew he would do what was expected of him. He would wed Selene so that their sons might bring peace to the war-weary lands of Argone and Mouldour.

Because he was an honorable man, he could not ask Kylene to be his concubine, though it would be within his right to do so when he took the throne.

Because he was an honorable man, because Kylene meant more to him than his own life, he would send her away from him. Better the pain of a clean break than the torment of seeing her each day and knowing she would never be his.

How could he send her away? How could he face the future, knowing he would never see her again?

Why did he have no bond with Selene, who was his rightful bride? Unless she was not meant to be his bride at all. But she was Carrick's seventh daughter . . .

He closed his eyes, his head pounding.

"What troubles you, my son?"

Hardane met his father's gaze. "Nothing. Everything. I do not wish to wed Selene."

Lord Kray released a deep sigh. "Sometimes it isn't easy to do what's expected, what's required. Sometimes one has to put the welfare of the many over the desires of one's own heart."

"It was a pledge made long ago," Hardane muttered. "Who knows if the prophesy is true? Perhaps there will never be peace between Mouldour and Argone. Perhaps, if it's meant to be, peace will be achieved no matter who I marry."

"Perhaps."

"I want Kylene for my wife. I've lived like a eunuch my whole life, Father. When I finally bed a woman, I wish it to be one of my own choosing, one who fires my blood."

"That's how the feud between our countries

175

started in the first place," Kray reminded his son.

"Then let it continue!" Too restless to remain seated any longer, Hardane stood up and paced the floor. "Who's to be offended? Her parents are dead. Her sisters have allied themselves to foreign nobles."

"What of my honor? I pledged my word that you would marry Lord Carrick's seventh daughter. Whether you find her desirable or not, she is still your betrothed. Would you shame her?"

"Won't having a husband who despises her bring her a greater, more lasting shame?"

Lord Kray shrugged. "Perhaps we should ask the lady in question."

Hardane came to stand in front of his father. "And if she agrees to release me from my vow?"

"I shall discuss it with your mother and with Druidia."

Hardane nodded. It wasn't much to hang on to, but at the moment it was all he had.

Kylene spent the day in the safety of her room. Lying on her bed, she stared up at the ceiling. She had a sister. All this time, she'd had a twin sister she hadn't known existed.

And that sister was betrothed to the man she loved.

It had been Selene the Interrogator was looking for. Selene who should have received Hardane's *tashada* in her dreams. Selene who would be his wife, bear his children, share his throne, his joys, and his sorrows.

Tears burned her eyes and she let them fall freely,

hoping they would ease the ache in her heart, knowing they would not. She loved Hardane of Argone with every fiber of her being, and she would never love again. She could not return to the Bourne Sisterhouse. It was unlikely that she would be able to return to the Sisterhood at Mouldour, but there were other empires, and other abbeys. She would ask to be sent to Bierly or Dunsmere. Both had large cloisters. Perhaps one of them could find a place for her.

But the thought of spending the rest of her life in selfless service to others no longer had the power to soothe her.

Glancing outside, she was surprised to see that night had fallen. When Hadj came to the door to tell her dinner was ready, Kylene pleaded a headache and begged to be excused.

Sitting back in her chair, she closed her eyes and sought to calm her troubled spirit by thinking of the vows she had made at the Motherhouse in Mouldour. But she no longer wanted to live a life of poverty, chastity, and obedience. She wanted to be Hardane's wife, to spend her nights in his arms, to spend her days surrounded by their children. How could she hope to lock herself behind high stone walls when her heart would ever be here, in Argone?

Soft clouds scudded across the sky as she made her way out of the castle into the welcome darkness of evening. The air was fragrant with the scent of night-blooming flowers, the grass damp beneath her bare feet as she walked to the small lake behind the castle and sat down on the stone bench. It was peaceful here, quiet. She stared at her reflection in the still water, gasped as a man suddenly appeared behind her.

"Hardane."

There was a world of longing, of sadness, in her voice.

"Lady." His hands caressed her shoulders, his thumbs lightly massaging the sensitive skin along her nape.

Ah, she thought, the magic in his touch. She tilted her head back and he bent forward to kiss her, his mouth covering hers. Somehow, he was on the bench beside her and she was in his arms. Her lips parted under his and she moaned softly as the latent fires between them burst into glorious flame.

He groaned her name, his hands moving restlessly over her back, and she pressed herself to him, wanting to be closer still.

And then, somehow, she was standing beside the lake, watching, and it was Selene in Hardane's arms, Selene's name that rumbled in his throat, Selene's hands twined in his hair.

"No!" She screamed the word, the sense of hurt and betrayal sharper than a dagger in her breast.

"No!" She cried the word again, and woke with the sound of her own voice echoing in her ears.

It had only been a dream, she thought, and then she frowned. Perhaps it hadn't been a dream, at all, but a vision of what was to come.

Rising, she bathed and changed her gown and then, reluctantly, made her way downstairs toward the dining hall. She heard a babble of excited voices as she approached the room, stared in wonder at the gathering that met her eyes.

Besides Hardane and Lord Kray, there were six men in the room, all talking and gesturing at once, their voices echoing off the walls like thunder.

Sharilyn sat at the foot of the long trestle table, her eyes glowing as she gazed at each man.

They could only be Hardane's brothers, Kylene thought. All had the same long black hair, the same tawny skin. But none were quite as tall, quite as handsome. And none had his eyes.

Hardane saw her then, his face lighting with a smile that was hers alone. "Kylene," he said, his voice warm with affection, "come and meet my brothers."

Feeling like a dwarf among giants, she crossed the room to Hardane's side.

"This is my oldest brother, Dubrey. The twins, Dirk and Garth, Morray, Liam, and Dace."

Kylene nodded to each one in turn, noting that they all had dark eyes, wondering how a woman as slightly built as Sharilyn had produced such a brood of strapping young men.

"And who," Dubrey asked with a wink at Hardane, "might this be?"

"This is Kylene."

Dirk and Garth exchanged knowing grins. "Kylene," they said together. "So, she is not your betrothed."

"No."

Dubrey stepped forward and took Kylene's hand. "I'm happy to meet you, my lady. Might I interest you in a walk through the gardens later?"

"Excuse me," Dace said, shoving his elder brother aside. "Might I interest you in a ride across the south meadow?"

Kylene glanced from one to the other, flustered by their attention, by the admiration in their eyes.

"Perhaps you'd sit with me at table this morning," Morray asked, sidling up beside her.

"That's enough," Hardane said irritably. Taking Kylene's arm, he drew her away from the others and ushered her toward the table, where he held her chair as she sat, then sat down beside her.

"Hadj!" he roared.

Moments later, the serving girl entered the room bearing a tray filled with hot honey bread and fruit.

"Where is Selene?" Sharilyn asked.

"Still abed, my lady," Hadj replied, setting the platter before Lord Kray.

Lord Kray grunted with disapproval as he took his seat at the head of the table. Still abed, he thought irritably, and then chided himself for his unkind reaction. The girl had had a hard time of it, what with her father dying and all. No doubt she needed the rest.

"All right, you louts," he called good-naturedly, "stop leering at the Lady Kylene like you've never seen a girl in skirts before and sit down. My meal grows cold. Dubrey, will you say the blessing?"

Kylene bowed her head, conscious of Hardane beside her. How many more days would she be allowed to stay at the castle? How could she bear to leave him?

With the blessing said, Hardane's brothers turned

their attention to the large platters of food that were forthcoming from the kitchens.

Gradually, as the men eased their hunger, Kylene became aware that the brothers were watching her speculatively.

"You never gave me an answer, my lady," Dubrey said after a while. "Will you walk with me in the gardens?"

"I . . . I don't know."

"Say you will," Dubrey coaxed. "You can bring Hardane along as chaperon if it will make you feel safer."

Kylene slid a glance in Hardane's direction. His dark brows were drawn together in a scowl of disapproval.

"You won't mind, will you, little brother?"

"Won't mind what?"

Kylene glanced over her shoulder to see Selene enter the room. She looked radiant this morning. Clad in a flowing robe of midnight blue, Selene seemed to float across the floor.

"And who's this?" Dace asked.

"Selene," Hardane answered curtly. "My betrothed."

Liam frowned. "But . . ."

As though pulled by the same string, six pairs of eyes gazed first at Kylene and then at Selene.

"Twins," Dirk mused, poking Garth in the ribs.

"Yes," Hardane acknowledged.

"One for each of us," Garth said to Dirk, "if we can just manage to get rid of our little brother."

Kylene blushed.

Selene laughed.

181

Hardane was not amused. He glared at his brothers, warning them to keep still.

"Here, Lady Selene," Liam said, rising. "Come, sit here beside me and let us get acquainted."

"Thank you," Selene said. She smiled graciously at Liam, apparently pleased by his request. Inwardly, she was fuming because Hardane had not made a place for her at his side.

"So," Lord Kray said, his gaze sweeping over the faces of his sons, "how long will you be home?"

Garth shrugged. "Until the wedding, at least. After all, it isn't every day that our baby brother marries."

"Indeed," Dubrey agreed. He looked at Kylene and smiled. "Perhaps, if I'm very lucky, we'll have a double wedding."

Hardane swore softly, his annoyance at his brother's implication bordering on soul-dark rage.

Dubrey stood up and extended his hand to Kylene. "Shall we take that walk, my lady?"

Because she could think of no polite way to refuse, Kylene placed her hand in Dubrey's and stood up.

"Will you accompany us, Hardane?" Dubrey asked.

"If you feel the need for a chaperon, take Dace," Hardane replied tersely, and rising to his feet, he left the room as though pursued by demons.

Dubrey chuckled softly. "Do you feel the need for an escort, my lady?"

Kylene looked into Dubrey's eyes and saw only merriment and a desire to bedevil his brother lurking in their depths. "No."

Dubrey bowed to his mother, nodded to his father, and led Kylene from the room.

Outside, they walked for a time in silence. Dubrey continued to hold Kylene's hand but she didn't object. She felt no threat from this man, only a sense of friendship.

"You care for Hardane deeply, do you not?" Dubrey asked after a time.

"Yes."

"It shows." Dubrey chuckled softly. "Just as it shows that he cares for you, and not for your sister."

"Did Hardane tell you that?"

"No, but we've always been close. I can see how he feels by the way he looks at you."

"It doesn't matter. He'll wed Selene soon."

"What will you do then?"

"I don't know. Go to Dunsmere, perhaps."

"Dunsmere? Why would you want to go there? It's a dreary place."

"They've a large cloister there. Perhaps they'll accept me, if I suit."

"Accept you? You'd lock yourself away from the world just because Hardane is marrying another?"

"No. I'm pledged to the Sisterhood at Mouldour, but I can't return there, so I thought perhaps Dunsmere Abbey would take me."

"You, a member of the Sisterhood? I don't believe it."

"It's true."

"But . . ." Dubrey frowned. "How did you meet Hardane?"

"It's a long story."

"I have nothing better to do." Dubrey paused before a low stone bench situated beneath a lacy tree. "Let us sit awhile and you can tell me the tale."

Hardane paced his room, restless as a caged tiger. She was out walking. With Dubrey. Of all his brothers, Dubrey was the one with the most charm, the most appeal. He was a brave knight, a man who had distinguished himself on the field of battle. A man who was rich in his own right, with a castle of his own, land of his own. A life of his own.

Hardane swore under his breath as he pictured Dubrey and Kylene, walking in the garden. Dubrey would tell her of his exploits in Chadray, make her laugh with tales of his childhood, bewitch her with his easy humor.

And if she didn't care for Dubrey, he had five other brothers who would be only too happy to court her. They'd take her for long walks, for picnics. They'd ply her with gifts of candied sweetmeats and feather fans. They'd serenade under her window, and recite poetry.

All the things he longed to do.

Could not do.

Filled with an all-consuming jealousy, he smashed his fist against the wall, swearing as pain exploded in his hand and splintered up his arm.

Breathing heavily, he stared at the blood oozing from his knuckles. It was bright red, like his anger.

The sound of laughter drifted through his bedroom window. Crossing the floor, he gazed into the garden to see Kylene and Dubrey walking hand in hand, smiling at each other as if they'd known one another for years instead of minutes.

Watching them, he felt the anger drain out of him, leaving him feeling cold and empty and more alone than he'd ever felt in his life.

Chapter Twenty-Two

Hardane walked beside Selene, only half listening to what she was saying. His thoughts, as always, were with Kylene who was, as always, in the company of one of his brothers, most likely Dubrey.

"What?" He focused his gaze on Selene, realizing she had asked him a question.

She gestured at the bench in a small arbor. "I asked if you'd like to sit awhile?"

Hardane nodded, knowing the time had come to say what was uppermost on his mind.

"You have a lovely home," Selene remarked. "I'm so glad to see it at last. To meet you." She gazed up at him, letting him see how much she admired him, how pleased she was that they were to be wed.

"Selene . . ." He ran a hand through his hair. "I . . . I wish to be released from my pledge."

186

"What?"

"I wish to marry another."

"That's impossible. We were destined from birth to be life mated."

"I know."

"Who is it, this woman you wish to take my place?"

"That's not important."

"Do you love her?"

"Yes."

"You had no right to give your love to another," Selene accused, her eyes bright with tears. "You belong to me."

"You won't release me from my vow?"

"No."

Agitated, he stood up and paced back and forth in front of the bench.

"Why?" he demanded. "Why do you wish to be mated to a man who desires another? There will be no happiness between us."

"Women marry for many reasons other than happiness," Selene answered coldly. "I want a home, children, security. I want what was meant to be mine, and I will have it."

"You may have my home," Hardane retorted, his voice as cold as the winter wind, "you may have security. But I will never give you children."

Selene smiled up at him. "I think you will," she murmured confidently. "You're a man, after all. An honorable man. Once we're wed, you'll not break your vow of fidelity. Sooner or later, you'll come to me."

"I will not," he said curtly. Turning on his heel,

he left her there, chilled by a terrible fear that she was right.

Hardane sat on the edge of his bed, staring into the hollow blackness of the fireplace. A week had passed since Selene's arrival. It had been the worst week of his life, and tonight didn't promise to be any better. Tonight, during the ball Sharilyn was giving in Selene's honor, Kray would introduce Selene to the local populace. It would give the people a chance to meet Hardane's betrothed, to mingle with the Lord and Lady of Argone, to pledge their loyalty and support to the House of Argone and its heirs.

He did not want to marry Selene. Duty had demanded he spend time with her this past week, that he show her around the keep, get to know her, let her get to know him.

But he didn't want to know her.

Even worse than spending time with Selene had been the torture of watching his brothers pay court to Kylene. Dubrey took her walking each morning. Dace deluged her with love sonnets that praised her beauty. Dirk and Garth sang duets under her window at eventide. Liam wrote poetry.

Hardane swore under his breath. He'd had no chance to spend time with Kylene, no opportunity to speak to her alone. And yet he didn't need to talk to her to know what she was thinking, what she was feeling. He knew. She thought he had deceived her, betrayed her. She was hurt by his lack of attention, pleased and confused by the sincere flattery of his brothers.

Though he'd been tempted to walk in her dreams, he'd restrained himself, his sense of honor refusing to let him be unfaithful to Selene, even though he felt nothing for her. He had, on occasion, tried to walk in Selene's mind, to see her thoughts, but to no avail. His inability to connect with her bothered him greatly, reinforcing his suspicion that she wasn't the woman meant for him.

He stood abruptly, the truth so obvious he wondered why he hadn't realized it before.

Selene and Kylene were twins, both seventh daughters, but he knew suddenly and without doubt that Selene had not been the firstborn of the two, but the second.

It explained everything.

Kylene sat in her room, staring dolefully at her reflection in the looking glass, wondering how she would endure the night to come. She would have to smile and look pleased when Selene and Hardane were presented to the people. She would have to bestow a sisterly kiss of affection on Selene's cheek, offer her congratulations to Hardane.

She had to leave this place. She could not stay here, see them together every day, know that Selene slept beside Hardane at night. Tomorrow, she would ask Lord Kray to send her to Bierly or Dunsmere, or even back to Mouldour. She would willingly face the Lord High Interrogator again rather than stay here and watch Selene gather happiness with both hands.

But first she had to get through the ball.

She smoothed her hands over her skirt. Her

gown was of pale ice blue, trimmed in white fur. A fine silver chain circled her neck. She had refused Hadj's offer to arrange her hair. Instead, she wore it loose around her shoulders because Hardane liked it that way.

Hardane. How empty this past week had been without him.

A knock at the door told her it was time to make her entrance. Taking a deep breath, she picked up a white feather fan and left her bedchamber, knowing that, if she could get through this night, she could face anything the future might hold.

The ballroom was aglow with the light of a thousand candles. Women gowned in all the colors of the rainbow danced with men clad in starkly elegant evening clothes. Music filled the air.

Feeling shy and completely out of place, Kylene took a place near the doorway, half-hidden by the lacy fronds of a giant fern.

As if by magic, her gaze was immediately drawn toward Hardane. He was dancing with Selene, and Kylene felt her breath catch in her throat at the sight of them. Hardane was dressed in black save for a white shirt that complemented his swarthy good looks and dark hair. He'd never looked more handsome, more desirable, more unapproachable.

Kylene looked at her sister. Wearing a gown of emerald green trimmed in white fur, Selene looked every inch a princess, a perfect mate for Hardane. Her eyes glowed as she gazed into Hardane's eyes.

Kylene looked away, unable to bear the sight of the two of them together. Soon, too soon, Selene would be Hardane's bride. Try as she might, she could not find it in her heart to be happy for her sister. Instead, she was torn with envy, so jealous she was almost sick with it.

She couldn't stay here, she thought, she couldn't listen to Lord Kray announce their official betrothal, couldn't lift her glass and join with the castle guests as they toasted Selene's health and happiness.

She was turning to leave when she felt a hand on her arm. She stilled instantly, knowing who it was that stood behind her. She would know the touch of his hand in the dark.

"Kylene."

"My lord."

"Look at me."

"No. Please, let me go."

"I can't. Dance with me."

"I don't know how."

"I'll teach you."

It was useless to argue. Helplessly, she let him draw her out onto the dance floor. It was heaven to be in his arms, to look into his eyes, to see him smiling down at her.

Before she quite realized what was happening, he had danced her onto the balcony. Taking her hand, he led her into the shadows.

"Kylene, we have to talk . . ."

"You never told me you had brothers," she said.

"And a sister. You'll meet her one day."

"Perhaps," Kylene said evasively. "Can all your brothers change shape as you do?"

"No."

"Can your mother?"

191

"Of course. I inherited the ability from her."

"How does your father feel about that?"

"I never asked him."

"Oh. I guess—"

"Kylene, stop it."

She looked up at him in wide-eyed innocence. "Stop what?"

"Stop your babbling. I know how you feel."

"Do you?"

"I never meant to hurt you."

"You promised me . . ." She turned away lest he see her tears. It didn't matter what he had promised. She'd known he could never be hers, that she could never be his. It had all been a silly dream, as tangible as a will-o'-the-wisp.

Hardane placed his hands on her shoulders. "I know what I promised," he said, the hurt he'd seen in her eyes making him forget, for the moment, what he'd brought her out here to tell her.

"Always and forever, you said," Kylene whispered. "Why did you make me hope when you knew it could never be?"

"I meant what I said. I'll not let you go again."

She whirled around to face him, tears of pain and fury shining in her eyes. "You can't keep me here against my will! I won't stay and watch you marry my sister. I won't, and you can't make me!"

"I'm the heir of Argone," he reminded her, his anger rising to match hers. "I can do whatever I wish."

Her rage melted like snow in the sunlight. "If you care for me at all, you'll let me go."

"Kylene, listen to me. Haven't you figured it out

yet? You and Selene are sisters, twins."

She looked up at him as if he weren't very bright.

"We've only Selene's word that she's the first-born. I think she's lying. Wait!" He held up a hand to silence her protest. "Just think about it. It's the only explanation that makes sense. It explains why I can read your thoughts, but not hers, why I can walk in your dreams. She isn't the firstborn. You are."

Kylene stared at him in speechless wonder. It sounded so logical, so sensible, she wondered why it had never occurred to her, but even as she grasped at the idea, she pushed it aside, afraid to hope.

"Surely if I was the firstborn, Selene would know."

"Of course she knows," Hardane said, his voice harsh.

"But . . . but that means she lied to you. To me."

Hardane nodded, his eyes dark with unspoken anger.

"But there's no way to prove it. Only her word against mine."

"There's a way, lady," he said, gathering her into his arms. "There's always a way."

"What is it?"

"You'll have to wait until the day of the wedding to find out."

"Why?"

She felt his arms tighten around her, as if to protect her.

"It's a test, of sorts," Hardane replied, his voice low and strained.

193

Kylene drew back so she could see his face. "What kind of test?"

"I can't tell you. It's a closely guarded secret, meant to insure that the heirs of Argone marry only the bravest and the best of women. Or, in this case, the right woman."

"Hardane? Hardane, are you out here?"

Kylene moved out of Hardane's arms, a guilty flush heating her cheeks at the sound of her sister's voice.

"Oh," Selene said, her gaze darting from Kylene's flushed face to Hardane's impassive one, "there you are, Hardane. Your father is ready to make the announcement."

She held out her hand, but Hardane refused to take it.

"Are you sure you want to go through with this?" he asked brusquely.

It was all Selene could do to keep from flinching under his cool stare. "Of course." She glanced at Kylene. "Dubrey is looking for you. I shouldn't be surprised if he proposes soon."

The sooner the better, Selene thought, annoyed. She'd seen the adoring look Kylene had bestowed on Hardane, the barely concealed jealousy in Hardane's eyes when he heard his brother's name mentioned in connection with Kylene's.

Selene placed a proprietary hand on Hardane's forearm. "Shall we go?"

Hardane shrugged Selene's hand from his arm, nodded briefly in Kylene's direction, and returned to the ballroom. Wordlessly, Selene turned to follow him.

Kylene stared after them for a moment, her mind in turmoil. Knowing she couldn't bear to hear Lord Kray announce Hardane's forthcoming marriage, she made her way to her bedchamber and closed the door.

Hardane thought she was the firstborn twin, that she was indeed his betrothed.

Could it be true?

Oh, please, let it be true!

Chapter Twenty-Three

With the seventh month rapidly approaching, the whole castle was in constant turmoil. The housemaids and the scullery maids were busy from dawn till dark, making sure that every tablecloth, every tapestry was brushed clean. The bed linens were washed and aired, the rushes replaced. All the silver was polished until it gleamed. The crystal sparkled like the sun.

The gardens were weeded, the shrubs pruned, the lakes and waterways cleaned of fallen leaves and debris.

Sharilyn toured the entire castle from the lowliest dungeon to the uppermost turrets, making certain that every cobweb, every speck of dust, had been thoroughly swept away.

The castle seamstresses sewed hour after hour, making new wardrobes: a dress of deep royal blue satin and silk for Sharilyn, a gown of forest green velvet for Kylene, a gown of soft shimmering silver for Selene. The royal tailors produced new clothes for Hardane and Lord Kray as well.

Amid all the fuss, Dubrey continued to court Kylene. He sought her company often and eagerly, his sincerity stealing her affection if not her heart. Of all the brothers, he was the most like Hardane, and sometimes, on dark, lonely nights in her room, she let herself wonder what it would be like to marry Dubrey. Even though she doubted Hardane would ever be hers, the thought of spending the rest of her life in the Motherhouse no longer held any appeal. And if she could not have Hardane, perhaps she might find a measure of happiness with Dubrey.

She was thinking of that now as she sat on the balcony outside her chamber. She had not seen Hardane alone since the night of the ball when he had promised he would find a way for them to be together. As much as she yearned to believe, needed to believe, she was afraid to trust him, afraid of being hurt again.

She had tried to search her own heart and soul, tried to find some deep inner sense that she was indeed the firstborn twin, but no such knowledge came forth. She had no memory of her childhood, only an abiding fear of water that she could not explain. The first face she remembered was that of Mother Dorissa bending over her bed, begging her not to cry, but she couldn't recall why she had been crying.

Later, growing up, she had always felt differ-

ent from the others, a woman apart, even though
she had been treated much the same as the other
members of the Sisterhood.

Thinking back, she tried to recall why she had felt
that way, but it was more of a feeling, a sense that
she had been destined for something else, rather
than anything that had been said or done.

Was she truly the firstborn twin, betrothed to
Hardane, as he believed? Had her sisters in the
Motherhouse known that she was a princess, born
to marry into the House of Argone? But if it was
true, why had no one ever told her? Why hadn't
Mother Dorissa prepared her? Why had her father
abandoned her? Where was her mother? Her sisters? For the first time, it occurred to her that
she must have six other siblings if she and Selene
were the seventh and eighth born. Perhaps she had
brothers as well, aunts, uncles, cousins.

She closed her eyes against the growing pain
in her head. So many questions. Surely someone,
somewhere, had the answers.

But it no longer seemed to matter. Tomorrow
was the seventh day of the seventh month.

The day of the wedding.

A knock at the door drew her from the balcony.
She'd expected it to be Hadj bringing water for
her bath. Instead, she saw Selene standing in the
hallway.

"May I come in?" Selene asked.

Kylene nodded. Since Selene's arrival, they had
been together only at mealtimes, never alone. There
was no bond between them. Selene had not sought
out Kylene's company, nor had Kylene sought hers.

Closing the door, Kylene led the way into the small blue and white sitting room.

"Sit down, won't you?" she invited, indicating the soft leather chair beside the window.

Selene shook her head, her gaze sweeping the room. To her delight, she saw that it was not as large or as lavishly appointed as her own chambers.

"I'm not staying long. I merely came to tell you not to attend the wedding."

Kylene stared at her twin, surprised at the hurt that washed through her. She hadn't wanted to attend the ceremony, knowing it would be agony of the worst kind to stand watching while Hardane married another. She had, in fact, spent the last several nights trying to think of a plausible excuse to avoid the celebration altogether, but being told not to attend, and by her own flesh and blood, hurt just the same.

"As you wish," Kylene agreed.

Selene nodded and turned to leave.

"Wait."

Selene glanced over her shoulder, a look of annoyance on her face. "What is it?"

"Where is my mother? My sisters?"

"Our three oldest sisters married knights from other empires long ago. The others died of a fever."

"And our mother?"

"She's dead. She died of the same fever that took our sisters."

Kylene stared at Selene, repulsed by the coldness in her sister's tone. Did the woman feel nothing over the loss of her parents, her siblings? Was there no love in her heart?

"Is that all?" Selene asked impatiently.

Kylene nodded. Her parents and three of her siblings were dead, but she wasn't alone in the world. She had three other sisters. The thought comforted her as she watched Selene leave the room. Surely they weren't all as cold and uncaring as her twin.

Sitting on the edge of the bed, she let her mind wander, imagining what it would be like to meet her sisters and their husbands. Their children, if they had any. She thought how nice it would be to spend the high holidays with family, to learn about her parents, her own childhood, of which she had no recollection.

A sound in the hallway drew her attention to the present. Rising, she went to the door of her chamber.

"Is someone there?" She listened a moment and then, quite clearly, she saw Hardane's image in her mind.

Her heart seemed to turn over in her breast as she put out her hand and opened the door.

"Kylene . . ."

"I knew it was you," she said even as she let her eyes look their fill. He wore a loose-fitting shirt that matched the gray of his eyes, black breeches and knee-high boots. And he was handsome, so breathtakingly handsome.

"You've been missing me," she said, startling them both. "You've come to ask me to go for a walk."

He looked down at her, his eyes bright with amusement. "Are you reading my mind, lady?"

"So it would seem."

"Will you walk with me?"

"You've always been able to read *my* mind," Kylene replied. "Surely you must know the answer."

He smiled down at her as he held out his hand.

Kylene smiled back as she placed her hand in his, and then she frowned, thinking that Selene wouldn't like his being there.

"Where's your betrothed?" she asked, unable to keep a note of bitterness from her voice.

His gaze moved over her face as his hand squeezed hers. "By my side, lady."

Kylene blinked back her tears, unable to speak for the joy those few words kindled in her heart.

Hand in hand, they left the keep and walked into the night. She knew without asking where they were going.

In the moonlight, the maze was even more magical, more beautiful. The topiary unicorn seemed to shimmer in the starlight, the leaves of the trees whispered secrets to the soft south wind, the tall grass swayed to the music of the night.

And when Hardane held out his arms, Kylene went to him without hesitation.

For a long while, he only held her close, his face buried in the wealth of her hair. She fit in his embrace as if a beneficent God had designed her with him in mind. A deep breath filled his nostrils with her scent, stirring his desire as no other woman ever had. He let his essence surround her, felt their spirits blend into a single entity as her thoughts met his.

No words were said. None were necessary.

Tomorrow was the seventh day of the seventh month.

Tomorrow, he would know if Kylene was truly destined to be his life mate.

Tomorrow, she would discover the truth of who she really was.

But tonight . . .

He stroked her hair, his fingertips lightly caressing her cheek as he murmured her name, only her name, over and over again. When he kissed her, it was more than a mere touching of his lips to hers, but the promise of a lifetime.

There was no need to read his thoughts now. She knew that, right or wrong, he had pledged himself to her, and only her.

In the silence of her mind, she made the same vow.

Thinking to find serenity in the rightness of it, she was startled by a sudden inner vision of flames rising up all around her, enveloping her, of a black wolf, its hackles bristling, its fangs bared . . .

With a cry, she pulled free of Hardane's embrace, her only thought to run away from what she knew was a vision of the future.

"Kylene, wait!"

"No." She began to run as she heard him coming up behind her. "Stay away from me!"

"Kylene! It's not what you think!"

But she could not banish the terror of the flames from her mind. She could still feel the heat overpowering her, burning her hair and skin, stealing her breath away. And the wolf, snarling at her, could only be Hardane.

She screamed when she felt his hand close over her shoulder. He tried to draw her into his arms, but she pummeled his chest with her fists as he drew her close.

"Kylene, listen to me, please."

"No." She shook her head, his nearness striking fear in her heart. He was the wolf.

"It's not what you think," he said again, his voice quiet, soothing. "Trust me. Please, lady."

"I can't."

"The flames are part of the test. You'll come to no harm, I promise you."

"And the wolf? What of the wolf snarling at me? Was it you?"

"I'd never hurt you, Kylene. You must believe me."

She stared up at him, wanting to believe, afraid to believe.

"I know in my heart that you're the firstborn. The flames will prove it. You have only to trust me, to believe in yourself, in our love."

"No. No, I can't. Please, let me go. I'm afraid."

"Of me?"

She stared into his eyes. They were gray and calm, so familiar.

"Kylene?" Seeing the fear in her eyes, reading it in her mind, he was tempted to tell her everything, and yet he couldn't tell her the whole truth. Not yet.

Feeling like the worst kind of coward, he drew her into his arms and held her close.

"Please," she whimpered, "please let me go."

"I can't."

"I'm afraid," she said, shivering uncontrollably. "So afraid."

"I know," he replied, his voice husky with concern, "but you have nothing to fear. The flames will prove who you are. It's a challenge you must face of your own free will."

She relaxed in the strength of his arms, feeling his courage bolster her own. "How? When?"

"Tomorrow night, at the Temple of Fire."

Kylene shuddered. "The Temple of Fire?"

"It's where all the heirs of Argone are life mated. Be there, Kylene. Don't let a promise made to your sister keep you away."

Tenderly, he cupped her face in his hands and gazed deep into her eyes. "Don't let your fears keep us apart."

Chapter Twenty-Four

Kylene sat in her room plagued by doubts and indecision. Should she do as she'd promised Selene and shun the wedding, or should she put her faith in Hardane?

Don't let your fears keep us apart, he'd said, and for the first time, she acknowledged that she was afraid. Not of the fire, as she'd claimed, but of learning the truth that she knew Hardane was hiding from her. But, more than that, she was afraid to be his wife, to take her rightful place at his side, to help him rule Argone when the time came. She'd had so little contact with people other than the Sisters at the Motherhouse. She was ignorant of the social structure of Argone, ignorant of its religion, its beliefs. She was Mouldourian. Perhaps the people of Argone would never accept her. Perhaps Hardane's parents would never accept her.

She buried her face in her hands. So many doubts. She was sure of only one thing, her unwavering love for Hardane. Did she have the courage to fight for him? Did she truly believe she was the firstborn twin, and if she did, if she was, was she going to cower in her room and let Selene marry Hardane?

"No!"

Rising, she took a last look at herself in the mirror. The green velvet dress was the most flattering gown she'd ever worn. It accented her breasts, complemented the color of her hair, and made her skin glow. She wore her hair loose about her shoulders because Hardane preferred it that way, even though mature women did not leave their hair unbound.

Her decision made, she hurried from the room before she could change her mind. She was already late.

The Temple of Fire stood on the crest of a hill. Made of highly polished moonstone, it glowed eerily in the light of the full moon.

Kylene thought it was the tallest, most beautiful building she'd ever seen. She was puzzled by the lack of windows, but decided there was probably a reason why one side of the building had no opening other than a massive door made of wood so dark it was almost black.

She was breathless when she reached the top of the rise. Pausing to catch her breath, she stared at the life-size figure of a wolf carved in the heavy wooden door before she turned the heavy brass handle and crossed the threshold of the temple.

She came to an abrupt halt as she closed the door behind her. She had expected to find herself in a church with stained-glass windows, candles, an altar, some holy artifacts. Now she saw that the Temple of Fire was not a building at all, but four high roofless walls that enclosed an emerald green meadow. Tall, slender trees clothed in shimmering leaves of gold and silver grew in scattered clumps.

For a moment, she stared at the murals painted on the walls. One portrayed a pack of wolves running across a grassy plain; another depicted a lone wolf howling at a bright yellow moon. A third showed the figure of a tall, bare-chested man with the head of a wolf.

But it was the mural on the fourth wall that caught and held Kylene's attention. It showed a woman being consumed in an orange flame while a pack of wolves stood in a circle around her.

Drawing her gaze from the painting, she saw that there was a long, low altar in the center of the meadow. The altar was covered by an iridescent cloth of green and gold.

Those who had been invited to the wedding, and they were few, were gathered behind the altar.

Hardane, looking resplendent in snug buff-colored breeches, high kidskin boots, and a white linen shirt, stood in front of the altar, on the right.

Selene stood to the left, with perhaps six feet of blackened ground between them.

Lord Kray and Sharilyn took their places behind Hardane.

A priest in long gray robes stood in front of the altar between Hardane and Selene.

"Are all those who were invited to attend present?" the priest asked.

Kylene saw Hardane frown as his gaze moved over the faces of the guests. And then he looked toward the doorway, smiling when he saw her.

"Yes," he said, his voice carrying clearly.

"Shall we proceed?"

You must challenge Selene's claim. Hardane's voice rang out in Kylene's mind. Looking over at him, she saw him nod.

"My Lord Kray," the priest said, "shall we proceed?"

Lord Kray nodded. "Yes."

"No." With as much dignity and courage as she could muster, Kylene made her way to the center of the meadow and stood beside Selene. "I challenge this woman's right to marry into the House of Argone."

"A challenge?" the priest exclaimed. "You wish to challenge?"

Selene glared at Kylene. "Are you mad?" she hissed.

Lord Kray took a step forward, his face dark with condemnation. "Kylene . . ."

"Let her speak, Father," Hardane said.

"By what right do you challenge this marriage?" the priest asked.

"By right of being the firstborn twin."

"Have you proof of this?" the priest asked.

"I . . ." Kylene looked at Hardane. *The fire will prove it.* "The fire will . . ." She glanced at the mural depicting the woman in flames, and then stared at the blackened ground at her feet.

Don't let your fears keep us apart. She sent an anxious glance at Hardane.

Hardane nodded at her, his dark gray eyes filled with love and reassurance.

"The fire will prove it," Kylene said.

An audible gasp broke the silence of the crowd.

Lord Kray frowned.

Sharilyn closed her eyes, a look of intense concentration on her face.

Selene continued to glare at Kylene, her eyes filled with malice.

"So let it be done," the priest said.

Holding his arms out to his sides, the Wolffan cleric began to chant softly. The words, low and musical, were foreign to Kylene's ears.

Though Kylene wanted to watch Hardane, her gaze was drawn to the priest. The air around him seemed to shimmer like heat rising from the desert floor. A low rumble, like the beating of distant drums, seemed to echo off the walls, and yet it wasn't so much a sound as a feeling of immense power rising up all around them.

Slowly the priest raised his hands, and Kylene saw that his palms were glowing, and when, moments later, he raised his arms over his head, twin walls of white fire sprang up on either side of him.

And now the priest stood in the middle of the twins walls of flame, with Selene and Kylene behind one flaming barrier and Hardane behind the other.

"Hardane, seventh son of Argone, born of Sharilyn and Kray here present, come forth."

The beat of the drumming grew louder, and Kylene glanced around, wondering where the sound was coming from.

She stared through the blaze, gasping in horror as Hardane took a step forward. For a moment, he seemed to be engulfed in a sheet of white flame, and then he emerged through the wall of fire, apparently unharmed, to stand at the priest's left hand.

"Selene, seventh daughter of Mouldour, rightful heir of Carrick and Joce, come forth."

Selene stared at the flames. They were orange now and they danced and swayed before her, their rhythm almost hypnotic. She told herself there was nothing to fear. Hardane had walked through the wall of fire unscathed. So could she. Reminding herself of all she hoped to gain, of the reward that would be hers, she took a step forward, her hands clenched at her sides.

She could feel the heat against her skin; the smoke filled her nostrils; the crackle of the flames rang like thunder in her ears.

She gazed through the barrier of fire to where Hardane stood beside the priest.

"Selene, seventh daughter of Mouldour, come forth," the priest repeated.

She couldn't do it, Selene thought in despair, not for the throne of Argone, not for Hardane, not for all the wealth of the world.

There was a long pause. A low murmur rose from the crowd as they looked from Selene to Hardane, wondering at her hesitation.

The priest bowed his head a moment and then, in a loud voice, cried, "Kylene, seventh daughter of Mouldour, rightful heir of Carrick and Joce, come forth."

Kylene glanced again at the mural of the woman engulfed in flames, at the blackened ground before the altar.

Don't let your fear keep us apart. Once again she heard Hardane's voice in her mind, strong and clear.

Taking a deep breath, she stared at him through the shimmering flames, surprised to see that the fire was no longer orange but a brilliant shade of white, and then, her gaze locked with Hardane's, she took a step forward.

There was a sensation of warmth, of being engulfed in a bright silver haze. For a moment, her mind was filled with all the colors of the rainbow, and then she saw the image of a black wolf running through the forest. She concentrated on the face of the wolf. He seemed to be smiling at her, beckoning her. Fearlessly, she followed him, and then she was through the fire, facing Hardane.

His deep gray eyes were filled with love and pride as he stepped forward and took her hand in his.

"As heir of Argone, I accept this woman as my wife and declare that we are life mated from this night forward."

The priest began to chant again, and this time the voices of those who had been invited to the ceremony joined in, until the night was filled with song underscored by the low rumble of a drum.

And while the anthem was still going strong, the priest placed his hands over theirs and spoke the ancient words that made them one.

As he blessed their union, the flames exploded in a burst of blinding white light and then disappeared.

Selene stared at Hardane and Kylene, her face a mask of hate and envy.

"You'll rue this day, Hardane of Argone!" she shrieked. "A curse upon you and all your house!"

And then, before anyone could stop her, she ran out of the temple.

For a moment, no one moved, and then Lord Kray and Sharilyn came forward to welcome Kylene into the family.

Hardane's brothers came next, each bearing a gift for the bride. A rope of exquisite blue pearls from Dubrey, a fine gold chain from Liam, a length of cloth of gold from Garth and Dirk, a jeweled dagger from Dace, a jewel-encrusted box from Morray.

After Hardane's brothers had welcomed her, the others came forward, wishing her health and happiness, bearing gifts of herbs and spices and flagons of wine, all of which were symbols of fertility and felicity.

Dazed, Kylene accepted the gifts, the hugs, the good wishes. Later, she would worry about Selene's vile threat, she would relive the fear and the magic of the flames, but for now she could think of nothing save the fact that she was Hardane's wife for now and for always.

Chapter Twenty-Five

"Come," Hardane said, taking Kylene by the hand.

"Where are we going?" She gazed up at him in surprise. She had thought there might be a celebration of some kind to honor their marriage.

Hardane smiled at his bride. She had never looked more beautiful. The gown of shimmering green velvet made her golden skin glow and deepened the red of her hair. Her eyes were sparkling with love and excitement. And she was his, for now and for always, this wondrous creature who had stolen his heart and his soul.

"Hardane?" She was gazing up at him, waiting for his answer.

"Tomorrow," he said. "Tomorrow night there will be feasting and dancing and tournaments," he explained as he led her out of the temple, "but tonight is ours alone. We will celebrate in our own way, just the two of us."

His words, softly spoken, brought a quick flush to Kylene's cheeks as she realized that what she had only dreamed of was about to become reality.

She felt as if every eye were watching them as they left the temple.

Hand in hand, they walked down the hill toward the keep. Caught up in the magic of the night, in the glow of being Hardane's bride, Kylene imagined that the wind was whispering her name, wishing her luck in her new life. It even seemed as if the moonlight were following her, wishing her well.

She grew increasingly nervous as they neared the castle. She was Hardane's wife now, his to do with as he pleased, and though her every thought had been centered around him since the day they met, it occurred to her that she really knew very little about him.

"I won't hurt you, lady," he vowed.

His words were low and reassuring; only the faint tremor in his voice betrayed his inner anxiety. With some relief, she remembered that he was as inexperienced as she.

Hardane slid a glance in Kylene's direction, wondering if she was as aware of his uncertainty as he was of hers.

They were still holding hands when they entered the keep and climbed the long, winding staircase that led to the sleeping quarters.

Hardane paused at the top of the steps and then, swinging Kylene into his arms, carried her down the hall to his bedchamber and opened the door.

Stepping into the room, he held her for a long moment, unable to believe that she was there, in his room, in his arms at last. His, to do with as he pleased. His, for now, for always.

He was glad now that he had never broken the vow he'd made to his mother, glad that he was as chaste as his bride. And yet, perversely, he wished he had some experience with women beyond what he had imagined.

Slowly he lowered Kylene to her feet, acutely conscious of every inch of her warm feminine form as her body slid across his.

Flustered by his nearness, Kylene took a step backward, and let out a little gasp of delight. The glow from a dozen candles filled the room with a soft yellow light. An engraved silver flagon of red wine and two delicate glasses stood on a silver tray next to the bed. And the bed . . . Kylene pressed her hand to her breast. The blue counterpane was covered with hundreds of snowy white rose petals. Their fragrance wrapped around her; their presence, and Hardane's thoughtfulness, made her heart ache with tenderness.

"When did you do all this?" she asked, touched beyond words by the romantic gesture.

"I asked Hadj to do it while we were gone."

"But . . . how did you know I'd be at the temple, that I'd brave the flames?"

"I didn't know. I only hoped."

Uncertain of what she expected of him, he was almost afraid to touch her, to surrender to the desire that was raging through him for fear he might hurt or frighten her. But even more com-

215

pelling than his desire was the knowledge that
had not been entirely truthful with her.

"Kylene, there's something I need to tell you
He gazed down at her, into eyes as soft and brow
as the earth, eyes filled with fire and mystery.

"Tell me, then," she replied quietly.

Hardane cringed inwardly, shaken to the core
the trust shining in her eyes. Would she still lo
him when she knew the truth?

Slowly, he shook his head. "Lady, I . . ."

Lifting her hand, Kylene caressed the rugge
outline of his jaw.

"I'm not afraid," she whispered, praying that s
would be forgiven for such a small lie. For she w
afraid; afraid of the unknown, afraid she wou
say or do the wrong thing.

Hardane raised one black brow as he took h
trembling hand in his. "Not afraid?" he chided ge
tly.

"Perhaps a little," she admitted.

"Of me?" His voice was hoarse; his eyes we
vulnerable.

"No, my wolf. Only afraid my ignorance w
displease you."

A low growl of denial rose in Hardane's thro
as he drew her hard against him and covered h
mouth with his.

He had never had a woman except in dreams

She had never had a man, and yet there was
awkwardness between them.

Gently, he began to undress her, his han
trembling with anticipation as he cast away la
er after layer of clothing until she stood befo

him, more beautiful, more desirable, than he had ever imagined. His fingertips slid over her silken flesh, curious and reverent as he marveled at the unblemished beauty of her skin, the fullness of her breasts, her slender waist and long, shapely legs.

Humbled by her beauty and by the acceptance in her eyes, he made a silent vow that he would never do anything to cause her pain, knowing he would rather die than cause her a moment's distress. Even now, he could hardly believe that she was here, that she was his. None of his dreams had prepared him for the reality of this moment.

Kylene gazed up at him. "One of us is overly dressed, don't you think?" she whispered, surprised by her boldness.

"Aye, lady," Hardane agreed, and sucked in a deep breath as Kylene began to undress him, his whole body aching with need as she removed his shirt.

Kylene felt herself blush as she slid his shirt from his shoulders, reveling in the way he trembled beneath her touch, in the knowledge that he was hers, that from this moment on she could touch him, hold him, kiss him as she had so often yearned to do.

Her fingertips lingered over the width of his shoulders, traced meaningless patterns in the swirls of black hair on his chest. Kneeling, she removed his boots, and then, taking a deep breath, she stood up and began to unfasten his breeches.

At the touch of her hands, he went suddenly still, and she felt a wondrous sense of feminine power and excitement, and then a little stab of apprehension as he stood gloriously naked before her.

Murmuring her name, Hardane swept Kylene into his arms and carried her to the big feather bed. No longer would he sleep alone, tormented by his desire for this woman above all others, plagued by shadowed images that woke him in the night.

He lowered her carefully to the bed, his body covering hers. She was warmth and comfort, the answer to every prayer, every dream he'd ever had. He kissed her and the spark in his loins burst into flame. And now, for the first time, he could let it burn without fear.

Kylene drew Hardane close, closer, delighting in the weight of his body, in the soft sighs of pleasure that escaped his lips as her hands stroked his back and shoulders. He was every desire she'd ever had, every wish come true.

She had been afraid that her untutored hands wouldn't know how to pleasure him, but she knew now that her fears had been groundless. She seemed to know instinctively how to please him and her heart swelled with love and joy as he murmured her name over and over again.

She gasped as his body became part of hers. Instantly, Hardane withdrew.

"Have I hurt you?" he asked anxiously.

"A little, but . . . but I think it's to be expected."

Hardane drew a deep breath, remembering that Jared had once told him that, should he ever be fortunate enough to bed a maiden, the woman would experience a moment of pain, that there would be blood.

Propped on his elbows, Hardane gazed into her eyes, needing her with an intensity that went beyond words.

"Lady," he whispered, "what shall I do?"

"Whatever you wish, my lord wolf." And then, knowing he was afraid of causing her pain, she drew him into her arms and kissed him.

The touch of her lips, the restless touch of her hands on his back, drove him over the edge. He kissed her hard as he plunged into her, knowing that nothing short of death could keep him from making her his.

Kylene moaned low in her throat as they became one, and then the brief discomfort was forgotten and she felt not only her own pleasure, but his as well.

For an instant, the image of the wolf flashed in her mind. The hair beneath her hand felt like fur, and she seemed to feel his tongue stroking her palm, whining softly as he brushed against her legs. Incredibly, there was an instant when she felt as though *she* were the wolf.

And then she was soaring, all her senses keenly alive, lost in the wonder of Hardane's touch and her own unbridled response. Higher, higher, she raced past the moon and the stars until she caught the rainbow and it shattered in her grasp, filling her whole being with all the colors and textures of life renewing itself.

Hardane let out a long, shuddering sigh. And then he smiled. Nothing Jared had ever told him, nothing he had ever imagined, had prepared him for the reality of what had just happened. Not only had his body merged with Kylene's, but his heart and his mind as well. There had been a moment, one breathless moment, when all he was, all his hopes and dreams for the future, had merged with hers, a single glorious moment when her essence had been interwoven with his.

Rolling onto his side, he drew Kylene into his arms and rained kisses on her eyelids, her nose, her mouth. He smiled at the husky sigh of satisfaction that whispered past her lips.

"You're very quiet, lady," he remarked, one finger toying with a lock of her hair.

"I know, but . . ." She lifted one shoulder and let it fall. "I don't want to spoil this moment."

"I didn't displease you, then?"

"Oh, no," Kylene answered quickly, fervently. She smiled up at him, her green eyes filled with mischief. "Of course, I have no other lovers to compare you with."

A low growl rumbled in Hardane's throat as he rolled her onto her back, his body pinning hers to the mattress.

"And you never will," he declared fiercely. "I'll flay the hide from any man who dares to touch you."

Kylene stared up into her husband's face, startled by his implacable tone. What she had said in jest had not been taken that way. His gray eyes were dark with fury. And jealousy.

"Hardane . . ." She smiled at him, hoping to erase the anger from his gaze. "I was only jesting. I want no one but you."

"I know," he replied, somewhat embarrassed by

220

his outburst. "But the thought of you with another man is more than I can bear." His hand caressed her cheek with infinite tenderness. "There were times in the last few weeks when I wanted to kill my own brothers. Especially Dubrey. Watching them court you, watching you smile at them, dance with them . . ." Hardane shook his head ruefully. "I could have cheerfully killed them all."

"They were only teasing you."

"I know, but it didn't make any difference." Hardane rolled onto his side and drew her into the circle of his arms. "But they were with you."

"And you were with Selene." Kylene sat up, frowning. "Where do you suppose she went?"

Hardane shrugged. "I'm sure she's in the castle somewhere. She has nowhere else to go."

"I know, but—"

"No more talk of Selene for now," Hardane admonished.

"One question?"

"Ask it."

"What would have happened if Selene had answered my challenge and braved the flames?"

"She would have been destroyed."

"I wasn't."

"She's not you, lady."

"But . . ."

Hardane drew Kylene down beside him once more. "I don't want to think about Selene," he murmured. "I don't want to talk about Selene. I want you, lady, only you, in my thoughts, in my heart, in my arms."

"Hardane . . ."

"Aye, lady?"

She twined her arms around his neck. "Read my thoughts, Wolf of Argone," she whispered, and molded her body to his just in case he had trouble reading her mind.

Kylene sat up, uncertain as to what had awakened her. A glance at the window told her it was still dark outside. Frowning, she reached out to Hardane's side of the bed and found it empty.

Murmuring his name, she slipped out of the huge four-poster bed, drew on her night robe, and padded barefoot to the window. Drawing the heavy midnight blue velvet drapery aside, she gazed into the courtyard below.

Certain she was imagining things, she rubbed her eyes and looked again.

And there, beneath a midnight moon, she saw two wolves frolicking in the night-damp grass.

She knew at once that the large black wolf was Hardane and knew, with the same certainty, that the smaller wolf was Sharilyn.

She'd been watching the pair for perhaps five minutes when a deep voice sounded from behind her.

"It's something you'll have to learn to live with."

Turning, Kylene saw Lord Kray standing in the doorway. "My lord?"

"It's in their blood, you know. You can't fight it. Nor can they."

"I don't object to Hardane taking on the shape of the wolf," Kylene replied. "I find it rather . . . fascinating."

Lord Kray stared at her for a long moment, and then, slowly, he shook his head. "You don't know, do you?"

"Know what?"

"It isn't a shape he assumes. It's a part of who and what he is."

Kylene felt a sudden coldness creep down her spine. "Are you trying to tell me my husband is a wolf?"

"Aye, in a manner of speaking."

"He told me once that the wolf shape is the easiest to assume," Kylene remarked.

"Of course. It's what he is."

"But Hardane told me his brothers can't change shape."

Lord Kray shrugged. "It's a trait that's passed only to seventh sons, or daughters. I don't know why the others don't possess it. Perhaps no one does."

"Did you know about Sharilyn when you married her?"

"Aye."

"It still bothers you, doesn't it?" Kylene guessed.

Lord Kray released a deep sigh. "Sharilyn has been my life mate for more than thirty seasons."

"You have not answered my question, my lord."

"Aye, child, sometimes it bothers me greatly."

Lord Kray crossed the room and stood beside his daughter-in-law, his gaze focused on the two wolves dancing in the moonlight.

"I don't believe it," Kylene said, though the proof was there before her eyes. "He can't be a wolf."

"You misunderstand me, Kylene. He isn't the

kind of wolf that prowls the forest and steals our chickens and kills our sheep. And yet . . ."

Lord Kray released a breath that seemed to come from the depths of his soul.

"And yet?" Kylene prompted.

"They are capable of killing."

For a moment, Kylene watched the two wolves in silence. They were beautiful in the moonlight. Graceful. Powerful. Almost mystical.

Deadly.

"Has . . . has Hardane killed people?"

"In the wolf shape? I don't know."

"But Sharilyn has. And that's what bothers you."

"Aye. She killed a man to save my life. I should be grateful, I know, and yet it was so savage." Lord Kray shook his head. "I've seen men killed before. Men have died by my hand, and yet . . . I know not how to explain it, Kylene. I know only that it troubled me greatly at the time, and I've never gotten over it."

My husband, Kylene mused.

The instant the thought crossed her mind, the big black wolf turned and stared up at the window, its fathomless gray eyes shining in the moonlight. And then, with a wave of its tail, it disappeared into the shadows. A moment later, the other wolf followed.

"Good sleep, daughter," Lord Kray said, and after giving her a fatherly hug, he left the room.

Kylene stood at the window for a time, and when Hardane still did not return, she began to pace the floor, Lord Kray's words replaying in her mind over and over again.

Something you'll have to learn to live with . . . in their blood . . . who and what he is . . .

A sound at the door drew her attention. Turning, she saw the wolf standing in the corridor. She took an involuntary step backward as the contours of the wolf's shape began to transform, the thick black pelt melting away to become sun-bronzed flesh as the four-legged creature took on its human form.

He crossed the threshold into their sleeping quarters, closed the door behind him, but didn't approach her.

Kylene saw the tension in his face, in his taut muscles as he crossed his arms over his chest.

"Does it change anything between us?" he asked, and she heard the wariness in his voice, saw the vulnerability, the fear, that lurked in the depths of his eyes.

"I don't know," she replied honestly, knowing she might as well speak the truth before he read it in her mind. "I knew you could take on the shape of a wolf; I didn't realize you were one." She clasped her hands together to still their trembling. "Why didn't you tell me?"

"I was afraid it would frighten you. Afraid you'd run back to the Motherhouse and I would never see you again." A melancholy smile tugged at the corner of his mouth. "And I was right. You are frightened."

"How can you be a wolf?" she exclaimed, her anguish evident in her voice. "I know what your father told me, but it's more than I can comprehend."

225

"I'm not a wolf in the way you think, and yet the blood of wolves, of the Wolffan, runs in my veins. I can't explain it any better than that."

"What of our children?"

"They will be like other children."

"Except the seventh one."

"Aye. It's both blessing and curse, Kylene. I can't change who and what I am, not even for you." He drew a deep, shuddering sigh. "Not even if I could."

Kylene bit down on her lip as she tried to gather her thoughts. She loved him, she could not leave him. She nodded as she made her decision.

"Then we'll have no seventh-born child."

"You forget, lady, that you, too, are a seventh-born child. Would you rather that you had not been born?"

"But no curse was born with me."

His eyes were as hard and gray as stone as he looked at her.

"You were born to be mine, lady," he said softly. "Perhaps that is curse enough."

The pain in his voice tore at her heart. She longed to run to him, to tell him it didn't matter, but she stood rooted to the floor.

A muscle worked in Hardane's jaw as he saw the uncertainty and confusion in her eyes.

Without a word, he turned on his heel and left the room.

The door closed softly behind him.

It sounded like a death knell in her ears.

Chapter Twenty-Six

Feeling as though he had received a mortal wound, Hardane left the keep.

For a moment, he stood in the moonlight, his head thrown back, his hands clenched as he fought the searing agony that Kylene's words had inflicted on his soul.

And then, because it was in his blood, because it had always been his way when he was troubled, he transformed into the wolf and began to run through the night.

There was solace in racing across the countryside. His senses were more keen, more alert, and he ran effortlessly, tirelessly. He caught the scent of rabbits, of squirrels, of deer and wild boar. The scent of feral wolves hunting in the dark of the night.

He had, on occasion, met his wild cousins in

the forest. They were wary of him, sensing that, though he shared their shape, he was not one of them. And yet he could communicate with them, and they with him.

But it was not wolves on his mind tonight. It was the look of disbelief in Kylene's eyes, the horror he'd read in her mind when she accepted the fact that he was as much wolf as man, that it wasn't merely a random shape he assumed at will, but a part of him.

For the first time, he had been ashamed of who and what he was.

And yet he could not blame her. He knew, deep inside, that he should have told her the truth long ago. There had been times when he'd been tempted, times when he'd been on the verge of telling her everything, but he'd lacked the courage to confess the truth.

To risk the possibility of losing her love, of watching the affection in her eyes turn to revulsion.

He ran on, his sides heaving, his breathing hard and fast.

Had he lost her forever?

After a time, he stopped running. Dropping to his haunches, he lifted his head and howled with misery.

And from the distance, like the echo of the pain in his heart, he heard the answering cries of his feral cousins as they lifted their voices to mingle with his.

Chapter Twenty-Seven

Kylene spent a long and sleepless night waiting for Hardane to return.

Sitting on the window seat staring into the darkness, she heard the far-off cry of a wolf. She knew instinctively that it was Hardane, that he was giving voice to his anger and frustration, to the agony her words had caused him.

Later, she heard other cries rise to meld with the first. Surprisingly, she could distinguish Hardane's cry from those of the other wolves.

The real wolves.

The wild wolves.

Hardane was a wolf, but not a wolf.

He was a man, but not a man like any other.

Could she live with him, knowing that?

Could she live without him?

If only he hadn't left her, if only he'd let her explain. And yet, what could she have said? She'd been appalled by what Lord Kray had told her, shocked to learn that the wolf form was not merely a shape he could assume at will but an inherent part of him.

If only he'd told her the truth sooner . . .

She shook her head ruefully. It would still have come as a shock and she probably would have reacted just as she had—with fear and revulsion.

Tears burned her eyes as she thought of how she had hurt him. He had never treated her with anything but tenderness and kindness, and how had she repaid him? By acting as if he were some sort of monster, unworthy of her trust, her love.

If only he would come home. If only he would give her another chance.

She sat at the window the rest of the night, watching the stars fade from the heavens, watching the sky brighten as night turned to day.

And still he did not come.

Burying her head in her arms, she closed her eyes and wept tears of regret and bitter self-recrimination.

A knock at the door roused Kylene from a troubled sleep. She mumbled permission to enter, and Hadj swept into the room, a covered tray in her hands.

"I've brought breakfast, my lady," Hadj said. She glanced around the room, obviously wondering at Hardane's absence.

"Did Lord Hardane request it?"

"No, my lady, I thought he was here . . ." Hadj's voice trailed off.

Kylene felt a blush climb into her cheeks. It was the morning after her wedding and she didn't even know where her husband was.

"Take the tray away," she said, not meeting the serving girl's eyes.

"Yes, my lady. Shall I draw your bath?"

Kylene nodded; then, swallowing her pride, she said, "Hadj, have you seen Lord Hardane this morning?"

"No, my lady."

Kylene bit down on her lip, wondering where he'd gone. There was to be a celebration tonight, a feast to honor their marriage. Surely he'd be there!

She spent the morning in her room, alternately pacing the floor and staring out the window.

Where was he?

Sharilyn knocked at the door later that afternoon to ask if anything was amiss. Kylene shook her head, and then dissolved into tears. In minutes, Sharilyn had heard the whole story.

"It was wrong of him not to tell you," Sharilyn remarked. "Does it change how you feel about him?"

"I don't know." Kylene averted her eyes, unable to meet her mother-in-law's probing gaze.

"In the old time, the Wolffan assumed the wolf form more often than the human form," Sharilyn said quietly. "There's a freedom to be found in the shape of the wolf that can be found nowhere else. I know not how to explain it better than that.

231

"In those days, sorcery and witchcraft were strong in the land, and many believed that evil wizards took on the shape of wolves. Ordinary men cannot discern between feral wolves and the Wolffan, and my people soon realized that it would be wiser, and safer, to remain in human form.

"In time, our ability to take on the shape of the wolf faded from the memory of the people and it became a fable, told to scare little children into behaving lest they be gobbled up by the Wolffan. Now, only a few know the truth."

"I hear your words," Kylene replied slowly. "I know that Hardane has the power to change shape. I've seen him do it, and still it's hard for me to believe that he's both man and wolf, that it isn't just a shape he assumes."

"It is a truth few people can accept. That is why only a few of our people have ever married outside the Wolffan clan."

"Then why was Hardane betrothed to a princess of Mouldour?"

"Because it was prophesied that such an alliance was the only way to bring a lasting peace to Argone and Mouldour."

Kylene nodded. She understood what Sharilyn was saying. Marriage had often been a way to forge a lasting peace between warring nations.

"Did Hardane say when he would be back?" Sharilyn asked.

"No. He left last night and hasn't returned."

"I see."

"Do you . . . do you know where he's gone?"

"No, but I'm sure he'll return soon. He loves you, daughter, you can be certain of that if nothing else."

Hardane didn't return that night. The celebration took place as planned, with Sharilyn and Lord Kray explaining that Kylene had not yet recovered from the ordeal in the Temple of Fire and that Hardane was comforting her.

In her room, Kylene stood at the window staring down into the garden below, wondering when Hardane would return. He had to come back, she told herself over and over again. After all, this was his home.

But the hours passed and still he did not return.

Chapter Twenty-Eight

It was late the next night when Hardane returned to the keep. Kylene was in their bedchamber, sitting in the window seat, her gaze focused on a distant star, when she felt his presence in the room.

Slowly, she turned around to face him. In a distant corner of her mind, she wondered how long he'd been back. Long enough to bathe and change his clothes, she thought as her gaze moved over him. He was a study in black, from the top of his head to the snug black breeches riding low on his narrow hips. His eyes were shadowed, and a day's growth of beard covered the lower half of his face.

Kylene stared at the thick black bristles on his jaw, at the long black hair that fell past his shoulders. Gradually, her gaze lowered to the mat of ebony-colored hair that covered his broad chest.

Wolf.

Hardane's jaw clenched under her scrutiny.

"Aye, lady," he said roughly, "a wolf stands before you in the guise of a man. Think you I'll tear out your heart?"

"You have torn it, my lord wolf," she retorted, unable to hide the resentment she felt. "Torn it until it bleeds with sorrow and remorse."

Hardane took a deep, steadying breath. She had a right to be angry. He should have told her the truth before the wedding. He should have warned her, prepared her.

"I never meant to hurt you, or deceive you," he said quietly, and wondered if she'd ever forgive him.

She looked skeptical. "Didn't you?"

"I should have told you everything," he admitted, his voice laced with regret.

"Yes."

A hurt deeper than pain lanced his heart as he tried to prepare himself to live without her, though how he'd face the future without her was beyond all comprehension, so quickly had she taken root in his heart, his very soul.

His gaze moved over her, committing to memory the fire that danced in her deep red hair, the dark brown of her eyes. Her skin was smooth and unblemished, her cheeks as pink as rose petals, her lips as red as a pomegranate seed. Kylene . . .

His hands curled into tight fists as he summoned the courage to ask the one question he dreaded.

"Will you leave me, now that you know the truth?"

Will you leave me, now that you know the truth?
She heard the pain in his voice and knew that her
leaving would cut him deeply. And knew, just as
certainly, that she'd rather die than live without
him. Wolf or man, she loved him utterly, completely. To live without him would be no life at
all.

"Kylene?" He stared into her eyes, his whole life
hanging on her answer.

"I'll not leave you, unless it is your wish."

"You'll stay?" he asked in disbelief. "In spite of
the curse of my bloodline?"

Running across the room, Kylene threw herself
into his arms. "A blessing, my lord wolf, not a
curse."

Hardane held her at arm's length, wanting to
make sure she understood that the Wolffan, like
their wild cousins, mated for life.

"Are you certain, lady?" he asked, his gaze holding hers. "Once my seed is growing within you,
there can be no turning back. Once our sons are
born, I will never let you go."

"Could you let me go now?"

Slowly, he shook his head. "No, lady, not even
if it meant my life."

"Then love me, Hardane," she murmured. "I care
not if you be wolf or man. Both or neither, only
love me now."

"As you wish, lady," he replied, his voice husky
with desire as he lifted her into his arms and carried her to their bed. "As you wish . . ."

And then, as gently as ever a man loved a woman, Hardane possessed her, and with every touch,

with every caress, he reaffirmed his infinite love for her. And Kylene, listening with her heart, heard every unuttered vow as clearly as if he'd spoken his love aloud.

"I heard you in the night," Kylene remarked a long time later.

She was lying in his arms, her head on his shoulder, her fingers lightly tracing a path through the hair on his chest.

"Did you? And what did you think?"

"I realized how deeply I had hurt you, and that, in so doing, I had hurt myself as well."

Hardane wrapped a skein of her hair around his hand, admiring its softness as he brushed it against his cheek.

"I wasn't going to come back, lady. I couldn't face the thought of living here without you."

"But this is your home," Kylene exclaimed softly. "Where would you have gone?"

"There's a wolf pack that hunts in the forest. For a time, I thought of joining them, of spending the rest of my life as a wolf."

"You wouldn't."

A faint smile curved his lips. "I had decided I didn't want a life without you, but I knew I had to see you one more time."

Kylene sat up, her eyes wide as she stared down at him. "And if I had sent you from me, you would have gone to live with the wolves?"

"Aye, lady. What would my life be if I couldn't share it with you?"

"Oh, Hardane," she murmured, her voice thick

with emotion. "You must know how much I love you."

"Sometimes love isn't enough."

Choking back a sob, Kylene snuggled against him once more, stunned to think he would have given up his home, the throne, the life he'd been born to live, all because of her.

She hugged him fiercely, determined to make him happy, to give him strong sons and beautiful daughters, to please him in every way a woman could please a man.

In the weeks that followed, they spent every moment together. Hardane showered her with gifts: jewels that reflected all the colors of the rainbow, lustrous silks and satins in fiery shades of red and blue and green. He took her to the stables and presented her with a horse of her own, a dainty, long-legged mare with a coat like black velvet and a mane and tail like ebony silk.

They took long rides together, sometimes traveling to nearby towns, sometimes spending the night near the waterfall.

On one such night, after they'd made love beneath a starlit sky, they walked hand in hand along the edge of the mountain. And there, silhouetted in the moonlight at the bottom of the falls, Kylene saw the Wolffan warrior who had ridden over the edge. And sitting on the boulder beside him, her wedding gown shimmering like liquid silver in the moonlight, was the woman who had chosen to join her beloved in death rather than face the future alone.

Kylene had stared up at Hardane, unable to

believe her eyes. "Do you see them?" she had whispered.

"Aye, lady," Hardane had replied, squeezing her hand. "And they see us."

And when Kylene looked again, she saw the two lovers gazing up at them.

The woman waved, her delicate hand` ghostly in the moonlight. And then the Wolffan warrior lifted his lady onto the back of his horse, swung up behind her, and rode off into the shadows beyond the falls.

Kylene had never known such happiness as she knew in those carefree days. It was as if she had been born anew the night Hardane returned to the castle, born into a world of light and laughter, a world of brilliant colors and sounds. Her regimented life in the Motherhouse seemed like a bad dream, a nightmare from which she'd been awakened by love's first kiss.

Like a princess in a fairy tale, she found herself married to a prince, waited upon by servants. She had only to ask for something and it appeared before her. A new gown. A glass of wine. A bowl of freshly picked snowberries. Every whim, every desire of her heart, was granted almost before she'd made it known.

But most wondrous of all was Hardane. He had become the center of her world, her life. She basked in his touch, felt her heart thrill anew each time she heard the deep timbre of his voice. His face was the first she saw in the morning, the last she saw at night. His kisses sent her off to sleep and woke her with the dawn.

She thought often of the sisters she'd never met. One day soon, she would ask Hardane to locate what was left of her family, perhaps invite them to Castle Argone, but not yet. She was too caught up in her newfound happiness to want to share it with anyone else. Soon, she would make time to meet her sisters and their families, but not now.

Occasionally, she wondered what had happened to Selene. No one in the castle had seen her sister since the wedding. The knowledge that her twin sister hated her, hated her enough to try to kill her, was hard to bear. Kylene tried to imagine how she would feel if the situation were reversed, but she knew, deep in her heart, that she would never have plotted against Selene.

But Hardane gave her little time to fret about her sister's treachery, and she gradually put it out of her mind.

These long golden days of sunshine and laughter, these glorious star-studded nights of ecstasy, belonged only to Hardane.

Chapter Twenty-Nine

Selene stood in the center of the Great Hall of Castle Mouldour, the rapid pounding of her heart the only sign of her inner tension.

She was risking her future, her very life, by being here, and yet she had nowhere else to go, no other course of action to take.

She took a deep breath as she heard footsteps in the outer hall, and then her uncle stood in the doorway. He was an impressive man, tall and brawny, with broad shoulders, and legs that looked as solid as tree trunks. A full beard and a mustache covered the lower half of his face. She could tell by the look in his frigid blue eyes that he wasn't happy to see her.

"Selene." He muttered her name as he stepped into the room.

She dropped a curtsey. "Uncle."

"Where's your father?"

"He's dead."

Bourke's eyes narrowed thoughtfully. With his brother's death, the throne became more secure. "And your sister?"

"She married Hardane of Argone a fortnight ago."

"You know that for a fact?" Bourke asked, obviously worried.

"I was there."

Bourke stared past her, unseeing, as he absorbed this information. Kylene's marriage to Hardane was an event that the Interrogator had assured him would never take place. Now it was an accomplished fact.

A wedding. A wedding night. Children . . . twins. Bourke grunted softly. The twins that had been foretold by prophesy. The twins who would steal his throne, his power.

"Why have you come here, Selene?"

"I need a place to stay."

"And you want to stay here?" Bourke looked skeptical.

"No. I want a place of my own, land of my own."

"I have no land to give away."

"Perhaps we can make a trade."

Bourke snorted disdainfully. "What would a mere woman have to trade?"

"My sister for Kildeene Castle."

Bourke's eyes glinted with interest. "How do you propose to get her away from Argone?"

"I know a way. Do we have a bargain?"

Bourke nodded slowly.

"I'll have your word, Uncle."

"You have it."

Selene smiled. At last she would have a place of her own, land of her own. She would have no need of a man to rule her. She would take her pleasure where she could find it, and answer to no one.

"There's a secret entrance that leads from Hardane's bedchamber all the way to the river on the west side of the keep," she said. "Unless your men are complete fools, they should be able to slip into the castle unseen, take Kylene, and make their escape without being caught."

Bourke studied his niece thoughtfully. They had more in common than mere kinship, he mused. Selene was a woman who knew what she wanted and was prepared to do whatever it took to obtain it, even if it meant betraying her own sister, as he had betrayed his brother to obtain the throne of Mouldour.

Bourke grunted softly. It was too bad they shared the same blood, he thought with regret. Selene would have made a fine queen.

Chapter Thirty

The Interrogator leaned over the rail, his gaze fixed on the sandy shore of the Argonian coast. The woman, Kylene, had set the prophesy in motion by marrying the future Lord of Argone, but she would not live long enough to bear his children. He would have her head when they returned to Mouldour, and the head of the Wolf of Argone as well, if it were possible.

The Interrogator rubbed his hands together. Once he had fixed it so the prophesy could not come true, the throne of Mouldour would be secure. Bourke's only child was a bastard by birth. She would be easily disposed of when the time came.

Frowning, the Interrogator stared at the waves lapping at the side of the ship. Once Kylene was eliminated, once the fulfillment of the prophesy was no longer possible, there would be nothing to stop him from taking over the throne. He could take the Princess Selene to wife. She would make a powerful ally. If she shared the throne, the people of Mouldour would more readily accept him as Lord High Ruler since she was Carrick's daughter, and Carrick had been the rightful Lord High Ruler of Mouldour. The people hated Bourke, but they would give their allegiance to Selene, and to the man who made it possible for her to obtain the throne.

It was worth thinking about, and he thought of little else as the ship made its way toward the Argonian coast.

It was after midnight when they dropped anchor in a placid cove.

In the distance, he heard the sound of a water-fall.

Kylene snuggled against Hardane. Drifting between waking and sleeping, she listened to the sound of the waterfall as it splashed over the rocky mountainside to the river below.

Through heavy-lidded eyes, she gazed at the stars, at the full yellow moon hanging low in the sky. In a few hours it would be dawn, time to return to the keep. Hardane had duties to perform this day.

A rebellion had sprung up in Chadray several days ago, and Lord Kray and his sons had gone to quell it, leaving Hardane in charge of the keep. Most of the able-bodied men of Castle Argone had accompanied Lord Kray.

In the days since his father's departure, Hardane had been busy from dusk till dawn with castle affairs, but yesterday afternoon he had spirited her out of the keep, insisting he needed a few hours away from the petty complaints of the people.

There had been no need to ask her twice. She had been more than eager to spend time alone with her husband in their favorite retreat.

Kylene turned her head to the side, her gaze moving lovingly over her husband's profile. It was a decidedly masculine face, all hard lines and planes, his jaw shaded with black bristles.

She ran her hand lightly over his jaw, loving the feel of his coarse black beard beneath her fingertips, and then her hand slid down his chest, lower, lower, toying with the curly black hair that ran straight as an arrow to that part of him that made him a man.

A growl rumbled in Hardane's throat, and she found her hand trapped in his, found herself staring into the depths of his gray eyes.

"You're asking for trouble, lady," he warned.

Kylene widened her eyes in mock innocence. "Trouble, my lord?"

"Aye, lady," he replied, and before she quite knew how it happened, she was tucked beneath him, her hands imprisoned in his as he bent to claim her lips in a kiss that seared her from head to heel.

"I could grow to like such trouble," Kylene murmured.

"Could you, wench?"

"Wench?" She glowered at him. "Wench, is it?"

Hardane grinned impudently. "A wife must be all things to her husband," he said arrogantly. "Friend, lover . . ." He pressed a kiss to her brow. "Mother, sister. Wench . . ." His lips brushed her cheek. "Lady . . ." His tongue slid across her lower lip. "Mistress."

Kylene blinked up at him, her expression serious. "Were you ever tempted to take a mistress, my lord wolf?"

Hardane grunted softly as he recalled the day Jared had taken him to the pleasure house of Karos.

"No," he answered honestly, remembering the disgust he'd felt at being in such a place. "Never."

He kissed her again. "You're all the woman I need," he murmured gruffly. "The only woman I'll ever need, or want. I . . ."

Abruptly, he released her hands and sat up, his head cocked to one side.

"What is it?" Kylene asked.

"Listen!"

Kylene frowned. "I don't hear anything."

"Someone's coming." Hardane stood up, his hand reaching for his sword. "Stay here."

On silent feet, he made his way toward the path that led to the waterfall, a muffled curse rising in his throat as he saw what looked to be a hundred well-armed men riding toward the castle.

He muttered a vile oath as he recognized the man riding at the head of the column. As he watched, a rider approached and the Interrogator signaled for the column to halt.

In the stillness of the morning, Hardane had no trouble overhearing what was said.

"We can take the castle with little trouble," the rider said. "Lord Kray and most of the men have gone to Chadray to settle a dispute."

The Interrogator smiled, obviously pleased with this unexpected bit of good news.

"I don't want the castle, only the woman," he said. "Everyone else is expendable, but the woman must be taken alive. Is that understood?"

"Yes, my lord."

"And Hardane," the Interrogator added. "I want him, too, if possible."

"Yes, my lord."

"We'll rest the horses for a quarter of an hour, then press on."

Hardane stared at the column, his mind racing. He could make a run for the keep and hope he could muster a defense with the men who had remained at the castle, but he knew that such a course of action would inevitably lead to a battle, a battle they couldn't win against such odds. Even if he managed to get a messenger to his father, even if he managed to hold the Interrogator off until Lord Kray returned from Chadray, there would be lives lost. He couldn't put Kylene or his mother at risk when there was a chance he could prevent it.

Hardane clenched his fists until his knuckles were white. The Interrogator wanted Kylene, only Kylene . . .

Turning on his heel, Hardane ran back to Kylene.

"What is it?" she asked, her brow furrowed with concern as he snatched up her gown and thrust it into her hands.

"Dress quickly." He shook his head as she reached for her undergarments. "There's no time for that now," he said. "Hurry." He was reaching for his breeches as he spoke.

"What is it?" Kylene asked anxiously. "Tell me, please."

"There's no time." Catching her around the waist, he swung her onto the back of his horse. "Ride hard for the keep. Tell my mother the Interrogator is riding toward the castle. She'll know what to do."

"The Interrogator? Coming here?" Kylene went cold with fear as she recalled her last encounter with the man. "Where are you going?"

"Kylene, I've no time to explain. I'll come to you as soon as I can. Hurry now!"

She wanted to argue, needed to know where he was going, but the urgency in his eyes, in his voice, kept her protests at bay. Leaning toward him, she kissed him once, hard and quick, and then she dug her heels into the stallion's flanks and headed for the castle, praying that he would soon follow.

Drawing a deep breath, Hardane willed his body to change. He shuddered convulsively as his large, hard-muscled frame assumed an unfamiliar form, transforming into something smaller, softer, rounder.

And then, praying that his ruse would work, he swung onto the back of Kylene's mare and urged the horse toward the trail that led to the waterfall.

"There!" The Interrogator pointed at the woman riding toward them, unable to believe his good fortune. "It's her!"

The Interrogator smiled as the woman reined her horse to a halt, then sawed hard on the reins, wheeling the mare into a tight turn, but it was too late. Before she could escape, four of his men had her surrounded.

One of the men grabbed the mare's reins and led her back to the Interrogator.

"So, my lady," the Interrogator said, his voice heavy with sarcasm, "we meet again."

"What do you want?"

"You, my lady," he replied, blessing the gods of Mouldour for this unexpected bit of fortuity. "Ivar, turn the column around. We return to the ship at once."

"What of Hardane?" Ivar asked.

"He'll come to us." The Interrogator smiled with malicious glee. "I'll have them both."

He chuckled softly. *And the throne as well,* he mused to himself. *All without spilling a drop of blood. The throne. Power. The secret of shape changing. Soon it would all be his.* "Bind her hands and bring her along."

Sharilyn stared at Kylene, hardly able to understand the girl's words as they tumbled from her mouth.

"The Interrogator. He's here. Send for Lord Kray. Quickly!"

"The Interrogator?" Sharilyn exclaimed, the very name striking fear to her heart. "What does he want? Why would he come here?"

"He wants me. I don't know why. And Hardane. He wants Hardane."

Sharilyn took a deep breath. "Where is Hardane?"

"He stayed behind. He said he'd come as soon as he could . . ." Kylene stared at Sharilyn. "You don't think . . ."

"Yes," Sharilyn said, confirming Kylene's worst fears. "That's just what I think."

"But . . . but he said he'd never taken on a woman's shape."

"It should be easy for him to assume yours, my daughter. He knows it as well as he knows his own."

Kylene shook her head, refusing to believe what she knew to be true. Hardane had assumed her shape. He had let the Interrogator take him not only so that she could reach the castle safely, but in hopes of preventing a battle.

"Oh, Hardane," she murmured. As the full impact of what he'd done hit her, she sank into a chair, staring sightlessly at the floor.

As from a great distance, Kylene heard Sharilyn giving orders to Teliford and the others, and when that was done, Sharilyn sent Parah to check with the lookouts, but all four reported that all was quiet, no enemy in sight.

Hardane's scheme had worked, Kylene realized. Thinking that he had her in his clutches, the Interrogator had returned to his ship. Even now, he could be making his way toward the Isle of Mouldour.

By the time the Interrogator realized his mistake, the element of surprise would be lost and the people of Castle Argone would be ready for him should he decide to return. A messenger had already been sent to Chadray to inform Lord Kray of what was happening. Riders had been sent to the outlying villages, ordering every village to send a dozen men to help defend the castle.

But none of that mattered to Kylene. Hardane was gone, perhaps forever.

A single tear slipped down her cheek as she wrapped her hands over her stomach in a protective gesture as old as time and began to rock back and forth.

Chapter Thirty-One

Hardane braced himself against the bulkhead as the ship cleaved through the waves toward the open sea. His satisfaction that his plan had worked warred with his regret at leaving Kylene in such haste. But it couldn't be helped. He could not put her life in jeopardy, not now.

He frowned as he looked at his body . . . her body, now. Always before, he had taken on the shape of a man, and with it, a man's physique and a man's strength.

He shook his head ruefully, remembering how he'd tried to struggle when they'd dragged him below decks. Kylene's slender, softly rounded arms lacked the strength he'd always taken for granted and he'd felt utterly weak and helpless as two of the Interrogator's men had wrestled him down the narrow ladder, their hands groping his flesh.

A wry grin twisted Hardane's lips as he glanced down. He had breasts now, a narrow waist, long, shapely legs. He had soft skin and a wealth of russet-colored hair, none of which could be used to defend himself.

He had known a soul-deep anger as one of the Interrogator's men had shoved him up against the bulkhead and caressed him. With his hands lashed behind his back, Hardane had been helpless to fight the man off. Until he'd resorted to an age-old feminine maneuver and kneed the man in the groin. He'd been unable to help wincing, himself, as he did so. Still, Hardane had felt a tremendous sense of satisfaction as the man instantly released him and doubled over, clutching his battered manhood.

That had been hours ago. How many hours, Hardane wondered as he gazed around his prison. It was an empty storeroom, four solid walls, no portholes, only one door.

With the ease of a man at home on the sea, he began to pace the floor, cursing the long skirts that hampered his every step even as he wondered how long he'd be able to maintain Kylene's shape.

He felt odd, as though he'd been stuffed into clothes that were too tight. And that was odder still, because he'd never felt that way when he had assumed male shapes, or the shape of the wolf.

For a moment, he toyed with the idea of becoming the wolf, of ripping out the throat of whoever first opened the door of his prison. But he dismissed the thought immediately. He couldn't kill the whole crew, and as long as he was imprisoned, he dared not change into another shape for fear of alerting the Interrogator to the fact that he hadn't captured Kylene at all.

Time. He needed to buy time. Time for his father to return to Argone.

A sound at the door brought Hardane to an abrupt halt and he backed against the bulkhead, waiting, wishing his hands weren't bound behind his back, wishing he had a weapon with which to defend himself.

And then the door swung open and the Interrogator entered the room, a smug expression in his ice blue eyes. Two men, well armed, stood watch in the companionway.

"What is the meaning of this?" Hardane demanded. The sound of Kylene's voice coming from his throat startled him for a moment.

"I am only reclaiming what was mine," the Interrogator replied coldly. "No one has ever escaped from the Fortress and lived to tell the tale. I could not have a woman be the exception."

The Interrogator closed the door and leaned against it. Drawing a dagger from his belt, he tapped the narrow blade against the palm of his hand.

"It was in my mind to dispose of you," he remarked, "but then I realized that you're the perfect bait to lure Hardane to Mouldour."

"Why do you want m . . . Hardane?"

"I want to learn the secret of shape shifting."

"It isn't a trick to be learned; it's a part of him, of who he is."

The Interrogator made a wordless sound of disagreement. "I don't believe that."

"It's true nonetheless."

"Perhaps. And perhaps a little torture, cleverly inflicted by one skilled in the art, will loosen his tongue. If not . . ."

The Interrogator smiled a cold cruel smile as he dragged a finger down Kylene's cheek.

"If his own pain will not pry the secret from him, perhaps the sight of his life-mate writhing in agony will do the trick. Either way, I shall enjoy the game."

With a cry of rage, Hardane lunged forward. In his haste, he tripped over the hem of his skirt. He fell forward, felt the edge of the dagger pierce his right shoulder as he stumbled into the Interrogator's blade.

Silently cursing his weakness and his clumsiness, Hardane reeled back, groaning softly as the Interrogator jerked the blade from his flesh.

"Stupid girl," the Interrogator snarled. "You'll be no good to me dead."

"Or alive," Hardane retorted.

He flinched as the Interrogator struck him hard across the mouth.

"Enough of your insolence, my lady. It matters not to me whether you spend this voyage in comfort or in chains. The choice is yours."

So saying, the Interrogator opened the door and left the room.

With a sigh, Hardane sank down on the floor. His shoulder throbbed monotonously. Blood continued to trickle down his arm, forming a small dark pool beside him.

He closed his eyes, fighting the pain as he concentrated on maintaining Kylene's shape. Only a few more days, he thought wearily; only a few more days and then it wouldn't matter.

Kylene sat in a soft leather chair before the hearth in her bedchamber, a heavy quilt drawn around her shoulders as she stared into the flames.

Sharilyn had sent a messenger to Chadray to advise Lord Kray of what had transpired. Other runners had been sent to the nearby farms, asking them to send men to help defend Castle Argone should it be necessary. The animals had been driven inside the castle walls and the gates shut and locked. Every precaution that could be taken had been put into effect, and now all they could do was wait—wait to see if the Interrogator returned, wait for Lord Kray and his sons to come home.

Kylene gazed out the window, wishing she could cry, but the emptiness she felt inside was too deep for tears. Hardane had assumed her shape so that she could get away, gambling with his life so that the Interrogator would be satisfied to leave once he'd captured the prize he came for. And it had worked, but at what cost. The Interrogator would no doubt execute Hardane once he realized he'd been duped. If that happened, it would no longer matter that she was safe, Kylene thought disconsolately. She'd have nothing left to live for . . .

She cut the thought off in midsentence, feeling as though she were betraying not only Hardane but a part of herself as well.

Closing her eyes, she concentrated on Hardane, and gradually, as if a fog were lifting from her mind, his image appeared before her. Only it wasn't his image at all. It was startling, like looking in a mirror. He was locked in a small room of some kind, his hands—her hands?—bound behind his back. Dried blood darkened his clothing.

Even as she watched, he stood up and took on his own shape, and then he began to pace the floor. So vivid was his image, she could feel the sharp pain in his shoulder, the chafing of the coarse rope that bound his arms behind his back. He seemed oblivious to the discomfort as he continued to pace the floor. She felt his anger, his quiet desperation. His satisfaction that he'd been able to deceive the Interrogator.

"Hardane . . ."

She spoke his name aloud, saw him pause, his head cocked to one side. Had he heard her, then? She called his name again, felt the bond between them vibrate.

"Come back to me, my lord wolf," she said, willing her love across the miles that separated them. "Please come back to me."

She heard footsteps approaching the room where he was held captive. In the blink of an eye, Hardane sank to the floor and assumed her shape as a knock came at the door.

The knocking came again and then again, and the images faded like shadows before the rain.

Disoriented, Kylene opened her eyes and looked around. Only then did she realize it had all been a dream, and that someone was knocking at her chamber door.

And then the tears came.

Chapter Thirty-Two

For Hardane, the hours seemed to crawl by, with each day the same as the last. He was given food and water and the opportunity to relieve himself twice each day.

It was an odd feeling, lifting layers of heavy cloth, then squatting over a wooden bucket to urinate when he was accustomed to standing. He tolerated the snickers of his guards, the occasional caress, wondering how women who sold their favors to strangers endured such intimacies.

He felt a deep sense of revulsion at being touched against his will. It galled him, being forced to endure the lewd stares of the Interrogator's men, having to listen to their coarse suggestions, knowing he was at the mercy of his guards, of the Interrogator, because, in his present form, he was smaller, weaker.

Late at night, when he was certain of being undisturbed, he transformed into his own shape. Resuming his own form was like slipping on a pair of old boots—comfortable and familiar.

In his own shape, Hardane prowled the confines of the small storeroom restlessly, hour after hour, his mind filling with images of Kylene. She had become the most important thing in his life. She was his woman, his wife. He longed to hold her in his arms once more, to feel the warmth of her body against his own.

Kylene. She was never out of his thoughts, his dreams. Once, he had imagined that he heard her voice pleading with him to return.

He kept track of the days as best he could. If his calculations were correct, they'd been at sea twelve days.

If his calculations were correct, they would reach Mouldour on the morrow.

And now it was night and the Interrogator had come to see him again, as he had each day, his expression smug, his ice blue eyes cold and unwavering.

Hardane stood with his back to the wall, his hands bound behind him, waiting, wondering what lay in store for him once they left the ship. Nothing good, he mused, judging by the look on the Interrogator's face. Somehow, he would have to escape his captors before they reached the Fortress.

"I had thought to execute you upon our arrival at Mouldour," the Interrogator remarked. He crossed the floor until he was less than an arm's length away from the woman he'd been sent to destroy. "But now . . ."

His eyes narrowed as he caressed her cheek. The skin was smooth and soft beneath his callused fingertips and he felt a sudden stirring in his loins. Surely, now that he had her away from Hardane of Argone, there was no need to dispose of her immediately.

Hardane jerked his head back to avoid the Interrogator's touch. "But now?"

"You would be wise not to annoy me, my lady," the Interrogator warned.

Reaching out, he caught Kylene's chin between his thumb and forefinger and gave it a cruel squeeze.

"Your life is in my hands, madam. I can let you live, or I can execute you now in any manner that amuses me."

Knowing it would be foolish to provoke the man, Hardane kept silent.

An oath escaped the Interrogator's lips. Insolent wench, he thought, and then, because she refused to cower, refused to beg, he slapped her hard across the face, taking perverse pleasure in the bright red stain that blossomed on her cheek.

"You might spend the night thinking of the last time you were a guest in the Fortress," the Interrogator suggested.

Hardane's eyes narrowed as he remembered the brutal whipping Kylene had endured at the hands of the Executioner.

"I see you've not forgotten the feel of the lash, or my promise to see you dead. Perhaps in the morning you will be more agreeable," the Interrogator mused. He placed his hand on Kylene's shoulder, let it slide suggestively down her arm, the back of his hand caressing her breast. "You might even think of some way to convince me to allow you to live."

"Don't count on it." Even as he spoke the words, Hardane knew it was a mistake, but some inner devil forced the retort past his lips, perversely determined to have the last word no matter what the cost.

Fury blazed in the Interrogator's ice blue eyes. Hardane reeled back as the Interrogator struck him across the face with the short crop he habitually carried.

The blow laid Hardane's cheek open almost to the bone, splattering blood in the Interrogator's face and over the walls.

Incensed that the man would strike a woman in such a fashion, his cheek burning with pain, Hardane spit in the Interrogator's face.

"You'll regret that," the Interrogator promised as he wiped Hardane's blood and spittle from his face. "I'll flay the skin from your body an inch at a time, madam, and then, if you're lucky, I'll let you die."

With a smug smile, the Interrogator opened the door and left the room.

Hardane waited until the Interrogator's footsteps had receded, and then he sank down on the floor, resting his head on his bent knees, his lacerated cheek throbbing from the Interrogator's blow.

The next morning, at the cry of "Land ho!" he transformed into the wolf.

He heard the sound of whistling as the crewman who brought him breakfast each morning approached the storeroom.

Hardane's hackles rose as the key turned in the lock. Had he been in human form, he might have laughed at the startled look on the man's face when he saw a wolf inside the door. But he wasn't a man now, and he was in no mood for laughter.

With a growl, he hurled himself at the hapless crewman, his mouth filling with the warm, sweet taste of blood as his teeth ripped into the man's shoulder. And then he was out the door, clawing his way up the narrow ladder, racing across the deck toward the gangplank.

He heard a shout behind him, felt a deep burning pain as an arrow pierced his right leg. And then, from the rigging, someone dropped a net over him and he knew he was well and truly caught.

Panting hard, he lifted his head to find the Interrogator staring down at him, a look of amazement in his cold blue eyes.

"Hardane," the Interrogator murmured. "Can it be you?" He turned to the seaman who had brought the wolf down with a single well-placed arrow. "Quetzel, go below and check on our prisoner."

Hardane remained where he was, bloody saliva dripping from his jaws, his gaze fixed on the Interrogator's face.

Drawn by the commotion, the other crewmen

gathered around, their faces reflecting astonishment at finding a wolf on board.

Moments later, Quetzel returned. "The lady's gone, my lord."

"And Ren?"

"Bad hurt."

The Interrogator nodded, his expression one of grim satisfaction. He had lost the lady, he mused. Indeed, it now appeared he'd never had the lady at all, but perhaps he had something far better.

"How'd a wolf get on board?" Quetzel asked, still eyeing the beast.

"It's not a wolf."

"Not a wolf!" Quetzel's hand tightened on the crossbow clutched in his hand. "My lord, you can see with your own eyes that—"

The Interrogator cut him off with a wave of his hand. "This, my friend, is none other than Hardane, Lord of Argone."

Quetzel stared at the wolf, at the thick black fur, at the bloody saliva, at the arrow jutting from the bloody wound, and then a slow smile spread across his broad face. Everyone knew the Interrogator had been seeking the Wolf of Argone for months. Surely there would be a large reward for the man who had brought him down.

The Interrogator nudged the wolf in the side.

"Will you go to the Fortress as wolf or man, Hardane?" he asked harshly. "The choice is yours."

Hardane stared at the Lord High Interrogator through unblinking gray eyes. Other than Kylene and his immediate family, no one had ever seen him transform from one shape to another.

With a shrug, the Interrogator turned away. "Niles, secure the net so the beast can't escape. Quetzel, there's a large sea chest in the hold. Bring it up and lock the wolf inside, net and all. Perhaps, by the time we reach the Fortress, he'll be more agreeable."

It was a three-hour journey from the coast of Mouldour to the Fortress.

For Hardane, trapped in the net and locked inside a chest only large enough to hold him, it seemed much longer. No one had bothered to remove the arrow from his leg, and he howled with pain as the wagon jolted over the rough road. The air inside the box grew warm, stifling.

Helpless, steeped in fury, he imagined sinking his fangs into the Interrogator's throat, drinking his blood to quench the awful thirst that plagued him.

He was only barely conscious when he realized that the motion of the cart had stopped. A short time later, the chest was unlocked, the lid was opened, and he was lifted out, net and all, and dumped into an iron-barred cell.

At the Interrogator's command, a half-dozen armed men surrounded him. Then, with a vicious smile lighting his face, the Interrogator took hold of the arrow and jerked it from the wolf's flesh.

Hardane roared with pain, his jaws snapping wildly as he struggled against the net in an effort to sink his teeth into his tormentor's throat.

But the Interrogator only laughed and then, still

chuckling with malicious glee, he motioned for his men to leave the cell.

Following them out, he closed and locked the heavy iron-barred door and pocketed the key.

With a wave of his hand, he dismissed the men, ordering two of them to remain out of sight but within calling distance.

When he was alone in the dungeon, the Interrogator pulled a stool up to the cell and sat down, his gaze fixed on Hardane. All his life, he had yearned to know the secret of shape shifting, had yearned to see it done. And now the time was at hand. Sooner or later, Hardane's control would slip and he would assume his own shape. And he would be there to see it.

Almost against his will, the Interrogator felt his gaze drawn to the wolf's eyes, and as he stared into the creature's unblinking gray gaze, he was gripped by a sudden terror as a primal fear of the ancient Wolffan race rose up within him.

Old tales, heard long ago in his childhood, flooded his mind. Tales of Wolffan males devouring human young, tales of female Wolffan luring innocent men to their deaths. Tales of Wolffan men and women mating with human men and women. Those tales he knew to be true. Hardane of Argone had been conceived from such a union. It was said the blood of the Wolffan could cure warts, that they could sicken a flock of sheep with a glance, that they drank human blood, and danced in the light of the midnight moon.

With a disdainful snort, the Interrogator shook such fanciful fables from his mind. The Wolffan had the power to assume other shapes, that was all. They weren't witches; they possessed no hurtful magic.

Feeling calmer, he sat back, his arms crossed over his chest, and waited.

Plagued by thirst and the constant throbbing pain of his wound, Hardane lay panting on the cold stone floor, the weight of the net growing heavier with each passing moment. He longed for a drink, one cool drink of water, to ease his thirst.

Closing his eyes, he whined low in his throat, feeling more miserable, more alone, than he'd ever felt in his life.

As though reading his mind, the Interrogator reached for the water jug on the floor beside him. He shook it several times, the water making a pleasant swishing against the sides of the jar, and then he took a long slow drink, letting a little of the water dribble down his chin.

A low growl of rage and frustration rumbled in Hardane's throat as the scent of the water reached his nostrils. Curse the man!

With a sneer, the Interrogator put the jug aside and rose to his feet. Taking up a three-pronged lance, he slid it through the bars and jabbed at the wolf's injured leg.

Hardane howled with pain as the sharp prongs pierced his already torn flesh. Rage exploded within him, and with it the primal urge to kill.

Knowing it was futile, he began to thrash about, but the movement only entangled him more deeply in the net's web.

The Interrogator leaned forward. "Change for

me, Hardane," he urged. "You'll have no food, no water, until you do."

A low-pitched snarl of frustration and rage filled the cell, and then, as the Interrogator jabbed him with the lance again, a long, anguished cry echoed off the cold stone walls.

"Change, Hardane," the Interrogator urged. "Change now, or I'll cleave your head from your body and send that fine black pelt to Kylene."

It was not an idle threat. One look into the Interrogator's cold blue eyes assured him of that.

For a moment, Hardane thought of giving up, of calling the Interrogator's bluff and putting an end to everything once and for all. But then he thought of Kylene, of the anguish his death would cause her, and he knew he could not do anything to cause her grief, not now.

He felt the transformation sweep over him, saw the Interrogator's eyes widen in stunned disbelief as wolf became man.

It took only moments, yet the Interrogator saw it all clearly, as if time had somehow slowed its pace. He saw the wolf's head change shape, saw the thick black fur disappear while the paws transformed into human hands and feet. And suddenly it was Hardane, clad in a pair of buff-colored breeches, trapped within the net. Blood stained his right thigh and dripped onto the stone floor. A long gash, black with dried blood, angled down his left cheek.

Teeth clenched against the pain throbbing through him, Hardane took hold of the net and threw it off. Then, summoning what little strength he still possessed, he stood up and faced his enemy.

The Interrogator stared at the man before him, shaken to the depths of his soul by what he'd just seen. He had always believed that the Wolffan could change shapes, he had spoken of it as if it were a known fact, but to actually see it happen was a truly frightening thing.

And then the fear left him, replaced by an immense desire to know how such an incredible feat had been accomplished.

"Tell me," he demanded. "Tell me the secret of changing."

"There is no secret," Hardane replied coldly.

"You lie! I will have the secret, or I will have your life."

Slowly, Hardane shook his head. "There is no secret," he repeated calmly. "If you wish to learn magic, seek a wizard."

"A wizard! I have no desire to learn the art of illusion or sorcery. I want to know the secret of shape shifting."

"Shape shifting is inherent in the Wolffan. It cannot be taught. It cannot be given away. It cannot be stolen."

A wordless cry of frustration rose in the Interrogator's throat. "We will see." He hissed the words through clenched teeth. "Perhaps you will sing a different song when your lady is here."

Hardane took a step forward, heedless of the pain that shot through his right leg. "What do you mean?"

"I mean to bring her here, my Lord of Argone."

"Here? Why?"

"To put an end to the prophesy for now and all time."

"You have only to kill me to do that. There's no need to bring Kylene into this. She cannot fulfill the prophesy without me."

"But I also wish to know the secret of the Wolffan."

"There is no secret! Wolffan shape shifting is inbred into all who are seventh born. There's no more to it than that."

"But I think there is. And when she is here, you will tell me what I wish to know, or her life will be forfeit before your own."

Hardane's hands clenched the bars. "I warn you, Renick, harm her and even the flames of Gehenna will not keep me from ripping out your heart."

The Interrogator took a step back, unable to mask his surprise. "You know my name."

"Aye, Renick of Britha. I know who you are."

With an effort, Renick wiped the surprise from his face. No one living knew his name. Born of a whore in the back alleys of Britha, he had never acknowledged the name his mother had bestowed upon him, or taken a new one. He was the Interrogator. It was his title and his rank. Men feared it, and him.

"How came you by this knowledge?"

Hardane shook his head. "Do you think I would reveal his name and thereby put his life in danger?"

"It matters not," Renick said. "What matters now is Kylene. Whether she lives or dies depends on you. You might think of that while we await her arrival."

"You're a fool. Do you think my father will let her come here?"

A sly smile curved Renick's thin lips. "Indeed, my lord wolf, indeed."

Hardane stared after the Interrogator as he left the dungeon, the words "my lord wolf" echoing in his mind. How often had Kylene called him that, her voice low and husky with affection, with desire? Kylene. The thought of her in Renick's clutches was more frightening than the thought of his own death, however painful that might be.

His hands tightened around the thick iron bars as he tried to convince himself he had nothing to fear. Kray would never allow Kylene to leave Argone. Knowing that Hardane had been captured, his mother and father would keep a careful watch over Kylene. The precautions that were taken in time of war would be followed. The castle gates would be locked and closely guarded. Strangers would not be allowed to enter the keep. The walls would be heavily manned at all times. Kylene would be safe. He had to believe that, or he'd go mad with worry.

With a groan, he sank down to the cold stone floor and rested his forehead against the bars. He was hungry and thirsty, weak from loss of blood. His leg ached as if all the fires of Gehenna had been kindled inside, and his cheek throbbed with a dull monotony. And he was weary, so utterly weary.

But, more than that, he ached with the need to see Kylene, to hold her, hear her voice, see her smile. The pain in his thigh was as nothing compared to the fierce pain in his heart when he thought of never seeing her again.

Closing his eyes, he summoned her image to mind, wondering if he could reach out to her from such a long distance. Her name repeated itself in his mind, and he seemed to hear her voice, soft and low, whispering that all would be well. He felt her hands soothing his brow, massaging the tension from his back and shoulders.

Kylene. Fervently, he prayed for her safety and for that of his family.

A short time later, one of the guards appeared. For a moment, the man stood staring through the bars. Keeping a wary eye on Hardane, he slid a loaf of hard black bread and a bowl of water into the cell, and then he hurried away, as if the devil himself were snapping at his heels.

Hardane stared at the coarse bread with distaste, remembering the rich pastries and rolls that Old Nan had prepared, but he was in no position to be choosy. He ate the bread slowly, drained the bowl of water, wishing it were wine.

He'd no sooner finished eating than Renick appeared, followed by four heavily armed guards.

Hardane struggled to his feet, wondering what Renick had in store for him now. He didn't have long to wait.

"Chain him up," Renick ordered, and the four guards entered the cell. One remained in the doorway, his lance at the ready.

Hardane fought them as best he could, but, unarmed and wounded, he was no match for three brawny men. Still, he managed to hold his own until one of the guards kicked his wounded leg out from under him.

Pain exploded in his thigh and he reeled back, fighting the nausea that rose in his throat.

In minutes, his arms were drawn behind his back and chained to the wall behind him. A thick iron collar was fitted around his neck, and then one of the guards dropped a noose over his head and snugged it tight before securing the other end to an iron ring set high above Hardane's head.

A muscle worked in Hardane's jaw. If he tried to change into the wolf, in an effort to slip his bonds, the noose would be drawn tight around his throat, slowly strangling him.

The Interrogator watched it all with an expression of supreme satisfaction. He chuckled softly as he left the dungeon. Soon, everything he'd ever wanted would be within his grasp.

Unable to sit down because of the noose around his neck, Hardane sagged back against the wall and shifted his weight to his left leg in an effort to ease the ache in his right thigh.

Alone, he stared into the darkness, fighting the urge to transform into the wolf, knowing that to do so would bring slow, strangling death. He knew of tales of Wolffan turning into everything from lizards to birds, but there was no truth to such stories. Wizards and magicians might turn into frogs or flowers, but the only inhuman shape the Wolffan could assume was that of the wolf.

He sighed as he heard the sound of footsteps in the corridor.

And then he heard the swish of skirts.

Curious, he opened his eyes, gasping when he saw the woman standing in the corridor.

For one heart-stopping moment, he thought it was Kylene. But his bride radiated goodness and light, while the woman before him seemed shadowed in endless darkness.

The woman smiled at him as she unlocked the cell door and stepped inside.

"So, my Lord of Argone, we meet again."

"Selene." He spoke her name as if it tasted bad in his mouth.

She nodded. "It's useless to fight him, you know. The Interrogator will have what he wants, and he cares not who he hurts to get it."

"It seems you have much in common."

Selene shrugged, untouched by his scorn.

Hardane stared at her, wishing it were Kylene who stood before him. Selene's eyes might be the same shade of brown, but they were as hard and cold as frozen earth. Her hair was as red as Kylene's, her skin the same creamy hue, her mouth as full and ripe, and yet she might have been as old and bent as Druidia for all the desire she sparked within him.

"What do you want, Selene?" he asked wearily. "Why have you come here?"

She stepped forward, close enough that her skirts brushed his legs as she traced the gash in his cheek.

"To gloat, of course. To see for myself that the prophesy will never come true, to assure myself that Kylene will never share your throne, or bear your children."

"She's your own flesh and blood. Why do you hate her so?"

"Why shouldn't I hate her? An accident of birth, and she was destined to have everything, everything, while I was to live in her shadow, simply because she was the firstborn twin."

"Do what you will, you cannot change destiny, Selene."

"You think not?" She ran her fingertips over his shoulder and down the length of one arm. "The Interrogator wants to know the secret of shape shifting. He'll do anything to make you tell him."

"There's nothing to tell."

Selene shrugged as she spread her hands over his chest. "It matters not to me. I came here to make a deal with you, Hardane of Argone."

"What kind of deal?" he asked, frowning as her hands slid down his belly.

"I want to be your life-mate, to share the throne of Argone."

"Such a thing is impossible."

"Is it?" She pressed herself against him, her hands drawing lazy circles on his shoulders. "I think not. You have only to send Kylene back to the Motherhouse at Mouldour and let me take her place at your side."

Hardane shook his head, repulsed by her nearness.

"No one else need ever know," Selene purred, grinding her hips against his. "I look like her. I sound like her. No one can tell us apart."

"I can."

"I'm offering you life, Hardane. All you have to

do is accept me as your life-mate."

"You mean all I have to do is betray Kylene," he retorted. "Make a mockery of the vows we took."

Selene took a step back. "You would rather die than do as I ask?" she exclaimed, unable to believe he would refuse her.

Hardane snorted softly. "I'd as soon bed a viper as share my life with you."

She slapped him then, the sound of her palm striking his cheek echoing loudly off the damp stone walls.

"So be it. But think on this, my arrogant Lord of Argone, when she dies an inch at a time at the hands of the Interrogator, the guilt will rest on your shoulders."

Hardane felt himself trapped in the web of Selene's gaze as she stared up at him through eyes so like Kylene's, and yet so different. He felt it then, the same swirling darkness that had permeated Kylene's bedchamber the night she had vowed to be his.

A mocking grin tugged at the corner of Selene's lips. "When she lies dead at your feet, remember that I offered you a chance to save her and you turned it down. Will you be able to live with that?"

He couldn't, and they both knew it.

"Think it over carefully, Hardane," she advised as she turned away and started down the corridor. "I shall come back in a day or two to see if you've changed your mind."

Chapter Thirty-Three

Kylene sat on a chair near the hearth, watching as Lord Kray paced the floor of the Great Hall. Sharilyn sat on a low-backed couch, a bit of needlework lying forgotten in her lap, while they tried to decide on a plan of action to rescue Hardane.

Stubbornly, Kylene had insisted that whatever strategy they devised, she be allowed to accompany them.

"No, no, no!" Kray said, wheeling around to face Kylene. "No matter what we decide, your coming along is out of the question. I won't hear of it."

"I'm going," Kylene replied quietly. "Nothing you can say will stop me."

Lord Kray's face softened at her show of bravado. "You love him very much, don't you?"

Kylene nodded, unable to speak past the rising lump in her throat. Ever since Hardane had

assumed her shape and gone off to decoy the Interrogator, she'd been plagued with dark visions—
faint images of Hardane being abused, tortured,
locked in the very cell that she had once occupied
in the bowels of the Fortress. He was in danger,
hurting and in pain, and she had to go to him.

When Lord Kray and his sons had returned from
Chadray two weeks earlier, she had expected them
to set sail immediately for Mouldour to rescue
Hardane. And that had, in fact, been their intent.

They had formulated several plans: they would
sail in under colors not their own; they would hire
the Norconian pirates to infiltrate the dungeon
and smuggle Hardane out of Mouldour; Jared
would go to Mouldour alone on the chance that
one man would not be noticed; Dubrey and his
brothers would disguise themselves as members
of the Mouldourian Guard, walk boldly into the
Fortress, and spirit Hardane away in the dead of
night.

Kylene had thought each plan had merit; Lord
Kray had found a flaw in each one. His most
convincing argument against rushing into anything was the very real fact that, since the Isle
of Coriantan had allied with Mouldour, Bourke
had twice the number of fighting men at his dis-
posal, twice the number of warships, as well.

And there was something else to be considered,
Lord Kray had reminded them. To attack Mouldour
now would only serve to break the tenuous peace
that had formed between the two countries while
they took time out to lick their wounds and regroup
from their last brutal encounter.

And there was one more thing to be considered, Lord Kray had remarked the last time they'd discussed the subject, and that was the fact that, as far as the Interrogator knew, he had captured Kylene. If she were to go to Mouldour, it would put both their lives in danger.

And so the days passed, and no decision was made. And then, that very morning, Dubrey had announced that all unauthorized ships were being turned away from the coasts of Mouldour. One ship, not heeding the warning, had been destroyed. And since there was no way to approach the island of Mouldour except by ship, the odds against rescuing Hardane now seemed insurmountable.

"So, what are we going to do?" Kylene asked, her gaze shifting from Lord Kray to Sharilyn and back again.

"We'll wait," Kray decided, though the inactivity was driving him to near madness, as it was everyone else. "The Interrogator must want something. A ransom, perhaps. Until we know what it is, we'll wait, and hope for the best."

A small cry of despair rose on Kylene's lips. Rising, the needlepoint in her lap falling unnoticed to the floor, Sharilyn crossed the room and put her arms around her daughter-in-law's shoulders.

"You must take better care of yourself, child," she admonished softly, kindly. "You do Hardane no good by refusing to eat. You need to keep up your strength, especially now."

Kylene nodded as she wrapped her arm around her belly. Everything Sharilyn said was true, but she had no appetite for food, and sleep offered no rest, only nightmare images of Hardane being tortured. Sometimes, she heard him crying her name as the Interrogator flayed the skin from his back, and sometimes, mired in a web of dreams and memories, it was her own screams that echoed down the corridors of her mind, her own back that cringed under the lash.

She ran from the room as nausea rose in her throat, nausea that had nothing to do with the fact that she was pregnant with Hardane's child, and everything to do with the awful images that had haunted her day and night since he'd been gone.

Chapter Thirty-Four

Renick paced his quarters, his brow furrowed, his rage a growing, living thing within him.

Curse Hardane! Why must the man be so mule-headed? Why did he refuse to reveal the secret of Wolffan shape shifting? A part of the heritage of a seventh-born child, Hardane had said, a part of their infernal religion. Renick had heard all that before. Perhaps it was true, but there was more to it than that. Shape shifting meant power, and Renick was a man who was obsessed with power, who craved it as some men craved women or liquor or the strange foreign intoxicants that made a man's mind wander.

Ah, to be able to change shape, to have the power to appear as a lowly servant or a highborn king. There was no end to the advantages such power would give him. And he meant to have it.

For the past twelve years, he had been a man of power and authority, second in command only to the Lord High Sovereign of Mouldour himself. And when he'd realized that Carrick's brother was about to steal the throne, he had, without a qualm, pledged his allegiance to Bourke. But now he was tired of taking orders, tired of doing Bourke's dirty work.

It was time to usurp the throne for himself.

He wanted the power, and the wealth that went with it.

He wanted the adulation of the people.

And it was all within his grasp. He would learn the secret of shape shifting, dispose of both Hardane and Kylene, thereby thwarting the prophesy, plot Bourke's death, and rule Mouldour.

In time, he might even conquer Argone.

The first step was to bring Kylene to the Fortress.

Chapter Thirty-Five

Hardane swayed on his feet as two of the Interrogator's men removed the shackles from his wrists, then quickly left the cell and locked the door.

He watched as Renick dismissed the guards, wanting nothing more than to curl up on the cold stone floor and go to sleep. He'd been on his feet for two days, unable to sit down, unable to do more than shift from one leg to the other because of the chains that bound him to the wall.

Two days, and he'd had nothing to eat or drink.

Two days, and the wound in his thigh throbbed incessantly, making it hard to think coherently.

Renick took a step forward. "I would see the wolf, Hardane."

For a moment, Hardane stared at the Interrogator and then, as easily as he drew breath, he transformed into the wolf, his gaze resting on the face of the woman who stood in the shadows.

A gasp rose in Selene's throat. Like all Mouldourians, she was familiar with the tales of Wolffan shape shifting, but she had always assumed they were no more than that, gruesome fables told to pass the time. She felt suddenly ill as she watched the transformation until all trace of Hardane was gone and a huge black wolf stood in his place.

Teeth drawn back in a snarl, the wolf sprang forward. Unmindful of the wound in its hind leg, it threw itself against the bars. Selene screamed as a froth of saliva sprayed across her face.

"He can't hurt you," Renick said with a sneer.

Selene nodded. Reason told her she had nothing to fear. The wolf couldn't break the bars. It couldn't escape from the cell. But knowing that such a thing was impossible could not stifle the primal fear that pounded in her heart, nor could she repress a shudder as she stared into the animal's cunning gray eyes.

He was bigger than an ordinary wolf, more frightening than anything she had ever seen in her life. He paced the cell, and she watched him in horrified fascination. Despite the ugly wound in one hind leg, the beast paced back and forth, its movements graceful, defiant. And when she looked into its eyes, eyes as gray as the clouds before a storm, she saw Hardane staring back at her.

"Make him change back," she urged. Unable to free her gaze from that of the wolf, she grabbed the Interrogator by the shoulder and shook him. "Make him change!" she cried, her voice rising hysterically. "Now!"

"Do as she says," Renick ordered brusquely.

With a low whine, the wolf shook itself. And then, his gaze fixed on Selene, the wolf took on human form once again.

"Do you still want to rule at my side?" Hardane asked disdainfully. "Do you still want to share my bed, bear my children?"

Shaking her head, Selene took a step backward, repulsed by the very suggestion. And then, knowing she was going to be violently ill, she turned on her heel and ran down the corridor.

With a snap of his fingers, Renick summoned the guards. "Bring him food and water. He'll be no good to me dead."

Though his wounded thigh was paining him a great deal, Hardane continued to stand, his gaze fixed on the Interrogator's face. He would not sit down, would not give in to the pain that made itself known with every beat of his heart, not while his enemy stood there, watching.

Minutes later, one of the guards returned with a tray of bread, a slab of smoked venison, a thick chunk of yellow cheese, and a small jug of wine, which he slid under the cell door.

Hardane's mouth watered and his stomach rumbled loudly, but he made no move toward the tray.

The Interrogator grunted softly, admiring the man's insolent pride in spite of himself.

"Very well, my Lord of Argone," he said with a sneer, "I'll leave you to dine in private. Enjoy your meal. You never know. It may be your last."

Only when he was alone did Hardane sink down on the floor. For a moment, he sat there, shivering convulsively from the stress of the last few days, the last few minutes. He stared at the blood encrusted on his thigh, a silent prayer of thanks in his heart that the wound hadn't festered.

And then, unable to help himself, he tore into the nearly raw venison, tearing the meat into strips like a wild thing. He devoured the bread in the same way. Only when he'd taken the edge from his hunger did he reach for the wine, and this he drank slowly, savoring each swallow. He ate the cheese last, relishing the tangy flavor.

With his hunger assuaged, his thoughts turned to Kylene, always Kylene. Head bowed, he prayed for her health, for the health of their unborn sons, for his father and mother. He prayed that Argone would not go to war because of him, that the tenuous peace between Argone and Mouldour, the first in over ten years, would not be broken, even though he knew it would not last indefinitely. It was merely a moment of serenity before the tempest that was sure to follow, a chance for both sides to regroup before the next assault.

Kylene . . . hear me . . . know that I love you . . . that I will love you with my last dying breath . . . and through all the endless days and nights of eternity . . .

He willed the words across the miles that separated them and then, with her name on his lips, he closed his eyes and surrendered to the awful weariness that engulfed him.

Kylene sat up in bed, Hardane's voice ringing in her ears. *Hear me . . . know that I love you . . .*

Tears flooded her eyes as the sound of his beloved voice filled her mind. He was still alive!

Slipping out of bed, she dropped to her knees and offered a fervent prayer to God, thanking Him again and again that her husband still lived, begging for a miracle to save Hardane.

She was still praying when there came a knock at the door and she heard Lord Kray's voice.

Rising, she opened the door to find Lord Kray and Sharilyn standing in the corridor.

"You've had news?" Kylene remarked. Bad news, she thought, judging from the redness of Sharilyn's eyes, the bleak expression on Lord Kray's face.

"We know what the Interrogator wants now." Lord Kray's voice was as solemn as his countenance.

He had not intended to tell Kylene of the Interrogator's message, but Sharilyn had insisted that Hardane's wife had every right to know of the Interrogator's commands.

"It's you, child," Kray went on heavily. "He's discovered Hardane's true identity, and he demands your presence at the Fortress."

Lord Kray paused, and for the first time Kylene noticed how pale he was. For a moment, he stared at the floor, as if gathering his strength.

"There's more, isn't there?" Kylene asked tremulously.

"Yes, child," Kray replied, his voice grave. "Should you refuse to do as he says, he has promised to send Hardane back to Argone. A piece at a time."

Kylene stared at her father-in-law, unable to speak as the horror of what the Interrogator threatened unraveled in her mind. For a moment, the room spun out of focus and she stumbled backward, a low moan rising in her throat until it burst forth in a scream of denial.

Immediately, Lord Kray gathered her into his arms and held her close. In vain, he tried to think of some words of comfort, of hope, but none came to mind.

"I'll leave at once," Kylene said, and though the mere idea of returning to the Fortress filled her with dread, she knew she would do anything within her power to help Hardane.

"I can't let you go," Kray said, his voice firm. "Hardane would never forgive me if anything happened to you."

"I've got to go."

Kray shook his head. "No, Kylene. Think of the prophesy."

"I don't care about the prophesy," Kylene exclaimed, twisting out of his arms.

"He's bluffing," Kray said, running a hand through his hair. "He's got to be bluffing. Even the Interrogator wouldn't dare execute a man of Hardane's station."

"He will," Sharilyn replied quietly. "You know he will, Kray. He'll do anything to assure that Bourke retains the throne."

"We can't let her go," Kray said, his voice thick with anguish. "She carries the promise of lasting peace within her womb."

"What do I care if there's peace in Argone if Hardane is not here to see it!" Kylene exclaimed angrily.

"Think of what you're saying," Kray urged. "Would you put the lives of your children at risk?"

"Yes, and my own as well. I can't let him die. I can't. I won't."

"Your sons will rule the thrones of Argone and Mouldour. Under their leadership, both lands will prosper."

"I don't care!"

"I forbid it!" Kray shouted. "Do you hear me? I forbid it!"

"Kray . . ." Sharilyn spoke slowly and deliberately. "You can't mean to let our son die."

"Do you think this is a decision that's easy for me? But you know the Interrogator's reputation! He'll kill them both to assure that Bourke holds the throne."

"I'm going," Kylene said. Squaring her shoulders, she lifted her chin defiantly. "It's my life, and my decision, and I'm going."

Sharilyn nodded, proud of her daughter-in-law's courage in the face of such overwhelming odds. The Wolffan were not given to waiting or lengthy contemplation. It was their way to attack first and ponder the wisdom of it at a later time. What did it matter what the Interrogator wanted, or what he hoped to gain, when Hardane's life hung in the balance?

And yet . . . Kray was right. Hardane would never forgive them if anything happened to Kylene. She glanced at Kylene, noting the dark circles that shadowed her eyes, the gauntness of her cheeks, the paleness of her skin. The look of determination on her face.

"I'm going!" Kylene repeated. "Nothing you can say will stop me."

"Listen to me . . ." Lord Kray said, his voice ragged with anger and frustration.

"No, Kray," Sharilyn said quietly. "You listen to me. I have a plan."

Lord Kray released a sigh that seemed to come from the very depths of his soul.

"I'll listen," he replied wearily, "because I have always listened to your counsel. But I think I know what you're about to suggest, and I tell you here and now, I'm against it."

"Come, Kylene, sit here beside me," Sharilyn said, sitting on the edge of the bed. "We have much to discuss."

It was near dawn when Lord Kray and Sharilyn bid Kylene good night.

Alone in her room, she stood at the window watching the last stars fade from the sky, and for the first time in days, there was hope in her heart.

Chapter Thirty-Six

Hardane woke from a restless sleep. For a moment, he stared into the utter darkness of his prison. His leg, though mending, was still painful when he put any weight on it. His arms, stretched over his head, ached from the strain, and his wrists were swollen from the constant chafing of his restraints. The noose and the thick iron collar around his neck made breathing difficult.

A heavy sigh escaped his lips. Being chained to the wall day and night gave him little opportunity to rest his injured thigh and made it virtually impossible for him to sleep for more than a few minutes at a time.

Heartsick, homesick, he murmured Kylene's name. And then, in a rush, he knew what had awakened him. He'd been walking in Kylene's dreams, holding her close, caressing the satin smoothness of her skin, his face buried in the silky mass of her hair as he breathed in her scent.

Kylene . . . She was near, he thought, near enough that he could walk in her dreams again.

He frowned as his mind filled with a myriad of images: his ship, the *Sea Dragon*, was under full sail as it made its way toward Mouldour, cutting through the water like a scythe through hay. He saw his father, a look of grim determination on his face as he paced the quarterdeck; he saw his mother and Kylene sitting in the captain's cabin, their faces shadowed with worry.

Kylene . . . he could see her clearly in his mind, her beautiful red hair flowing, unbound, down her back. Because he liked it that way. Her eyes, warm and brown, were dark with concern. His gaze caressed her face, then moved to the gentle swell of her belly. His sons rested there, within the safe haven of her womb.

Kylene . . . she seemed so near, his whole being yearned toward her, aching to hold her, to be touched by her.

"Go back," he murmured. "Go back to Argone before it's too late."

Closing his eyes, he willed her to hear his thoughts. He'd been so certain his father would realize the necessity of keeping Kylene safe in Argone, and now they were all en route to Mouldour, determined to free him.

He tugged against the chains that bound him, cursing softly as the heavy irons cut into his flesh.

He had to get away before it was too late, before everyone he loved was at Renick's mercy.

He groaned low in his throat as he realized there was nothing he could do. Nothing at all.

Kylene lay curled on her side on Hardane's bunk in the captain's cabin, her eyes closed as she hugged his pillow to her breast. If she breathed deeply, she could detect his scent, though faint.

Kylene sighed heavily. Hardane's brothers had wanted to accompany them to Mouldour, threatening to tear the Interrogator limb from limb, but Lord Kray had insisted they stay behind to guard Castle Argone should the Interrogator return. Dubrey, Liam, and Morray had castles of their own that would also need protecting in the event of an attack.

Kylene had been surprised to learn that some of Hardane's brothers had their own castles. She'd once asked Dubrey if he didn't occasionally feel jealous that his youngest brother would one day inherit the throne. It was then she'd learned that Hardane's three oldest brothers had land and holdings of their own.

"There's no need for us to be jealous," Dubrey had assured her. "We knew from the day of his birth that he would rule Argone. There's always been something special about Hardane. Not just the fact that the blood of the Wolffan is strong within him. The people love him. As you do."

As you do . . . The words repeated in her mind.

"Please, let him be all right," she prayed fervently. "And please," she added as her stomach churned with nausea, "please let this voyage be over soon."

She'd been sick ever since they lost sight of land, and nothing seemed to help, but she didn't care. She knew she'd endure anything, take any risk, to free Hardane from the bowels of the Fortress. She thought of him constantly, praying that he was well, that he was still alive.

Her nights had been filled with nightmare images of the ship filling with water, slowly sinking beneath the waves. She felt the cold water closing over her, heard the sound of terrified screams, her own and those of her unborn children.

Just one good night's sleep, she thought. If she could just have one good night's sleep . . .

"Kylene."

His voice, deep and vibrant, called to her.

"Hardane?"

"Lady."

Relief, sweeter than Mouldourian honey, washed through her as he took her in his arms and held her close.

"I love you," he murmured, his voice low and husky.

She nodded, unable to speak for the rush of emotions that swelled within her breast. She gazed into his eyes, warming herself in the love she saw reflected there. His hands stroked her arms, caressed her breasts, rested on the slight swell of her belly.

"I've missed you." He lifted one hand to cup the back of her head as he bent toward her, his mouth slanting over hers.

He kissed her with such exquisite tenderness it brought tears to her eyes, and she pressed herself against him, needing to feel his nearness, his strength, wishing she could somehow slip inside of him and never let him go.

"Love me," she begged. "Love me now."

He breathed her name as he swept her into his arms and carried her to bed. Gently, he kissed and caressed her, his hands playing over her willing flesh until she was on fire for him, until she had to touch him in return. He filled her senses, until there was nothing in all the world but the sight and taste and touch of Hardane, the sound of his voice murmuring that he loved her, would always love her.

Caught up in the never-ending wonder of his nearness, she followed him up, up, to the heights of desire, his name a cry on her lips as their bodies merged, heart to heart and soul to soul.

She was drifting, floating on a sea of sensation and satisfaction. He was here, beside her, and nothing else mattered . . .

"Go back."

She frowned at the urgency in his voice.

"Kylene, you must tell my father to return to Argone."

She woke abruptly, her body sheened with perspiration. "Hardane?"

"Tell my father to turn the ship around. There's nothing you can do."

She sat staring into the darkness for several moments, stunned by the realization that it had all been a dream.

But there was nothing imaginary about the voice in her head, Hardane's voice, warning her to turn back.

Sitting up, she shook her head. "No, my lord wolf," she murmured into the darkness. "I'll not leave you there."

"Go back, lady . . . go back . . ."

His voice, filled with pleading, grew faint and then was gone.

Sharilyn listened quietly as Kylene told of hearing Hardane's voice warning them to turn back. He was alive, at least, she thought, relieved.

"You don't think it was just a dream, do you?" Kylene asked.

"No, child."

"Don't tell Lord Kray," Kylene begged. "I'm afraid he'll insist we go back to Argone."

"Nothing will make us turn back, Kylene. You needn't worry about that. We'll reach Mouldour tomorrow night." Sharilyn placed her hand over Kylene's. "How are you feeling?"

"I'll be all right."

"You don't look well."

"I'm fine, really. Just a little queasy."

"We'll find him, Kylene. I promise you that." Sharilyn gave Kylene's hand a squeeze. "Get some rest, child. And try not to worry."

As she watched Hardane's mother leave the room, Kylene prayed that their plan, as impossible as it seemed, would work.

She gazed out the window, staring at the far horizon where the land met the sea. The thought of returning to the Fortress filled her with dread. Too clearly, she recalled the ugly little cell the Interrogator had locked her in, the constant oppressive darkness, the foul stench of excrement and vomit, the cruel sting of the whip on her back, the smell of her own blood and fear.

And now Hardane was there, perhaps in the same dreary cell. He was hurt, alone, and yet his thoughts were only for her safety.

With a sob, she buried her face in his pillow and willed him to find comfort in her love, to know that he would not be alone much longer.

Chapter Thirty-Seven

Naked save for a scrap of cloth knotted around his loins, Hardane stood in the middle of the inquisition chamber, his wrists tightly lashed to a thick iron bar suspended over his head. The end of the noose around his neck was also secured to the iron bar to discourage him from turning into the wolf. Should he do so, the noose would tighten, and he would be left hanging in midair while the rope choked the life from his body.

How long had it been since Kylene had stood in this very room, in this very spot? How long since the Executioner had laid a whip across her tender flesh?

Hardane's hands curled into tight fists as he stared into the eyes of the man who had replaced the former Executioner. He was a tall man with a long narrow face and cruel brown eyes. But he was a master with the long black whip in his hand.

For the last twenty minutes, he had plied the lash with infinite skill, sometimes sending the whip though the air so that it flicked lightly, painlessly, at Hardane's groin. At other times, the lash cracked through the air to land with sickening force across his bare back, cutting deep into sweat-sheened flesh and quivering muscle.

He was a man who enjoyed his work, this new Executioner, Hardane had to give him that. And he was good at it, able to command the whip so that it fell soft as a caress, or sharp as the bite of an adder.

Hardane tensed as, from the corner of his eye, he saw the Executioner lift his arm, saw the whip slither through the air. His stomach clenched with dread and his mouth filled with the sharp taste of fear as the lash snaked through the air with a sharp whistling sound to bite deep into the backs of his legs.

He choked back the urge to cry out as the thick black whip fell again, slicing into the half-healed wound on his right thigh.

Head hanging, his breath coming in labored gasps, Hardane closed his eyes, his whole body trembling convulsively as he waited for the lash to fall again.

But there was only blessed silence. And then he heard a faint creak as the door to the inquisition chamber slid open and he knew the Interrogator had arrived, come to ask the same question he'd asked every day and every night since their arrival at the Fortress.

Renick stepped into the room and closed the door behind him. Tapping a short black riding crop against his thigh, he circled the prisoner, a glimmer of satisfaction in his eyes. The Lord of Argone would break soon. No man could possibly endure what he'd endured and continue to resist. It was only a matter of time.

"I don't want him dead," Renick remarked as he walked around the prisoner. Face impassive, he observed the blood dripping down Hardane's back and legs. "Only cooperative."

"Yes, my lord."

With a grunt, Renick dismissed the man, then went to stand in front of Hardane. Lifting his crop, he delivered a stinging blow to Hardane's chest.

"Look at me!"

Wearily, Hardane opened his eyes and stared into the face of the Interrogator.

Dressed in a light gray wool shirt, dark gray breeches, and black boots, his face cleanly shaven, Renick looked fit and well rested, as if he hadn't a care in the world. His eyes, as blue as an icy river, held a keen look of anticipation.

"The secret, Hardane," Renick said brusquely. "I would know the secret of the Wolffan."

"There is no secret."

"She'll be here soon," Renick said, tapping the butt of his crop against Hardane's chest. "The *Sea Dragon* has been seen off the northern coast. If you wish me to spare her life, you will tell me what I wish to know."

"There's nothing to tell!" Hardane exclaimed, the pain that racked him swallowed up in his fear for

Kylene. "Don't you think I'd tell you if there was?"

"We'll soon see, won't we?"

"Renick, for the love of God, leave her alone. Kill me now and be done with it, but don't touch Kylene. If I'm gone, the prophesy can't be fulfilled. You and Bourke can rule Mouldour. Cut me down and I'll write my father a letter, extracting his promise that he'll never attack Mouldour again. If necessary, I'll have him send Bourke half of all our crops, all our goods. . . ."

Hardane groaned deep in his throat as the Interrogator shook his head, his expression one of boredom and disbelief.

"Renick, if that's not enough, I swear I'll give you everything I own." He took a deep breath, knowing even as he prepared to humiliate himself by begging that it wouldn't be enough. "Please, Renick, please don't harm Kylene."

The Interrogator stared up at the prisoner, his eyes narrowed thoughtfully.

"What aren't you telling me, my lord wolf?" he mused. "There's more here than concern for your woman. What are you hiding?"

"Nothing."

"You're lying."

"No." Hardane took a deep breath. "Kylene and I are life-mated. There's a bond between us. I don't know how to explain it, except to say that she's a part of me, closer than my own blood kin."

"What causes this bond?" Renick asked, his earlier conviction that Hardane was hiding something forgotten as he considered the implications of this new bit of information.

"It's peculiar to seventh-born Wolffan offspring," Hardane answered cautiously.

"If I should mate with a seventh-born Wolffan, would my mate and I share such a bond?"

A feeling of unease, a premonition of disaster, skittered down Hardane's spine.

"I don't know." The lie slid smoothly past his lips.

The Interrogator's eyes narrowed ominously. "I think you do."

Renick tapped the crop against his thigh, his brow furrowed thoughtfully. Perhaps, if he were to life mate with a seventh-born Wolffan woman and share the bond of which Hardane spoke, he might also be granted the secret of shape shifting. Perhaps he didn't need the heir of Argone after all.

"Tell me, Hardane, does this bond pass to all seventh-born Wolffan?"

Hardane kept silent, the sense of impending danger growing stronger.

Without warning, Renick struck his crop against the half-healed wound on Hardane's right thigh. "Answer my question, Wolffan."

Fighting the urge to vomit, Hardane shook his head.

"Answer me," Renick demanded, "or what happened here today will be as nothing compared to what will happen on the morrow. Does this bond pass to all seventh-born Wolffan?"

Hardane licked lips gone dry. "No."

"You're lying."

"No." Hardane gasped as Renick wielded his crop again.

"Explain!"

Hardane stared at the blood trickling down his thigh. Bright shafts of pain darted the length of his right leg, making it hard to think coherently.

"Explain," Renick repeated softly. "Only tell me what I wish to know, and I promise no harm will come to Kylene."

Hardane swallowed the bile in his throat. "Your word?"

"Of course. Only tell me what I wish to know and I'll send someone to bind your wound. You'll have food and wine. A blanket to turn away the cold."

"Kylene . . ."

Her name whispered past his lips, soft as a sigh, and for a moment he saw her face, her warm brown eyes filled with concern, her lips moving in a silent prayer.

"Kylene . . ." He was fighting to stay conscious now. His hands curled around the bar over his head, and he stared at the Interrogator through a red haze of pain, felt the room begin to sway, felt himself falling into the darkness that hovered all around him.

Impatient to hear what Hardane had to say, Renick plied his quirt one more time.

Hardane gasped, his body twitching convulsively, as a fresh wave of pain jerked him from the brink of unconsciousness.

"I'll do her no harm, Wolffan," Renick said. "Only tell me now, quickly, what I wish to know."

"Only the seventh born . . . of one who . . . is also . . . seventh born."

"Your mother!" Renick exclaimed, wondering why he hadn't thought of it before. "Of course."

But Hardane was past hearing.

When he woke, he was lying on the floor of his cell, his arms chained behind his back. He groaned softly as he struggled to sit up. His wounds had been treated and bound. A blanket of coarse wool covered his nakedness. A plate of cold sliced mutton, vegetables, and a loaf of freshly baked bread were on the floor beside him, along with a large bowl filled with wine.

A wry smile tugged at Hardane's features as he received Renick's silent message.

You're a wolf. Eat like one.

His pride, the only thing the Executioner hadn't whipped to shreds, rebelled at the idea of eating off the floor like a dog, but his hunger soon overcame his self-esteem.

It was awkward, eating off the floor with his hands chained behind his back, but he managed it well enough to take the edge off his hunger.

After quenching his thirst, he sat back against the wall, closed his eyes, and summoned Kylene's image to mind. He would die content, he thought, if he could only hold her one more time, inhale her warm womanly scent, touch the silk of her hair, taste the incredible sweetness of her lips.

Kylene. He ached for her in the depths of his soul; his heart feared for her safety.

Kylene. She was near. The *Sea Dragon* had been seen off the northern coast of Mouldour.

Perhaps she was here, even now.

*   *   *

"Ready?" Sharilyn asked.

"Ready," Kylene replied firmly, though her hands were shaking and she wondered if her legs would support her.

"We'll be right behind you," Lord Kray said, his hand resting on the hilt of his sword.

Sharilyn embraced her husband. "If anything goes wrong, remember how much I love you."

Lord Kray nodded. "As I love you." He gazed deep into his wife's eyes. "Should it become necessary to make a choice, you know what to do."

"Aye, my lord," Sharilyn whispered. "Are you ready, Kylene?"

"Yes."

"Jared?"

"Let's go," he replied tersely, and settled the helmet more firmly on his head.

There was a moment of silence, and then the four of them disappeared into the darkness that surrounded the Fortress.

Chapter Thirty-Eight

Hardane stirred restlessly on the cold stone floor. The pain in his thigh made it difficult to get comfortable; concern for Kylene made sleep impossible.

Through heavy-lidded eyes he stared at his right thigh. It was a mass of torn and swollen flesh, and he wondered absently if he would die from the Executioner's whip or from the infection slowly spreading through him.

Steeped in despair, he gazed into the darkness, cursing Renick, cursing himself. If anything happened to Kylene . . .

He frowned as he saw a faint light illuminate the far end of the corridor. He heard footsteps, and then he saw Renick and Selene walking toward him, trailed by a guard bearing a torch.

Hardane's hands curled into tight fists as he

wondered what mischief had brought his enemies to the dungeon at such a late hour.

Abruptly, he stood up, the pain in his leg momentarily forgotten. As the three figures drew near, he leaned forward, his eyes narrowed, his instincts telling him that all was not as it seemed.

"Kylene!" he exclaimed softly.

And then he frowned as he took a closer look at the Interrogator and he knew that it wasn't Renick at all, but Sharilyn in Renick's form.

"Mother?" Hardane shook his head, wondering if he was dreaming.

"We'll have you out of here soon, Hardane," his mother promised. "Hurry, Jared."

Hardane's gaze moved over the guard. "Jared!"

The guard set the torch in the holder outside the cell, then lifted the visor on his helmet. "The same," he said.

Slipping a fine piece of wire from his pocket, Jared inserted it into the lock.

A moment later, the door swung open and Kylene hurried into the cell.

"Hardane, Hardane," she murmured, her hands fluttering over him like butterfly wings, "what have they done to you?"

She bit back a cry of dismay as she noted the raw skin on his wrists, the bloodstained bandage on his thigh, the hollows in his cheeks.

"I'm fine," he mumbled, his gaze fixed on her face while Jared worked his magic on the shackles that bound him to the wall.

"Can you walk?" Kylene asked.

"I don't know."

"We'll get you out of here if I have to carry you," Jared muttered.

"Hurry, now," Sharilyn urged.

"A moment, mother mine," Hardane said, and bracing himself against the wall, he drew Kylene into his arms and kissed her.

The heat of her body against his, the warmth of her kiss, chased the ache from his thigh and filled him with hope.

"Hardane!" Sharilyn said impatiently. "We don't have time for that now."

Hardane gave Kylene one last kiss and then, with regret, let her go.

Immediately, Jared stepped forward. "Put your arm around my shoulders and let's get out of here while we can."

Sharilyn, still in the guise of the Interrogator, went first, carrying the torch. Kylene followed her. Jared and Hardane came last.

"Where's my father?" Hardane asked.

"Keeping guard at the entrance to the dungeon."

"And the Interrogator?"

Jared shrugged. "Asleep in his chambers, I hope. We didn't dare take the time to explore the sleeping quarters upstairs."

Kylene glanced over her shoulder again and again as they made their way down the narrow corridor, assuring herself that Hardane was really there, repeatedly thanking the Father of All that he was still alive.

After what seemed like an eternity, they reached the stairway that led out of the dungeon.

For Hardane, each step sent fresh splinters of

pain shooting through his thigh, but he managed to make it to the top.

Lord Kray sighed with relief when he saw the four of them emerge from the bowels of the Fortress.

Stepping forward, he gave his son a fierce hug. "Thank the Father," he murmured.

Silent as wraiths, they made their way through the dark hallway that led to the entrance of the Fortress.

Kylene held her breath as Lord Kray approached the big double doors that led to freedom. They were going to make it.

Kray's hand was on the latch when a dozen men materialized out of the shadows, their lances glinting in the light of the torch.

The captain of the guards surveyed the group assembled near the door, then addressed the Interrogator. "Is something amiss, milord?"

Sharilyn shook her head. "All is well. Return to your post."

"Stand fast, Rynell. Brant, secure the door!"

Sharilyn and Kray exchanged uneasy glances as Renick entered the room.

"Take them, you fools!" Renick ordered brusquely.

Looking confused, the guards glanced uncertainly from one Interrogator to the other.

"He's an impostor!" Renick said, pointing at Sharilyn.

"He's the impostor!" Sharilyn countered imperiously.

Renick snorted derisively. "Take them, I say!"

Still, the guards didn't move, their expressions mirroring their confusion as they stared at the two men, both of whom claimed to be the Lord High Interrogator of Mouldour.

"So," Renick said, his gaze on Sharilyn's face, "if you are the Interrogator, as you claim, then you can tell me the name of each man in this room."

The guards looked at Sharilyn expectantly.

Kray smiled at her. "Looks like we're well and truly caught, beloved," he murmured.

Sharilyn smiled back. "May the Father of All grant that we may meet again in the clouds of Paradise," she murmured, and then she shouted, "Jared, run!"

Pivoting on her heel, she threw the torch into Brant's face, then drew her sword from its scabbard and whirled around to face the man who had come up behind her.

At the same time, Kray yanked the door open and pushed Jared and Hardane outside. Kylene followed hard on their heels.

"Make for the ship!" Kray shouted at Jared, and slamming the door, he drew his sword and took a place beside Sharilyn.

Rynell picked up the torch and placed it in a wall sconce while the other guards stared at Sharilyn. It was obvious the men were still perplexed by the presence of two men claiming to be the Interrogator.

"Take them!" Renick shouted, and the authority in his voice spurred his men into action.

Kray squeezed Sharilyn's hand and then, with a

cry, drove his sword into the heart of the nearest man.

Sharilyn's cry echoed that of her husband as she lunged forward to parry a thrust in her direction.

Kray fought valiantly, his sword slicing through the air with great and deadly skill. For an instant, he admired his wife's ability. She wielded her sword with the dexterity and proficiency of a seasoned warrior.

Between them, they dispatched four of the Interrogator's men and disabled three others in a matter of minutes, and then one of the guards slipped past Kray's defenses, his blade driving into Kray's chest.

A cry of distress rose in Sharilyn's throat as she saw her husband fall. Filled with rage, she whirled on the man who had wounded her husband, her sword slashing through the air like heat lightning until it found its mark.

"I want him alive!" The Interrogator's voice rang out over the harsh sounds of battle, and the five remaining guards drew back to form a circle around Sharilyn, careful to stay out of reach of her blade.

For a long moment, Renick stared at the man standing beside the fallen Lord Kray. It was a bit unnerving, staring into one's own face. Was it Hardane? Renick studied the impostor's right leg. The man didn't fight as if he'd been recently wounded.

Renick frowned, and then smiled. "Take him!" he ordered, and the five guards walked toward the impostor, slowly closing the circle.

With a savage cry, Sharilyn transformed into the wolf. Startled, the guards fell back, their mouths agape as they stared at the creature who had appeared to be a man only moments before.

Jaws snapping, Sharilyn lunged past the guards and hurled herself at the Interrogator, her only thought to rip the throat from the man who had harmed those she loved.

Renick reacted instantly. Drawing his knife, he faced the charging wolf and as the beast hurled itself at his throat, he buried his knife in the wolf's belly.

A high-pitched shriek, more human than animal, echoed off the cold stone walls.

Jared swore under his breath, the short hairs rising on the back of his neck, as a long, agonized scream rent the stillness of the night.

Kylene shuddered as the heartrending cry rang in her ears. Never in all her life had she heard a cry filled with such terrible anguish.

She stared at Hardane, seeing the agony that slashed across his face as his mother's soul-shattering scream faded into the quiet of the night.

He threw back his head, a howl of equal pain rising in his throat, and Kylene shuddered again, knowing she would never forget that awful sound, or the look of torment on Hardane's face.

"Let me go!" Hardane demanded, trying to shake off Jared's hold.

Jared shook his head as he tightened his grip on his friend's shoulder. "There's nothing you can do.

We've got to get Kylene out of here."

"I can't leave them here!" Hardane argued, silently cursing the wound that rendered him too weak and light-headed to break Jared's grasp on his arm.

"It's what they wanted."

Hardane swore under his breath, torn between the need to go back and fight alongside his parents and the need to protect Kylene.

In the end, he had no choice at all. Leaning heavily on Jared, he followed Kylene toward the shore where a small boat waited to carry them out to the *Sea Dragon*.

Kylene sat on the edge of the bunk, her hand enfolded in Hardane's as the ship's doctor examined the deep puncture in his thigh.

The wound had festered and she turned her head away as the doctor probed the swollen mass of mutilated flesh.

She let out a small gasp as Hardane's hand tightened around hers.

"Sorry," he muttered hoarsely, and loosened his grip.

Kylene smiled at him. "It's all right."

He looked up at her, his gray eyes narrowed with pain, his face pale and haggard. "We've got to go back."

She didn't say anything, only stared down at him, noting the dark shadows beneath his eyes, the deep lines of pain and weariness in his face.

A night and a day had passed since they escaped from the Fortress. Hardane had ordered the *Sea*

Dragon to put out to sea, then dropped their sails when they were safely out of sight of Mouldour.

He'd slept through that first night and well into the next day, his arms locked around Kylene's waist as if he would never let her go, as if he feared that, should he release his hold on her, she would disappear forever.

And now it was night again, and in spite of Hardane's assurances that he was fine, she had insisted that the doctor be called to examine his thigh.

The ship's physician had confirmed her worst fears: the wound was infected. Unless something was done, the poison would spread and Hardane would die.

And now she sat beside him, trying not to vomit as the doctor lanced the wound, unleashing a river of thick yellow pus and blood so dark it was almost black.

Kylene leaned forward, wiping the sweat from Hardane's brow with a cloth soaked in cold water. He was hurting, and hurting badly. She could see it in the depths of his eyes, in every taut line of his body. His hair, as black as a midnight sea, was damp with perspiration. One hand held hers in a viselike grip as the doctor probed deeper into his flesh, but she made no protest, knowing that he was hurting far worse than she.

She blinked back her tears, wishing there was something she could do to comfort him, to ease the awful pain that tormented him.

"Your . . . presence . . . comforts me," he gasped.

"It will be over soon," she promised. "Cry if you want to, my lord wolf. Scream if you must. I'll not think the less of you for it."

"Kiss me," he whispered.

"Now?"

"Now." The word was a groan.

Obligingly, she bent down and slanted her mouth over his. His lips were warm with fever and he tasted of the ale they'd given him in hopes of dulling the pain. He trembled convulsively as the doctor forced the poison from his flesh, and she kissed him harder, wishing she could draw his pain into her own body.

His hand cupped the back of her head, his fingers curling in her hair as the kiss lengthened and deepened, and Kylene felt the tension drain out of him, felt his body begin to relax.

Into her mind came a vision of the waterfall at Argone. She could hear the mighty roar of the water as it raced over the edge of the mountain, smell the earth, feel the spray of the falls against her face. She saw herself sitting on a flat rock, with the moonlight shining in her hair. And at her feet sat a big black wolf with eyes as gray as a winter sky.

"That should do it." The doctor's words shattered the illusion.

Hardane's hand fell away from her head and Kylene sat up, momentarily disoriented. "What?"

"'Tis done."

The doctor pointed at the wound. He had cut away the ragged edges of flesh and forced all the pus from the wound. The blood that oozed from the wound was no longer dark but a bright healthy red.

"I'll just stitch up the wound, and he'll be fine in a day or two."

"Stitch him?" Kylene mumbled, staring at the needle the doctor had removed from his bag. "Now?"

"Aye, now."

She couldn't watch, Kylene thought frantically. She could not sit there and watch while the ship's physician poked that needle into Hardane's torn flesh. She simply couldn't.

Rising, one hand still clasped in Hardane's, she glanced at the cabin door, anxious to be gone from the room.

"Kylene . . ." His voice reached out to her.

She stared down at him. "I . . . I'll be back in a minute."

"Don't leave me."

"Please," she begged. "I can't stay. Don't ask me."

Understanding dawned in the smoky depths of his eyes. "You'll come right back?"

Kylene gazed into his beloved face, seeing the harsh lines of pain and fatigue etched around his mouth and eyes. Surely the pain of stitching would seem like a small thing to endure when compared to the probing of the wound, she told herself in an effort to alleviate the guilt she felt for wanting to leave the room.

She looked down at their joined hands, knowing she lacked the courage to draw her hand away, to leave him there to suffer alone.

With a sigh, she sat down on the edge of the bunk

once more and poured Hardane another glass of ale.

"I won't leave you, my brave wolf," she promised. "Not now. Not ever."

Feeling as though she'd been run over by a team of horses, Kylene settled into a tub of hot water, sighing as the enervating warmth eased the tension from her taut muscles.

Hardane was sleeping peacefully, thanks to his utter weariness and the amount of ale he'd consumed.

It had been horrible, sitting at his side while the doctor stitched the raw, angry edges of the wound together. She'd kept her gaze fixed on Hardane's face, trying not to imagine the needle piercing his flesh. Hardane had endured the sewing as he had endured everything else, in tight-lipped silence.

He was here, he was safe, but their troubles were far from over.

She thought of Lord Kray and Sharilyn, of Selene, of Bourke and the Interrogator. Of the children growing beneath her heart.

With a sigh, she closed her eyes. Somehow, they had to rescue Lord Kray and Sharilyn. But how?

Unable to think clearly, she stepped from the tub and dried herself off. Slipping into one of Hardane's shirts, she sat in the captain's chair beside the bunk and closed her eyes.

Hardane was here, and he was safe. For now, that was all that mattered.

Chapter Thirty-Nine

Renick and Bourke stood in the doorway, watching as Bourke's physician treated the wound in Sharilyn's abdomen.

"Will she live?" Renick asked curtly.

"Aye."

"And the other one?" Renick asked.

The physician shrugged. "He's bad off, milord. If he survives the night . . ."

The doctor shrugged again as he contemplated the unconscious man locked in the cell across the narrow corridor.

"I've done all I can for the man. The rest is up to him."

Renick grunted softly. If Kray died, so be it. But the woman had to live. She was the seventh-born child of a seventh-born child. Heir to the secret of mind-bonding and shape-shifting, and who knew what other mystical feats. He would mate with her, acquire the bond, and discover for himself how such miraculous deeds were accomplished.

He glanced at Sharilyn thoughtfully. Perhaps he should dispose of Kray. The woman might be more agreeable to mating if her husband was dead. Then again, she might be more manageable if she thought her husband's life depended on her cooperation.

"Hardane is getting away," Bourke muttered irritably, "and you stand here doing nothing."

"Are you questioning my judgment, my lord?"

"Perhaps. And perhaps you've forgotten that my throne will not be secure until both Kylene and the heir of Argone are dead. The people are growing weary of war. Many are looking forward to the peace promised by the prophesy."

"Fear not, my lord. I will yet have Hardane's head. We have his mother and his father," Renick said with a sneer. "Hardane is a man of honor. He will feel it is his duty to return for his parents. When he does . . ." He shrugged. "He won't get away again."

"What of Selene?"

"What of her?"

"It is her ambition to rule Argone."

"A woman, rule Argone?" Renick asked in amazement. "Impossible."

"Not if you were to rule at her side."

"My lord," Renick murmured with feigned astonishment. "I'm honored that you would consider such a thing."

Bourke's green eyes narrowed. "Are you? Or have you perhaps already thought of doing just that?"

"My lord, you wound me deeply with your lack of trust."

"I know you well, Renick. You're an ambitious man. One without scruples or conscience."

"My lord . . ."

Bourke cut him off with a wave of his hand. "Those qualities have served me well in the past, Renick. See that they don't overcome your judgment."

Renick bowed his head in a show of servitude. "You have nothing to fear from me, my lord," he said humbly.

"But you have much to fear from me, Renick. Remember that."

Renick murmured an obsequious farewell as Bourke left the dungeon, but inwardly he was seething with barely suppressed fury. Much to fear, indeed! Once he knew the secret of shape shifting, he would be indestructible. He would be able to take on any shape, be it man or beast, and slip past Bourke's defenses, infiltrate Bourke's secret chambers.

A slow smile played over his lips. He would be able to take on Bourke's shape; indeed, he'd be able to take Bourke's place if he so desired! It was a heady thought.

Bourke was naught but a weak-minded fool. He'd taken his brother's throne by trickery and then, instead of disposing of Carrick as he should have, he'd banished the man from Mouldour. And now the peasants were crying for peace, and if he wasn't careful, Bourke would give it to them!

Renick grimaced with disdain. Peace! What profit was there in peace? You couldn't lay heavy taxes
on the people in times of peace. You couldn't send
your armies to plunder foreign lands, robbing their
coffers of gold and silver and precious stones in
times of peace. You couldn't take prisoners and
sell them for slaves, or kidnap a beautiful woman
who caught your fancy.

Peace! Bah! Tapping his quirt against the palm
of his hand, he paced the floor. He'd been ruling
Mouldour for months now, planting his ideas in
Bourke's mind, coaxing him to see things his way,
gradually winning Bourke's guards to his way of
thinking. Perhaps it was time to rid himself of
Bourke once and for all. . . .

A slow smile crept over his features as he contemplated ruling the lands of Mouldour and Argone.

He was still smiling when he left the dungeon.

A low groan, the smell of stale sweat and excrement. Frowning, Sharilyn opened her eyes to darkness. Where was she? A sharp pain rocked her
when she tried to move. Instinctively, she reached
for the source of the pain, only to find that her
hands were strapped at her sides.

And then, in a rush, it all came back to her. They
had managed to free Hardane from the dungeon
and in so doing, Kray had been killed.

The pain of her loss struck her like a blow and
then as quickly disappeared. He wasn't dead.

"Kray?" She reached out to him, her *tashada*
searching for her life-mate, her soulmate. With

relief, she realized he was imprisoned in the cell across the corridor.

"Sharilyn?"

"I'm here, beloved."

"Are you well?" he asked, his voice betraying his concern.

"Well enough. And you?"

"I'll survive," Kray said grimly, "at least until my sword has tasted the Interrogator's blood."

"For that you must wait your turn," Sharilyn replied.

"Ah, wife, you have the heart of a warrior," Kray murmured, "and you have my heart as well."

"As you have mine," Sharilyn replied fervently. "Do you think Hardane made it to safety?"

"Aye, beloved."

"Then I shall die content."

"Will you, wife? Have you no desire to see your grandchildren?"

A pain sharper than the one inflicted by the Interrogator's blade pierced Sharilyn's heart. Never to see Hardane's twins! Ah, that would be a bitter blow. Still, it was a sacrifice she was willing to make, if only Hardane was safe.

Hardane, her seventh-born son, her favorite son because the blood of the Wolffan ran strong in his veins. Hardane, who shared her love of the wild, who danced with her in the light of a midnight moon. The future of Argone depended upon his survival.

"Sharilyn?"

"Aye?"

"He'll come back. You know that."

"Aye, beloved. I . . ." She broke off in mid-sentence as the sound of footsteps sounded in the passageway.

Moments later, the Interrogator was standing in the corridor outside her cell, a torch in his hand.

"Ah," Renick exclaimed, pleased to see that Sharilyn had regained consciousness.

He glanced over his shoulder, a low grunt of satisfaction rumbling in his throat when he saw Kray staring back at him.

"What is the meaning of this?" Kray demanded, tugging against the chains that bound his hands and feet.

"You break into my stronghold and have the gall to ask why you are imprisoned?" Renick retorted.

"You had my son."

"Yes. And I will have him again."

Kray stared at the Interrogator, chilled by the vicious look in the man's eyes. "Do as you wish with me, only let my wife go free."

"I think not," Renick mused. "I have need of her."

"To what purpose?"

"I wish to know the secret of the Wolffan," Renick said, his voice hard and implacable. "It is my intention to mate with your woman, to share the mind bond, to learn the art of shape shifting."

"Mate with you!" Sharilyn exclaimed. "I'd as soon mate with a pig as with a creature such as yourself."

"Indeed? And would you withhold yourself from me if it meant your husband's life would be forfeit?"

"What a coward you are, my lord Interrogator, to think to threaten me with my husband's life."

"Coward, am I? Think what you will, but you will give me that which I desire, or I will kill your husband an inch at a time, and your son as well."

"You're mad," Kray exclaimed in horror. "Don't you think if the secrets of the Wolffan could be given to others that Sharilyn would have long ago shared them with me?"

Kray's words pierced Renick's anger. What if Kray spoke the truth? And what if he was lying in an attempt to gain his freedom and that of his wife?

"We shall see," Renick mused. "When the woman's wounds have healed, we shall see. Sewar!" Renick called, speaking to the guard waiting at the far end of the corridor. "Advise the men we'll be leaving for Castle Mouldour at first light."

A cry of impotent rage rose in Kray's throat as the Interrogator took the torch and stalked out of the dungeon, plunging them into darkness as deep as his despair.

Chapter Forty

"Get back into bed!" Kylene glared at Hardane, her hands fisted on her hips. "Right now!" she said, practically shouting the words.

"I've been in this blasted bunk three days. That's long enough!"

"Hardane of Argone, you are the most stubborn man I've ever known."

"I'm the only man you've ever known!" he retorted irritably. "Now give me my breeches so I can get up."

"No."

"By all the saints, Kylene, I've a mind to turn you over my knee."

His dark gray eyes really looked like thunder-clouds now, she thought.

"Kylene!"

She cocked her head to one side, a smile flitting

over her lips. "Are we having our first fight, my lord wolf?"

He grinned back at her. "So it would seem." He swung his legs over the bunk, biting back an oath as the movement sent long tendrils of pain skittering up and down the length of his thigh. "And I mean to win it."

"Please, Hardane, just one more day in bed. You need the rest."

"I can't, Kylene. I can't leave my parents in that dungeon another day. Don't ask it of me."

She relented immediately, touched by the pleading in his eyes, the urgency in his voice.

"I'm going with you," she said, handing him his breeches.

"No."

"Yes."

"Kylene . . ."

"Hardane . . ."

He glared at her as he pulled on his breeches and then, with a sigh of resignation, he drew her into his arms. Ah, but it felt good to hold her close, to inhale the sweet scent that was hers, and hers alone. Her skin was soft and smooth under his hands. As always, her body molded itself to his, two halves of the same whole, the same heart.

Closing his eyes, he buried his face in the wealth of her hair. When he'd been locked in the dungeon of the Fortress, certain he'd never see her again, he had dreamed of holding her like this just one more time. And now she was here, in his arms, and her very nearness made all his senses come alive.

Kylene wrapped her arms around Hardane's

waist and held him tight. No matter what happened, she vowed she would not be parted from him again. Not in life. Not in death.

She drew away as there came a knock at the door, followed by Jared's voice advising them that the coast of Mouldour was in sight.

Sharilyn blinked several times in an effort to bring her vision into focus. She'd been drugged, she thought absently, a sleeping potion of some kind.

She glanced around the room, and the movement, slight as it was, made her head ache. She was lying on a large, circular bed in a narrow, low-ceilinged room. There were bars at the windows.

Sitting up, she saw that the bed took up a good portion of the floor space in the middle of the room. There was no other furniture save for a small rough-hewn oak table that held a white porcelain bowl and a pitcher of water.

How long had she been here? Two days? Three?

Slipping her legs over the edge of the mattress, she stood up and went to the door. It was locked, as she'd known it would be. Turning, she crossed the floor to the window. Outside, she saw the high walls and towers of Castle Mouldour.

Her first coherent thought was for Kray. Closing her eyes, she summoned her husband's image to mind. A low cry of despair welled in her throat when she saw him. He was locked in a dark cell in the lowest dungeons of Mouldour. The wound in his chest, located high, near his right shoulder, was festering. Lying on the cold stone floor, he tossed restlessly, his body racked by chills and fever. She called out to him, willing him to respond, but he seemed unable to hear her.

She whirled around at the sound of her door being unlocked, took an involuntary step backward as the Interrogator entered the room, closing the door behind him.

"So, what do you think?" Renick asked, his hand making a gesture to indicate the room.

"I think you'll regret this."

"Indeed?" His hand rested on the hilt of his sword. "I mean to have you as my mate," he said coldly. "Should you refuse, should you do anything other than what you're told, your husband's life will surely be forfeit."

"He's nearly dead now," Sharilyn retorted.

The Interrogator's eyes gleamed with interest. "How do you know that?"

Sharilyn glared at him.

"You will tell me, or Kray will suffer for it."

"He's suffering now!" she exclaimed, and even as she spoke, she could feel the fever raging through Kray's body, feel the hard, cold floor beneath him. He was only barely conscious.

"I want to know the secret of that bond," Renick said. "If we mate, will it pass to me?"

"No."

"You're lying."

Sharilyn shook her head. "It's the truth. The bond cannot be taken by force. I cannot give it to you."

"Then what is the secret?"

"The bond can only be shared between those who are predestined to be life-mated, my lord,"

Sharilyn answered quietly, "or by those who are joined by bonds of love. My mind bond with Kray was forged out of our regard for each other. Had I been forced to wed against my will, no bond would have been possible, even though I have the power."

Renick frowned. "I don't believe you, but there are ways to get the truth."

"No! Leave Kray alone. I'm telling you the truth, I swear it on the lives of my children."

"Tell me the secret of shape shifting."

"There is no secret. As Kray said, it cannot be given away. It is inherent in the seventh born of one seventh born."

Renick stared at the woman, a vile oath whispering past his lips. She was telling him the truth. He knew it without doubt.

Rage and frustration welled up within him. He had spent a lifetime in pursuit of the secrets of the Wolffan, only to learn that he'd been chasing something with no more substance than a rainbow.

Crossing the floor, he snatched the bowl from the table and hurled it against the wall. The pitcher followed, and then the table.

With a wordless cry, he grabbed Sharilyn by the arm and threw her down on the bed, his body covering hers to hold her in place.

"If I can't have the secret of the Wolffan, then I'll have you," he muttered, his hands tearing at her clothes.

Sharilyn screamed as the Interrogator's hands clawed at her bodice. She scratched at his face, pummeled his body with her fists, and when her puny efforts to protect herself failed, she transformed into the wolf and lunged for his throat.

Renick cursed his lack of foresight as he found himself straddling a wild-eyed she-wolf. Instinctively, he threw up one arm to ward off the wolf's attack, screamed with pain and terror as he felt the wolf's fangs sink into his shoulder.

Scrambling to his knees, he jumped off the bed and ran for the door, the sound of the wolf's growls and snapping teeth spurring him onward.

The wolf's jaws closed around his ankle as he opened the door. Panic added strength to his limbs and he lashed out at the animal with his free foot, catching the beast in the side and flinging it across the floor.

With a gasp, Renick ran out of the room, slammed the door behind him, and twisted the key in the lock.

Panting, he slumped against the wall. By all the saints, he thought, staring at the bloody gashes in his arm and ankle, he was lucky to be alive.

Hardane led the way toward the Fortress, grateful for the clouds that hung low in the sky. Kylene was behind him, followed by Jared and three of the crewmen from the *Sea Dragon*.

Silent as drifting shadows, they made their way to the outer wall. Jared and the crewmen overpowered the guards at the gate. One of Hardane's men stayed behind to make sure the guards didn't alert anyone to their presence.

Crossing the courtyard, they made their way to

the dungeon. Hardane drew his sword as they reached the entrance to the dungeon, but there were no guards stationed at the doorway.

Frowning, he glanced back over his shoulder to make sure Kylene and the others were behind him, and then he started down the long stone stairway that led to the nethermost cells.

Each step he took sent a jolt of pain shooting up his right thigh. Perhaps Kylene had been right, he admitted grudgingly; perhaps he should have waited another day. But even as the thought crossed his mind, he knew he couldn't have waited any longer. He knew what it was like to be imprisoned in the bowels of the Fortress, knew he couldn't leave his parents there a minute longer than necessary.

He paused at the bottom of the steps. Head cocked to one side, he listened to the darkness, his nostrils testing the air, before he started forward.

He knew, even before he reached the first cell, that his parents were gone, the dungeon was empty.

"What is it?" Jared called.

"They're gone."

"Gone?" Kylene said. "Gone where?"

"I don't know."

"Do you think he . . . that they're . . ." She broke off, not wanting to say the words aloud.

"I don't know."

"Now what?" Jared asked.

"Castle Mouldour," Hardane mused aloud. "Renick must have known I'd come as soon as I was able. I think he would have taken them there."

"But why?"

"It's practically impregnable," Hardane replied, his voice thoughtful. "But one man might be able to steal inside."

"One man?" Jared mused, frowning. "Do you think that's wise?"

"I don't know, but I won't put Kylene's life at risk again. Come," he said, taking her by the arm, "let us go back to the ship."

He was limping badly by the time they returned to the *Sea Dragon*.

Kylene insisted that Hardane go to bed at once, and he didn't argue. He dutifully drank the warmed white wine she offered him and then he sank back against the pillows, his eyes closed, while she removed his shirt, boots, and breeches.

He sighed with pleasure as she began to massage his thigh. Her hands were warm, her touch as light as down as she gently rubbed the soreness from his leg.

Kylene felt her heart swell with love as she massaged Hardane's thigh. What a brave man he was, her warrior wolf.

Thinking him asleep, she started to draw away, but his hand closed lightly over her arm.

"Don't stop," he murmured.

With a wordless murmur of assent, Kylene began to massage his other leg, her fingers straying of their own accord higher and higher along the inside of his thigh.

She felt a quickening low in her belly as he moaned with pleasure. Boldly, she let her fingers knead the hard muscular plane of his chest and belly, the width of his shoulders, pleased by the little sounds of delight her touch elicited.

She let her hands slide over his strong, sturdy neck, and then over his shoulders again, marveling at his hard-muscled flesh. His skin was smooth and warm.

Impulsively, she began to press feather-light kisses to his neck, his shoulder, his navel.

With a groan, he caught her around the waist and pulled her onto the bed until she was sprawled across him.

"Lady," he murmured, and his voice was low and husky with desire.

"My lord?"

He cupped the back of her head with one hand and drew her toward him. Eyes still closed, he kissed her, a long, slow kiss that gradually grew in heat and intensity until she was clinging to him, everything forgotten but the power of his touch, and her need for him.

Without taking his mouth from hers, he somehow managed to ease her out of her dress and undergarments. When she would have pulled away to remove her boots and stockings, he shook his head, unwilling to let her go for even a moment.

He caressed her, his hands gentle, entreating. As if she would refuse him, she thought, overcome with a rush of love for this man who had risked his life for her, who knew her, and loved her, body and soul.

She basked in the adoration she read in his eyes,

thrilled to his touch. He was a big man, hard-muscled and strong, yet he made love to her with infinite care, mindful of the new life she carried beneath her heart. His hands worshiped her; his kisses fanned the fire between them.

"Lady," he murmured, raining kisses along the side of her neck. "Ah, lady, you're like fire and silk in my hands."

"Am I?"

"Aye, lady." He groaned deep in his throat as her fingertips skimmed over his chest, trailing fire.

Kylene drew back. "Are you in pain, my lord wolf?" she asked, afraid she had accidentally jarred his injured thigh.

Hardane gazed up at her, a wry grin on his lips. "I'm in pain," he muttered, "but not where you think."

Kylene frowned at him, and then grinned, her cheeks growing warm as she took his meaning.

"Think it's funny, do you?" he growled. "To torment me with your nearness and then pull away?"

Before she could answer, he rolled them over and tucked her beneath him.

Careful not to crush her, he kissed her again, groaning softly as she arched against him. Her skin was smooth and soft, unblemished and beautiful. Her scent rose all around him, warm and musky. She moved restlessly beneath him, the friction of her skin against his inflaming his desire until he was trembling with need.

"Now, my lord wolf," she crooned softly, her

hands gliding restlessly up and down his broad back, her nails lightly raking his flesh.

"Now," he agreed, and buried himself deep within her welcoming warmth.

Chapter Forty-One

Sharilyn paced the floor of her prison hour after hour, her mind in turmoil. Kray was unconscious and his mind was closed to her, but at least he was still alive.

She cursed herself for refusing to bed the Interrogator. What did it matter if he had his way with her body? She could have sent her *tashada* to Kray while the Interrogator defiled her. Instead, she had angered him, and she knew Kray would pay the ultimate price for what she'd done.

She paused as she heard footsteps in the corridor. It was the guard who brought her meals. Instantly, she took on the shape of the Interrogator and began pounding on the door.

"Let me out of here!" she hollered, hammering on the door again. "Hurry, you fools!"

There was the rasp of a key turning in the lock, and then the door swung open. Two guards stood in the passageway. One held a covered tray in his hands; the other held a sword.

"What is it, my lord?" asked the man bearing the tray.

"The woman! She's escaped!"

Sharilyn marched boldly out of the room, knocking the tray from the hands of the near guard.

"You!" she shouted, gesturing to the armed guard. "Follow me!"

Without waiting for a reply, she hurried down the corridor, her inner sense leading her to the dungeons, and to Kray.

He waited in the shadows, not daring to breathe, as he watched the man move cautiously through the night. The darkness made it impossible to see the man's face, impossible to tell if it was friend or foe, though he doubted he had many friends left in Mouldour.

He closed his eyes for a moment, one hand pressed to his chest. He was still weak from the blood he'd lost, but he was determined to have his revenge, to plunge his knife into Bourke's traitorous heart, to feel the man's blood on his hands. He had endured exile and betrayal at the hands of those he had loved and trusted, and he would have his moment of vengeance if it was the last thing he ever did.

Tonight, he thought. Tonight he would destroy Bourke, or die trying.

*　　*　　*

Hardane paused in the shadows of Castle Mouldour, his eyes and ears attuned to the slightest movement, the slightest sound. He had left Jared offshore in a small boat; the *Sea Dragon* sat at anchor out of sight behind a high promontory.

On silent feet, he made his way to the back of the castle and through an ancient wrought-iron gate that was heavily overgrown with vines.

He paused every few feet to sniff the wind, to listen to the sounds of the night.

At last he reached the rear door that led into the dungeons. Using a bit of wire that Jared had given him for just this purpose, he unlocked the door and stepped into the musty darkness.

For a moment, he transformed into the wolf, using the animal's superior senses to locate his father's whereabouts. Then, assuming his own shape once more, he made his way down the dark corridor until he came to the cell that imprisoned Kray.

Hardane shrank against the wall as he saw a light coming from the opposite direction, swore softly as he saw Renick and an armed guard halt outside Kray's cell.

"Open the door," the Interrogator ordered imperiously.

Hardane held his breath as the cell door swung open and the Interrogator and the guard stepped inside. Then, drawing his sword, Hardane rushed forward, closed the prison door, and took the key from the lock.

The guard swore as he whirled around.

"Hand me your sword," Hardane ordered.

"Do as he says," the Interrogator commanded.

"Are you sure, my lord?" the guard asked, his gaze fixed on Hardane.

"Quite sure," the Interrogator said.

With a look of disgust, the guard handed his sword through the bars.

Instantly, Sharilyn took on her own shape.

"Mother!" Hardane gasped.

"My son," she replied with a smile.

Hardane stared at his father, who lay unmoving on the cold stone floor, his hands and feet shackled to the wall.

"Is he . . . is he dead?"

"No, only unconscious."

There was no need for further discussion. Sharilyn used her sash to tie the guard's hands behind his back, then stuffed her kerchief in his mouth. When that was done, Hardane unlocked the door, removed the shackles from his father's hands and feet, then slung his father over his shoulder and led the way out of the dungeon.

When they reached the top of the stairs, they paused a moment to listen, and then Sharilyn opened the door and stepped into the darkness beyond the dungeon.

As soon as she stepped outside, a heavily muscled arm wrapped around her neck, choking off her breath.

Hardane, still hidden in the shadows, carefully lowered his father to the ground, then drew his sword and pressed the point between the shoulder blades of the man holding his mother.

"Release her."

"Drop your sword, or she's dead."

"Release her," Hardane repeated, putting pressure on the sword so that it slit the man's shirt and pierced his flesh.

The man gasped as the point of the blade split his skin, but his arm remained around Sharilyn's throat.

"A deal, then," Hardane suggested. "I'll put up my sword and you let the woman go."

"Your word?"

"My word in exchange for yours."

"Done," the man agreed.

With more than a little reluctance, Hardane lowered his blade.

A moment later, and with just as much trepidation, the man released his hold on Sharilyn and whirled around to face Hardane.

"Bourke!" Hardane exclaimed as he saw the man's face. Raising his sword again, he placed the point in the hollow of the man's throat.

"You fool," the man said, his voice thick with contempt. He gestured at his clothes, which were ill-fitting and covered with mud. "Has Lord Bourke taken to dressing in rags these days?"

Hardane frowned. "If you're not Bourke, who are you?"

"His brother, Carrick. Rightful ruler of Mouldour."

"Carrick is dead," Sharilyn remarked, coming to stand beside Hardane.

"Not quite, madam," the man replied with a low bow.

"Carrick would not dare to show his face here,"

Hardane said, his gaze fixed on the man's face, his sword steady at his throat. "Bourke and the Interrogator would kill him on sight."

The man nodded. "As I plan to kill them."

"Maybe he's telling the truth," Sharilyn mused.

Hardane grunted softly. "Maybe, but there's no way to prove it."

"Let's take him with us."

"Very well. Bind his hands and we'll take him along."

The man shook his head. "I came here to kill my brother, and I'm not leaving until it's done."

Hardane took a step forward, the tip of his blade pricking the skin at the man's throat.

"You can come with us, or die here. The choice is yours."

"I'll go," the man said, and stood quietly while Sharilyn bound his hands behind his back.

Handing his sword to his mother, Hardane settled his father over his shoulder once more and they made their way toward the shore where Jared waited with the boat.

Jared jumped to his feet, his sword in his hand, as he heard the sound of footsteps. He stared into the darkness, and then frowned.

"What the devil!" he exclaimed upon seeing the prisoner. "Bourke! You brought Bourke here?"

"He claims to be his brother, Carrick," Hardane said. "Here, help me get my father into the boat."

In moments, they had Kray settled in the bow, his head cradled in Sharilyn's lap. The prisoner sat on the deck in the stern while Jared and

341

Hardane rowed out to sea.

"What's going on?" Jared asked. "What happened to Lord Kray? Where's the Interrogator?" He jerked a thumb in the prisoner's direction. "Where did you find him?"

"Enough," Hardane said, exasperated. "I don't have all the answers myself. But I intend to get them as soon as we reach the ship."

Kylene was waiting for them topside. She ran forward, her cloak falling unheeded to the deck as she threw her arms around Hardane.

"Are you all right?" she asked, pressing kisses to his lips, his chin, his cheeks.

"I'm fine," Hardane assured her. He took her hand in his and gave it a reassuring squeeze. "But my father's ill. Go with my mother and see what you can do for him. I've got to talk to Kruck. I'll join you as soon as I can," he said, releasing her hand. "Jared, take the prisoner to the brig."

Hardane gave Kylene a quick kiss on the cheek, and then he was gone.

It was only when Jared gave the prisoner a shove toward the forward hatch that Kylene took a good look at the man's face.

"Jared, wait!"

She took a step forward, her narrowed gaze probing the man's face. Was it possible? Could it be . . .

"Papa?"

"Selene! What are you doing here?"

"I'm not Selene," she replied, disappointed that he didn't recognize her even though there was no reason why he should.

"No, it can't be . . . Kylene, my dear girl, is that you?"

"Papa? Oh, Papa!" She threw her arms around him, her joy at his presence overshadowing a lifetime of questions.

"What's going on?" Hardane threw a glance at Jared, and then stared at Kylene, who was hugging the prisoner for all she was worth.

"Seems this is the long-lost Lord Carrick, after all," Jared replied with a grin. "Should I cut his throat or cut him loose?"

An hour later, Kylene sat beside her father, unable to take her eyes from his face.

Earlier, Hardane had cut Carrick's hands free and had allowed him to bathe and change into clean clothes, and now they all sat in Hardane's cabin while Carrick told of what had transpired since Bourke usurped the throne. He told of being hunted, of hiding out in caves and abandoned buildings, of having to scavenge like a predator for food.

"But Selene said you were dead," Kylene exclaimed, taking her father's hand in hers. "That you'd died in a cave."

Carrick shrugged, not wanting to believe that his daughter had coldbloodedly left him in that cave to die.

"I'd been sick with a fever," he said slowly. "Drifting in and out of consciousness. Perhaps she thought I was dead when she left me there."

"You're lucky you didn't die, sick as you were, with no one to help you," Hardane remarked, still doubting the man's identity.

"I had someone to help me," Carrick answered.

"Oh? Who?"

"A wolf," Carrick said, his gaze moving from Hardane to Kylene.

"A wolf?" Sharilyn leaned forward in her chair, her eyes suddenly alight with interest.

Carrick nodded. "A she-wolf found me there. She shared her kills with me." He shrugged. "The raw meat restored my strength."

"A wolf." Sharilyn looked at Hardane as she murmured the word.

"You don't believe me?" Carrick said, a challenge rising in his eyes.

"I believe you," Hardane said. "Tell me, why was Kylene sent to the Motherhouse?"

"To keep her safe."

"To keep her safe?" Hardane asked suspiciously. "Or to make sure the prophesy would never be fulfilled?"

"To keep her safe," Carrick repeated emphatically.

"Safe from whom?"

"Her sister." Carrick gave Kylene's hand a gentle squeeze. "Selene was always jealous of you. She knew she would always live in your shadow because you were the firstborn twin, the one destined to share the throne of Argone, to fulfill the prophesy that would bring lasting peace to Mouldour. She tried to hurt you on several occasions. Your mother and I thought it was just childhood jealousy until Selene tried to drown you in the bathtub."

At his words, Kylene's hand flew to her throat. The bathtub! Of course, it all made sense now.

Her horrible fear of water, of drowning. It all came back in a rush, as clear as if it had happened only yesterday instead of years ago.

They'd been playing in the tub, having a contest to see who could stay under the water the longest. It had been Kylene's turn. She'd been just about to come up when she'd felt Selene's hands on the back of her head, refusing to let her come up for air. She remembered the horror of it, the awful panic when she realized her sister wasn't playing. She'd been almost unconscious when her mother lifted her out of the tub. Until now, she'd blocked the whole incident from her mind.

"Soon after that," her father went on, "we realized there were others who wanted to destroy you so that the prophesy could not be fulfilled, just as we realized that, to keep you safe, we would have to send you away until it was time for you to marry."

"Are you telling me that you wanted the prophesy to be fulfilled?" Hardane asked. "That you want peace?"

"Aye."

"You're lying! Everyone knows that the House of Mouldour has refused all offers of peace, that they have pursued war with a vengeance."

"Not I." Carrick met Hardane's accusing stare. "I have always spoken for peace. It was the main cause of contention between Bourke and myself. He wanted to conquer Argone, to put his bastard daughter on the throne. I refused."

"And so he took the throne by force," Hardane mused.

"Yes. With a little help from the Interrogator and the witch of Britha, Bourke managed to steal my throne."

Hardane grunted softly as he pondered Carrick's explanation. One thing still troubled him. "Why didn't Kylene know who she was?"

Carrick shook his head. "Understandably, Kylene was never the same after her sister tried to drown her. I think she refused to acknowledge who she was because it was too painful, or maybe she simply didn't want to remember." He shrugged. "As it turned out, it made it that much easier to hide her. She couldn't remember who she was, and except for the Mother General, no one in the Motherhouse knew who she really was."

There was a moment of silence, and then Carrick turned to Kylene. "Where's your sister?"

"I'm not sure. At Mouldour, I would imagine."

Carrick grunted softly. Holding Kylene's hand, he glanced over his shoulder at his son-in-law.

"What do you plan to do with me now?"

Slowly, Hardane shook his head. "I don't know."

"I think we should all get some sleep," Sharilyn suggested, rising to her feet.

She glanced around the room. Kylene looked to be on the verge of emotional exhaustion. Carrick was thin and pale, obviously not yet fully recovered from his sickness. There were fine lines of pain etched at the corners of Hardane's mouth and eyes. Of them all, only Jared looked fit and strong.

"I think you're right," Hardane agreed, rising to stand beside his mother. "Jared, take Lord Carrick to the brig. We'll talk more in the morning."

"The brig!" Kylene protested. "Hardane, he's my father. I won't have him locked up."

"Kylene . . ."

She jumped to her feet, her hands planted on her hips, her eyes defiant.

"If he goes to the brig, I'll go with him!"

"Very well," Hardane relented. "Lock him in the aft cabin."

"Hardane . . ."

"I know he's your father," Hardane replied wearily. "But I don't know whose side he's on, and until I do, he'll have to be locked up, at least at night."

She wanted to argue with him. She would have argued with him if she hadn't seen the utter weariness in the depths of his eyes, heard the barely suppressed pain in his voice. She remembered then that the wound in his thigh was not yet fully healed, that he should still be in bed, resting his leg.

"Good sleep, Father," Kylene said, kissing his cheek, and then, smiling sweetly, she put her arm around Hardane's waist, giving him the benefit of her support without anyone being the wiser.

Sharilyn bid them good night and hurried to her cabin to check on Kray, leaving Jared to escort Carrick to the aft cabin.

Alone in his quarters with Kylene, Hardane sat down, his head resting against the back of the chair. His leg ached incessantly, his head throbbed, and all he wanted to do was sleep. But he couldn't rest. Too many troublesome thoughts were churning through his mind. His father was badly wounded and might not recover. . . . Carrick was not dead, after all. . . . He was here. . . . He said he wanted peace, but could he be trusted. . . . Bourke wanted to rule Argone. . . . Renick intended to have it all. . . .

He closed his eyes and summoned the image of the wolf. Putting everything else from his mind, he imagined the freedom of running across the fields in the dark of night, of dancing in the light of a midnight moon.

A low growl of pleasure rose in his throat as he felt Kylene's hands soothe his brow, felt her fingertips knead the stiffness from his shoulders. Her fingers slid down his arms, and then began to work their magic on his injured leg, her touch soft and soothing, the warmth of her hands banishing the pain from his taut muscles.

"Sleep, my lord wolf," she murmured, and her breath fanned his face. "Sleep, beloved. All will be well."

And because he loved her, he believed her.

Chapter Forty-Two

Bourke sat on the tall, intricately carved throne, his hands resting on the arms, which were covered with rich purple velvet.

"He's alive, I tell you. Someone saw him leaving the castle. With Kray. And Sharilyn." Bourke dragged a hand across his brow. "And the wolf of Argone."

"It's impossible!" Selene exclaimed. "I was with him when he died."

"Then he must have risen from the grave." Bourke was practically shouting now. "What say you, my Lord Interrogator? How is it that Kray managed to escape from the dungeons?"

"It is obvious to me that his wife took on my shape and effected his release," Renick replied calmly. "Never fear, my lord, we will have them."

"You're a fool, Renick," Bourke retorted angrily.

"We've lost everything." He ran a hand through his hair, then drummed his fingers on the carved arm of the throne. "We'll have to flee the country. Find sanctuary. He'll never forgive me—"

"Stop babbling, you fool!" Renick snapped. "We've lost nothing!"

Bourke glared at the man who had held the title of Lord High Interrogator for the last twelve years.

"If you think that, Renick, then you're a bigger fool than I imagined. The people have always loved Carrick. Now that he's returned, they won't rest until he's restored to the throne."

"This is all your fault, you spineless dolt. If you'd killed him in the first place, as I suggested, we'd have nothing to worry about now."

Bourke stood up, his face flushed with rage. "You dare to call me such names! Jance! Arrest this man!"

"There will be no need for that, Jance," Renick said.

A slow grin spread over the Interrogator's face as he drew his sword and climbed the three steps that led to the throne.

"Jance!" Bourke screamed, staring past Renick to the guard who stood at his right hand. "Arrest this man at once!"

"I'm afraid Jance no longer takes orders from you," Renick said with mock regret. "I bought his loyalty a long time ago."

"This is an outrage!" Bourke sputtered.

"Indeed?"

With a cry, Bourke reached for his sword.

It was the move Renick had been waiting for.

Face void of all expression, he drove his sword into Bourke's heart and gave it a short hard twist.

For a long moment, Bourke stood there, his body impaled on the Interrogator's sword, his eyes staring at the blood that dripped from the blade, and then his eyes glazed over and he fell forward.

Renick put out a hand to stop Bourke's fall. Withdrawing his sword from Bourke's chest, he gave a gentle shove and the body teetered backward and dropped with lifeless grace onto the throne.

Slowly, Renick turned to face Selene. She was watching him, her face drained of color, her eyes wide with disbelief.

"My lady," Renick said, holding out his hand, "how would you like to share the throne of Mouldour?"

Chapter Forty-Three

For the first time in her life, Kylene felt a sense of coming home as they entered the Great Hall of Castle Argone.

Parah, Teliford, and Hadj had hurried out to meet them on their return, their smiles of welcome quickly turning to expressions of concern when Hardane's father was lifted from a litter and carried inside.

Lord Kray's condition had worsened during the voyage. He had drifted in and out of awareness during the first ten days; since then, he'd been unconscious. His face was as pale as moonstone, his cheeks were gaunt, there were dark shadows beneath his closed eyes.

News of their liege's illness quickly spread throughout the castle and kingdom. Almost immediately, gifts began to arrive—dried flowers, sachets filled with healing herbs and spices, prayers and good wishes written in the ancient language of Argone.

The castle physician had been called to attend Lord Kray's injury. Grim-faced, he had drained the wound and cut away the putrid flesh.

The Wolffan priest came, offering what comfort he could. All of Hardane's brothers had come home, lending their strength and support to Sharilyn.

Druidia had been summoned, but for once none of the witch's unguents or potions had any effect, and now, three days after their arrival, Lord Kray remained unconscious.

In his father's illness, Hardane sat upon the throne of Argone. Kylene had been startled the first time she entered the Great Hall and saw her husband sitting in his father's place.

Lord Kray's throne was massive. It had been fashioned from the same dark wood as the doors of the Temple of Fire. The arms were carved in the likeness of wolves lying on their bellies, heads resting between their paws. The back of the throne was in the shape of a wolf's head.

Sharilyn's throne was the same as Kray's, only slightly smaller.

And now it was the night of the third day and Kylene was wandering through the castle. The servants had gone to bed long since. Sharilyn was sitting beside Kray. She'd hardly left her husband's bedside since their arrival. Hadj had to remind her to eat. Old Nan, the cook, prepared all Sharilyn's favorite dishes in hopes of tempting her appetite, but to no avail. Sharilyn ate only a few bites at a time, never taking her eyes from Kray's face, never leaving his room except when absolutely necessary.

Kylene's father had been given free run of the castle with a thinly veiled warning that the dungeon awaited him should he try to escape. Kylene had spent her days with Carrick, getting to know him, listening to stories of her mother and sisters.

On one occasion, Carrick had reminisced about his childhood, about the happy times he'd had as a boy growing up in Castle Mouldour. Bourke had once been his best friend, he had confided. They had explored the castle together, from the topmost turrets to the hindermost regions of the dungeons. They had played tricks on the housemaids, learned to ride together, to fight together, shared secrets. Being twins, they had tried to fool their parents and friends, laughing with delight whenever their mother mistook Bourke for Carrick. Their closeness, the bond they had shared, had made Bourke's treachery all the more painful for Carrick to accept.

Kylene saw little of Hardane. He was burdened with the affairs of Argone, and when he had a free moment, he sat with his father. Kylene could not help feeling guilty because her own father was here, strong and healthy, while Lord Kray hovered in the netherworld between life and death. She tried to tell herself she had no cause to feel guilty. She'd been years without a father; surely no one could begrudge her the time she spent with him now.

Kylene sighed heavily as she made her way to the Great Hall. She needed to see Hardane, to feel his arms around her, to feel his strength.

He was there, sitting on his father's throne, a sable cloak wrapped around his shoulders.

She stared at him from the doorway, wishing there was something she could do to ease the pain in his heart.

She had been there only a few moments when Hardane looked up, his gaze finding her in the shadows. Wordlessly, he held out his arms and she hurried toward him, climbing onto his lap to pillow her head against his shoulder.

They sat that way for a long time before Hardane spoke. "I was missing you," he murmured, one hand burrowing in her hair. "I'm glad you're here."

Kylene snuggled deeper into his arms, hoping her presence would comfort him.

"Why don't you come to bed?" She traced the outline of his jaw with her fingertip. "It's been a long day."

Hardane grunted softly. Bed, he thought. A nice soft bed with Kylene to warm him.

"A hot bath to relax you," Kylene suggested, "a glass of wine, and then a good night's sleep."

Hardane nodded. Effortlessly, he stood up and then, carrying Kylene with him, he made his way up the winding stairway that led to their bedchamber.

He closed the door behind them. A tub of scented hot water awaited him. A flagon of wine stood on the bedside table. The blankets were turned back, and his pillows had been plumped.

"Thank you, wife," he murmured, kissing her cheek.

"You're welcome, my lord wolf. Will you put me down now?"

"If you wish."

He let her slide through his arms until she was standing in front of him, her body pressed to his.

Kylene smiled up at him as she began to unfasten the laces of his shirt. Lifting the garment over his head, she tossed it onto a chair, then knelt to remove his soft leather boots and breeches.

Taking him by the hand, she led him to the tub, trying not to notice his body's reaction to his nudity and her nearness.

When he was settled in the tub, she dropped to her knees beside the tub, took up a soft cloth, and began to wash him.

Hardane groaned softly.

"Is something amiss, my lord wolf?" she queried, dragging the cloth across his chest and down his belly.

"Nay, lady."

"You don't seem very relaxed," Kylene mused, noting the taut muscles in his arms, the tension in his jaw.

He gasped as the cloth brushed the inside of his thigh. "You can hardly expect me to relax with you so near."

She had not meant to arouse him, only to soothe him. "I did not mean to torment you," she remarked, not certain whether she was causing him pleasure or pain.

"Ah, lady," he muttered hoarsely as her hand hovered dangerously near his groin, "it's torment of the sweetest kind, I assure you."

"Shall I stop?"

"No." He ground out the word, his body aflame as the soapy cloth moved over him, teasing, tantalizing.

His nostrils filled with the scent of the water, and with Kylene's own sweet scent, which was more intoxicating than ale, more potent than Mouldourian wine.

Lifting a hand, he cupped the back of her head and drew her toward him, his mouth covering hers. She was his woman, his life-mate, overflowing with life. His free hand moved to the soft swell of her belly. She was life renewing itself, and he needed that reassurance, needed it badly.

Kylene sighed with pleasure as his lips moved over her face, her neck, and then, abruptly, his arms went around her waist and he buried his face in the cleft of her breasts. She felt his shoulders shake and realized he was crying.

"Hardane." She dropped the cloth and wrapped her arms around him, her heart aching for his sorrow.

She held him close until his sobs subsided and then she coaxed him from the tub, dried him with a square of heavy toweling, and led him to bed.

Undressing, she slid in beside him, turned onto her side, and drew him to her breast.

Like a fox to its den, Hardane snuggled against her, his arms locked around her waist, his face buried in the warm softness of her breasts.

For a time, he didn't move, only lay there beside her, content to be held in her arms. The warm womanly fragrance that was hers and hers alone rose all around him. He could hear her heart beating a soft tattoo beneath his cheek.

He lay still for so long that Kylene thought he'd fallen asleep. Gently, she smoothed his hair, caressed his cheek, her heart swelling with such an outpouring of love it was almost painful. She wished she could do something to ease his sorrow, and the knowledge that there was nothing she could say or do brought tears to her eyes.

"Why do you weep?" Hardane murmured.

"Because you're unhappy and I . . . I love you so much and . . . and there's nothing I can do to help."

"Your presence comforts me, lady, as nothing else can."

His words, so clearly spoken from the depths of his heart, brought a fresh wave of tears to her eyes.

Rising on one elbow, Hardane kissed the moisture from her cheeks, and then his mouth covered hers. As always, her nearness fanned the embers of desire until he felt as though his very blood were afire.

Hardane caressed her with his lips and his eyes, and everywhere he touched, her body came to life. She wrapped her arms around his neck, her thighs parting to receive him. And for a brief moment, there was nothing in all the world but the two of them, life reaching out to life as their hearts and souls entwined, love engulfed by love.

Something was wrong. Kylene sat up, her heart pounding with dread. In the darkness, she reached out for Hardane, only to find the bed empty beside her.

Truly worried now, she lit a candle and glanced around the chamber. There was no sign of Hardane.

Frowning, she slipped out of bed and drew on a heavy fleece-lined wrapper. Holding the candle in one hand, she crossed the floor, opened the chamber door, and peered into the corridor. All was dark.

She hesitated for a moment and then, as though guided by an invisible hand, she made her way down the stairs, through the main hall, and down the passageway that led to the gardens behind the keep.

When she reached the narrow door that led to the gardens, she blew out the candle and left it on a nearby table. Then, taking a deep breath, she lifted the latch and stepped into the yard.

It was like stepping into another world. Overhead, the moon was full and bright, almost blinding in its intensity. A fountain bubbled in a corner of the yard; tall trees stood like sentinels in the darkness, their leaves whispering a requiem to the dead.

The rich scent of flowers and earth hung heavy in the air. And there, in the midst of the garden, she saw a half dozen wolves gathered together. One lay beside the fountain, its head between its paws, while the others stood around it, their tails lowered. She hadn't made a sound since she stepped into the yard, yet one wolf, the tallest of them, immediately swung around to face her.

It was Hardane. In spite of the distance between them, she felt the touch of his eyes on her face, felt the heavy sadness that permeated his whole being, and she knew, without being told, that Lord Kray had passed away in the night.

Hardane, I'm so sorry. She spoke the words in her mind, and the wolf nodded its head. She glanced at the prone wolf and knew that it was Sharilyn; knew, without knowing how she knew, that the other wolves were related to Hardane's mother, that they had come to share her grief in the loss of her husband.

She was turning to go, to leave them to mourn in private, when she heard Hardane's voice in her mind.

Stay. I need you here.

She met his gaze and nodded. There was a small wrought-iron bench beside the doorway and Kylene sat down, wanting to remain unobtrusive.

For a long time, the wolves simply sat there, and then, one by one, they lifted their heads, their voices rising on the night wind in a long lament that bespoke their sorrow, their loss.

The anguished cries sent a shiver down Kylene's spine, and she thought she had never heard anything as sad, as heartbreaking, as the sound of those melancholy howls as members of the Wolffan clan mourned the passing of a loved one.

One by one, the wolves stepped forward to lick Sharilyn's face, and then, like shadows before a storm, they disappeared into the darkness until only Sharilyn and Hardane remained.

With a low growl, Sharilyn rose to her feet. She rubbed against Hardane a moment, whining softly, and then trotted away.

Almost immediately, Hardane assumed his own shape.

As always, the incredible sight of wolf transforming into man trapped Kylene's breath in her throat. It was an amazing thing to watch, mesmerizing, frightening.

And then Hardane was walking toward her, and her breath escaped in an audible sigh of relief that he was again the man she knew and loved.

She rose to meet him, her arms outstretched to enfold him.

"I'm sorry," she murmured, drawing him to her, "so sorry."

"He went in his sleep," Hardane said, his voice thick with unshed tears. "He never woke up. My mother . . ." He took a deep, steadying breath. "She's grieving, not only for his death, but because she was denied the opportunity to tell him goodbye."

Kylene's arms tightened around him. There was nothing she could say to comfort him, to make the loss any easier to bear.

They stood there, in the waning moonlight, for a long time. Hardane rested his head on Kylene's, his arms wrapped loosely around her waist, finding solace in her nearness, in her quiet understanding of his grief.

His father had been a man in his prime. He should have ruled Argone for years to come, should have lived to see the birth of his grandchildren, to see lasting peace forged between Mouldour and Argone.

You'll pay for this, Renick, he vowed, his arms tightening convulsively around Kylene. *You'll pay in blood.*

"No!" Kylene drew back, shaking her head vigorously as the image of a bloodstained sword flashed through her mind. "No, Hardane, please."

"I must."

"Why?"

"Why?" He looked at her as if he'd never seen her before. "How can you ask that after what he did to you? To my father? Not to mention what he did to my mother. To me."

Releasing her, Hardane ran a hand through his hair, then began to pace the yard. "My father's blood cries out to be avenged."

Kylene wrapped her arms around her swollen belly. "And what if you're killed? What do I tell our sons?"

Hardane whirled around to face her, his jaw rigid. "You tell them the truth, that I died avenging their grandfather's death."

"And do you think that will comfort them? That it will bring *me* comfort on cold nights?"

"Kylene, try to understand."

She shook her head, her long auburn hair swirling around her shoulders like a thick fiery mist.

"I understand that vengeance means more to you than I do."

"That's not true!" Hardane exclaimed, suddenly angry.

"I don't want to raise our sons alone."

"Have you so little faith in my ability to defend myself that you already fancy yourself a widow?"

"Fighting Renick will solve nothing. Your father's gone, and the Interrogator's death will not bring him back."

Closing the distance between them, Kylene laid her hand on her husband's arm. It was as unyielding as stone.

"Please, Hardane . . ."

With a sigh, he drew her into his arms again, his chin resting lightly on the top of her head.

"Lady, you don't know what you ask."

Taking his reply for assent, Kylene rested her cheek against his chest and closed her eyes.

The next few days would be long and difficult for all of them.

Chapter Forty-Four

Lord Kray's body lay in state for three days and three nights while people came from near and far to pay homage to their fallen liege. Hardane had sent a runner to advise his sister of her father's illness as soon as they had reached Argone; another runner had been sent to advise her of his death.

Sharilyn, clad in a dress of charcoal gray, her head and face covered with a gossamer black veil that hid the dark shadows beneath her eyes, greeted the farmers, the townspeople, the curious, and the grieving who came to pay their final respects to her husband. Dry-eyed, she accepted their words of sorrow, their embraces, their tears.

Food was provided for the mourners; beds were offered to those who needed shelter until after the interment.

Hardane's sister, Morissa, arrived late in the afternoon on the day before the funeral. She was a lovely woman with curly black hair and light brown eyes.

Morissa welcomed her new sister-in-law into the family with a warm smile and a hug, immediately putting Kylene at ease.

"I'm so pleased to meet you at last," Kylene murmured, feeling as if she'd known Morissa for years instead of a matter of moments. "I only wish it could have been under happier circumstances."

Morissa nodded. She wrapped her arms around her swollen girth as she apologized for her absence at the wedding.

"I understand," Kylene said. "When is your baby due?"

"At the end of the month." Morissa placed her hand over Kylene's stomach. "And yours?"

"In late spring, I think."

"I'm glad my time is almost here." Morissa pressed a hand to the small of her back, a brief look of pain flitting across her face.

"Is something wrong?" Kylene asked anxiously. "Maybe you should sit down?"

Morissa sighed heavily. "I'm fine. Just a twinge. Eben wanted me to stay home, but I couldn't. I couldn't." She blinked the moisture from her eyes. "I can't believe Father is gone."

"He was a fine man," Kylene said sympathetically. "I wish I had known him better."

"He was always so good to us. To Mother."

Kylene glanced across the room to where

Sharilyn stood talking to several mourners. "How's your mother doing, really?"

Morissa shook her head. "I don't know. I haven't had any time alone with her. No one has, except Hardane. He's always been her favorite, you know."

Kylene made a vague gesture, not knowing what to say.

"It's all right," Morissa said. "I don't mind. None of us do. Hardane and my mother have always shared a special bond, but Mother's never given any of us reason to be jealous. I . . ."

Morissa's words trailed off as her husband came up beside her and slipped an arm around her waist.

"I think you should go upstairs and get some rest," Eben suggested. "The funeral is set for tomorrow morning."

Morissa inclined her head in Kylene's direction. "It was good to meet you at last, Kylene. See if you can't persuade Hardane to go to bed early. He looks tired."

Kylene nodded. "I'll try."

She watched them out of sight, her thoughts wandering. Lord Kray had passed away, but his daughter would soon give birth to a new life. And in a few months, Hardane's sons would be born. It was an endless cycle, life and death. She wondered if Morissa was as apprehensive of childbirth as she was.

At length, the last visitor had paid his respects and all the house guests were bedded down for the night.

Sharilyn refused to leave her husband's side. She stood there, her face wan, her eyes dry, as Hardane and Dubrey closed the lid of the carved oak coffin and covered it with a cloth woven in bloodred and black, the colors of the House of Argone.

"Mother," Hardane said, "you should go to bed."

Sharilyn shook her head. "No. I can't leave him here alone, not tonight."

"We'll stay with you, then," Hardane said, indicating his brothers, who had gathered around.

"No. I want to be alone with him."

Dace laid a hand on his mother's. "You shouldn't be alone now."

"Leave her," Hardane said.

Dace immediately lifted his hand from Sharilyn's arm and, after giving his mother a kiss on the cheek, left the hall. One by one, the other brothers embraced their mother and then followed Dace from the room.

Hardane was the last to embrace Sharilyn. He held her for a long moment, one hand stroking her hair, and then he took Kylene by the hand and led her out of the room, leaving his mother standing beside the casket, alone in the Great Hall.

The morning of the funeral dawned dark and cold. Heavy black clouds lowered in the sky, promising rain before the day was through.

It was fitting, Kylene thought, for the dreary weather matched the mood of everyone in Castle Argone.

367

The funeral was held in the Church of Alysha, half a league from the keep. Named after the wife of one of Argone's former rulers, it was an enormous edifice, made of huge blocks of pink-hued stone and black oak. The double doors were ten feet tall. The windows, of every shape and size, were of stained glass.

Inside, beneath an arched window, was an altar three feet high and twelve feet long. Huge candlesticks were set at intervals along the outer aisles.

The Wolffan priest who had officiated at the Temple of Fire stood behind the altar. He was clad in a hooded white robe tied with a crimson sash. Kylene had thought it odd that a Wolffan priest would conduct the service until Hardane told her that Kray had embraced the Wolffan religion in the belief that, if he did so, he would be united with Sharilyn in the afterlife. It was fortunate, Kylene thought, that the people of Argone respected a man's right to worship as he saw fit.

When everyone was seated, Hardane and his brothers carried the coffin into the chapel and placed it at the foot of the altar.

The service was not overly long. Prayers of consolation were uttered, a choir of monks clad in somber black sang a dirge in a language Kylene did not understand. And then each member of the immediate family went forward and laid a white winter rose upon the casket.

Hardane was the last to approach the altar. Reverently, he placed his rose upon the cloth-covered coffin and then, to Kylene's horror, he drew a dagger from inside his shirt and cut a shallow gash in the palm of his right hand.

Turning to face the mourners, Hardane held his bleeding hand over the casket. Bright drops of blood splashed over the white roses.

"By my blood here spilt, I vow to avenge my father's death."

There was a long silence, and then the priest began to chant softly, and as he did so, he sprinkled Hardane's head and shoulders with ashes.

Stunned, Kylene stared at Hardane, at the blackened ashes scattered over his head and shoulders, at the blood dripping from his hand.

He had lied to her. He had promised he would not leave her to avenge his father's death and now, before half the countryside, he had vowed to avenge Lord Kray.

There was a final prayer, and the funeral was over. The mourners, somber in their silence, filed past the coffin and out of the chapel.

A gentle rain was falling; a cold, bitter wind blew from the north as Hardane and his brothers carried the casket into the graveyard behind the church.

The grave had already been dug. The earth waited to receive its own.

Kylene stood beside Sharilyn, her mind and heart numb as Hardane's words echoed and re-echoed in her ears: *By my blood here spilt, I vow to avenge my father's death.*

The church bells began to ring as the coffin was lowered into the ground.

It was then that Sharilyn's outward composure cracked. With a sob, she fell to her knees and buried her face in her hands.

The sound of her tears rose above the wail of the wind.

It was a sound that Kylene knew would haunt her dreams for days to come.

She watched as Hardane drew his mother to her feet and gathered her into his arms.

By my blood here spilt . . . Kylene shivered as an image burst upon her mind, an image of another coffin, Hardane's coffin, being lowered into the ground.

Choking back a rush of nausea, she left the graveyard and returned to the church. Inside, she dropped to her knees in front of the altar and began to pray.

It was Dubrey who found her there. Dubrey who took her home.

Kylene sat in the bedchamber she shared with Hardane. Sitting in the window seat, she stared into the darkness, the ache in her heart too deep for tears.

He had lied to her, had let her believe that he meant to forgo his quest for vengeance. She had trusted him, and he had betrayed that trust. He was going after the Interrogator, to kill or be killed, and she would never forgive him. Never.

For the first time since their marriage, she felt no joy at the sound of his footsteps approaching their room, nor did she run to the door to greet him.

She heard him enter their chamber and close the door, heard him cross the floor toward her, felt his hand caress her shoulder.

Without turning around, she pushed his hand away.

"What's wrong, Kylene?"

"Wrong?" She drew her hurt around her like a cloak. "Why should anything be wrong simply because you lied to me?"

"I never lied to you."

"You did!" She whirled around to face him. "You promised me you wouldn't go!"

"I never promised any such thing."

"You did," she insisted. She tried to remember that night, tried to recall exactly what he'd told her, but she was too hurt to think clearly, too steeped in despair to bandy words with him now.

"It's late," Hardane said quietly. "Come, let's go to bed. You'll feel better in the morning."

"No." Rising, she folded her arms over her breasts. "I wish to sleep alone."

"Kylene . . ."

"Get out."

"Listen to me."

"No, I listened to you before, and you lied to me. You let me believe that I meant more to you than some useless need for vengeance."

"How could you have believed I would let my father's death go unavenged? How could I live with myself if I didn't try to bring Renick to justice?"

"Justice! What do I care for justice? Will justice feed my children if you are killed? Will justice warm my bed?"

"Kylene, please try to understand."

He reached out to take her in his arms, but she

darted past him, anger and hurt warring in her heart. "Leave me alone!"

"Damn, lady, be careful you don't say something you'll regret."

"The only thing I regret is trusting you."

He took a step toward her, one hand outstretched, but she backed away from him, her eyes shining with unshed tears. "Don't touch me!"

Hardane stared at her for a long moment, his gray eyes turbulent, and then, without another word, he left the room, quietly closing the door behind him.

In the fortnight following the funeral, Kylene rarely saw Hardane except at meals. It seemed there were always people crowding into the Great Hall. Some were merely anxious to see their new ruler, but most of them came with problems: a land dispute, stolen cows or pigs or sheep, a need for help of one kind or another. She'd never realized how much time and effort went into the running of a country.

Under other circumstances, she might have resented the many hours he spent away from her. But not now. She was hurt and angry because he was determined to avenge his father's death no matter what the cost.

For the first time, she was glad that she had a room of her own where she could hide and lick her wounds.

How could he be so uncaring of her feelings? How could he even consider doing something that would put his life in jeopardy when he would soon be a father? Was shedding the blood of the Interrogator more important than being there for his sons?

And what would she do if he were killed? Argone was not her home. Much as she loved Sharilyn, as much as she adored Hardane's brothers, she had no desire to remain in Argone without Hardane. In spite of everything, Mouldour was her home.

She spent long hours with her father, expecting him to console her, to take her side. Instead, Carrick urged her to be forgiving, to try to see things from Hardane's point of view. His father had been killed. His mother had been held captive. Hardane, himself, had been imprisoned and badly abused. Even Kylene had felt the wrath of the Interrogator. Did she truly expect her husband, a man born and raised to be a warrior, to ignore such treachery?

"Yes!" Kylene had exclaimed. "I should mean more to him than revenge."

"He's a man, daughter," Carrick had replied quietly. "A man of courage and honor. He must do what he thinks is right."

Right! Kylene had stamped her foot, too angry for words. What difference did it make if avenging Lord Kray was the right thing to do if it cost Hardane his life?

She had sought out Dubrey, certain he would take her side, certain that he could make Hardane understand how she felt, that Dubrey would speak to Hardane and make him see things her way.

But Dubrey had agreed with Carrick. And so had Hardane's other brothers. Every one of them.

Most shocking of all was the fact that Sharilyn

also thought Hardane was in the right. And that
bewildered Kylene. How could Hardane's mother
even think of letting Hardane go off to Mouldour
to avenge Kray's death? Sharilyn had just lost her
husband. Did the possibility of losing a son mean
nothing? Did the Wolffan put vengeance above
everything else?

Now, sitting in the window seat of her chamber,
Kylene rubbed her temples in an effort to ease the
throbbing in her head. She was lonely and unhappy. She wanted to be in Hardane's arms, to feel his
strength, to bask in his love, but she couldn't bring
herself to go to him. And he wouldn't come to her.
Not after the way she'd behaved the night of the
funeral.

Night after night, she'd gone to her lonely bed
only to lie awake, staring into the darkness, wondering how she could miss him so much when
he'd lied to her. Knowing he had no intention
of keeping his word, he'd promised he wouldn't
seek revenge, and then he'd broken his pledge and
vowed to avenge his father's death.

Hadn't he? She tried to remember what he'd said
when she'd begged him not to go after Renick.
Slowly, the words he'd spoken came back to her.

Lady, he'd said, *you don't know what you ask.*
He'd never promised her anything, she realized.
She'd only heard what she wanted to hear. The
realization had filled her with a deep sense of
shame and an ever-growing need to apologize.

Knowing he could read her thoughts, she had
silently begged him to come to her. Each time she
heard his footsteps in the adjoining chamber, she

had hoped he would open the connecting door, that he would sweep her into his arms and beg her forgiveness, that he would forget his blood vow and put aside his need for vengeance.

And night after night, the door between his bedchamber and hers remained closed.

And her arms remained empty.

One night she had tried to walk in his thoughts, but his mind had been closed to her, as solid as the door that shut her from his presence.

With a sigh, Kylene wrapped her arms around her belly, now burgeoning with new life. Closing her eyes, she let the tears fall, weeping with regret for the harsh words she had spoken in haste and in anger, crying because she was lonely and unhappy, because she couldn't bring herself to swallow her foolish pride and beg his forgiveness, because she wanted him to come to her.

The tears fell harder, faster, as she imagined the days and weeks slipping by while the abyss between her and Hardane grew ever wider, ever deeper, until bridging it became impossible.

Perhaps it was already impossible.

The hours slipped by. The moon rose in the sky, shedding her bright white light on the gardens below, inviting Kylene to come outside and wander in the moon-dappled night.

Rising from the window seat, she made her way down the staircase and out into the darkness. The fragrant scent of winter roses filled the air, reminding her of the hundreds of white velvet petals that had covered their bed on the night of their wedding.

"Hardane, forgive me," she murmured as she plucked a white rose and breathed in its sweetness. "Please forgive me."

Lady, come to me.

His voice, low and resonant, whispered like a nearly forgotten melody in the quiet corridors of her mind.

Lady . . .

The flower fell, unnoticed, from her hand as she turned to follow the siren call of his voice, her pulse racing with hope and trepidation.

She found him in the heart of the maze, standing beside the small stone bench beneath the ancient willow tree.

Her heart gave a little leap of joy at seeing him. He was so tall, so incredibly handsome. The moonlight played in his hair, that long black hair that she so loved to touch. He wore a forest green shirt that complemented the color of his hair and skin. Fawn-colored breeches clung to his legs, outlining his muscular thighs. Knee-high kidskin boots covered his feet and hugged his calves. Never had he looked more masculine. More unapproachable.

Her gaze was drawn to his face. To eyes that were deep and dark and gray. Eyes that had once held secrets she longed to know. Eyes that had once viewed her with warmth and affection. Now, they regarded her without expression, and that was more frightening than anything else.

The silence stretched between them. Kylene plucked at the folds of her skirt, conscious of the gentle bubbling of the crystal geyser, of the sweet scent of the marsh flowers that grew in rich profusion around the edge of the maze. Tall green and gold ferns swayed to the music of the breeze.

He continued to watch her, his arms folded across his chest, his dark gray eyes unfathomable. Was he waiting for her to break the silence?

"You summoned me, my lord?" she said at last.

"Aye, lady."

"I'm here."

He nodded, his gaze sweeping over her from head to heel, missing nothing. "Are you well?" he asked gruffly.

"Well enough."

Hardane ran a hand through his hair, then released a heavy sigh. "I've missed you, Kylene."

"Have you, my lord?" she asked tremulously.

"Aye, lady," he replied quietly. "More than you'll ever know."

"Why didn't you come to me?"

"Why didn't you come to me?"

"I was afraid you'd send me away . . ."

"Kylene . . ."

"You shut me out of your thoughts." She made no effort to conceal her pain, or to stem the tears that welled in her eyes. "I thought you didn't love me anymore. I wanted to go to you, but my pride . . . I was too proud, too afraid . . ."

Too afraid he'd reject her. "Lady . . ."

The word was laced with sorrow and self-reproach. Each tear she shed was like a knife in his heart. On the night of their wedding, he'd made a solemn promise that he would never cause her pain, and now, only a few months later, he had broken that vow. He could see the anguish in her

377

eyes, hear it in her voice, read it in her thoughts.

His throat grew thick with unshed tears as he held out his arms.

"Forgive me, Kylene," he murmured. "Please forgive me. I never meant to hurt you."

Feeling as though a crushing burden had been lifted from her heart, she crossed the short distance between them, and when his arms folded around her, it was like walking out of darkness into the light.

She wept then, copious tears that washed away all the hurt of the past.

"Forgive me?" he asked again.

"Aye, my lord wolf, if you'll forgive me."

"There's nothing to forgive, Kylene. You were right to be angry with me."

"Then you won't . . ." She bit back the words, afraid to make him angry by mentioning the Interrogator.

A muscle worked in Hardane's jaw. How could he let his father's death go unavenged? Truly, she didn't know what she asked. And yet . . . how could he leave her? He let his mind walk in hers, reading the deep-seated fear that she had not acknowledged. She was afraid he would leave her, as her father had left her. Afraid of being alone and unloved.

He gazed into her eyes, seeing the love, the fragile hope. Was she really asking so much?

Hardane drew her up against him, taking pleasure in her nearness, her warmth. His hand slid between them, resting on the warm swell of her stomach. And there, beneath his callused palm, he felt the life stirring within her.

His sons. He had no right to do anything that might deprive his sons of a father's love and protection. No right to put his need for vengeance above the needs of his bride.

"I won't go after Renick," he said quietly.

It was the hardest decision he'd ever made.

Kylene gazed into his eyes, her expression solemn. "But what of your vow?"

"The vows I made to you in the Temple of Fire on the night we wed are more binding, Kylene. My place is here, with you. I'll not leave you to bear our sons alone while I seek vengeance against Renick. I swear it to you on the lives of our unborn children, and on my love for you."

Humbled by his words, by the depth and strength of his love, she buried her face against his chest so that he couldn't see her tears. She had cursed him and wrongfully accused him of lying to her, refused him his place in her bed, and he had begged her forgiveness.

"I'm sorry, Hardane," she sobbed, "so sorry."

"Don't weep, lady," he murmured. "Please don't weep."

Feeling helpless, he lifted her into his arms and carried her out of the maze toward the keep, and all the while he whispered that he loved her, would always love her, that nothing had changed between them.

Up the winding staircase, through the long narrow corridors, to his bedchamber, he carried her, absorbing her nearness, welcoming the weight of her in his arms.

His room was dark, but he moved unerringly toward his bed. Lowering her gently to the mattress, he stretched out beside her and drew her into his arms.

"Promise me," he said urgently, "promise me we'll never again sleep apart."

"I promise."

"Tomorrow I want you to move your things in here. We can use the other room as a nursery, if you like, but I don't want you to have a room of your own anymore."

"Whatever you wish, my lord wolf."

"Tell me you love me."

She stroked his hair, his cheek, traced the line of his jaw. "I love you."

"Kylene . . ."

Whispering her name, he covered her mouth with his, drinking in her sweetness, savoring the taste of her on his lips, his tongue.

Kylene ran her fingers through his hair, loving the way it felt in her hands. She reveled in his easy strength, in the power that flexed and relaxed at the mere touch of her hand. His arms and legs were long and corded with muscle; his belly was hard and flat.

Their clothing fell away and she let her hands explore every inch of his hard-muscled body, reacquainting herself with the width of his shoulders, the contours of his broad back, the springy black hair on his chest.

She murmured his name as she pressed kisses to

his lips, his brow, his fine straight nose, his strong square chin. And when she was on fire for him, quivering with need and desire, she wrapped her legs around his waist and guided him home.

Chapter Forty-Five

Gradually, life at the castle returned to normal. Hardane's brothers and sister took their leave one by one, returning to their own lands. Morissa promised to send word as soon as her child was born.

In the days that followed, Kylene noticed that her father and Sharilyn were spending more and more time in each other's company.

She often saw them strolling through the gardens, walking side by side, so close that Sharilyn's skirts brushed against Carrick's legs, though they never touched hands. On rainy days they could usually be found sitting in one of the small anterooms, companionably quiet as they watched the wind and the rain.

When she remarked on it to Hardane, he simply shrugged. They were of a similar age, he remarked.

Carrick was in a strange land. Sharilyn was in need of solace. It seemed logical that they would seek each other out.

As time went on, the despair and sadness that had been etched on Sharilyn's features lessened. She began to smile again. She listened to Kylene's ideas for turning the bedroom adjoining Hardane's into a nursery, and began to spend her evenings sewing things, not only for Morissa's baby, which was due any day, but for Kylene's twin sons as well.

A fortnight after the funeral, a messenger arrived to announce that Morissa had been delivered of a healthy baby girl. Sharilyn left Castle Argone the next morning, and Carrick went with her.

For the first time, Kylene found herself in charge of the keep. It fell to her to decide what would be served at meals, to settle a dispute between the scullery maid and the cook, to determine if new rushes should be laid in the Great Hall.

It was a new experience, being the mistress of a castle. All her life, she had been accustomed to taking orders, not giving them.

Sharilyn had been away only a few days when another messenger arrived at the keep. Though the hour was late, he insisted on seeing Hardane.

Kylene sat up in bed, yawning as she watched Hardane pull on his breeches.

"Go back to sleep," he said, ruffling her hair. "I won't be long."

With a nod, she snuggled under the covers and closed her eyes. These days, she needed little encouragement to sleep. It seemed she was tired all the time. And when she wasn't sleeping, she was eating everything in sight.

With a wry grin, she spread her hands over her belly. She was as big as a horse, she thought, but Hardane didn't seem to mind. He still looked at her as if she were the most beautiful thing he'd ever seen. Often, in the evening, he spread his large hands over her swollen belly, smiling with delight as the life within her moved under his fingertips. Sometimes they walked in the gardens, spinning dreams of the future.

She was almost asleep when she heard the door open. Scooting over to Hardane's side of the bed, she waited for him to join her.

She frowned when he didn't come right to bed. Sitting up, she saw him standing at the window staring down into the garden below.

"What is it?" she asked. "What's wrong?"

"Bourke's dead."

"Dead? How? When?"

"I'm not sure. It took the messenger over a fortnight to get here with word of his death."

Kylene stared at Hardane's profile, her mind whirling at the implications of what he'd said.

"That's not the worst of it," Hardane remarked. "Renick has married Selene, and she's claimed the throne."

Slipping out of bed, Kylene crossed the floor to stand behind Hardane, her arms wrapped around his waist.

"What will happen now?"

"I don't know. It seems the people of Mouldour have accepted Renick as Lord High Sovereign and acknowledged Selene's right to the throne through your father's bloodline."

"This means war, doesn't it?"

"Perhaps," Hardane said with a shrug. "And perhaps Renick will be content with Mouldour."

"But you don't think he'll be satisfied to rule Mouldour for long, do you? You think he'll want the throne of Argone as well?"

Hardane nodded. Mouldour was a cold and barren land, and though it was rich in ore and other valuable minerals, it lacked the verdant valleys and wooded hillsides of Argone. Sheep and cattle flourished here. The land was rich and fertile, and there was fresh water in abundance. For years untold, the people of Argone had defended their homeland against invaders. So far, they'd managed to drive their enemies away.

Kylene pressed her cheek against her husband's back. She could feel his concern, his worry for her, for his people.

Drawing away, she began to rub Hardane's back, her fingers kneading deep into his taut muscles. War, she thought bleakly. But surely Hardane would not go to battle. He was the Lord High Ruler of Argone. If he went out to fight, who would stay behind and defend the throne?

"Put your mind at ease, lady," he murmured. "I won't leave you unprotected."

Turning to face her, he drew her into his arms, his chin resting lightly on the top of her head.

Kylene wrapped her arms around his waist and held him tight as her mind filled with images of bloodshed, of men dying, of women weeping.

"Don't dwell on it, beloved," he chided softly. "Tomorrow I'll send Jared and a handful of men to Mouldour to look around. I've already sent runners to my brothers and Eben to warn them to be ready. There's nothing else to be done until we know what Renick's intentions are."

She knew he meant to soothe her, to ease her fears, but she couldn't help remembering the implacable hatred in the Lord High Interrogator's eyes when he spoke of Hardane, the look of greed on his face when he spoke of conquering Argone.

"He killed Bourke, didn't he?"

"I don't know, but I wouldn't be surprised."

"And he'll kill you, if he gets the chance."

"Kylene . . ."

"We'll never be safe as long as he lives, will we?"

Hardane expelled a deep breath. There was nothing to be gained by lying to her. She'd felt the wrath of the Interrogator; she knew what atrocities he was capable of.

"Let's not speak of it now," Hardane said. Swinging her into his arms, he carried her to bed and drew the blankets around her. "Go back to sleep."

Kylene caught his hand in hers. "Come to bed."

It was in his mind to refuse. He was too keyed up to rest. He had plans to make, people to consult with. He needed to speak to Kruck, to Jared, to Teliford. He needed to send messages to his brothers, to Morissa, to his mother. The people of Argone needed to be warned so that they could round up their animals, arm their men, fortify their homes. So much to do. And yet, as he gazed into Kylene's eyes and saw the love and concern reflected there, he knew he could not deny her this one simple request.

Slipping under the covers, he drew her to him and held her close all through the night, and as he drifted to sleep, he prayed that war could be avoided, that he might be able to spend tomorrow night, and every night, lying in Kylene's arms.

Chapter Forty-Six

Selene rested her hands on the arms of the throne and smiled. At last she was where she had always wanted to be.

She glanced down at her gown of spun cloth of gold, at the rings glittering on her fingers, the wide gold band on her left wrist. There was a bejeweled crown on her head, a rope of pearls around her neck. And in her chambers there were boxes and boxes of jewels, of gold, of silver. The wealth of the kingdom. And it was hers.

She slid a glance at Renick, seated on the throne beside hers. He would have been a handsome man but for the scar on his left cheek. Still, he possessed an air of virility, a latent sense of danger, that excited her. She had been his wife for nearly a month now, and she knew the shape of his body, the texture of his short blond hair, the way his icy blue eyes blazed with desire when he took her in his arms.

She knew the touch of his hands upon her willing flesh.

She toyed impatiently with a fold in her skirt, waiting for him to finish the business at hand. Spies had recently returned from Argone and she was anxious to hear the news.

Earlier, she had listened intently as Renick conferred with the minister of war, silently agreeing with every decision her husband made. When the time was right, when their army had been gathered together, when their allies had arrived, they would attack Hardane and the riches of Argone would be theirs.

Renick had indicated it might be necessary to dispose of Kylene as well as Hardane. He had looked at her closely, his cold blue eyes probing deep into her soul, as he awaited her reply. She knew he had expected her to shrink from such a possibility, to object to anything that would harm her sister, but then, he didn't know she had once tried to drown Kylene in the bathtub. She had met his level gaze with one of her own.

You must do whatever is necessary, my husband, she had replied.

At first, he had been stunned by her answer, and then he had smiled, obviously pleased to learn that they were much alike.

She glanced at him again. They were well suited, she mused. Both sure of what they wanted. Neither afraid to do what had to be done. The day after Bourke's funeral, his two-year-old daughter had been sent from the castle, given into the care of a farmer and his wife who had been warned that their lives would be forfeit should they ever divulge the child's identity.

Soon, Selene thought, soon she would rule the countries of Mouldour and Argone. With Renick at her side, nothing and no one would be able to stop her.

Chapter Forty-Seven

Sharilyn gave Morissa a last hug, pressed a gentle kiss to her granddaughter's cheek, and hurried from the keep, tears stinging her eyes. Her visit, which was to have lasted several more weeks, had been cut short by an urgent message from Hardane.

She blinked back her tears as Carrick handed her into the closed carriage, then followed her inside and shut the door.

A moment later, the carriage lurched forward.

For a time, they traveled in silence. Sharilyn gazed out the window, her mind troubled. Bourke had been killed, and Renick had seized the throne of Mouldour. Deep in her heart, she knew that only misery and bloodshed would come of such a coup. And Selene ruled with him.

Selene and Renick. Truly a match made in the bowels of Hades.

"I'm sure everything will be all right," Carrick said after a while.

Sharilyn smiled at him. He was a kind man, good to the depths of his soul. It was no wonder Bourke had managed to steal the throne. Carrick saw only the good in the people he cared for. With him on the throne of Mouldour, there might have been peace, but Bourke and Renick wanted only war, needed war as an excuse to plunder the wealth of other, weaker lands.

With a sigh, she stared out the window. What a godsend Carrick had been to her in the days following Kray's death. He had ever been there for her, willing to hold her while she cried, willing to listen while she talked about Kray and the good times they had shared, their laughter, their tears.

And when she had shed her tears, he'd told her of his exile, how Bourke had robbed him of the throne, how he and Selene had spent the last few years hiding in caves and farmhouses on the islands surrounding Mouldour.

Looking away from the window, she met his gaze, felt her heart flutter within her breast. He was a handsome man. His hair was a dark, dark red sprinkled with gray, his eyes the same warm shade of brown as Kylene's. The first time she'd seen him, he'd been pitifully thin and pale, but he'd gained weight from weeks of eating Nan's good cooking; nights of resting without fear had brought the color back to his face.

She chided herself for being attracted to a man when Kray had been gone such a short time, and yet it was not the Wolffan way to mourn overly long for the death of a loved one. Life was a gift to be lived to the fullest; it was not to be wasted in sorrow or regret.

"What will you do now?" she asked.

"Fight for what's mine," Carrick replied. "The throne of Mouldour belongs to me. I'll not have Renick rule in my stead. Not now. Not ever."

Leaning forward, Sharilyn placed her hand on his arm. "Be assured that the people of Argone will fight with you, Lord Carrick."

A smile curved his lips as he covered her hand with his. "Did you ever think, my lady, that perhaps it isn't a mating between your son and my daughter that will bring peace to our lands? Perhaps it isn't our grandchildren who will be the ones to bring an end to war, but an alliance between us."

Sharilyn stared at him, stunned by his words. "Between us, my lord?"

"Aye, my lady," he said with a captivating smile. "Between us."

"Are you . . . are you speaking of marriage?"

"Aye, lady, when the time of your mourning is past."

"But . . . what of my Wolffan blood?"

"What of it?"

"It doesn't bother you?"

"No."

"But we've only just met. I hardly know you."

"Search your heart, Sharilyn of Argone. You know me well enough."

He wanted to marry her. The thought of it, the wonder of it, lingered in Sharilyn's mind all the way to Argone.

Chapter Forty-Eight

It was raining when Sharilyn and Carrick arrived at Castle Argone. Jagged flashes of lightning rent the angry black clouds as they hurried into the keep.

After Sharilyn and Carrick had changed out of their traveling clothes and had something to eat, the family met in the Great Hall.

Sharilyn quickly gave the details of the birth, assuring Hardane that Morissa and the babe were well. They drank a toast to the newest member of the family, and then Carrick stood up, his hands clasped behind his back.

"Is it true about Bourke?" he asked. "Did the message come from a reliable source?"

"Yes," Hardane said. "There's no doubt of his death, or of the fact that Selene and Renick now hold the throne."

"What will you do now?"

"Wait. My brothers have all been warned. The next move is up to Renick."

"Wait?" Carrick exclaimed. "That's all, just wait?"

"My men have been preparing for battle ever since we heard of Bourke's death," Hardane replied, the edge in his voice indicating he didn't care for Carrick's implication that he didn't know what he was doing. "Supplies are being brought into the castle in case of a siege. The townspeople and farmers are making what preparations they can. Have I forgotten anything?"

Carrick grinned sheepishly. "No."

"It's late," Sharilyn said, rising to her feet. "I'm going to bed."

"Good sleep, Mother," Hardane said, giving her a hug.

"Rest well, son. You, too, Kylene." She turned to Carrick. "Good evening to you, sir."

"Madam." Carrick bowed formally, a smile playing over his lips as he watched Sharilyn leave the room, and then he, too, took his leave.

It was a look that was not lost on Kylene. "Well," she said, "what do you make of that?"

"I think your father's in love with my mother."

"And do you think she's in love with him?"

"I know it."

"You know it? How?"

"I just know."

"But . . . but she's still in mourning. Isn't she?"

"Perhaps."

"Do you think they'll get married?"

396

Hardane nodded. "Before the year is out, I should think."

Rain or shine, Hardane's men trained in the inner courtyard. From dawn to dusk the sounds of sword against sword and sword against shield rang in the air until Kylene no longer noticed it.

Hardane often trained alongside his men. Whenever possible, Kylene watched them from the parapet above the courtyard. Though she hated to think he would actually go to war, she loved to watch Hardane in action. He moved with such assurance, such inborn grace, that she never tired of watching him. He swung his sword as if it were made of rolled parchment instead of heavy steel, easily besting every opponent.

She watched with pride as her father took to the field. Despite the fact that he was older than many of the other men, he fought tirelessly, and was rarely defeated.

Even the servants took their turn on the training ground. Parah was clumsy and less than enthusiastic, but Teliford wielded his sword with vigor.

Best of all, Kylene enjoyed watching Hardane put his big gray war-horse through its paces. The stallion moved effortlessly, wheeling, rearing, turning left and then right, horse and rider so keenly attuned to one another they seemed like one being. So beautiful were they to watch, it was almost as if they were dancing instead of practicing for battle.

In the evening, she watched the furtive glances, the shared smiles, the touches that passed between her father and Sharilyn. A blind man could have seen that they were smitten with each other. Kylene was happy that her father had apparently found someone to love, but she couldn't help being a bit shocked at how soon Sharilyn seemed to have gotten over her husband's demise.

In Mouldour, it was customary for a woman to remain in seclusion at least a year after the death of her husband. But this wasn't Mouldour.

"The Wolffan don't stop living when someone dies," Hardane told her one evening. "The grief is still there, the pain lingers, but they don't mourn the way your people do. It doesn't mean she didn't love my father, or that she doesn't miss him. It's just that the Wolffan have a deeper understanding of how brief our life span is. It may seem disrespectful to you, but not to us. Why should my mother waste a year of her life in seclusion when it changes nothing? When she could be spending that time with your father?"

"And would you be so quick to marry again should you find yourself suddenly widowed?" Kylene asked tartly.

Hardane shook his head, and then he took her hand and placed it over his heart. "There will never be another woman for me, beloved. I understand my people's beliefs, but in this instance we disagree, and even though I understand how my mother feels and wish her every happiness, I'll never marry again."

"I didn't mean that," Kylene said. "I wouldn't want you to spend the rest of your life alone. It just seems that everything is happening so fast."

Lifting her hand, he brushed her knuckles with

his lips. "You're the only woman for me, Kylene," he murmured fervently. "Now and forever."

It was on the first day of spring that a messenger arrived at the castle with the news that everyone had been dreading: more than two dozen warships flying the black and gold flags of Mouldour and the green and orange flags of Corianton had been seen approaching the coast of Argone near Dubrey's holdings.

Other messengers had carried the news to Hardane's brothers and sister. Farmers from nearby towns arrived at the keep in droves. The men would help defend the castle in exchange for protection for their women, children, and livestock.

The first battle was fought by Dubrey's warrior knights. Badly outnumbered, they put up a fierce fight before retreating to the protection of the castle. Dubrey sent a runner to Castle Argone to warn Hardane that Renick's men were heading in his direction.

Kylene read the end of Dubrey's message over Hardane's shoulder:

We inflicted severe damage to Renick's army, but our own losses were far greater than his. Assure my mother that I'm well . . .

Kylene felt as though a cold fist were wrapping around her insides when she saw the look in Hardane's eyes.

"What are you going to do?" she asked.

"What would you have me do?"

She hesitated to answer even as she refused to meet his piercing gaze. She wished that she possessed the same stalwart courage that Hardane and his family seemed blessed with, but she could not control her fear. For most of her life, she had lived in seclusion, protected from even the mildest acts of violence. The thought of fighting and bloodshed were foreign to her, against everything she had been taught. But overriding all other concerns was her fear for Hardane.

Hardane placed a finger beneath her chin and forced her to meet his gaze.

"What would you have me do, lady?" he asked again.

"I don't know. I only know that I'm afraid. For you. For us."

Hardane put his arm around her shoulders and drew her close. "I know," he murmured absently. "I know."

"Please don't fight him."

Hardane drew in a deep breath, knowing that this time he could not accede to her wishes. Had he fulfilled his vow to avenge his father, Kylene's life would not now be in danger.

"Hardane?"

"Do you want me to run away?" he asked, struggling to control his anger.

"Would you?"

"Not this time, lady. There are too many people depending on me."

She heard the barely suppressed fury in his voice and was swamped with a sudden sense of guilt, knowing that he was blaming her because Renick was here. Because of her, he had not fulfilled his vow to avenge Lord Kray. Because of her, the Interrogator was here now, threatening the lives of everyone in the castle. Because of her . . .

Before she could apologize, before she could tell him how sorry she was for her cowardice, Carrick entered the room, closely followed by Jared, Sharilyn, and Teliford.

"Well, what are we going to do?" Jared asked.

"Defend ourselves," Hardane replied curtly. "I want every available archer on the parapets. I want six of our best swordsmen at the gatehouse. Jared, I want you and a dozen of your best men to patrol the keep. Advise Kruck to have the *Sea Dragon* ready to sail at a moment's notice. Mother, if Renick's men should make it into the keep, I want you and Kylene to leave immediately."

"No." Both women spoke at the same time.

"I'm not asking you, I'm telling you. I want you both to take the tunnel in my room and leave the castle. The *Sea Dragon* is anchored in the cove east of the waterfall."

"I won't leave you," Kylene protested.

Hardane placed his hand over her swollen belly. "Please, lady, don't argue with me about this. If Renick breaches our defenses, I want you to leave Argone."

Kylene shook her head. "No."

"Mother?"

"Don't worry about us, Hardane," Sharilyn replied quietly. "We'll do as you say. Won't we, daughter?"

Kylene turned mutinous eyes in her mother-in-law's direction and then, seeing the warning there, knowing that Hardane would be able to fight better if he wasn't worrying about her, she nodded. "Yes."

"Good. Once the fighting starts, I want the two of you to go to my room and stay there." He looked down at Kylene, imprinting her image on his mind. "Promise me?"

"Aye, my lord wolf," she murmured. "I promise."

Carrick cleared his throat. "Hardane?"

"Is there a problem?" Hardane asked, his gaze still on his wife's face.

"No. I . . ." Carrick's voice trailed off and a flood of red swept into his cheeks. "I want to marry your mother. Now. Tonight."

Hardane looked up, frowning.

Kylene gasped in surprise. Get married! So soon?

Hardane glanced at his mother. Her cheeks, too, were flushed, but her eyes were sparkling.

"Is this what you want?" he asked.

Sharilyn took Carrick's hand in hers. "Do we have your blessing?"

Hardane nodded. "Aye, mother mine. But are you sure you don't want to wait until my brothers and Morissa can attend you?"

"We don't want to wait," Sharilyn answered.

Hardane nodded again, readily understanding her urgency. She was afraid Carrick might be killed in battle, afraid that they might never be able to consummate their love.

"Teliford, summon the priest. We'll hold the ceremony in the castle chapel in an hour."

"And you, daughter?" Lord Carrick asked. "Do we have your blessing as well?"

"Yes, Father," Kylene replied quietly. "I hope you find the same happiness with Sharilyn that I've found with her son."

An hour later, they gathered in the small family chapel. The Wolffan priest stood behind the tall white stone altar. He was clothed in a long black robe. In one hand he held a pink candle, in the other, a sachet filled with vervain, yarrow, rosemary, basil, and lovage.

Sharilyn and Carrick stood side by side. She wore a full-skirted pale blue gown that emphasized the ebony of her hair and eyes; he wore a pair of fawn-colored breeches and a wine-red shirt.

Hardane and Kylene stood behind their parents. Behind them, seated in the first pew, were Jared, Hadj, Teliford, Parah, and Nan.

"Sharilyn of Argone, is it your wish to wed Carrick of Mouldour, here present?"

"It is."

"Wilt thou forsake all others, and honor his name from this time forward?"

"I will."

"Carrick of Mouldour, is it your wish to wed Sharilyn of Argone, here present?"

"Aye."

"Wilt thou forsake all others? Wilt thou honor and protect her from this time forward?"

There was a heavy silence as Carrick pondered those words. Protect her. Protect her from harm, from Renick. Aye, he'd protect her with his life, if necessary.

"I will," he answered solemnly.

"Then I bless this union in the name of the Father of Us All and decree that thou art life mated from this night forward." The priest nodded in Carrick's direction, a faint smile creasing his aged face. "My lord, you may kiss your bride."

Kylene felt tears well in her eyes as her father placed his hands on Sharilyn's shoulders and looked deep into her eyes.

"All that I have, all that will ever be mine, I will gladly share with you," he murmured, and then, very gently, he kissed her.

Kylene glanced up as she felt Hardane's hand on her arm. "Why do you weep?" he asked.

"It's so beautiful," she said, sniffling. "I don't remember my mother, and I'm . . . I'm just happy that my father has found someone to share his life with."

Hardane bent to kiss her cheek, and then he went to embrace his mother and offer his congratulations to Carrick.

From the chapel, they went into one of the family's private rooms to drink a toast to Sharilyn and Carrick. It was obvious that, even though they'd known each other only a short time, the bride and groom were very much in love. Sharilyn couldn't keep her eyes from her new husband, and Carrick found numerous excuses to touch his wife's arm, her shoulder, her hand.

No one was surprised when Carrick announced, rather abruptly, that he was tired. Sharilyn's cheeks were a becoming shade of pink as she bid Kylene and Hardane a good night, then followed her husband upstairs.

Teliford and the other servants also took their leave.

"So," Hardane said, "alone at last."

"They seem happy, don't they?"

"Very. And you, lady, are you happy?"

"Very, but . . ."

"But?"

"I'm worried, Hardane, worried and afraid."

"I know."

"Why won't Renick leave us alone? Why can't he be happy with the throne of Mouldour?"

"Some men are never satisfied. No matter how much land they own, they always want more. More land. More gold. More silver. I fear Renick is like that. If he conquers Argone, he still won't be satisfied."

Kylene rested her cheek on Hardane's chest. "It isn't just Argone he wants," she remarked, "and you know it. He wants your power."

Hardane grunted softly.

"Can't you give him what he wants? What difference does it make if he can turn into a wolf?"

"No difference, perhaps, but I told him the truth. The secret of the Wolffan isn't a trick. It's not a magic spell that can be passed from one man to another. It's what I am, Kylene, not something I do."

"But . . ."

"He knows he can't obtain the power, Kylene. That's not why he's here."

"Then why?"

"The prophesy, Kylene. He'll never rest easy on the throne of Mouldour so long as we live."

"What are we to do?"

What are we to do? Hardane gazed down into her eyes, his heart and soul overflowing with love for her.

"Do?" he murmured as he swung her into his arms. "We're going to bed, lady, that's what we're going to do."

Lowering his head, he kissed her, savoring the sweetness of her lips, delighting in the way her breath caught at his touch.

"We're going to forget about Renick," he whispered. "For this night, we're going to forget about everyone and everything else."

Swiftly, he carried her up the winding staircase to their room. Hadj had already been there, lighting the candles, laying a fire in the hearth, turning down the bedclothes. A jug of wine awaited their pleasure.

With infinite care and tenderness, Hardane sat Kylene on the edge of the bed and then he undressed her, pressing butterfly-soft kisses to her neck, her shoulders, her breasts. His hands caressed her rounded stomach, his heart swelling with happiness as he thought of his sons resting there beneath Kylene's heart.

He glanced up at her as he felt a lusty kick. "Does it hurt you?"

Kylene smiled at him as she shook her head. "No. It feels wonderful."

"I love you," he murmured.

"I love you."

She ran her fingers through his hair, loving the way it felt in her hands.

And then she undressed him, her breath quickening as her gaze moved over him. He was beautiful to see, she thought, her hand skimming over his broad chest and flat belly. His skin was dark bronze, smooth and even, his muscles rippling beneath her touch.

She was ready for him when he pressed her back against the soft feather mattress. His breath was warm against her cheek as he whispered her name, telling her that she was more lovely than the sunrise, that he loved her, that he needed her more than his next breath.

Tears filled her eyes as he became a part of her, making her whole and complete at last.

It was only later, when Hardane lay sleeping in her arms, that she remembered the Interrogator was near.

Chapter Forty-Nine

Kylene woke to the sounds of battle—men yelling, the harsh echo of wood striking wood as a battering ram crashed into one of the castle's huge wooden portals.

She sat up, her glance sweeping the room. Hardane stood at the window, gazing out. Wearing a suit of light armor, he was buckling on his sword.

She whispered his name, her voice betraying the fear that was rising within her.

Wordlessly, he turned away from the window and crossed the floor. Gathering her into his arms, he buried his face in the wealth of her hair, his nostrils filling with her scent. He tightened his hold around her waist, clinging to her as if he knew it was for the last time.

"He's here, isn't he?" Kylene whispered tremulously.

Hardane nodded. So much to tell her, he thought, so much to say, and no time to do it. He could only hope she knew how much he had cherished their time together, how much he cherished her.

A knock at the door told him it was time to go. Reluctantly, he drew away.

"Remember what I told you," he said, his gaze intent upon her face. "Stay here. If Renick's men breach the walls, you're to leave the castle immediately. Kruck will take you and my mother away from Argone."

Kylene stared up at him, a terrible fear engulfing her. "Hold me," she begged. "Please hold me. I'm so afraid."

He wrapped his arms around her, drawing her tight against him. How well they fit together, he mused. His hardness complemented her soft curves; her body molded to his as if she'd been created with him in mind.

"I love you," he murmured. "Never forget that."

"I love you," she replied fervently. "I loved you when you were only a dream." Her fingertips traced the line of his mouth. "Be careful, promise me you'll be careful."

Hardane nodded, flinching as another knock came at the door.

"I've got to go, lady." He cupped her face in his hands and kissed her softly, sweetly, one last time. "Take care of yourself, beloved. If I never see our sons . . ."

Kylene covered his mouth with her hand, stilling

his words. "Don't! It's bad luck to speak of death! You'll come back to me. I know you will."

Hardane nodded, his heart heavy as he saw the tears welling in her eyes. His own throat was thick with emotion. "Kylene . . ."

"Hardane! We need you outside."

Jared's voice called to him, reminding him that the people of Argone were depending on him.

"I've got to go," Hardane said.

He brushed his knuckles over her cheek, then kissed her one last time, quickly, fervently.

"Pray for me, lady," he murmured, and turning on his heel, he left the chamber.

Pray for me. His words seemed to hang in the air. Immediately, she dropped to her knees beside their bed and began to plead with the God of Argone to watch over her husband, to protect him in battle, to return him to her safe and unharmed.

Hardane followed Jared out of the keep. The courtyard was swarming with men, mostly farmers, whose fear was evident on their faces as they ran for cover from the arrows and rocks that were raining into the courtyard.

The castle walls were manned by Hardane's fighting men. Climbing onto one of the parapets, Hardane stared down at the enemy. Hundreds of armored men swarmed around the castle walls. Some were firing arrows. Others lobbed rocks from a catapult. Others were obviously seeking for a way into the castle.

Agonized screams slashed through the air as some of Hardane's men poured a cauldron of boiling oil onto a group of Renick's men who were battering the main portal.

The fighting went on for hours, but Hardane's men managed to keep the armies of Mouldour and Corianton at bay.

The sun climbed in the sky, and still the fighting went on, with neither side gaining an advantage until Renick's men began shooting fire arrows over the wall, igniting several bales of straw, as well as one of the outbuildings that was being used to house some of the women and children from the village.

In minutes, the courtyard was filled with confusion as women and children ran out of the burning building screaming in panic.

"Jared, get those fires out!" Hardane hollered.

Shouting his acknowledgment, Jared rounded up a dozen men and put them to the task.

Swearing softly, Hardane went to check on conditions at the rear of the castle.

From a distance, Renick watched the battle, not caring that his losses were heavy. He must seize the lady Kylene. Only when she was dead, only when it was certain that she would never bear Hardane's sons, would the throne of Mouldour be secure.

And once he had Kylene, he would have Hardane as well. He would execute them both once he had them safely aboard his ship, thereby forever putting an end to the prophesy. It would be his children, his and Selene's, that ruled Argone and Mouldour.

Renick nodded with satisfaction. Even now, four of his most trusted men were making their way through the tunnel that led to Hardane's chamber. Soon, he thought, Kylene would be in his custody. And when he had the woman, the man would follow.

In the meantime, his men had been ordered to take as many lives as they could, but to inflict as little damage as possible to Castle Argone, which would, after all, soon be his.

Kylene sat at the window, her hands fisted in her lap as she watched the activity on the castle walls and in the courtyard below. Occasionally, she caught a glimpse of Hardane. Even in a crowd, she had no trouble picking him out. Taller than most of his men, he moved with a purpose and assurance that set him apart from the others. The fighting had been going on for hours, but so far Renick's men had been unable to breach the walls.

Sharilyn had spent the morning at her side, but now, with the coming of dusk, she had gone downstairs to make sure that food was being prepared for the men.

How much longer, Kylene wondered, how much longer could Hardane's men repel Renick's army? Hadj had come to her every hour, bringing news of the battle. Losses on both sides had been few, though many had been wounded. Several small buildings within the bailey had been burned to the ground. A child had been trampled to death when a frightened horse jumped a corral fence.

Three women had suffered severe burns in the fire; a fourth had died.

With a sigh, Kylene buried her face in her hands. When would it end?

Thinking it was Sharilyn returning, she didn't look up when she heard footsteps coming up behind her.

A scream was trapped in her throat as someone dropped a sack over her head. Rough hands pulled her to her feet, and then she was being dragged across the floor.

She cried Hardane's name, her nails digging into the arms of the man who held her. She heard him curse, and then he hit her hard, his fist striking her on the side of the head. Bright lights danced before her eyes, and a sudden nausea rose in her throat.

Abruptly, the floor beneath her feet changed texture and she knew they were in the tunnel that led from Hardane's bedchamber to the sea.

She began to struggle again, fear and desperation adding strength to her limbs. She lashed out with her feet and her fists, sobs racking her body. She had to get away. Her life, the lives of her children, depended on it.

She felt her fist strike flesh, and then a blinding pain exploded in her head and she felt herself falling, falling, into darkness blacker than the night. . . .

Hardane braced one hand against the wall of the keep, his forehead pressed to the cold stone. With the coming of night, Renick's men had retreated.

The glow of their campfires could be seen against the night sky.

With a sigh, he pushed away from the wall. The fighting was over for now, and he had only one thing on his mind, to see Kylene, to wrap himself in her arms and forget, at least for a little while, that the battle wasn't over.

He'd just stepped into the Great Hall when his mother came running toward him.

"She's gone!" Sharilyn cried.

"Gone? Where?"

"I don't know. I left her for a few minutes to make sure Nan had everything under control in the kitchen, and when I got back, she was gone. I've looked everywhere."

Hardane frowned. Why would she leave? Where would she go? She'd promised to stay in his room until he came for her.

He took the stairs two at a time, his weariness forgotten in his concern for Kylene. He paused inside the door to their room, his gaze sweeping the chamber, and then, after taking several deep breaths, he closed his eyes and sent his *tashada* to find her.

Kylene, where are you?

The answer, when it came, was exactly what he'd feared.

Renick! She was on his ship, locked in a small cabin, her hands tied tightly behind her back. The left side of her face was swollen, her cheek badly bruised. He felt her pain and her fear, felt the nausea that churned in her stomach as the ship rocked at anchor in a small inlet west of the waterfall.

He fought down the rage that boiled up inside him, forcing his mind to be calm as he willed his thoughts to her.

I'm coming, lady. Don't be afraid.

No! Her cry screamed in the back of his mind. *It's you he wants. Please, Hardane, if you love me, stay away.*

Lady, you know I love you. I'll see you soon.

No. She sobbed the word. *No, please. He'll kill you.*

He'll try. In his mind, Hardane reached out to caress her, his shade surrounding her, enfolding her, infusing her with his strength. *We'll be together soon,* he promised, and regretfully withdrew his presence.

Sharilyn touched her son's shoulder. "Hardane?"

"Renick has her. I've got to go."

"You know that's what he wants."

"I know. I—"

He broke off as Jared burst into the room.

"This just came for you," Jared said, handing Hardane a message written in Renick's bold scrawl.

Hardane read the missive, then handed it to his mother.

"He wants you to come to his ship," Sharilyn said, reading quickly. "Tonight, alone and unarmed."

Hardane nodded.

"You're not going?"

Hardane met his mother's worried gaze. "What other choice do I have?"

"You know he won't let her go."

"I know."

"By Minock's beard," Jared exclaimed, "the man wants you both dead!"

"You think I don't know that?"

Sharilyn laid a comforting hand on her son's arm. "Have you a plan?"

"I plan to kill him. That's the only plan I have."

Jared and Sharilyn exchanged glances. Before they could speak, Carrick stepped into the room. "Renick's men are withdrawing."

"What?"

"They're marching toward the sea."

"All of them?"

"As far as I can tell." Carrick crossed the room and put his arm around Sharilyn's shoulders. "What do you think it means?"

"It means he has what he came for," Hardane replied curtly.

"He has Kylene," Sharilyn explained. "He sent a message demanding Hardane's presence at his ship tonight, alone."

"I see." Carrick dragged a hand across his jaw as he studied Hardane's face. The man looked as though he'd been to Gehenna and back and was being asked to go again. "What are you going to do?"

Hardane stared at Carrick, his expression bleak. "What do you think?"

Carrick nodded. "It's suicide to go alone."

"He's threatened to kill her if he sees anyone else," Hardane said, his voice ragged.

"He'll kill her anyway."

"I know that!" Hardane drove his fist into the wall, hardly feeling the pain that splintered through his knuckles. "Don't you think I know that? But what else can I do?"

"I have an idea," Carrick said slowly. "It might work. It might not . . ." He shrugged. "What have you got to lose?"

Chapter Fifty

Alone and unarmed, Hardane made his way down the narrow dirt path that led to the inlet where Renick's ship was anchored.

With every step he took, he became more aware of Kylene's presence, her nearness. Again and again, he spoke to her mind, assuring her that all would be well.

As he neared the Interrogator's ship, the gang-plank was lowered and a dozen men brandishing swords and crossbows surged toward him.

One, a tall seaman wearing a bright red eye patch, jabbed the point of his blade into Hardane's back. "Get aboard!" he said curtly. "The Lord High Interrogator doesn't like to be kept waiting."

A muscle worked in Hardane's jaw as he climbed the gangplank, his feet quickly adjusting to the gentle roll of the ship.

"That way," Eye Patch ordered, shoving Hardane forward.

Hardane's breath caught in his throat when he saw Kylene. She was tied to the main mast, her long red hair blowing gently in the evening breeze.

Renick stood beside her, a long-bladed dagger in his hand.

"I'm here," Hardane said. "Let her go."

Renick's laugh was filled with disdain. "Let her go? I think not."

"What do you want?"

"I want you dead."

"I'm here," Hardane repeated, his hands curling into tight fists. "Only let Kylene go free, as you promised."

Slowly, the Interrogator shook his head. "You're a threat, Hardane. The throne of Mouldour will never be secure as long as you're alive."

"Then kill me and be done with it. But let Kylene go."

"You're a fool," Renick said with a sneer. "You know the prophesy."

Renick laid the flat of the dagger on Kylene's swollen belly, and Hardane took a step forward, murder in his eye. But before he could reach the Interrogator, two men grabbed his arms.

"She's obviously pregnant," Renick said. "I might have let her live if you hadn't planted your seed in her, but now . . ." He shook his head. "Both of you must die. The only question is, who'll go first?" Renick frowned. "I wonder, which of you will suffer the most by watching the other die?"

"Renick, for the love of heaven, let her go! You've

got the throne of Mouldour. I'll abdicate the throne of Argone, I'll have my mother and brothers swear allegiance to you so long as they live. I'll do whatever else you ask, only let her go."

"Hardane, no." Kylene strained against the ropes that bound her, her heart aching with pain and love for the man who was pleading for her life, and for the lives of their sons.

Hardane struggled to free himself from the two men who were still holding him. He grunted as a third man struck him across the side of the head.

"Enough!" Renick roared. "We'll make no bargains, Hardane. I'm not fool enough to believe that your mother or your brothers would do as you say. I've waited too long for the throne of Mouldour to risk losing it now. The woman dies, and you with her."

"I beg of you, let her go!" Hardane cried.

"Do it and be done with it!" Selene exclaimed.

Kylene gasped as her sister moved out of the shadows to stand beside the Interrogator.

"You're in such a hurry, perhaps you'd like to do it, my love," Renick said, handing the dagger to Selene.

Selene's eyes narrowed. "Do you think I won't?"

Renick shook his head. "I don't doubt for a minute that you will. I'm only curious as to which one you'll chose to die first, the sister you hate, or the man who spurned you."

Selene's head jerked up. "You know about that?"

"I know everything that transpires in the Fortress, my dear." Renick stroked her cheek, his eyes mere slits of ice blue. "Never forget that. Now, which will it be? The lady or the wolf?"

"The lady," Selene said without hesitation. "I want to watch him suffer as she dies."

"Again, we think alike," Renick said with a pleased grin.

Hardane began to struggle fiercely as Selene raised the dagger and took a step toward Kylene.

All the color drained from Kylene's face as she watched her sister cross the deck toward her. Cold, implacable hatred radiated from the depths of Selene's eyes, and Kylene's heart began to pound a frantic tattoo. She was going to die, here and now, by her own sister's hand.

Trembling violently, she turned toward Hardane, wanting to imprint his face on her mind so that she might carry the memory of it with her into eternity.

From the corner of her eye, she saw a narrow shaft of moonlight glint on the blade clutched in Selene's hand.

"Wait!" Renick's voice broke the ominous stillness. "I'll give you one last chance to save her, Hardane. Only tell me the secret of Wolffan shape shifting, and I'll let the woman live."

"I don't believe you."

"I give you my word."

Hardane snorted disdainfully. "What good will your word be when I'm dead?"

"None, perhaps. On the other hand, it's the only chance the woman has. Are you willing to take it, or will you let her die when you might have saved her?"

Hardane's gaze swept over the ship as though he

were considering the Interrogator's offer. Renick's crew was on deck, gathered in a loose half-circle behind him. Selene stood beside Kylene, her knuckles white around the haft of the knife, her eyes filled with impatience.

He heard a faint sound near the foredeck and knew it was now or never.

"Very well, Renick," Hardane said quietly. "I'll show you how it's done."

The words had barely left his lips when he transformed into the wolf.

The men who had been holding him fell back, mouths agape, as Hardane sprang forward.

With a growl, he hurled himself at Renick, his jaws closing around the man's throat.

At that moment, Jared, Carrick, and thirty of Argone's best warriors swarmed over the rail of the foredeck, their swords cutting a wide swath through Renick's men.

With a cry of frustration, Selene whirled around, her arm raised, the knife in her hand poised to strike.

Kylene's eyes widened with fear as she saw the dagger plunging toward her heart. And then, as if the world had suddenly slowed, she saw Selene stagger backward, a bright crimson stain blooming around the arrow that protruded from her breast.

Selene stared in horror at the arrow that had pierced her heart. The dagger fell from her hand, a hand that no longer had the strength to hold it.

"You," she murmured, her voice thick with accusation as her gaze fastened on the face of the man who had killed her. "I thought you were dead."

Tears welled in Carrick's eyes as he ran forward, his arms wrapping around Selene as the life slowly ebbed from her body.

Kylene turned away, choking back the bile that rose in her throat, hardly aware that Jared was cutting her hands free, that the fighting was over. Renick's men had been disarmed and were being herded below to the brig.

Arms folded protectively over her stomach, she looked around for Hardane, felt a fresh wave of nausea churn through her as she saw the wolf prowling the deck.

It took all her courage to look at the Interrogator's body. She had expected to see a great deal of blood, had feared that Hardane, in his fury, had ripped out the man's throat. Surprisingly, there was no blood to be seen, and she wondered if the Interrogator was, indeed, dead.

"Hardane."

The wolf turned at the sound of her voice; then, with a wave of its tail, it disappeared into the shadows.

Kylene started to follow, and then she heard the sound of her father's tears, saw him sitting on the deck with Selene's body cradled in his arms.

She stared after Hardane for a moment; then, knowing he didn't want to assume his own shape in front of his men, she knelt beside her father and put her arms around his shoulders, wondering, as she did so, if he would hate her for being the cause of Selene's death.

Jared came to stand beside them. Not knowing what to say, he patted Kylene's shoulder, then went to see if he could help with the wounded.

A moment later, Hardane lifted Kylene to her feet and drew her into his arms. "Are you all right, lady?"

"Fine." Her gaze searched his eyes. "Are you?"

His arms tightened around her. "Aye."

"Did you . . . is he . . . ?"

"Dead? No."

In spite of all the Interrogator had done, in spite of what he'd meant to do, she was relieved to learn that Hardane hadn't killed him.

"What will happen to him now?" she asked.

"He'll hang."

Kylene swallowed. "When?"

Hardane glanced over his shoulder to where three of his men were pulling Renick to his feet. "Now."

With quiet efficiency, Renick's hands were lashed behind his back; a rope was thrown over the yardarm.

The Interrogator stood with his head high, his ice blue eyes filled with contempt as the noose was placed around his neck. There was no sign of fear on his face.

"Any last words?" Hardane asked.

Renick shook his head. A look that might have been regret flickered in the depths of his eyes as he stared at Selene's blanket-draped body, and then he shrugged.

"Just get on with it," he said tersely.

Hardane nodded at the four men standing behind Renick, and they took hold of the loose end of the rope and began to walk toward the stern. When Renick's feet cleared the deck, they secured the end of the rope to one of the stern cleats.

Kylene buried her face in Hardane's shoulder, unable to watch as the noose grew tight around Renick's neck, slowly choking the breath, the life, from his body.

There was a long silence punctuated only by the sighing of the wind and the gentle slap of the sea against the hull of the ship.

"Shall I cut him down?"

Hardane turned to face Jared. "Aye."

"And the body?"

"Throw it into the sea."

With a curt nod, Jared went to do as ordered.

"What about . . . what about my sister?"

Hardane's jaw clenched. Had it been up to him, he would have pitched Selene's body into the sea with that of her husband.

He was about to say as much when he looked up and met Carrick's anguished gaze. Kylene's father looked as if he'd aged ten years since he'd come aboard the Interrogator's ship.

"If it's all right with you," Carrick said, his voice ragged with pain, "I'd like to take Selene home, to Mouldour."

"As you wish," Hardane replied quietly. "Take the ship. Jared and my men will accompany you when you're ready."

Carrick nodded his thanks. "I'll leave on the morning tide." A deep sigh escaped his lips. "Tell Sharilyn I'm going to spend the night here, with Selene."

"Would you like me to stay the night with you?" Kylene asked.

"No, but I thank you for the offer."

"I'm sorry," Kylene said, her voice thick with unshed tears.

"I'm not blaming you, daughter," Carrick said. "I did what I had to do, and I'd do it again." He swallowed hard, his mind replaying that agonizing instant when he'd had to choose one child over another. "I need this time to be alone with her, to say good-bye."

"Do you . . . would you like me to go with you to Mouldour?"

Carrick glanced at Hardane, knowing the final decision rested with him.

"I don't think a sea voyage is a good idea in your condition," Hardane said.

"I'm fine," Kylene insisted, her gaze on her father's face.

"I'm afraid I agree with Hardane," Carrick said, squeezing her arm affectionately. "Perhaps you might come for a visit after . . . ," he swallowed a sob, "after your twins are born."

Kylene nodded. Twins, she thought, pressing a hand over her womb. She and Selene had shared their mother's body, but nothing else. Fervently, she prayed that her sons would share more than a blood bond, that they would learn to love and respect one another as equals, that there would be no jealousy between them.

Rising on tiptoe, Kylene pressed a farewell kiss to her father's cheek.

"Let's go home, lady," Hardane said.

Removing his cloak, he draped it over her shoulders, slid his arm around her waist, and led her down the gangplank.

When they reached the foot of the hill, he swung Kylene into his arms and carried her up the narrow, winding path. His war-horse nickered softly as they crested the hill.

Effortlessly, Hardane lifted her into the saddle, then swung up behind her and turned the stallion toward home.

There was a flurry of activity when they reached the keep. Sharilyn, Hadj, Parah, Teliford, and Nan met them at the door, all talking at once, until they saw Kylene. Her face was devoid of color, her eyes red-rimmed and shadowed with grief.

Hadj immediately went upstairs to turn down Kylene's bed and lay out her nightclothes, while Teliford lit a fire in the hearth. Parah went out to look after Hardane's horse. Nan hurried into the kitchen to brew a pot of strong black tea.

"Where's Carrick?" Sharilyn asked anxiously.

"He stayed on Renick's ship," Hardane replied, and after settling Kylene in one of the big chairs beside the fireplace, he took his mother aside and quickly related all that had happened.

Sharilyn looked thoughtful as she studied Kylene's face. "Is she all right?"

Hardane shrugged. "I don't know. She hasn't said a word since we left the ship." But maybe that wasn't so strange, after all she'd been through.

"And Carrick?" Sharilyn asked.

"I think he needs you."

Sharilyn glanced at Kylene again. Dared she

leave the girl to go to her husband? And yet, how could she stay? She couldn't begin to imagine the pain, the anguish, Carrick must be feeling. Taking Selene's life must have been like destroying a part of himself.

"Go," Hardane said. "He shouldn't be alone. And he'll want you there beside him when he resumes the throne."

"He was right," Sharilyn mused. "He was right all along."

"About what?"

"When he asked me to marry him, he remarked that maybe it wasn't your sons at all, but our marriage, that would forge a lasting peace between our countries."

"It would seem he was right, mother mine. Because of your marriage to Carrick, peace will come to Argone and Mouldour far sooner than anyone expected."

Sharilyn smiled. "And my grandsons will be able to grow up in a land blessed with peace."

"You'd best go now," Hardane said. "Carrick sails with the dawn tide."

"He'll wait for me," Sharilyn said with a knowing smile.

Hardane grinned. "So, the bond is already forming."

Sharilyn nodded. "And you, my son, may soon have a little brother."

Hardane stared after his mother as she left the hall, but there was no time to ponder her words. Sweeping Kylene into his arms, he carried her upstairs.

A tub filled with scented water awaited her. A cozy fire crackled in the hearth. The covers had been turned down, and a hot brick had been placed at the foot of the bed to warm it. A pot of tea and a plate of honey bread sat on a tray by the bedside.

Kylene stood quiescent as Hardane undressed her, then lifted her into the tub. Gently, he washed her, his gaze lingering on her breasts as he imagined his sons suckling there.

When he looked up, he saw that she was crying. Her tears, as silent as the night, filled him with pain.

Lifting her from the tub, he dried her off, and then, wrapping her in a blanket, he sat beside the hearth with her in his arms.

And still the tears came.

Feeling helpless, he stroked her hair while she cried, shedding bitter tears for the sister who had hated her so much that she had tried to kill her, weeping for the father who had sacrificed one daughter to save another.

Attuned as he was to her every thought, the depths of her sorrow pierced Hardane's very soul.

He held her all through the night, until her body's need for rest overcame her grief and she fell asleep in his arms.

Chapter Fifty-One

Kylene gazed into the darkness, her lips pressed together to still the cry that rose in her throat.

She was in his arms and nothing could hurt her. She repeated the litany until the spasm passed. How long, she wondered, how many hours had passed since the first twinge awoke her? How long had it been since that first mild twinge turned into claws that threatened to tear her apart?

She gasped as another pain knifed through her, sharper than any of the others.

"Kylene?" Hardane awoke immediately. "What's wrong?"

In the grip of a strong contraction, she could only grasp his arm.

"Kylene?"

"It . . . it hurts."

"I know," he said. And he did know. He could

feel it, the pain that started low in her back, gathering in intensity as it swept forward.

"When did it start?" he asked.

"I don't know."

She groaned softly, certain she was going to die. She felt Hardane's hands gently turning her on her side, felt his strong fingers begin to knead the tension from her back and shoulders.

When the contraction was over, he slid out of bed and lit a fire in the hearth. Then, giving a tug on the bell pull, he summoned Hadj, instructing her to fill a pot with water, to bring Kylene a cup of watered wine.

When that was done, he returned to Kylene. Sitting on the edge of the bed, he took her hand in his, felt her body tense as another contraction ripped through her.

There was a knock at the door, and then Hadj entered the room. She placed the pot of water on the hearth to warm, then handed Hardane a small cup of wine.

"Shall I stay, my lord?" she asked, trying not to stare at Kylene, who was writhing on the bed.

"No. Send Teliford after Druidia."

"Yes, my lord."

Kylene clutched at his arm. "You won't leave me?"

"No, lady."

He brushed a wisp of hair from her brow, felt the shudders that racked her body as the pains grew stronger. Connected by the bond between them, his own body tensed as her pain communicated itself to him.

"Don't be afraid, Kylene," he murmured, wondering how she could endure such pain. "Everything will be all right, I promise you."

She gazed into his eyes, touched by the love and concern she saw there. She moaned as another pain knifed through her, saw her own agony mirrored in the depths of his eyes, felt the tremor that shook his body as her own convulsed.

For the next hour, he massaged her back, held her hands when the contractions grew unbearable. His voice soothed her fears; his touch spoke of love and caring.

Hadj arrived with the news that Druidia had gone to Chadray.

"Then summon the physician."

"No!" Kylene shook her head. "I don't want anyone but you. Please, Hardane. He frightens me."

"Are you sure, lady? I've never delivered a baby."

"I'm sure."

Hardane glanced at Hadj, who shrugged.

"It won't be long now, I'm thinking," Hadj remarked. "I'll go fetch some fresh linens."

Hardane nodded. Of all the times for his mother to be gone, he mused bleakly. He'd never needed her more than now.

The next hour was the longest of his life. He felt her every pain, his heart echoed her every cry, as Kylene labored to bring his sons into the world.

Her fingernails raked his arms, leaving long bloody furrows, but he hardly felt the pain, so minor was it when compared to what she was suffering.

Like most men, he had never given much thought

to the process of birth. A man spilled his seed in mindless pleasure, but it was reaped in a river of pain and blood. It was beyond comprehension that his mother had endured such agony eight times.

It was near dawn when the first infant, tiny and red-faced, slid into his hands. Hardane's eyes were damp with unshed tears as he cut the cord and handed the child to Hadj, who tied a bit of red ribbon around one tiny wrist, identifying it as the firstborn. A short time later, his second son entered the world, its tiny fists flailing the air.

As he gathered the afterbirth into a pail to be buried later, Hardane felt a sense of awe, of reverence, not only for the miracle of birth, but for the woman who had walked through the shadow of death to bring new life into the world.

With brisk efficiency, Hadj changed the bed linens, then bathed and swaddled the infants.

When that was done, she offered Kylene a glass of cold goat's milk and gave Hardane a cup of strong wine. Then, with a last glance at the new parents, she left the room.

Kylene smiled wearily as Hardane sat on the edge of the bed, a baby in each arm. Her heart swelled with such love and tenderness it couldn't be contained. Tears welled in her eyes and trickled down her cheeks as she gazed at her husband and sons.

"They're beautiful, Kylene," Hardane murmured. "You're beautiful."

She held out her arms and he handed her one of the twins, watching as she carefully inspected the baby from the top of its head to the soles of its feet, marveling over the thatch of thick black hair, counting each tiny finger and toe.

When she'd made sure the baby was perfect, she took the other one and did the same thing. They were identical. Perfect in every way.

"What shall we name them?" Hardane asked, thinking he'd never seen anything more lovely than Kylene as she sat against the pillows, a child nuzzling her breast.

"I thought we'd name the firstborn Kray, after your father."

"He would have liked that," Hardane murmured. "And the other?"

"After my father?"

"Kray and Carrick." Hardane nodded his approval, then grinned as the child in his arms began to cry. "I think this one's hungry, too."

"Here, give him to me."

It took some maneuvering, but in a few moments she had a child at each breast.

Kylene grinned up at her husband, happier than she'd ever been in her life.

"Perhaps we'll have a daughter next year," she mused.

Hardane looked stricken, and then he shook his head. "Nay, lady, I don't think I could endure such agony again."

Kylene grinned at him. "If birthing were left to the men, the race would have ended long ago."

It was true, he thought. He'd rather face an army with only his bare hands to defend himself than vicariously suffer the pangs of childbirth again.

"I love you, my lord wolf," Kylene said quietly.

"And I love you, lady, more than you can imagine," he replied, and knew he'd ask nothing more of life than to share it with this woman who had filled his heart and soul with love and laughter.

Epilogue

Kylene sat on the grassy bank, watching Hardane and her twin sons splash in the river's shallow depths.

Two years had passed since the Interrogator's death. Two years of peace and happiness.

In that time, she'd seen all her dreams come true. Her father was happily married to Sharilyn and they were expecting their first child in the fall. She had met her sisters and their families. To her delight, she had eleven nieces and nephews, and three cousins by marriage.

Best of all, she was pregnant again. The child was due any day. She knew Hardane hoped for another son, but Kylene knew in her heart that it was a daughter with hair as black as night and eyes as gray as a winter sky.

She smiled as Hardane and the boys scrambled

up the bank toward her. Her sons flung themselves into her arms, showering her with water and kisses, exclaiming over the monstrous fish their father had almost caught with his bare hands. And then, too filled with energy to sit still, they ran off to the woods to look for lizards and squirrels and whatever else they could find.

Shaking the water from his hair, Hardane sat down on the grass beside her.

"How do you feel?" he asked as he placed one hand over her swollen girth.

"Fine."

"No pains yet?"

"No."

She smiled up at him, touched, as always, by the love and concern in the depths of his eyes. The bond between them had grown stronger in the last two years, so that she often felt as if a part of herself was missing when he was not nearby.

Kylene let her fingertips glide over his cheek. "Do you think *you're* ready?"

Hardane grunted softly, remembering how her pains had become his during the birth of their sons.

"I'm ready," he said gruffly, and knew he'd walk through the fires of Gehenna if it was what she desired.

Gently, he pressed kisses to her forehead, to the tip of her nose, to each cheek, and then, to her lips.

"I promised to love you for all time," he murmured, "in joy or sadness . . ."

"In good times and bad," Kylene added, threading

437

her fingers through his hair.

"In happiness and pain," Hardane finished.

"I love you," she murmured.

"And I love you," he replied.

Lifting her to her feet, he drew her into his arms and kissed her with all the love in his soul, and then, hand in hand, they walked toward the woods, drawn by the happy laughter of their sons.

"Powerful, passionate, and action-packed, Madeline Baker's historical romances will keep readers on the edge of their seats!"

—*Romantic Times*

A creature of moonlight and quicksilver, Leyla rescues the mysterious man from unspeakable torture, then heals him body and soul. The radiant enchantress is all he wants in a woman—gentle, innocent, exquisitely lovely—but his enemies will do everything in their power to keep her from him. Only a passion born of desperate need can prevail against such hatred and unite two lovers against such odds.

_3490-5 $4.99 US/$5.99 CAN

CHEYENNE SURRENDER

MADELINE BAKER

Author Of More Than 4 Million Books In Print!

"Powerful, passionate, and action packed, Madeline Baker's historical romances will keep readers on the edge of their seats!"
—Romantic Times

Callie has the face of an angel and the body of a temptress. Her innocent kisses say she is still untouched, but her reputation says she is available to any man who has the price of a night's entertainment.

Callie's sweetness touches Caleb's heart, but he and the whole town of Cheyenne know she is no better than the woman who raised her—his own father's mistress. Torn by conflicting desires, the handsome half-breed doesn't know whether he wants her walking down the aisle in white satin, or warm and willing in his bed, clothed in nothing by ivory flesh.

_3581-2 $4.99 US/$5.99 CAN

FIRST LOVE, WILD LOVE

MADELINE BAKER

"Lovers of Indian romance have a special place on their bookshelves for Madeline Baker!"
—Romantic Times

From the moment she catches sight of him working on the road gang, Brianne knows the Indian is forbidden to her. He is a prisoner, a heathen, a savage male animal who will have no mercy on her tender youth and innocence. Yet one look into his dark, fathomless eyes tells Brianne he'll capture her soul.

From the moment he escapes the white man's chains, Brianne knows she must go with him. He is her life, her fate, and one touch of his sleek, bronzed body tells her she wants no mercy...only the searing ecstasy of his savage love.
_3596-0 $4.99 US/$5.99 CAN

A WHISPER IN THE WIND

MADELINE BAKER

"Lovers of Indian Romances have a special place on their bookshelves for Madeline Baker!"
— *Romantic Times*

Michael Wolf returns to his tribe to share with the Cheyenne the glory and the heartache of the last golden days before the Battle of Little Big Horn, and to find the beautiful woman who haunts his dreams.

Refined and innocent, Elayna shares every civilized woman's fear of Indians, until she is kidnapped by the darkly handsome Cheyenne. Slowly, her disdain changes to desire beneath his bronzed body, and she vows to make any sacrifice to keep him by her side forever.

_3075-6 $4.95 US/$5.95 CAN

THE QUEEN OF WESTERN ROMANCE

MADELINE BAKER

When Lacey Montana began her lonely trek across the plains behind her father's prison wagon, she had wanted no part of Matt Drago. Part Apache, part gambler, Matt frightened Lacey by the savage intensity in his dark eyes, but helpless and alone, she offered to tend Matt's wounds if he would help find her father. Stranded in the burning desert, their desperation turned to fierce passion as they struggled to stay alive. Matt longed to possess his beautiful savior body and soul, but if he wanted to win her heart, he'd have to do it Lacey's way.

__2918-9 $4.50

MIDNIGHT FIRE

MADELINE BAKER

Three captivating stories of love in another time, another place.

MADELINE BAKER
"Heart of the Hunter"

A Lakota warrior must defy the boundaries of life itself to claim the spirited beauty he has sought through time.

ANNE AVERY
"Dream Seeker"

On faraway planets, a pilot and a dreamer learn that passion can bridge the heavens, no matter how vast the distance from one heart to another.

KATHLEEN MORGAN
"The Last Gatekeeper"

To save her world, a dazzling temptress must use her powers of enchantment to open a stellar portal—and the heart of a virile but reluctant warrior.

__51974-7 *Enchanted Crossings* (three unforgettable love stories in one volume) $4.99 US/
$5.99 CAN